"His pressure's dropping, Doctor."

The responsibility for the patient was fully in Kate's hands. New anxiety welled up in her. She didn't need this. She'd had more than she could handle already tonight.

"Get the crash cart in here!" Kate yelled, and motioned for a syringe to administer medication straight to the heart. Her own heart was in her throat. Panic made her hands shake. For the third time that night, she was presiding over a dying patient.

"What's the deal here?"

Kelly turned with relief. "Dr. Lincoln! Thank goodness you're here. We have an acute MI."

Ward Lincoln, tall and arrogantly confident, shot Kate a sharp look. He shouldered past her and gazed on the gray face of the patient. "Why the hell haven't you administered the clot buster?"

Kate stared in disbelief. Joseph Carmello's heart had stopped. The drug would be useless. "But Dr. Lincoln—"

"You've done enough, Dr. Madison," he snapped. "Now get out of my way and let me see if I can save this man's life."

Stunned, Kate moved back. After a split second of hesitation, her team began to respond to Dr. Lincoln's curt, confident orders. But overhead, the monitor still screamed in unrelenting electronic panic.

Several minutes later, after a scathing look at Kate, Dr. Lincoln called time and all activity ceased. As he stripped his gloves and tossed them in disgust in the waste bin, the team stood awkwardly silent. Every bleak face mirrored the toll of their failed effort to save Joseph Carmello. Nobody looked at Kate.

Also available from MIRA Books and
KAREN YOUNG

GOOD GIRLS

Karen Young
Full Circle

MIRA

RECYCLED PAPER · RECYCLED PAPER

ISBN 1-55166-471-2

FULL CIRCLE

Copyright © 1999 by Karen Stone.

Printed in U.S.A.

To my family.

I owe several people who helped me in the development of this book: My niece, Lauri Grady, for the medical stuff. Fellow writer friends Emilie Richards, Erica Spindler and Celeste Hamilton, for thoughtful insights and suggestions. My agent, Evan Marshall. And always, always, Maureen Stonehouse, my ever-encouraging, especially supportive editor. My sincerest thanks.

ONE

"That's the way... Good, good." Kate Madison nodded with approval as a shaky intern attempted to insert an airway into the throat of a bruised and bloody patient. "Okay. Cup his chin with your left hand, Betsy—like so. That's it. Now tilt it—try not to traumatize the throat. That's it. There! It's in."

"Wow, I did it!" The intern let out a sigh before turning to look at Kate, searching her face for a clue. "Now what?"

"You tell me, Betsy."

"He'll need a CAT scan."

"Right." The patient—a sixteen-year-old male—had sustained serious head trauma after going through the windshield of a car. Since arriving at the E.R. ten minutes ago, he'd been drifting in and out of consciousness.

"But he'll need to be stabilized before we send him up, right?"

"Yes." Kate signaled to another intern. "Felix, take over here, will you?"

Moving away, she sighed tiredly as she pulled the surgical gloves from her hands and tossed them into a bin on her way to the coffee room. Not only had she not had time for coffee tonight, but she'd had nothing to eat except a candy bar since coming on duty at seven that morning.

Friday nights were horrendous in any hospital E.R. and St. Luke's was no exception. In spite of rigid gun-control laws in Boston, already her team had treated two gunshot victims. Following in rapid-fire succession were a four-year-old boy who'd been attacked by his neighbor's Rottweiler, a fifty-two-year-old female in a diabetic coma, a couple of overdosed crack addicts, a prostitute who'd been badly beaten by an impotent john and three college students found unconscious in their fraternity house with blood-alcohol levels triple the legal limit. A team was on standby now for an incoming traffic-accident victim via Lifeflight—compound fractures below both knees, facial lacerations and skull trauma, crushed larynx. Estimated time of arrival—six minutes from now. So far, no patient had died, although the accident might change that. With Felix to monitor the teenager, Kate could just possibly grab a cup of coffee and make a pit stop at the bathroom.

The coffee in the lounge was bitter, black and sweet, but it injected adrenaline into her flagging system, along with acid and empty calories. She tore open a pack of saltines—not because she was particularly hungry, but her stomach had been rebelling lately at her diet of caffeine and junk food on the run. After eating only one, she tossed the rest into the trash and vowed to have something healthy when she got home. Although she'd already put in a fourteen-hour shift, God only knew when that would be.

Glancing at her watch, she thought of calling her apartment to pick up her messages. Maureen Reynolds, her lawyer, had been trying to meet with Robert's lawyer for a month. Kate's divorce was six months old and she still hadn't received the settlement check from the sale of their house. She needed to know, too, if her mother had called. She'd tried twice before leaving this morning and frequently the day before, without success. Her mother refused to get an answering machine. Why Victoria resisted such a convenience baffled Kate. But many things about her mother baffled Kate.

As she left the lounge, a flurry of activity drew her gaze to the emergency entrance. Pulsing red lights flashed intermittently across the walls as an ambulance turned in at St. Luke's E.R.

"Dr. Madison, code one. Dr. Madison, code one."

Oh, shit. Kate bent her head, pinching the bridge of her nose. Pushing aside her anxiety, she went to the nurses' station.

"What's up, Ricky?"

Ricky Hall fielded all calls to the E.R. from a complicated phone setup in the nurses' station. Sultry eyed, with creamy skin and a mop of dark, wild curly hair, Ricky looked more suited to pushing makeup for Lancôme at Filene's, yet Kate had never seen her blanch at anything passing through the trauma unit. "Sorry, Dr. Madison, I know you haven't had a minute tonight, but—"

"It's okay. I'll survive."

"Domestic dispute. Wife battered by estranged husband. Multiple contusions, nosebleed, dislocated shoulder. The usual."

The usual. Kate put a hand on her stomach. "Jake is up for the accident victim, right?"

"Right, Doctor. Due any minute on Lifeflight."

"Okay, I'll take this one. See if you can find Eric to assist Jake. I didn't like the sound of that head trauma."

"Gotcha."

Kate ducked quickly into the women's toilet. When she came out of the stall, she washed her hands and then spent fifteen seconds staring at her reflection in the mirror. Something about women who were browbeaten and battered by brutal men until they were almost unrecognizable cut straight through her defenses. It baffled her that she hadn't learned to steel herself against certain aspects of her profession. As a physician, she was always going to encounter battered women; the trauma unit was a revolving door for them. Drawing a deep breath, she headed for the nurses' station.

"Kelly Mareno's standing by if you need her," Ricky said as Kate approached.

"Did Jake's accident arrive?" Kate asked.

Ricky nodded, motioning toward a busy cubicle where a team of doctors and nurses worked frantically over a bleeding man. "Dr. Grissom has everything under control in 6A."

"Good." Kate stood watching for a moment. Jake Grissom was exploring the area where the patient's skull had made contact with the windshield. He moved carefully and methodically, unfazed by the urgency of others in the team. Kate moved on.

The board was due to make a decision between Kate and Jake for chief-resident status. She'd psyched herself up for it when the board had met a week ago, but the action had been tabled. Now it would be another month before the meeting reconvened. The waiting was difficult. Accepting the decision philosophically would be more difficult. Kate wanted the job more than Jake, who didn't share her all-consuming passion for work. He wouldn't feel the sting of rejection as much as she would. And for Kate, the promotion was more than the next step up the ladder; with her personal life in shambles, her career was everything to her now.

"You okay, Doctor?"

Kate managed a smile. "I'm fine." She glanced at the big clock over Ricky's head. "It's been a long night."

"Don't I know it."

Both turned as the double doors burst open and a stretcher was pushed in by two EMTs. Pete Renfroe, a sea-

soned trauma technician, hurried alongside, holding an
IV bag while his partner guided the gurney. On it lay a female patient whose white face was made grotesque by an
ugly bruise on her right cheek, one swollen eye and a bul-
bous upper lip oozing blood. A scared-looking woman
followed close behind the stretcher, holding the hand of a
small girl. Kate guessed she was a neighbor or a relative.
The child's face was blank and pale. Her sneakers
squeaked faintly on the polished tile as she was hustled
along at a pace too fast for her short legs.

Still focused on the patient, Pete began reeling off information to Kate. "Female, age thirty-two. Couple of
bruised ribs, but her lungs are okay, I think. I popped her
shoulder back, but it's hurting her. BP's a hundred over
seventy. She was out for a few minutes, according to her
sister, but she's stable now. Talked a little in the ambulance. Worried about her kid."

But not worried enough to remove the child from a violent environment. Kate pushed the thought away and
touched the patient's arm. "What's your name, miss?"

"Charlene," she murmured. "Charlene Miller."

Kate parted the woman's shirt and delicately probed
the bruised rib cage. The woman groaned and fluttered
her eyes.

Pete gestured with his head. "That's her sister back
there with the kid."

"The patient's child?"

"Yeah."

Kate stepped aside, allowing Pete and his partner to
wheel Charlene Miller into a vacant cubicle. With the help
of two nurses, they transferred her onto a hospital
stretcher, hung the IV bag and moved back.

"She's all yours, Dr. Madison." Pete leaned over,
touching the woman's shoulder. "You're in good hands

now, Charlene." He spoke in a hearty tone, intent on re-assuring her.

"Will she be all right? She's my sister." Anxiously, the woman with the child tore her gaze from the patient to look at Kate.

"We'll do our best," Kate told her, adjusting the drape to cover the patient's bruises as the child looked on. "You'll need to wait outside, miss," she added, inspecting the IV on the back of the woman's hand. Kate glanced at Kelly Mareno, who wrapped a pressure cuff on the patient's left arm and took a reading.

"Still stable?" Kate asked.

"Uh…falling." Kelly moved the electronic stethoscope, listened intently. "Ninety over sixty-five."

Ignoring Kate's request to leave, the sister edged closer. "Her ex did this. I told her not to let him back in, but she always does."

Preoccupied with the blood-pressure problem, Kate hardly heard her. One of the E.R. staff usually ushered family members out.

"Possible internal bleeding," Kate murmured, pulling the drape down to check the woman's abdomen. Fresh bruises over old, faded ones. The sister gasped and Kate made an irritated sound. "Someone show this woman where to wait."

Pete, still collecting EMT property, touched the woman's elbow. "Come on, miss. Let Dr. Madison do her job."

"You'd think she'd consider how this affects Lindy," the sister complained. "Letting him slap her around like that." She allowed Pete to walk her and the unresisting child toward the door. "Lindy's gonna grow up thinking this is the way normal people act." She raised the child's hand. "Look at her. She's been exposed to so much violence between Charlene and Vinny that she doesn't even react anymore."

"My baby…" A weak murmur came from the patient.

"Your sister has your little girl," Kate told her. "She's okay."

"No, no… Baby…" She touched her abdomen.

"Are you pregnant?" Kate asked sharply as tears trickled from the corners of Charlene's eyes. "Charlene? Are you pregnant?"

"Please…don't want…to lose…"

Kate jerked the drape down past the woman's thighs. "Damn!"

"Hello," Kelly murmured.

"My God!" Through the window the sister was staring at the bright red bloodstain soaking the pad under the woman's buttocks. "I can't believe you let Vinny get you pregnant again, Charly!"

"Get her out of here," Kate muttered, probing gently to check the fetus. When she withdrew her hand, fresh blood gushed onto the pad beneath Charlene's buttocks. She turned to the nurse holding the chart. "Buzz Dr. Steinberg, Celie." Marv Steinberg was the OB-GYN resident on call.

In spite of Pete's efforts to draw her down the hall, the sister was craning her neck to see inside the cubicle. One hand was pressed to her mouth; the other anchored the child to her side. "She told me she wasn't gonna let him touch her that way again!"

Ricky appeared—thank God!—and said something to the woman, slipping an arm around her waist. Then, smiling at the little girl, she urged them toward the waiting room.

With her stethoscope pressed to the patient's abdomen, Kate watched them go, her eye on the little girl. There was something about her…. Trailing behind her aunt, the

child gave one last look over her shoulder at Kate with
wide dark eyes that were too solemn. Then her gaze
shifted to her mother. No fear, no curiosity, no expectation; just...nothing. A dark memory stirred deep in Kate's
mind—a quick picture that flashed, then just as quickly
receded. She resisted it fiercely. These odd lapses in con-
centration had been happening more and more frequently lately. Blinking to bring her attention back to the
bruised body now in her hands, she listened intently for
the sound of a fetal heartbeat.

"What's her pressure now, Kelly?"

Kelly manipulated the stethoscope and strained for a
reading. She shook her head. Another nurse finished the
connection to the monitor and Charlene's heartbeat became a visible green line, weak and uneven.

"She's getting shocky," Kelly warned.

"Get Dr. Steinberg, stat!" Kate called, reaching for an
airway. "I'll intubate her." Spotting Jean Sharpe, the
night charge nurse, Kate ordered a crash cart and a cardiac team to stand by, just in case. Sharpe indicated with
a nod that she'd anticipated the order.

Kate moved back to the head of the examining table
and delicately inserted the tube that would breathe for
Charlene Miller if necessary. The falling pressure could
be caused by hemorrhaging from the aborted fetus, but
there wasn't enough bleeding to convince her that that
was the problem. Kate suspected the heart had sustained
a bruising blow from the battering. If so, that could cause
pericardial tamponade—blood pooling between the heart
muscle and the pericardial sac that surrounded it. The
malfunctioning heart was causing progressive shock. But
there could be internal bleeding elsewhere. This was one
of those fateful cases where gut instinct guided the physician's call as much as experience and technology.

As Kate studied the patient with rising anxiety, Kelly

made an urgent sound. Abandoning the stethoscope, she felt for the carotid artery on the woman's neck.

"Nothing, Doctor. We're losing her!"

Quickly, Kate ordered epinephrine. With the patient's traumatized chest, massage could easily fracture a rib and puncture a lung. The night charge nurse appeared, slapped the medication into Kate's palm and watched her administer it. Then all eyes were again on the monitor. Still nothing.

The sister, noting the urgent activity in the unit, had stopped in her tracks. "I thought you said she'd be all right!" she cried. Trying to shake free of Ricky, she struggled to get back to her sister. "Don't let her die, Doctor. Don't let her die!"

"Where's that crash cart!" Kate called.

"On the way," Jean Sharpe said.

Commotion in the hall signaled the arrival of the cardiac team. As they set up, Kate examined Charlene's pupils and found them fixed and dilated. A renewed surge of anxiety added to the weight of responsibility as the E.R. team worked urgently toward one goal—saving a life.

"Stand back." Neal Winston, nephew of one of Boston's premier cardiovascular surgeons, shouldered in close and squirted jelly from a tube in two spots above the woman's breasts.

"Careful!" Kate said to him sharply. "She has possible fractured ribs and a bruised heart."

He rolled his eyes. "Which means nada if we can't jump-start her. Besides, from the look of her, she's no stranger to rough handling."

Kate choked off a sharp retort. She understood why interns wisecracked, but Kate had glimpsed pieces of Charlene's life—her little girl, her abusive history, her frantic sister.

"All clear!"

A sharp snap of the paddles and Charlene's body convulsed like a rag doll tossed by a child.

All eyes fixed on the monitor.

Nothing.

"Again. All clear!"

Another brutal electrical jolt. Then the green line on the monitor jiggled. Jiggled again, then it shifted weakly into uneven movement. Standing beside Charlene Miller's battered body, Kate breathed a sigh of relief.

Ten minutes later, Kate stripped off her gloves and threw them into the wastebin before heading toward the waiting room where Charlene Miller's sister had finally been persuaded to stay. The room was empty except for the child.

The little girl was curled up in the chair, her feet tucked beneath her, her hands lying limp and unmoving. She stared straight ahead, her large unblinking blue eyes too big for her face. Too old for her years. What was it about this little girl? As Kate moved to approach her, a buzzing sound suddenly filled her head and rose to a deafening roar until all her other senses were overpowered. White light popped and flashed in her vision. Then fragments, like clips from a movie, came and went, too rapid and disjointed to pin down. Rising water. Fire. Screams. God, what was happening? A deep, dark abyss opened at her feet. Terror rose in her throat. Dizzy and faint, Kate reached out blindly, and found the edge of the chair beside tiny Lindy Miller.

The chair felt reassuringly solid. Aware of the child, Kate tried desperately to overcome her panic. Gasping, she rode the turmoil inside herself, calling up techniques she'd recommended to panicked patients. Breathe in...breathe out...in...out...

"Is my mommy going to die?"

She heard the child's question as if through a sound

tunnel. Rubbing her face with both hands, Kate took a deep breath before turning to look at the little girl.

"Is she going to die? I wanna know."

"Everything all right here, Dr. Madison?"

Kate looked up to find Jean Sharpe eyeing her narrowly. Kate clutched at her stethoscope, steadied by the familiar feel of it. "Yes. Thanks, Jean."

"Well…" There was lingering doubt in the nurse's shrewd gaze.

Kate pulled herself up straight in the chair. "Were you paging me?"

"No." Jean glanced at the child with thin-lipped disapproval. "Where is the aunt?"

"I'm not sure, but I'll sit with Lindy for a while."

With a reluctant nod, Jean finally walked away.

"Where is your aunt, Lindy?"

"Gone to the bathroom." Lindy looked at Kate solemnly. "He hurt her real bad this time, didn't he?"

This time? Outrage stirred in Kate, almost displacing the lingering reaction of her bizarre panic attack. "She's hurt, but we're here to help her, Lindy."

After a moment, Lindy asked, "Who're you?"

Kate put out her hand, but the child made no move to take it. "I'm Dr. Madison."

"Is she gonna die?" Lindy repeated.

"She's upstairs with another doctor now. They're doing all the good things doctors and nurses know about to help people like your mother."

Kate withstood the child's frank scrutiny for a moment. She could see Lindy weighing her words, sifting grown-up double talk through a sieve of countless meaningless promises. How many more senseless, brutal batterings would this child witness? Already she'd been robbed of her innocence.

"Would you like some hot chocolate?" Kate asked as

the aunt hurried toward them from the rest room. "We have a special pot in that little room right over there where we fix it."

"No."

"Oh, Doctor, is Charly going to be okay?" The aunt's face was anxious and worried.

"She's holding on. She's—"

"Dr. Madison, code one. Dr. Madison, code one."

Kate glanced distractedly toward the nurses' station, where Ricky was beckoning to her. "I'm sorry, Miss—?"

"McNeal. Gloria McNeal."

"Your sister's upstairs," Kate said, already at the door. "She's in the cardiac-care unit on the second floor. They—"

"Cardiac care? Doesn't that mean a heart attack? She didn't have a heart attack, did she?"

"She's had a cardiac event, Ms. McNeal, and fortunately the cardiac team arrived just in time."

"'Event'? What does that mean?"

"Cardiology isn't my specialty, but someone in CCU will explain. She is critical, Ms. McNeal, so for the next few hours, I think it's advisable for you to stay close by."

"Omigod. He's killed her."

"Not yet."

"Dr. Madison, code one. Dr. Madison, code one."

Ricky's voice on the intercom was insistent.

"I'm sorry," Kate said, touching the woman's hand. She took a step back. "I really have to go."

Still shaken from the strange panic episode, Kate hurried down the hall. She longed for a minute to collect herself, but an EMT crew was already wheeling a patient into the cubicle vacated by Charlene Miller. One look at the stretcher and Kate knew there was no time to waste; it was a small boy.

"This one's bad, Dr. Madison."

Kate sighed. Peter Wilkins was another crack EMT, and his judgment was seldom off. She lifted the blood-soaked bandage, and adrenaline kicked in as she had a look at the neat bullet hole just above the nipple. Blood pulsed from the wound with every heartbeat.

"Twelve-year-old boy found his father's handgun and was showing his friend how it worked," Peter said. "BP thirty-five over twenty, pulse faint, shocky. I intubated him in the unit. I'm gonna go see his dad. If he doesn't calm down he'll be your next patient."

"Deserves to be," Kelly Mareno muttered, slipping the pressure cuff on the small arm. Beside her, Celie Franks was hooking the boy up to the monitor, her face grave. The instant he was connected, the green line went flat and the ominous one-tone sound struck dread into every heart in the E.R.

"Get the crash cart!" Kate cried, running desperate hands over the small bloody rib cage toward the back to find the exit wound. She closed her eyes as her fingers found it, large, grotesquely lacerated, fatal.

"Crash cart on the way!" Jean Sharpe responded. Again the charge nurse had anticipated Kate's requirements.

Kate explored the exit wound, her fingers encountering torn flesh, mangled veins, bits and pieces of bone.

"Where's the bullet?" Kelly asked. Her eyes, visible above her mask, were worried.

"Went clean through," Celie replied, her large brown eyes solemn and sad. Only two months before, her grandson had died in a drive-by shooting.

"Not clean," Kate murmured. "But it went through."

The crash-cart team exploded through the doorway. It was Neal Winston again—this time with no wisecracks. His face grim, he moved to the boy's head. Kate shifted her hand and exposed the exit wound high on the left

side. Overhead, the monitor screamed in flat-line alert
mode.

"It's no good, Kate," Neal said softly. "You need to call
him."

"No!" She made to reach for the paddles herself just as
Jake Grissom appeared.

"Jake, I need you to take a look," she said, lifting the
boy slightly to give Jake a view of the wound. Overhead,
the monitor shrieked on. With his signature calmness,
Jake examined the wound, then studied the boy's pupils.
They were fixed, dilated. He shook his head. "Call him,
Kate. He's gone."

"No." She had the paddles now, but her hands were
shaking too much to perform the procedure. "No, Jake,
he's so little. He's just..."

She felt the curiosity of the team surrounding the table.

"No one could have survived that wound, Kate. The
bullet blasted through his ribs and lungs and stomach before nicking his heart."

"It's a miracle he survived the ambulance ride," someone said softly.

There was silence all around.

Neal took the paddles from Kate's hands. "Can't buy a
miracle today, it seems," he said, storing the equipment
in the cart. "We lost Charlene Miller ten minutes ago in
CCU."

Kate refused coffee from one of the aides as she came
out of the bathroom a few minutes later. Shaken and
heartsick, she knew her knotted stomach would reject caffeine. She must look like hell, but it had been hell to lose
that little boy. And then to have to tell the father. God,
would this night never end?

She pressed her hands to her abdomen and sat down
behind a desk in the physicians' lounge. Her mother. She

needed to call her again, and this time if she didn't get an answer, she was trying Leo Castille. Leo would know, and if he didn't, she'd send him next door to check.

With shaking hands, she punched the number in and waited through six rings. She drew a sigh of relief as Victoria Madison finally answered.

"Hello, Mother, this is Kate."

"Kate. This is a surprise. Just a minute... My goodness, I was dozing, reading a book, but it was so boring I drifted off for a—"

"I know it's late, but—"

"Oh, I keep late hours, you know that. How are you?"

"Actually, I'm calling to ask you the same thing, Mother." Eyes closed, Kate made an effort to steady the tremor in her voice. But the face of Charlene Miller kept intruding. "Are you sure everything's okay?"

"What kind of question is that, Kate?" Victoria's voice gained strength, and when she spoke again, it was in her usual no-nonsense tone. "Of course I'm fine. Why would you think otherwise?"

"Amber left a message on my machine a couple of days ago, Mother. She said you haven't been looking well."

Victoria huffed with annoyance. "I don't know what Amber was thinking to upset you like that!"

"Maybe she was thinking I've been neglecting you. And she's right. I should have managed to get down to Louisiana before now, Mother. I just—"

"Boston is fifteen-hundred miles away, Kate," Victoria interrupted with impatience. "Besides, I don't want or need coddling. You know I hate that."

"I do know." Her mother prided herself on her independence. She lived alone and liked it. She didn't need Kate and made no bones about it. "I suppose if there's any coddling to be done, Leo's more than willing to do it."

"I don't know about 'coddling,' but he certainly nags and fusses so much that I sometimes want to send him off on a very long cruise."

"And he'd probably go if you'd go with him."

"What a preposterous suggestion, Kate."

"I was teasing, Mother." Kate rubbed her forehead tiredly. Her mother and Leo had insisted for years that their relationship was strictly friendship in spite of the fact that Kate and Amber had fantasized since they were schoolgirls that Victoria and Leo would someday marry, making them sisters. "But since you mention it, what is Leo nagging and fussing about?"

"Oh, the usual." Victoria's tone was dismissive. "You know how he is."

Kate heard rustling and the telltale click of Victoria's lighter, then the soft rush of air as she exhaled. "Are you smoking again, Mother?"

"I've almost quit." She made an impatient sound. "Do we have to waste time talking about this, Kate? You're so busy in that job, we hardly ever talk, so when you do call, I'd love it if we didn't get off on subjects that we can't agree on. Like smoking. Lord knows, the rest of the world is obsessed enough about that."

"With good reason, Mother," Kate said, closing her eyes. She agreed with her mother about one thing—she wished their conversations could be easy and loving and warm, not complicated by underlying strain and some other indefinable emotion, the source of which had always baffled and distressed her.

"What exactly did Amber say?" Victoria asked.

"Just that you didn't look well." An ache had started at a spot between her eyes. "You would tell me if something was wrong, wouldn't you, Mother? I could fly in to New Orleans and be in Bayou Blanc within hours. All you have to do is say the word."

"You're overreacting, Kate. I think you should concentrate on getting your own life together, then we'll talk about me. They say a divorce is one of the most traumatic of life's crises, and yours is barely six months old."

Kate turned to see a flurry of activity at the entrance to the E.R. and missed the next few words of her mother's lecture. As the patient was wheeled past her by two EMTs, Kate signaled to Betsy to follow them.

"Kate? Kate!"

"Sorry, Mother, but a patient has just arrived. I'm next up, so they'll probably be paging me. What were you saying?"

"Gracious, girl. How can you consider visiting me when it's difficult just to talk for a few minutes on the phone?"

"I'm at work now, Mother. I've tried for a couple of days to call you from home, but you haven't answered."

"Well, like you, Kate, I have things to do and places to go."

"Have you been away?"

"Just here and there. People have to get out, you know."

"Dr. Madison, code one. Dr. Madison, code one."

"There's the page, Mother. I'm sorry, but I must go. I'll call sometime tomorrow morning. After I grab a few hours' sleep, okay?"

"What happened with your promotion?"

"It's on hold. I'm sorry, Mother, I really—"

"Oh, go ahead then, Kate!" There was a clunk, then silence. Kate looked blankly at the receiver in her hand. Her mother had hung up.

"Didn't you hear the code call, Dr. Madison?"

Kate replaced the receiver before turning to acknowledge Jean Sharpe. "Thank you, Jean," she said dryly.

Sharpe's question had been both a prod and a reprimand. The woman was a stickler for procedure. She believed new residents should be indoctrinated at the outset on the importance of the nursing staff—a completely unnecessary precaution in Kate's case. She already had monumental respect for the role played by nurses. Perhaps Sharpe sensed Kate's feeling that she had overstepped her bounds.

"We have a critical patient in 4A cubicle," Sharpe snapped. "Dr. Grissom is occupied in 6C with a crushed femur and tachycardia. I hope you're recovered from your...emotional reaction over the gunshot wound, because 4A is a heart attack."

"Are you certain of that?"

"As certain as I can be after thirty years' experience," Sharpe said with a sniff.

"Then see that we have the clot buster handy," Kate ordered curtly, turning on her heel to head for the trauma area.

"You don't have to tell me how to do my job, Dr. Madison."

Shaking her head, Kate refused to be drawn further. Jean Sharpe had shrewdly noted Kate's fragile state tonight and wouldn't hesitate to push her to the edge. Kate knew that, in the nurse's opinion, it had been an inexcusable lapse of professionalism for Kate to reveal her distress when the young boy had died. Kate could only imagine what the woman would think if she'd witnessed her bizarre panic attack in front of little Lindy Miller a few minutes ago.

In cubicle 4A, Kate shoved the curtain aside. There were hours to go before she could leave and try to put this horrible night behind her. Instead of relieving her mind, the call to her mother had added to her concern about Victoria. Something was definitely wrong. She was going to have to make a trip to Louisiana. And soon.

She rubbed her head wearily, uncertain what she'd needed from Victoria other than to hear her voice and be reassured that she was okay. Instead, she was more depressed and anxious than ever—emotions that had no place in the E.R.

One look at the patient and Kate felt her dismay rise. The accumulation of hours of stress was telling on her. The patient was an elderly man, husky with a huge, distended belly, which was common in cardiac patients. Thanks to Kelly and Celie, he was already hooked up to the monitor, but he was sitting straight up, gasping for breath.

"I'm having a heart attack, Doc," he said, his face gray with pain.

"We've given him morphine," Kelly said. "His EKG shows some irregularities, but it doesn't confirm that he's having a heart attack."

"I'm having one, goddamn it! I couldn't be in this kinda pain unless it was a heart attack. I can't stand much more of this."

"Have we got his stats?" Kate asked Kelly as she fitted the earpieces of her stethoscope in place.

"Yes, but there are no enzymes in his blood yet."

"The hell with enzymes and blood!" the patient groaned. "I'm dying, here. Do something!"

"Just be calm, Mr.—" Kate looked at the plastic strip on the man's wrist. "Mr. Carmello. If you are having a heart attack, the worst thing you can do is to panic. We need a—"

"Just gimme one of those clot busters to head it off," Carmello said. "I read about it. How come you're not using it? Jesus, it hurts like hell."

Kate nodded at Kelly. "Give him another three of morphine while I try to hear..." She trailed off, straining to analyze the rushing sound of Carmello's heartbeat.

"His pressure's dropping, Doctor."

Kate nodded. "Have we called cardiology?"

Jean Sharpe appeared, looking cool and disapproving. "I've paged Dr. Lincoln, but he hasn't responded."

Sharpe could afford to be cool, Kate thought, looking first at the monitor and then at the trauma team clustered around Carmello. The responsibility for the patient was fully in Kate's hands.

New anxiety welled up in her. She was far from certain that Carmello was a cardiac case. Many men feared a heart attack when they were simply suffering from indigestion. If that was the case, administering streptokinase could be fatal. On the other hand, if it *was* an MI—myocardial infarction—enzymes dumped into the bloodstream from the damaged heart muscle would show in his stats. And that was the only way she could be entirely certain.

"I need that clot buster," Carmello said again. He'd fallen back on the stretcher and was bathed in sweat. "I got good insurance."

"It's not that, Mr. Carmello. Just be calm…"

"We can't wait for Dr. Lincoln," Kelly said in a low, urgent tone, her eyes on Kate.

"I can't give him the streptokinase," Kate snapped. "Not yet." She shot a look at the cardiac pattern on the monitor. It was erratic. Dangerously so. She drew in a sharp breath as the line went flat.

"He's coding!" Kelly said.

"Get the crash cart in here!" Kate yelled as the team moved into a well-practiced drill. With her eye on the monitor, she motioned for a syringe to administer medication straight to the heart. It was too late for the streptokinase; Joseph Carmello's heart was in full arrest.

"Nobody in cardiology on the way, Doctor," Celie said after taking a quick look down the hall.

"I've called," Jean Sharpe informed them, directing the crash cart to the stretcher. "Three times. They're apparently busy up there, too."

The team was good, coordinated and quick. The syringe Kate had called for was in her hand in seconds. Her own heart was in her throat. Panic made her hands shake. For the third time that night, she was presiding over a dying patient.

"What's the deal here?"

Jean Sharpe turned with relief. "Dr. Lincoln! Thank goodness you're here. We have an acute MI."

Ward Lincoln, tall, lean and arrogantly confident, shot Kate a sharp look. "Have you administered the buster?"

"No, I—"

He shouldered past her and gazed on the gray face of the patient. "Why the hell not?"

"We didn't get an enzyme read in his blood. Giving streptokinase without—"

"Oh, for God's sake!" He motioned to Kelly. "Have you got it ready?"

Kate stared in disbelief. Joseph Carmello's heart had stopped. The drug would be useless. "But, Dr. Lincoln—"

"You've done enough, Dr. Madison," he snapped. "Now get out of my way and let me see if I can save this man's life."

Stunned, Kate moved back. After a split second of hesitation, her team began to respond to Ward Lincoln's curt, confident orders. Everyone fell to the tasks barked out by the cardiologist. But overhead, the monitor still screamed in unrelenting electronic panic.

Seven minutes later, after a scathing look at Kate, Ward Lincoln called time and all activity ceased. As he stripped his gloves and tossed them in disgust in the wastebin, the team stood awkwardly silent. Every bleak face mirrored the toll of their failed effort to save Joseph Carmello. Nobody looked at Kate.

TWO

Kate paused at the door of Dr. Charles Winslow's office, gathering herself for what would probably be an uncomfortable interview. She assumed she was here to present to the administrator her account of Joseph Carmello's death in the E.R. on Friday night, which he would in turn pass on to the board. She had the statement with her in a large manila envelope, just in case.

She'd spent the weekend worrying. All mortalities were routinely reviewed. It was difficult to anticipate how such a dicey call would be viewed by physicians who hadn't been there. The worst that could happen would be a written reprimand, depending on how critical Ward Lincoln's opinion proved to be. If he felt she wasn't justified in holding off on administering streptokinase and said as much to the board, she could kiss the promotion to chief resident goodbye.

She was still reeling from the combined effects of the shift from hell on Friday night. After Carmello's death, she'd fled to the doctors' lounge, but the damage had been done. The expressions on the faces of her team—curiosity, disgust, sympathy—were like a deck of Tarot cards foretelling her fate.

With a humorless huff, she wondered what her co-workers in the E.R. would say if they knew how close to the edge she had come, lately. Hopefully they never would. Drawing a deep breath, she rapped smartly on Winslow's door.

The administrator of St. Luke's Hospital was standing when she stepped inside his office. He greeted her, waved her to a seat directly opposite his desk, then sat down and for a few moments studied some notes on a lined legal pad in front of him.

Finally he locked the fingers of his hands together, rested them on the pad and raised his eyes to hers.

"I've just completed a conference call with members of the board, Dr. Madison. I'm afraid you were the subject of our discussion."

She managed a smile. "I hope I shouldn't infer anything negative from the word 'afraid,'" she said.

"You've had some stress in your personal life lately. Your divorce is quite recent, I understand."

"Yes, but—"

"Sorry about that." He was nodding solemnly. "Five years in trauma care takes a toll, as well," he said, shifting his hands to glance at his notes.

"Some days I wish I were an accountant." It was another weak attempt at humor, but Winslow didn't crack a smile. She felt a pang of unease. "I'm kidding, of course," she added.

He lifted a page on the pad, checking something, then dropped it. "Friday night seemed to be one of those times if the account I've been given is accurate."

"Yes, we lost three patients in a row. It was…difficult." Without a doubt, she'd appeared unprofessional on Friday night. Weeping and uncontrollable shakes were unacceptable reactions to life-and-death situations in the E.R. She still winced, recalling her behavior.

He was studying his notes again. "The young boy was critical upon admission."

"A senseless accident with a handgun."

"Yes, yes. Tragic."

"I was very upset when we couldn't save him," Kate said, suspecting that Winslow had already heard details of her emotional reaction from Jean Sharpe. She might as well admit it. "It's always hard when we lose a child. But his wound—"

"Yes. No one could have saved him. Or the battered woman. Senseless. Absolutely senseless." He unlocked his fingers and leaned back in his chair. "But Joseph Carmello is the reason we needed to have this discussion."

"You've spoken to Ward Lincoln?"

"Yes. The board wanted to hear from him directly."

Kate leaned forward to give him the envelope. "My account of the event is written up in the report in this envelope. Mr. Carmello presented with severe chest pains. He—"

"Yes, I have the account from Dr. Lincoln and the charge nurse on duty that night."

Kate settled back in her chair, her heart sinking. "Jean Sharpe."

He took the envelope and slipped it, unopened, into a file. "I understand you have some concerns lately about your mother." He adjusted his bifocals and ran his finger down the notes on the pad. "She's in—ah—Louisiana?"

"Yes. She lives in a suburb of New Orleans. But how did you—"

"How did we learn your mother isn't well? These things get around, Dr. Madison, when people work in close proximity. I think of the dynamics in an E.R. as similar to those in a large family. Everyone has his or her duties and we all must work together to keep the family cohesive, happy, productive."

Winslow was a joke among trauma specialists. He'd enjoyed a very undistinguished career as a surgeon in internal medicine, specializing in the removal of gall bladders

before endoscopic techniques revolutionized the procedure. Clumsy and slow, he'd never learned the technique
of wielding minuscule scalpels while viewing everything
on a video monitor. Consequently, he'd moved into hospital management. His bloodless personality was far
more suited to crunching numbers and calculating the
profit margin than dealing with sick people.

"Louisiana," he continued, tapping his glasses on the
legal pad. "Yes, indeed, a very interesting culture.
Unique. I was there once for the Mardi Gras."

"Dr. Winslow, did the board discuss the chief trauma
resident slot?"

"Yes, as a matter of fact." The glasses went back onto
his face. "I'm afraid they decided to offer the position to
Jake Grissom."

"Oh."

"Yes, I know you had hopes there, Dr. Madison, but after Friday night... Well, as I said, trauma work takes a
toll."

"Are you suggesting the job went to Jake because the
board considered me too emotional?"

Winslow frowned and shook his head. "I don't believe
you heard me say anything like that, Dr. Madison. However, the events of Friday night did convince the board
that you might benefit from taking some time off."

"Excuse me?"

"As you know, physicians in the E.R. must be quick
and confident. They can't give in to the—ah—stress. Take
the case of Joseph Carmello, for example."

"Yes, do let's take that example, Dr. Winslow." With
fear knotting her stomach, Kate leaned forward, pointing
to the envelope with her report. "I believe my actions that
night will prove correct. Although Dr. Lincoln seemed to
think I should have administered the streptokinase earlier, we didn't have anything from Mr. Carmello's blood-

work that indicated he was in fact having a myocardial infarction. He—''

Winslow held up a hand. "He was a forty-one-year-old male with three children still in secondary school. Because of your hesitation, Dr. Madison, those children are now fatherless. His wife's a widow."

"Dr. Winslow…" She drew a breath. "As you know, that drug is extremely powerful and can be life-threatening if—''

"What could be more life-threatening than what happened at your hands, Dr. Madison?"

"I made a prudent decision!"

"Dr. Lincoln was most emphatic in expressing his opinion to the contrary. I know physicians can disagree, but in this case it proved a regrettable decision on your part to withhold the drug. The patient died, Dr. Madison," he reminded her almost gently.

"I stand by my decision," Kate repeated doggedly. "The drug was contraindicated under the circumstances."

"And, of course, you have that right—''

"Did Ward Lincoln say I was responsible for Mr. Carmello's death?"

Winslow looked pained. "You know I can't reveal what was said in a closed meeting, Dr. Madison."

"Even though it puts a black mark on my record here at St. Luke's?"

"Well, now, that's something we need to discuss." He lifted the pad and turned the page. "When something like this happens, we begin to wonder if it might happen again. We can't just let—''

"Something like what?" Kate cried. "I made a good decision based on my experience and on accepted medical protocol."

"Yes, yes, but your competency has been questioned by some members of the board."

"Based on a single dissenting opinion by Dr. Lincoln and a biased individual who has held a grudge against me from day one here at St. Luke's," Kate stated.

Winslow began collecting the material in front of him. "Unfortunately, we can't just disregard something like this, Dr. Madison. There's always the concern for exposure. We can't afford a lawsuit." The file folder, legal pad and Kate's unopened report were now in a neat stack.

With her fingers tightly laced in her lap, Kate asked quietly, "What exactly are you telling me, Dr. Winslow?"

"I'm afraid that the board has decided to suspend your privileges at St. Luke's."

She stared at him. In spite of everything she'd endured Friday night, she hadn't expected anything like this. "You can't be serious," she whispered.

"I'm authorized to tell you that once you've... ah...overcome the stress, we might consider reviewing the decision."

"'Might.'"

A tight smile touched his lips. "No guarantees, of course. There can't be in matters like this. You understand."

"You're suspending me." She searched his face in disbelief.

He stood. Clearly the interview was over, as well as her chance to argue her fate. "Naturally, the board and I wish you success in your next position, Dr. Madison. Wherever that might be."

But not at St. Luke's.

"Check with my secretary as you leave." He began edging his way from behind his desk. "She has your final check."

After closing the door of Winslow's office, Kate stood

with her heart pounding so frantically that she was light-headed. Unable to think, she simply stood with one hand at her throat and the other clenched around the familiar shape of her stethoscope—the symbol of her profession; the tool that signaled to the world she was a healer.

But no more. Charles Winslow had just pronounced the death knell to her career at St. Luke's, no matter how he tried to spin the message. Where was she going? What was she to do? She felt like the child she'd once been, needing the warmth and security of a mother to shield her from nameless terrors. But she was no longer a child. She was an adult. A physician.

And then deep, deep emotion welled up in her chest and she fought a terrible need to scream with outrage. Anger and panic and grief combined, numbing her as she made her way to the exit, desperate to escape before she brought even more disgrace upon herself. Dear God, if her career was over, so was her life!

THREE

A week later Kate stood on Dr. Leo Castille's front porch ringing his doorbell with a touch of anxiety. She'd rushed the last leg of her drive from Boston to Louisiana, but the closer she'd gotten to Bayou Blanc, the more her spirits had lifted in anticipation of being home again. Her mother hadn't exactly sounded thrilled over the timing of the visit, but Kate had refused to dwell on that. Still, she'd expected Victoria to be at home and had been a little concerned to find the big house on Vermilion Lane empty.

She heard sounds somewhere in Dr. Leo's house and smiled, anticipating her reunion with Amber's dad. But it was Amber Russo herself who answered the door.

"Kate! What're you doing here, *chère?* We've all been expecting a call from the airport. God, you look so good to me!" She pulled Kate inside and threw her arms around her. "I can't believe I happened to be at home when you got here, darlin'. Another hour and you'd have missed me."

"Hi, Amber." Smiling, Kate stood holding both Amber's hands. "Surprise."

"Come into this house, Katy-did," Amber said. Following her through the foyer and the hall, Kate found herself in the wide-beamed family room at the rear of the sprawling Acadian-style house. After urging Kate to a barstool, Amber headed for the fridge. "I'll bet you want something cold. It's hot as hell outside, but you probably noticed that the instant you stepped off the plane, huh?"

"How are you, Amber?"

Amber flashed a bright smile as she took a pitcher from the fridge. "I'm fine, of course. Tickled that you've decided to visit. You didn't give us much notice. How'd you get here? Victoria wondered about flight arrivals and so on. I bet you rented a car. You didn't need to do that, Kate. But you're so independent."

"I didn't rent a car. I have my own. And I didn't fly, I drove. But speaking of my mother, where is she?"

"You drove?" Amber repeated in astonishment. "All the way from Boston?"

"It's a long story. So, do you know where Mother is?"

"Uh, she's with Dad, I think," Amber said, waving a hand. "They're somewhere, who knows? But this is so…bizarre. You drove. God, that's what—two thousand miles! What do you mean it's a long story? And don't say you're heading back to Boston before I'm able to plan something to welcome you home."

Kate held up both hands. "Please, no parties. Not just yet, okay, Amber? Besides, we have time. I'm in no particular hurry to get back."

"Really?" Amber paused, the pitcher suspended over a glass. "How'd you manage that? I thought you E.R. types were always on a frantic schedule."

"Even we E.R. types have to stop and regroup eventually. In fact, as I passed the exit for the cottage, I realized it's been a long time since we were there." Her family and Amber's jointly owned a cottage on the north shore of Lake Pontchartrain. During their childhood, they'd spent many summer weekends and most holidays there. Even after she and Amber were married, they'd still managed to spend a few days together at the cottage once a year. Kate was reminded of the good memories as she'd passed the exit to get there on the interstate. "How long has it been, Amber?" Kate asked, unable to recall.

Amber arranged a sprig of mint in a glass of iced tea and pushed it across the bar to Kate. "Three years."

"Wow. About two too long, huh?"

"It hasn't been easy scheduling private time since I married Deke," Amber said, her voice changing. "When I was married to Ethan, he never cared one way or the other what I did, so long as it didn't interfere with bank business."

"You knew what he was when you married him, Amber."

Amber made a face as she sprinkled sweetener into her tea. "I knew he was rich and eligible. I didn't know he would be so boring."

Kate was shaking her head, smiling. "He was fifty-one and you were twenty-two!"

"Well, that's no excuse! I don't think Ethan ever knew how to have fun, even when he was young."

"You knew he was a man whose business came first."

Amber sighed. "I know, I know. I was a 'trophy wife' before the term was invented." She giggled. "I'm just grateful he didn't make me sign a prenuptial. I was so young and stupid I probably would have done it and then when I divorced him I wouldn't have gotten half of everything!" She made an impatient sound. "Oh, that's enough about Ethan! It was over fifteen years ago, for heaven's sake!"

"There's been a lot of water under the bridge for us both since then, hasn't there?" Kate said quietly.

Amber touched her hand. "I was sorry to hear about your divorce, Kate. Is your heart broken?"

"Not really. Which says something about my character, but I'm not sure what."

"Oh, you always were so hard on yourself. Besides, I

never liked Robert much. Oops, can I say that?" Amber scrunched up her shoulders as she used to do when they were kids, as if waiting for a scolding.

"Actually, toward the end I didn't like him very much myself." Kate twirled the mint sprig, smiling. "So, how's Deke these days?"

"Speaking of men we don't like? Same as ever. Although he has his fans."

"You don't like him?"

"Even in perfect marriages, don't women sometimes get a little fed up?"

"I wouldn't know, considering I didn't have a perfect one." Kate took the napkin Amber passed to her, then added, "Mother told me Deke's radio show is very well-known."

"Like I said, he has his fans."

But Amber wasn't one of them? Kate hadn't been around Deke much, but in the few times she had, he'd been just a little too full of himself for her to warm up to him. "Mother also tells me that your career is taking off big-time. Amber Lifestyles is fabulously successful, plus you're now a regular on morning television…and you write a weekly column for the newspaper." Kate smiled. "All I can say is, wow! And congratulations, Amber. What does Deke have to say about his talented wife?"

"Not much." With a short laugh, Amber turned to take the pitcher back to the fridge. "He's so wrapped up in his own stuff that I honestly don't know what he thinks about mine."

"He can't help but recognize your phenomenal success, Amber." Kate curved her hands around the cool glass. "Actually, it's pretty unusual to have two celebrities in one family. Maybe he's feeling a little professional jealousy."

"Maybe." Amber shrugged and with a toss of her black

curls walked back to the bar. "Then he's just gonna have to get over it, because I'm having a ball!"

"Good girl." Kate found herself studying the small extras placed here and there in Leo's kitchen and den. Evidence of Amber's talent for the unique and tasteful was everywhere. For Deke to deny her the pleasure of his approval smacked of a selfishness and indifference to his wife's needs that was unflattering, to say the least. Why couldn't he share their dual celebrity with her?

Kate finished her iced tea and tucked the corner of her napkin alongside the empty glass. "We were talking about finding time to go to the cottage. I'd love to do that. Do you think you can?"

"Maybe you should wait until you've seen Victoria before we make any plans, Kate."

"Something's wrong, isn't it, Amber? Mother sounded evasive when I said I was coming home. We don't have a cozy relationship like some mothers and daughters, but I've always felt welcome even though she doesn't say it in so many words. What's going on?"

Amber came around the bar to walk with Kate toward the door. "Victoria's always been complex, Kate, and so has your relationship. It's totally wrong to think she doesn't want you. Once you've seen her, you'll know that." At the door she frowned as Deke's Range Rover turned into the drive. "Uh-oh. Daddy's home."

"Gotta run," Kate said, brushing cheeks with Amber and kissing the air. After discussing Deke, she didn't particularly want to see him. She started down the steps. "Give Deke my best and tell him I'll see him later."

"Okay. Wait! One more thing," Amber called from the top of the steps. "We're doing the Fais Do-Do Festival the weekend of the sixth. Did Victoria tell you about it? Food, fun, frolicking... You'll still be in town then, won't you?

There'll be dancin' in the streets, *chère*. Deke and I are the headline act."

Kate smiled, walking backward. "What is it with the faux Creole accent, Amber?"

Amber pushed her curls up with one hand and batted her green eyes. "It's my trademark, *chère*. Don't I look Cajun-Creole?"

"Yeah, only I happen to know your ancestors came from England and Spain."

Amber grinned impudently and put a finger to her lips. "Shh. Don't tell my adoring public. And don't miss the Fais Do-Do, you hear? You want to see Deke and me onstage, don't you?"

"Hometown girl makes good, hmm? I wouldn't miss it." Kate smiled, lifting her hand to wave. "Enjoyed the chat and the tea."

"Bye, Kate."

Kate's brow was wrinkled in thought as she picked her way across the broad stretch of Leo's lawn. She'd looked forward to catching up with Amber, but she hadn't anticipated hearing there was trouble in her marriage. Or had she read more into Amber's chatter than was warranted? Amber had always been overly dramatic. Which reminded Kate of Amber's insinuations about Victoria. Where was her mother? She needed to see for herself that everything was okay.

When she crossed the small footbridge built by Leo years ago, the outline of her mother's house became visible. But there was no sign that she had come home. Kate's anxiety returned.

"Was that Kate I saw hightailing it across the lawn?" Deke Russo removed his sunglasses and stuck them in his shirt pocket. "What's the matter? She only likes half of the Russo team?"

Amber Russo fixed a smile on her face, stepping back from the door as Deke came inside. "She wasn't here for a visit. She was looking for Victoria. You won't believe this, Deke. She drove all the way from Boston!"

"Alone?"

"Yeah. At least I think so." Amber plucked a less-than-fresh bloom from a mass of glads in a tall vase in the foyer, then jiggled a couple of others here and there. Stepping back, she surveyed the arrangement. "Put it this way. She didn't mention anyone being with her. And guess what? She's not going back right away, either."

"Yeah, right." Deke loosened his tie as he headed for Leo's den and the bar, unbuttoning his shirt collar as he walked. "She's planning an extended stay in Bayou Blanc when she hasn't been able to fit in a weekend for more than two years?"

"I'm just telling you what she said, Deke."

"Well, if Kate says it, there's nothing else to be said, is there?"

From the window off the sunroom, Amber studied the patch of roofline just visible through the trees. "She's worried about Victoria."

"It's about time." Deke went behind the bar and selected a decanter of Scotch. "Fortunately for her, if Victoria's needed tender loving care, you've been around to supply it."

Amber sighed at the resentment in his tone. Deke was so possessive. Sometimes she thought he'd be happy if there was no one else in her life at all, not even her father. She moved to the bar beside Deke and filled a glass with ice cubes from a built-in automatic icemaker.

"Kate lives in Boston, Deke. I'm right here in New Orleans, forty minutes from Bayou Blanc. And Victoria's right next door to Daddy. It's natural for me to look in on her. She's been like a mother to me since I was six."

"You make my point, Amber." He removed the top of the decanter and sniffed the liquor inside, then poured himself a generous drink in the glass Amber provided. "You've always been more tied to Kate's mother's apron strings than Kate ever was."

Amber stared at a grouping of family photographs on the piano in the corner of the den. More than one of the pictures was of Victoria. "I'm not that close to Victoria, Deke." Behind her, he made a derisive sound and she added defensively, "And even if I am, how would you feel if your mother had died when you were six?"

"Ah, poor baby." He chucked her under the chin on his way to a big recliner. "You had everything as a kid, Amber—money, family, a fabulous house in the right neighborhood. Your daddy pampered you and spoiled you rotten. What if you weren't even sure who your daddy was?"

"What are you talking about, Deke? Your daddy was a policeman."

"That's what I always thought, but hell, women lie."

"Your own mother? Come on, Deke." He was obviously in one of his moods. After finishing the day's broadcast, he'd driven with her and Stephen across the lake and then gone to an "appointment." Whatever it was, it must not have gone well.

Amber reached beneath the bar for a coaster, then took it over and placed it under Deke's glass. She was continually reminding him to be careful of things, for all the good it did. "What's wrong, Deke? Have you had a bad day?"

"Every day is a bad day at that goddamned circus."

"The radio station? You didn't say anything on the way over here."

"Because I didn't want to think about it." He fumbled for the handle on the side of the chair, drawing up the footrest with a thump. "You know what they did? The station hired a new call screener and he's a nitwit. He let some left-wing wacko through on the show today. The guy was giving me hell about a spot we ran last week. Seems he thought I was unduly critical of the NOPD." Deke's mouth thinned with spite. "What I'd like to know is, how do those bleeding-heart liberals expect to keep the streets safe when they're the ones responsible for the police department's revolving-door policy? The cops arrest these lowlifes, give 'em a cup of coffee just like they were human, then blow their noses and let 'em go."

"Because that's the way the law is written, Deke."

"Then it's a stupid-ass law!" He released the footrest and rose out of the chair. "Besides, what the hell do you know about real life? Your old man's a doctor, for Chrissake! When my old man was on the force, they knew how to get the attention of the scum doing the crime."

"He's your father again now, huh?"

"He knew some shit, Robbie Russo did."

"Rubber hoses and sweatboxes."

"It worked, didn't it?"

She wanted to roll her eyes in distaste, but she resisted the urge, knowing it would send him off on a round of name-calling and pointless complaints about the New Orleans Police Department that could go on for an hour. When Deke was feeling disagreeable, she'd learned to hold her tongue. It took very little for him to cross the line into out-and-out cruelty. No matter how she told herself that words couldn't really hurt her, they did.

"I need another drink," he said, heading for the bar.

"Do you think you should have another, Deke? We still have to make the trip home."

"You can drive." She watched him throw ice into his glass and pour more Scotch. He added a scant amount of water and tossed off a good portion of the drink in one swallow.

"So what was the appointment that was so all-fired important we had to drive over here today?" she asked, hoping to divert him.

"I wanted to interview a call screener. I'm replacing the idiot they hired, count on that. This guy sent his résumé to me personally. Otherwise they'd probably throw it out with who knows how many other qualified people to hire some kiss-ass handpicked by Dick Rogers."

"Dick Rogers?" Had she missed a twist in his tirade?

Deke gulped some of his drink and gazed angrily into the glass. "You know what that asshole Rogers did? He came into the studio about five minutes before airtime today and told me the ratings for 'Talk the Right Way' were down." Still clutching the glass, he pointed a finger at her. "What I wanna know is, who the hell are they getting to do these polls? My ratings are as hot as they ever were. Deke Russo *is* talk radio in New Orleans. Nobody, but nobody, knows this town like I do. I've got connections at the NOPD, at city hall, at the chamber of commerce. You name it, baby. I know somebody big there. They think they can get some new hotshot in from who-the-hell-knows-where and he can bring in an audience like Deke Russo, they're full of shit!"

He was pacing as he talked, using his hands for emphasis. Once, she'd watched his broadcast and been amused as he waved and punched and slashed the air behind the mike to make a point. Now his mannerisms seemed boorish. Why had she ever thought his bad-boy charm attractive? How had she made such a ghastly mistake?

"Dick Rogers better watch his ass if he starts messing with me," he grumbled.

So that was it. He was feeling the sting of a downturn in ratings. For almost eight years, Deke had owned daytime talk in New Orleans. The core of his audience was extremists—on the political right. They were fiercely loyal, but no show could survive without other listeners—people who could be entertained by Deke's schtick but whose views were more moderate.

"Have they actually mentioned bringing someone else in?" She was careful to keep her tone neutral.

"No, but I can read that son of a bitch's mind." Deke was standing at the French doors now, staring out.

"Dick Rogers always seemed very professional to me, Deke. Are you sure you—"

He turned and nailed her with a fierce look. "Whose side are you on, Amber?"

"Yours, of course, but—"

"So you like Dickie, hmm?"

"I hardly know him, Deke."

"Just don't forget, sugar, that I opened the door for you at Channel 3—not Dick Rogers. Amber Lifestyles would still be a hobby and your only customers a few Yuppie friends if I hadn't paved the way for you to get that TV spot."

"I've always acknowledged the fact that you helped me, Deke," she said quietly.

"Damn right."

But her career had never been a hobby, and she resented Deke's insistence on dismissing everything she'd accomplished until he'd decided to take a hand in it. In fact, she'd worked like crazy to put Amber Lifestyles on the map and had actually made her reputation before Deke even noticed.

He was shaking his head, the worst of his bad temper mellowing out. "It beats me how the elite of New Orleans pay such humongous fees for that shit you think up."

Inside, she seethed. Deke didn't know the first thing about gracious living, about art, about the sheer joy of creating an environment in a home that made it a pleasure to step inside the door. But she kept her thoughts hidden, kept her opinion to herself. Once, she'd recklessly taken issue with his arrogance and she'd gotten more than she bargained for. Now she didn't care what he thought, so long as he didn't interfere; so long as he didn't jeopardize what she'd so carefully built for herself—by herself.

Deke watched her straighten a few magazines and anchor them with a paperweight. "So, what's up now that Kate's gonna be around for a few days? Y'all planning on going out to the lake?"

"I miss those outings at the lake," Amber murmured, looking again at the collection of photos. "It's been three years." One of her favorite pictures was a snapshot taken when she and Kate were about ten years old. The cottage was in the background. Amber picked up Deke's coaster and took it back to the bar. "Kate hasn't even seen Victoria yet," she told him. "When she does, I don't imagine she'll be interested in going to the lake."

He opened a hard briefcase with a loud snap of its twin locks. "Good. That'll save you from having to decline," he said, pulling out some papers. "You're not a swinging single anymore."

She didn't rise to the taunt. Deke knew she couldn't fool around even if she wanted to. He kept a tight rein on her comings and goings, and he had a vast network of "friends" who'd like nothing better than to keep an eye on his "little woman" for him.

Amber watched him studying the papers and felt nothing but resentment. Another divorce was out of the question, of course. She tried to recall what it was that had attracted her to Deke in the first place. At forty-two, he was strikingly handsome. Black hair and blue eyes added to the rakish charm that he claimed came straight from his Italian ancestors. The truth was, she didn't think Deke knew anything about his ancestors. And even though his job was almost exclusively sedentary, he was still as lean and rugged looking as he'd been five years ago when they'd married. Of course, the tan was artificial—several hours a week in a booth gave him the look of a dedicated sports fisher or a sailing enthusiast. But Deke was no sportsman, his love of guns notwithstanding. Maybe the wicked gleam in his eye had appealed to something reckless and undisciplined in her. And sex, of course. That, at least, had been good.

While he pored over his papers, Amber drifted around the room repositioning objects, plumping cushions, twitching magazines. As she refolded an afghan, she said, "I picked up the messages from my office, and guess what, Deke? Maison Belle wants me to endorse a line of linens and things for their stores."

"Hmm." Without looking up, Deke scribbled a note on the margin of a page.

Amber straightened a tall candle on the mantel. "They'll market them from all their New Orleans-area locations, plus they've acquired some new stores in Florida. Isn't that something?"

"I thought that guy gave me a phone number to reach him in Baton Rouge."

"Who, Deke?"

"The call screener. Damn it, Amber. Don't you ever listen to anything I say?"

"What do you think about Maison Belle? I'm calling Sidney Rosenthal as soon as we get back to town. I want to be clued in before we start talking contract terms. This could really turn into something lucrative, Deke. Bed linens, kitchen stuff, window treatments—the possibilities are endless!"

"I must have left that shit in my car," Deke muttered. He got up and moved to the door of the sunroom, where

Leo had a television set. Beyond the room were the pool and hot tub. The area was empty. "Where's Stephen? He can go out and get it for me."

"He's at the computer in Daddy's office. You heard him say that he had a new game he wanted to try."

"What the hell is it with that kid? When I was fifteen years old you would've had to hog-tie me to the bedpost to keep me inside on a summer day. Hell, school's out, girls are sashayin' around advertisin' it, and my kid's holed up in his room like some nerd."

"He's not like you, Deke." *Thank God.*

"He's not like you, Deke," he repeated, throwing his pen down in disgust. "You're damn right he's not like me. And as long as you keep encouraging him to spend his summer vacations mooning in his room, he'll never have a clue what the real world is like. Sometimes I think he'd be better off if his real mother was still alive."

There was no point in arguing that it wasn't her fault Stephen chose solitude over more sociable teenage pursuits. "You want me to get him?" she asked.

"Hell, I'll go get it myself. If it's not a computer or something that spits out weird-sounding music, he wouldn't recognize it, anyway."

Amber lay back against the softly patterned rattan sofa in the sunroom. Outside, Deke's Range Rover started up with a roar, then backed out and accelerated down the street with a reckless squeal of tires.

Have a nice day, darling.

"Is he gone again?"

Amber dropped her fingers from her temples and turned to see her stepson standing at the French doors. He held a CD case in his hand and had a fierce expression on his face.

"Yes. Something he forgot, or so he said. So we'll be

here awhile longer. I hope you aren't missing something at home."

"And what about you? Did he ask if staying over would be a problem for you? You've got responsibilities, too, you know."

She was shaking her head with a small wry smile. "No, he didn't ask that, Stephen."

At fifteen, the promise of the man Stephen would be someday was strong. He had Deke's well-proportioned limbs and broad shoulders. His hair was as black as his father's and his eyes were blue, but dark with secrets—more intense and complex secrets than any that had ever troubled his father.

Stephen had been ten when she married Deke, only a year after Jeanne Russo had died in a car crash. The boy was convinced even then that he was unwanted by both his parents, and nothing in his experience since had changed that conviction. He'd responded shyly but eagerly to Amber's friendliness, and by the time she'd been married to Deke for a year, Stephen had become her slave.

"Come here. Sit with me." She patted the space beside her on the sofa, and as he came over, she wondered how a father and son could have so little in common. Amber couldn't imagine the teenage Deke ever spending hours alone in a room sitting at a computer accompanied by sounds of obscure jazz musicians as he explored the Internet. Nor could she see Deke pondering the mystery of why his father virtually ignored him, as Stephen constantly did.

"I heard him just now," Stephen said, sitting down. "You were so happy about the Maison Belle thing and he didn't even notice. I don't think he even heard you. I don't know why you let him get away with that. You have to listen to him toot his own horn until it's sickening. He could have said something, like 'Good for you, Amber.' But no, he was too busy trying to find some jerk's phone number.''

"He said he'd had a bad day, Stephen."

"Other people have bad days but they don't act like him."

She took in a long breath. "You shouldn't let it get to you. I guess I can live without hearing him congratulate me."

"Yes, but a wife shouldn't have to." Stephen turned the CD case over and over in his hands. "I don't know why you keep defending him. He doesn't deserve your loyalty."

She turned her gaze to the bright surface of the pool, visible from the window walls of the sunroom, thinking of her words to Kate today. "If you could read my mind, you wouldn't call me loyal, Stephen."

"Good. I'm glad to hear it. At least that's something."

"Yes, something." She put her hand over his, and the movement of the CD case stopped as he turned to look at her. "What goes around comes around, Stephen. Remember that."

FOUR

Victoria still hadn't returned. Kate climbed the front-porch steps of her mother's house and stood for a moment before going inside. She'd always thought of the house on Vermilion Lane as belonging to Victoria. Although situated on three acres of land in a neighborhood carefully chosen by John Madison forty years earlier, her mother's personality was everywhere, from the art on the walls and the Aubussons on the floor to the antiques gracing every room. Her father had been an architect with offices in downtown New Orleans, but he'd never cared to live there. Instead, he'd built the house in Bayou Blanc to duplicate one of the old mansions off St. Charles Avenue in the Garden District. It was after Kate was in her teens that she'd learned John Madison had stayed in town during the week and come home to Bayou Blanc only on weekends. Her memories of her father were vague and insubstantial, probably, she told herself, because she had been only six years old when he died.

Standing on the porch, she was struck by how still everything was. No birds fluttered in startled flight at her arrival, and nothing stirred the leaves on the trees. Even the ceiling fans on the porch were quiet. It reminded her too much of her quiet girlhood. Next door, Amber's house had rocked with noise day and night—loud music had blasted from the stereo, hosts of kids had laughed and chattered, souped-up cars had come and gone. But not where Kate had lived. And certainly not today. There was no movement behind the tall windows. Shaking off the melancholy memories, she opened the front door.

Lemon oil, candles, carpet freshener, cigarette smoke—all familiar smells. From the mantel in the living room, only the soft chime of a striking clock broke the silence. Feeling let down by the solitude of her homecoming, Kate headed upstairs to unpack, when she heard her mother entering from the back door.

Leaving the foyer, she hurried through the house and stopped short just as Victoria sank into a chair and dropped her head wearily against the back.

One look at her mother and the worst of Kate's fears were realized. Victoria's face had the sallow, hollow-cheeked look of prolonged illness. Dark circles carved half-moons beneath her eyes. Deep creases bracketed her mouth. But it was the scarf artfully wrapped around her mother's head and tied at one side that pierced Kate's heart.

"Mother…"

"Kate." Victoria's eyes flew open. Kate went numbly to her, bent and kissed her cheek, grasped her hands. "Mother, what's wrong? What's happened?"

Victoria sighed, shaking her head. "Do we have to discuss it before you even sit down, Kate?"

Kate pulled a small ottoman close and sat down. "Now I'm sitting, Mother."

Eyes closed, Victoria murmured, "You were always so impatient."

"I'm a doctor, Mother. I know the signs of chemotherapy. And yes, of course we have to discuss it. How can I ignore something like this?"

"I'm nearly done with the chemo now." Victoria touched the scarf with a wry twist of her mouth. "A few more weeks and I might have had hair again, too. But you seemed set on coming now." She shrugged. "I suppose it was time you knew."

Kate was unprepared for the keen shaft of pain that came with her mother's words. She was a physician. In this one arena, surely it was reasonable to expect that Victoria would confide in her; might even need her.

"What is it, Mother?" she asked quietly.

"The cancer, you mean?" Victoria reached for a cigarette, ignoring Kate's dismayed protest. She lit it, drawing the smoke deeply into her lungs. "Ovarian, if you can believe that. Maybe I should have heeded the advice of my friends and had everything plucked out years ago when they were all doing it."

"What I can't believe is that you're still smoking."

"Oh, Kate, don't start." Victoria exhaled and then fell into a fit of coughing. She fumbled for a glass on the small table beside her. Kate intercepted her and held the glass while her mother sipped, then sat, stunned, as she continued, "It's hardly going to do any more damage than has already been done."

"What's the prognosis, Mother? I can't believe any doctor sanctions such a fatalistic attitude. I'll bet Leo is on your case something fierce." She paused, looking narrowly at Victoria. "Or does he know you're smoking?"

"He's worse than you are."

"Because he cares about you."

"He should be worrying about himself," Victoria said tartly. "His cholesterol is sky-high."

"How do you know that?"

"I got it from Ruby."

"Ruby Zeringue?"

"How many Ruby's do you know who work for Leo?" Victoria made an impatient sound. "Please, Kate, you're home for the first time in so long. We haven't seen each other in ages. Let me just enjoy your company for a day or so, and then you can become a doctor again."

Kate had an odd flashback to Victoria's visit eight months before, when they'd taken the train from Boston to New York for a weekend. Preoccupied at the time with her divorce, Kate wondered now if the signs of her mother's illness had been there. If so, what kind of daughter did that make her?

"I'm stunned, Mother," Kate said. "When I think…"

Victoria reached over and patted her hand. "I know, dear. It's a shock finding me like this, and I don't want you obsessing over it—as a physician, I mean. The truth is, I don't think the chemo is going to make much difference, but Leo insisted. He's been like a maiden aunt. Actually, he bullied me into it. But I'm glad you're here, Kate. Maybe you can convince them—"

"Them? You're seeing a specialist, I assume?"

"For what it's worth."

"You have to fight it, Mother! I've seen patients overcome unbelievable odds. Ovarian cancer is serious, yes, but there are many variables. Depending on whether or not there's any metastasis, we can—"

Victoria gave Kate's hand a firm shake. "Oh, stop with the medical stuff, Kate. I get enough of that from Leo. He's always going on about pathology and prognosis and protocol and medication. You wouldn't believe the regimen he'd like to foist on me."

"Because he wants to see you get well again," Kate replied firmly.

"I had the surgery and I consented to the chemotherapy. That's enough."

"You had surgery and you didn't even tell me?" Kate was aghast.

"You were going through a divorce, Kate." Her mother succumbed to another fit of coughing, crushed out her cigarette and leaned back, looking pale and drained. When she was able to talk, she said, "I never liked Robert, you know."

"You never told me that." Kate was beginning to wonder how many other things Victoria hadn't told her.

"He fell in love with you because you were beautiful and smart and committed to your work. And then—" She bent forward to pick up the glass and sipped "—I'll bet he complained of feeling neglected, right?"

"More or less," Kate murmured, wondering how her mother could have been so astute where Robert was concerned when she'd hardly spent half-a-dozen days getting to know him.

"Then he looked for solace elsewhere, right?"

In spite of herself, Kate had to smile. "Have you been reading my mail, Mother?" As Victoria rolled her eyes, Kate said, "Robert dumped me for a blonde who's seventeen years younger than me."

"Lucky you."

"I try to think that," Kate said, rubbing her forehead with a sigh. Her mother had enough problems without having to listen to hers.

"So tell me about St. Luke's," Victoria said. "When are they going to make you the senior trauma resident?"

"They aren't, I'm afraid." Kate took the glass from her mother, then moved to the bar. Turning partially from Victoria's keen gaze, she lifted a beautiful Baccarat pitcher and refilled the matching glass with ice and lemon-flavored water. When she turned back to her mother, her smile was in place. "The job went to Jake Grissom. You met him, remember? Tall, thin, wears little-bitty round glasses, has blond hair and—"

"As I recall, he has no hair, Kate." Victoria sat up a little straighter. "What do you mean they gave the job to Grissom? He seemed…adequate, but he isn't in your class, darling."

"Thank you for that vote of confidence, but—"

"But what, Kate?"

"Nothing, Mother." She held the smile. "The choice has been between Jake and me all along, I told you that. The board met—this past Monday morning, actually—and they chose him. That was it." *After I killed Joseph Carmello.*

Kate set the glass within Victoria's reach and moved toward the arched doorway. "Will you be okay while I go out to the car and get some more of my things?"

"We'll have to make arrangements to get the car back to the rental agency," Victoria said. "You can use mine while you're here."

"It's not a rental, Mother. I drove myself down from Boston."

Victoria looked astonished. "You drove all the way from Boston?"

Kate faked another smile. "It's interstate all the way."

But Victoria was studying her narrowly. "Just how long is this visit going to be, Kate? If you drove—"

Kate shrugged. "How long can you put up with me?"

"For as long as you care to stay," Victoria said without hesitation.

Kate smiled. "Well, it's nice to feel welcome."

With a small sound, Victoria leaned back against the chair and Kate crossed the room in a rush. Her mother's lips had no color and she was damp with a fine film of perspiration. "Nausea, right?" Kate murmured, and Victoria nodded weakly, eyes closed. "Take some slow, deep breaths, Mama." The childhood name came as naturally as the deep rush of emotion inside her. "That's it. Breathe slowly and deeply—in…out…in…out…."

After a few moments, Victoria's lashes fluttered and

she opened her eyes. Squeezing Kate's hand, she whispered, "Kate, Kate, I'm so glad you're home."

Kate thought for a minute that she had drowned. Then she swirled up out of her nightmare, gasping and groping at thin air, trying to get a grip on something besides cold seawater. What she found as her arms flailed wildly was the glass of water on her bedside table. It toppled over, soaking the tangled sheets. When the turmoil inside her subsided, she realized the noise she'd heard wasn't the roar of waves in a Gulf squall, but blank noise from the television's snowy picture. She wasn't in a bunk in her parents' cabin cruiser, but in her old room in Victoria's house. She wasn't six years old. She was an adult, long past the age of being spooked by nightmares. She'd had too much strong chicory coffee after dinner tonight. Or something.

Using the remote, Kate turned the TV off then threw the damp sheets aside and got out of bed. The hour tinkled from the small ormolu clock on a piecrust table across the room. Three in the morning. Her heart was still racing from the terror of the nightmare. Absolutely no more of that coffee Louisiana was so famous for.

In the bathroom she refilled the water glass. Or maybe it wasn't the coffee, but the remnants of an incident that had happened more than thirty years ago that was ruining her first night at home.

"God, I'm really losing it," she murmured, rubbing both temples. Looking up, she decided she resembled someone who'd survived a disaster, but barely. Her dark hair was damp with perspiration and clung to her cheeks and forehead in a look her stylist had never intended. Fear and terror still lingered in her gray eyes, and her mouth—in Kate's estimation always a little too full and vulnerable—wasn't completely steady yet.

The dream was always about the day her parents' sleek new forty-foot cabin cruiser had gone down in the Gulf. And the recollection was never clear. No matter how hard she tried to bring it together, all she really had was a hodgepodge of confusing impressions—loud voices, things falling, chaos, men shouting and her mother's screams. It always ended the same way—with the shock of a cold plunge into the Gulf and the panicked certainty she was drowning.

The nightmare had occurred frequently during her childhood and had surfaced again when she was going through her divorce. Now it had followed her home to Bayou Blanc. She turned the faucet on and splashed cool water on her face. Burying her face in a lavender-scented towel, she vowed not to allow herself to come undone. Her mother's condition had to be her first priority. Next, she'd think about salvaging her career. But sooner or later, before she left Bayou Blanc, she would find out once and for all what had happened on the boat that night thirty-three years ago.

FIVE

The next morning, Kate was at Leo Castille's office when it opened. Ruby Zeringue, receptionist in Dr. Leo's practice for at least twenty years, smiled broadly at Kate through the glass window separating the waiting room from the clinic's inner sanctum. "Well, would you look who's here!" She opened the door and grabbed Kate, giving her a huge hug. "This is one big surprise, yes. We thought you liked that Yankee weather too good to come home to Bayou Blanc ever again." She stepped back to study Kate, her black curly head shaking. "Ooo, my-oh-my, you're beautiful as ever, *chère*."

Kate found herself smiling. "Hi, Ruby. You look wonderful, too."

"Uh-huh." Ruby cocked her head. "So, you gonna come to work for us now?"

Kate laughed. "I'm afraid not, Ruby. I'm just visiting."

Ruby nodded. And kept nodding.

Still smiling, Kate asked, "What does that look mean, Ruby Zeringue?"

"You better watch out visiting Bayou Blanc right at Fais Do-Do time, *chère*. Somebody might put a hex on you, and you'd find yourself staying on here right where you was meant to be, yes."

"I don't think so," Kate said dryly.

"Well, you just remember what I'm sayin'."

"Kate! It is you, Katie." Leo Castille spotted her as he

left an examining room. "I thought I heard your voice. Vicky said you were coming, but I didn't think it would be so soon. Come on in here and let me give you a hug, darlin'." He caught her up in a warm, hard embrace, and Kate's throat went tight. He smelled of starched lab coat and Betadine and cigars.

Holding both her arms, he studied her much as Ruby had done. "You're supposed to be hobnobbing with those elite medical types in the Northeast, Kate. You finally see the light?"

"I saw the need for a few days off, Leo."

"Ah, well, I know that feeling."

"It was a sudden decision, actually." She tucked her hair behind one ear and smiled at him. "I got in late yesterday."

"I bet your mama was happy to see you."

Kate nodded, her smile fading. "That's why I came over this morning. Leo, I want to know everything. I—"

"Let's talk in here." He took her arm and guided her to the familiar dark blue leather wing chair that faced his big desk. While he took a seat, Kate studied the Audubon pelican print that hung behind him. And the collection of carved birds perched on the shelves of an antique étagère. And the books—medical texts, journals, reference works—dozens of volumes that she'd pored over for hundreds of hours. From the time she was ten years old, Kate had known she wanted to study medicine. Dr. Leo Castille had been her mentor. And her surrogate father.

"What exactly is going on with my mother, Leo?"

"What did she tell you?"

"That the diagnosis is ovarian cancer. That she's had surgery and is undergoing chemotherapy. But no details, Leo. And she's smoking! It's appalling. I've begged her for years to give up the habit, but she's never paid any attention. Now she says there's no need."

"She can be pretty stubborn, all right."

She looked at him. "That's an understatement if I ever heard one."

"Your mother has the right to make her own choices, Katy-did."

"But smoking!"

"Is it the smoking or the shock of finding Vicky so sick, darlin'?"

Kate's eyes filled instantly. She bit her lips, struggled with the urge to burst into tears and finally found her voice. "Why didn't she tell me, Leo? Would she have just…just d-died without even telling me anything?"

"It's not quite so bad as that, *chère*. She's never liked to worry you, you know."

"Then why didn't *you* tell me, Leo? You could have picked up the phone. If it weren't for Amber—"

"Is that why you're home? Because Amber called?"

"I was thinking about coming anyway." She studied her linked hands. "It's been a while and…I needed a break."

Leo chose a cigar from a box. "Well, I for one am glad you've come. Vicky may not have called you, Kate, but it's a good thing having you here." He didn't light the cigar, but simply rolled it between his fingers, savoring the feel of it. "I don't suppose you can stay very long, right? I know how it is in those big-city trauma centers. They're always understaffed—especially when it comes to experienced people like yourself. How long before you leave again?"

Kate stood and moved to the étagère. With her finger, she traced the graceful neck of a white heron. "I'm not actually on a vacation. I'm on a leave of absence. Sort of."

She waited for a moment or two, then turned to look at him. "You know what they say about us trauma specialists. We all burn out after a few years. Well, it looks like

I've burned out." Her smile was wobbly as she wrapped her arms around herself. "I guess I just needed a little time to regroup."

Leo had the cigar in his mouth now, but he still hadn't lit it. He removed it slowly, studying her keenly. "You're saying you need time off from that particular job at St. Luke's, or time off from practicing medicine? Which is it, Kate?"

Kate studied the brown pelican behind his head. "Time off from St. Luke's."

He nodded. "Well, St. Luke's loss can be Bayou Blanc's gain, as they say, darlin'."

"What do you mean?"

He clamped the cigar between his teeth. "How'd you like to sample the practice of medicine in a small town, Kate?"

"What? Here? At the hospital?" Kate doubted whether the Bayou Blanc hospital even had a trauma center. And if they did, they certainly couldn't afford a full-time trauma specialist. But her heart was beating fast at the thought. She would be the one and only. There would be no Jake Grissom to fall back on if a judgment call came up. She'd be on her own.

And what about the lives of the patients in her hands?

"Heck, no, not at the hospital," Leo said firmly. "I meant right here, Kate. I've been toying with the idea of retiring. You could step in, pick up the slack while I try it."

She stared. "Are you serious?"

"About having you here or the retirement bug?"

"Uh, both, actually. You can't retire, can you? What would this town do without their Dr. Leo?"

"Same as they've been doing for the past couple of years, I imagine. Turn to Sam."

"Sam?"

"Sam Delacourt. If I were the jealous type, I'd feel bad already, the way he's picked off some of my favorite patients." Leo wiggled the cigar to the side of his mouth. "Your mama, for one. Says Sam's a lot smarter than me. But what it is, is that he's just younger and prettier. I can see right through Victoria and I told her so."

Now Kate's heart was racing. "Sam Delacourt is my mother's doctor?" she asked in a faint voice.

"That's right." He snorted. "Seems she felt it'd be stressful having me treat her cancer, so she arranged to let Sam do it."

"You've been friends a long time," Kate murmured, but her thoughts were veering wildly in another direction. "It probably would have been difficult."

"I could've handled it," Leo blustered, removing the cigar. He scowled at it, thinking, then added, "But I'll admit it's hard seeing her suffer after one of those blasted chemo treatments."

"How often is Sam here?"

"Didn't Vicky tell you? He's moved lock, stock and barrel to Bayou Blanc. He bought a house on Vermilion Lane—Jacques Gautreau's place."

A ten-minute walk from her mother's house. Kate stood again and pulled an old issue of the *Journal of the American Medical Association* from Leo's bookcase and pretended to thumb through it. Of all the doctors Victoria could have chosen, Sam Delacourt was Kate's last choice. She wouldn't want Sam Delacourt treating her mother for an ingrown toenail, let alone a life-threatening cancer!

"Looking for something in that old *JAMA*, darlin'?"

Kate threw it down and turned to Leo. "Are you saying Sam's practicing full-time here in Bayou Blanc?"

"Not just in Bayou Blanc. He's here."

"Here?" She glanced at the door. "In your office?"

"*Our* office. He bought into the partnership, darlin'."

"What about his partners in New Orleans?" Kate asked, appalled. Oh, not on behalf of his partners, but for purely selfish reasons. She'd always run to Leo when she needed the nurturing that Victoria seemed incapable of giving her. Now, with Sam here—in Leo's office!—there would be no refuge for her. Anywhere.

"Isn't there some contract clause that prohibits a physician from joining a competitor within a specific length of time?" she asked.

"Not if the originals decide to pull out. Which Sam's partners did." Leo leaned back. "Wasn't quite enough business to keep an office going with the kind of overhead they had. So when he approached me to see if I was interested in having a partner, I jumped at the chance. Sam's tops in his field, you know."

Kate grunted something. Sam would never get any kudos from her. "But what I don't know is why he would decide to bury himself in Bayou Blanc after building such a spiffy reputation in the city."

"Considering his circumstances, I think he's probably reassessing his priorities. If you know what I mean."

She looked at him. "Why would I know what you mean?"

Leo returned her look quizzically. "I thought you might identify with a man rethinking his priorities, seeing as you're taking a leave of absence and shying away from putting a time limit on it. That sounds to me like somebody doing a bit of reassessing."

She refused to meet his gaze. "I just find it hard to see Sam Delacourt doing much second-guessing of his career goals, Leo. He's an ambitious, single-minded, arrogant—"

"Brilliant internist, Katie. Come, come, girl." Leo hitched his chair a little closer to his desk. "You sound as if you have some personal dislike for Sam, which sur-

prises me. Most women find him appealing—more than
appealing, if the patients in this office are anything to
judge by. As for 'arrogant,' no. I'd simply call Sam self-
confident—and with good reason. It was a lucky day for
me when he said he'd like to join my practice. He could
have written a ticket to any number of practices in half-a-
dozen states, but with his wife gone now and Mallory at
such a delicate age, well..." Leo sighed. "Yes, sir, that
kind of hard luck can make a man rethink his life and
where he's going."

"Elaine's dead?" For a moment, Kate didn't breathe.

Leo frowned. "I thought you knew, Kate. Surely Victoria would have—" He shook his head. "No, she probably
wasn't thinking about anything but that blasted chemotherapy when it happened. It's really been hard on her,
you know. Some patients breeze right through it, but
Vicky is laid low for days afterward. She had her last
treatment Monday. That's nearly a week. Takes her about
that long to settle down. Thank God it's over."

"Yes, thank God," Kate murmured, only half of her
mind registering that Leo talked more like a husband
than Victoria's good friend. The other half of her mind
was caught up in thoughts of Sam and Elaine. And Mallory. "His daughter's a teenager now, isn't she?"

"Mallory? Yes. She just turned fourteen, I think. She
took her mother's death very hard."

"Of course."

Leo gazed at his cigar, his eyes crinkled in thought.
"Not to dismiss the passing of an individual with any less
heartbreak and pain than another, but it seems to me that
Elaine's death was a blessing for both of them. Oh, I don't
think either of them would ever say that, or even think it,
but for five years the woman was in another world, you
know."

"No, I don't.... I didn't...." The whole thing was such a

stunner, she couldn't seem to form a coherent thought. Elaine, dead. Dear Lord. Then Leo's words repeated in her mind. Five years in another world? "Did the cancer reach her brain?"

"Her brain? No, it was lymphoma. Finally went to her bones."

"You said she'd been in another world for five years."

"I meant she'd never really recovered after the suicide attempt."

"I didn't know she'd...done that." Kate got to her feet and went again to the birds trapped behind glass. Beautiful, still, lifeless. "It must have been devastating for...for Mallory."

"And Sam, too. Although they brought her back once she was taken to the hospital, there was simply too long a span without oxygen. She functioned with severely diminished capacity, I believe."

"I didn't know."

"Well, how could you, darlin'? You didn't know Sam or his family at that time. But enough about Sam." He tossed his chewed, still-unlit cigar into the trash and folded his hands on his desk. "Let's talk about you and your plans."

"I have no plans, Leo. I'm going to take some time off and eventually look around for a new location, I suppose."

If I can find a hospital that'll have me. It was a huge black mark on any physician's career to be suspended for any reason, and Kate still hadn't made up her mind whether or not to file a lawsuit against St. Luke's. First of all, she needed to reassess if she was even cut out to be a doctor. Having to accept responsibility for the death of a patient had forced her to look closely at herself—to question her ability to make split-second, life-or-death decisions. She longed to discuss it with Leo, but she couldn't reveal the circumstances that had forced her out of St. Luke's, not even to Leo.

"How about spending some of that time off around here?" he prompted. "I meant it when I suggested you fill in for me while I sample retirement. I can't leave the practice outright. Sam's good, but there're more patients than one man can handle."

"Then get another 'man,'" Kate said.

He stood and headed around his desk, grinning. "Why bother when I've got another chance at a big-time, ambitious, single-minded, brilliant physician?" His arm went around her shoulders.

Kate smiled reluctantly. "But is there room for two like that in your practice?"

"We'll make room, darlin'."

"I really would like to do it, Leo, but—"

"Don't decide now. Think about it."

Oh, she was so tempted. With her reputation under a cloud at St. Luke's, easing into Leo's small-town practice was probably her best option to continue practicing medicine. It would give her time to work through this…"difficult period." That was all it was, she told herself—a temporary reaction to fatigue and the emotional upheaval of her divorce, added to the buildup of stress after five years of trauma duty, had done her in. It was definitely a temporary thing, because she could never commit to working around Sam Delacourt otherwise. Not even to salvage her career. Leo could sing his praises until hell froze over and it wouldn't change what she knew about Sam: he was heartless, a man capable of shameless deceit and betrayal.

"I wouldn't want to sign a formal contract, Leo."

"No problem. How about we play it by ear for a while—say the summer? Then—"

Suddenly the door to an examining room opened. A

tall man stepped into the hall. He was trim, with dark hair
graying at the temples, near-black eyes. His white lab coat
was open, showing a navy pullover, khaki Dockers and
running shoes. His attention was on the chart in his hand.
"Leo, I've got one of your patients in the—" Looking up,
he stopped short.

And for the first time in five years, Kate came face-to-
face with Sam Delacourt.

SIX

For a moment, Kate's stomach felt as if she'd jumped off a cliff. Her face grew warm with a rush of emotion as she forced herself to meet the gaze of the man she'd once loved with all the passion in her soul. Emotion—fierce and hostile—flared in his eyes. Discomfited, she realized that any dislike on her part was returned in spades. She wasn't sure what she'd expected, if they ever met again, but why he should harbor any animosity toward *her* was mystifying. She was the one who'd been wronged. As she looked at him, he schooled his expression into something resembling courtesy and gave her a curt nod. "Kate."

"Sam," she murmured in return.

Leo beamed, clearly missing the drama. "Sam, I see you remember Kate Madison. Don't I recall the two of you met while she was interning at Tulane? Yes, well, she's just in from Boston, taking a few days' vacation."

As they faced each other, Kate sensed that her sudden appearance made Sam as uncomfortable as she felt. But there was only distant courtesy in his tone when he asked, "St. Luke's, isn't it?"

"Yes."

She glanced at a still-beaming Leo, no doubt Sam's source of information. Just then a nurse approached Sam with a prescription, which he signed, then handed back before remarking, "I understand their trauma-care unit is first-rate."

"Location probably has a lot to do with that," she said. "It's comparable to Charity in New Orleans. Like most places nowadays, so much violence is concentrated in the inner city, and St. Luke's is right there."

Leo gazed at her fondly. "She's talking about making a change from all that, Sam," he said, pulling out another cigar. Fishing a tiny tool from his pocket to snip the end off, he didn't seem to hear Sam's grunt. "However, it's our lucky day. Kate's considering filling in while I take a shot at retirement."

Sam shot him a quick look. "'Filling in'? Here?"

"You bet. When she told me she was tired of that high-stress job at St. Luke's, I jumped at the chance to ask her to practice here for a while."

Sam folded his arms and tucked the patient's chart beneath his armpit. "Ours is a small clinic," he told her. "And we're essentially a family practice. Unlike what you're used to in a large urban hospital with anonymous patients, most of the people we see have been coming here all of their adult lives."

"I have a specialty in trauma care," Kate said stiffly, "but I'm a fully qualified M.D." *As you well know.* While earning those credentials, she'd been sleeping with Sam Delacourt.

His shoulders straightened. "We don't get a lot of gunshot victims in Bayou Blanc."

Her chin came up a notch. "Then you're lucky."

Sam shifted his gaze from Kate to Leo. "I didn't know you were serious about retiring, Leo."

The doctor studied his cigar. "Well, maybe I am and maybe I'm not. I figure to sample it and see how I like it. Play a little golf, sleep in, read the *Times Picayune* at one sitting, drink more than a single cup of coffee in the morning."

"Nothing's firmed up," Kate said coolly, but something

inside her flared angrily at Sam's obvious reluctance. It wasn't her credentials or lack thereof that made him disinclined to have her around, she suspected, eyeing him with open dislike. No, she was an uncomfortable reminder of a time in his life he'd like to forget.

Apparently missing the hostile byplay between Kate and Sam, Leo clamped the cigar between his teeth. "I've always hoped Kate would come back here to practice, Sam, but the chance of that happening always seemed pretty slim. She graduated near the top of her class, you know. She had her pick of jobs and locations." Still smiling, he was shaking his head. "No surprise she picked St. Luke's in Boston."

"Leo..." Uncomfortable, Kate moved to let a nurse slip past them. "I haven't decided to leave St. Luke's. I'm just...thinking about it." *Liar, liar.*

"Ward Lincoln practices there, doesn't he?" Sam asked suddenly.

Oh, God. "Yes."

Still watching her, Sam added, "And Cliff Matthews. He's chief of staff now, isn't he?"

Did the man know everyone? "Yes. Have you met them?"

"Only casually. We meet at conferences and the like. From time to time."

Kate winced inwardly, recalling her last encounter with Dr. Matthews. It was after the infamous exit interview with Charles Winslow. Unwilling to accept Winslow's word as final, she'd wanted some hint of her options should she hope to return to St. Luke's, but Matthews had resisted her attempt to define the terms of her banishment. St. Luke's options, not Kate's, were left open. If Sam called either Cliff Matthews or Ward Lincoln, she was dead.

Touching Leo's sleeve, she managed a smile. "I'll see you later, Leo, okay?"

He nodded, covering her hand with his. "Don't talk yourself out of staying home awhile, Kate."

"I won't." She waited for a second, then said to Sam, "If you have the time, I'd like a word, please."

Sam handed the chart over to Leo. "Talk to this patient, will you, Leo? I don't like the look of her X rays. She's showing severe bone deterioration and needs a hip replacement, but she flatly refused when I suggested it."

As Leo shuffled off, head down, to study the chart, Sam indicated a door farther down the hall, then waited for Kate. Brushing past him, she caught the scent of his shaving lotion and was assailed by emotions she'd thought long dead and buried. As she met his eyes directly, she and Sam were caught in a moment that both acknowledged and rejected their history. For Kate, the affair that had begun with such passion and hope had ended in bitterness and a badly bruised heart. She had fled to new and distant surroundings and married on the rebound. But Robert had turned out to be nothing like the fantasy husband she'd believed him to be. Meanwhile, Sam had returned to the wife and daughter Kate hadn't known he had. A part of her wanted desperately to blame Sam for everything—for the mess her life was in—but deep down she was beginning to wonder if there were other forces at work.

She let him usher her into his office, but before he closed the door, a nurse emerging from an examining room stopped him. "Sam, there's a patient in room 4A you should see."

"In a minute, Diane."

Kate suddenly recognized the nurse, who flicked a cold glance at Kate before addressing Sam again. "It's Captain

Chastain, Sam. He's been waiting for quite some time, and he's getting very testy."

"Not right now, Diane. There are two patients ahead of him, and I need a word with Kate before I can see anybody."

Diane Crawford. Kate had been an intern at Charity Hospital in New Orleans when she'd first met Sam's longtime nurse. It was no surprise that he'd persuaded her to relocate when he'd decided to join Leo's practice. Kate suspected the woman had been in love with Sam for years. With Elaine gone, maybe Diane would be the next Mrs. Sam Delacourt. As far as Kate was concerned, she could have him.

"How are you, Diane?" Kate asked politely.

"Fine," Diane returned with a glacial smile. "It's been a long time."

Kate turned to Sam with a faint smile. "Ambrose Chastain? Leo's old chess partner? Lord, is he still alive?"

Sam chuckled dryly. "Old sailors never die."

"Apparently not. He must be over ninety."

"No, only eighty-eight."

"Sam..." Diane said irritably.

"I can come back later if it would be more convenient," Kate offered.

"Not necessary." Sam turned back to Diane. "Tell the captain I'll be another half-hour. If he objects to that, ask Leo to look in on him."

Diane's ice-blue eyes narrowed, but after a moment's hesitation, she snatched Ambrose Chastain's chart from the wall rack and went back into the examining room.

Closing the door, Sam motioned Kate to a chair. She refused, expecting him to go to his desk, but he didn't. Instead, he stayed at the door watching her.

She was angrily aware of how she must look to him. Intent on seeing Leo, she'd dressed quickly that morning.

Her denim skirt, T-shirt and skimpy sandals made her feel at a disadvantage. She'd only taken time for a touch of lipstick and some blush. Her hair, cut at a posh salon in Boston to look sleek and sophisticated, was probably a mess. For work she usually confined the longish sides by pulling them up and anchoring them with a barrette at the crown of her head. Now she resisted an impulse to smooth it. She didn't give a damn what Sam Delacourt thought of her looks. What she wanted from him was information—as one professional to another—nothing more.

Sam arched an eyebrow. "You probably don't see a lot of old eccentrics at St. Luke's."

"No, but I'd trade old eccentrics for drug addicts, gunshot victims and battered wives any day."

He tugged on his earlobe, his dark eyes solemn. "Not many bullet wounds in Bayou Blanc, but we've got some drug problems, just like most places. As for battered wives, we have plenty of those."

Kate quelled the feeling that was sneaking back. How easy it was to fall into conversation with Sam. Their unique rapport had been one of the reasons she'd believed something lasting would come of their attraction when they'd first met. It still rankled, how naive she'd been.

How could she not have been suspicious when Sam's ideas for their weekends had always taken them away from New Orleans? But, no, she'd been thrilled and flattered over junkets to Mexico or a resort on the Alabama coast or a trip to Walt Disney World. Once, he'd even arranged a whole week in New York. It was only after the affair was over that she'd realized he couldn't be seen in New Orleans with the woman he was sleeping with because he had a wife.

"I didn't know you were working with Leo," she said coolly.

"And does it matter?"

"Ordinarily it wouldn't, but under the circumstances, it matters, yes."

Still resting one shoulder against the door, he crossed his arms over his chest. "What circumstances would those be?"

"My mother's illness," Kate replied.

"Ah...you're concerned about your mother?"

"Of course!"

"Well, better late than never, as they say."

Her hand froze. "What does that mean?"

"Your mother's been sick for more than ten months and you haven't found the time to make a single trip home. A person could infer from that that you aren't particularly concerned."

Kate stood stunned for a moment, then sank blindly into the nearest chair. "Ten months? Mother's been sick for ten months?"

Sam still watched her keenly. "Are you saying you didn't know?"

She shook her head. "I can't believe this. Why would she keep something like that from me?"

"A good question, Kate. Why would she?"

Kate sprang up again and began to pace. "She was with me at Christmas in Boston. She looked fine. She was fine."

"Christmas..." Sam moved from the door and went around to his desk. He sat down and folded his hands. "That would have been a couple of months after she was diagnosed."

Stricken, Kate stared at him. "She never said a word."

"She must have had her reasons."

But what would they have been? What could have convinced Victoria that Kate didn't have the right to know? It wasn't as if the illness wasn't going to affect Kate's life, too. Her mother might die! What if she'd learned of her mother's cancer when it was too late? What if she hadn't come home? Kate almost shuddered at what might have happened. If she hadn't been experiencing these odd flashbacks...if she hadn't screwed up in the E.R....

"Maybe something was going on in your life that made her hold off telling you something that would upset you," Sam suggested.

She stared at him blankly. "What?"

"Weren't you getting a divorce about then?"

God, did Leo tell him everything? "May I see her chart, please?" she asked, ignoring his question.

"You know better than to ask that, Kate."

"Excuse me?"

"You heard me. You know I can't violate that basic trust."

"Victoria Madison isn't just a patient, Sam. She's my mother, for God's sake! And I want to see her chart."

"I don't care what connection there is between you, you don't get her chart unless she tells me I can give it to you." He stood, raking a hand through his hair, and sighed. "C'mon, Kate, I don't want to argue with you over this. If it were anyone else, you wouldn't even ask."

"If it were Leo treating her," Kate said bitterly, "as it should have been, then there would be no reason to ask. Leo would hand it over without a word."

"Which could be the reason Victoria chose me and not Leo to be her physician."

"Stop it!" Kate smacked the desktop with one hand, then drew a shaky breath. "Look, I don't know what your problem is, Doctor, but I need to see my mother's records. I'm going to be the one caring for her and I want to know the extent of her illness. I'm fully qualified to understand anything you might have found regarding her condition, any tests, treatment, bloodwork, any p-prognosis—" She stopped, feeling her throat close and the threat of tears behind her eyes. What was the matter with her, for God's sake? She couldn't seem to do anything anymore without going into an emotional tailspin.

"Ah, Kate..."

Whirling, she walked to the door but didn't pull it open. A moment passed while she composed herself, then she turned and looked at him. "What is it, Sam? Do you think that if you're heartless enough where my mother is concerned, I'll get discouraged and throw up my hands? That I'll just vanish out of your life the way I did five years ago? Well, it won't happen. This is my mother's life and I'm here for the long haul, so you'd better get used to it. And while you're getting used to that, get used to the fact that I'll be right here in the office with you. I'm going to take Leo up on that offer to practice in your precious clinic."

"Leo had no right to make such an offer!" Sam retorted.

"Yes, well, if you want to crush an old man's plans for a well-deserved retirement, I'll let you be the one to tell him. For someone who didn't blink at cheating on his dying wife, telling an aging doctor that you don't give a damn about his plans or his dreams should be a piece of cake!"

If Sam had a reply, she didn't hear it. She yanked on the doorknob and stalked out, almost colliding with Diane Crawford. She brushed past the nurse, but at the end of the hall, she couldn't resist a last backward glance—just in time to see Diane slip into Sam's office, smiling.

She got all the way to her car before reaction set in. In spite of the blistering heat, she was in a cold sweat. The last thing she'd expected when she'd left the house this morning was to find herself committed to joining Leo's practice. And the last person she'd ever expected to prac-

tice with was Sam Delacourt. After starting the car, she sat
hunched over, holding the wheel in a death grip. Staring
blindly at a bright pink crepe myrtle directly in front of
her, she tried to figure out what scared her more—holding the lives of patients in her hands or being with Sam
every day. Whichever it was, she knew she had to be
ready.

That, of course, was exactly the problem. She wasn't
ready. She was wondering if she ever would be again.

SEVEN

Sam was on his way home when he spotted his daughter with a teenage boy at the intersection of Vermilion and Cocodrie. With a muttered obscenity, he pulled over abruptly, startling them as they leaned on their bikes at the curb. Just what he needed to cap off an already rotten day—his daughter breaking restrictions. He'd been anticipating a strong Scotch and water, a peaceful meal and an evening without stress. Since his confrontation with Kate that morning, a dull rage had simmered inside him. What the hell was Leo thinking, making Kate an offer without clearing it with him? His contract clearly spelled out the terms to be agreed upon before inviting another physician into the practice. He didn't want the complication of Kate Madison now—or ever.

And now, here was Mallory openly defying him.

He got out of his Range Rover and headed across the newly mowed shoulders of the road toward the two teens, neither of whom had acknowledged him beyond the slow straightening of the boy.

Hoping to ward off a classic teenager-versus-parent dispute, he tried for a reasonable tone. "Mallory, what are you doing here? You know you're restricted to the house for three more days."

She gave him a hostile look and said to the boy, "Can you believe this, Cody? We'd better write it down someplace. My dad's on his way home and it's still daylight."

The boy eyed Sam warily.

Sam glanced at him, then addressed his daughter. "Do I know your friend, Mallory?"

She sighed, rolling her eyes. "Cody, meet my father the doctor. Dr. Delacourt, meet Cody Santana."

"Hello, Dr. Delacourt," the boy said, looking uncomfortable.

"Hi, Cody." Sam turned again to his daughter. "Get in the car, Mallory."

"I'm on my bike, Dad." She spoke as if he were a nitwit. "What'll I do, just drop it here in the middle of the intersection?"

"We'll put it in the Range Rover."

"No way." Mallory tossed her tawny head defiantly. "I rode it over here, I'll ride it home."

"Careful, Mallory," Sam said softly. "I don't think you want to make a scene here and now. Let's get the bike loaded and we'll talk about why you broke restriction when—"

"Broke restriction! Why do you talk to me like that, Dad? It's so dumb. I 'broke restriction,' because I should never have been 'restricted' in the first place! I didn't do anything that all my friends aren't doing."

"Your curfew was 11:00 p.m., Mallory. You knew the rules and you broke them. If all your friends are staying out past 1:00 a.m., I guess you'll just have to be different. Next time, I hope you'll think twice about whether you want to go along with the group and suffer the consequences, or whether you'll abide by our rules and enjoy the perks when you're good."

"When I'm good." She glanced at Cody. "You hear that, Cody? He talks to me like I'm still six years old!" She turned on her father again. "Stop treating me like I'm a stupid kid. Besides, it's so bogus when you try to act like a real parent. It's bullshit! You never even noticed me when I was six years old."

"Hey, Mall…" Shifting uncomfortably, Cody lifted his shoulders in pained protest. "Be cool, okay? He's your dad."

"Only on my birth certificate," Mallory said bitterly.

Sam released a tired sigh. "Mallory, this is not the time or place…"

She laughed harshly. "No kidding."

He was torn between wanting to give her a stern shaking and wanting to gather her close and give her one of the warm hugs he should have found more time for when she was little. He did neither. A familiar rush of disappointment and failure held him back along with the fear that he had indeed waited too late. So he walked to the back of the Range Rover and opened it. "Roll your bike back here, Mallory," he ordered.

"Didn't you hear me? I'm not going with you!" She tightened both hands on the handlebars. "I'm riding my bike home!" Cody Santana stood watching, his dark eyes shifting from father to daughter.

Sam stalked over to get the bike himself, but Mallory moved onto the seat defiantly, preparing to ride off. Suddenly pushed beyond his limit, Sam reached out and grabbed her elbow. With a startled cry, she twisted and tried to free herself. "Let me go!"

"That's enough, Mallory. Don't make me—"

"You're a bully!" she screamed. "A dictator! I don't have to do what you say! I hate you!"

Sam's anger dissolved into a dull, sick ache. Her elbow felt as fragile as a bird's wing. The moment triggered flashes of memory from when she'd been very young— when he would arrive home late at night during his residency and she'd be sleeping, her arm curled around a favorite stuffed animal. He would lift the tiny elbow and tuck it beneath the blanket. Sometimes she would blink, half awake, then reach up with a smile and pull him down for a butterfly kiss, too sleepy to say a word.

What had happened? How had he lost her? How had he let it come to this?

Sam turned her loose and caught the bike she shoved at him, then watched while she stalked around to the passenger side of the Range Rover and climbed inside. With Cody's help, Sam hefted the bike into the back and closed the tailgate. When he drove off with Mallory, he saw the boy in the rearview mirror, watching with a troubled look.

"Mallory—"

Her hair flew wildly as she whipped her head around to look at him. "Are you satisfied now, Dad? I can never look Cody in the face again!"

"I can't allow you to defy me, Mallory. Whether you like it or not, I'm your father, and raising you is my responsibility."

She settled back, looking straight ahead and scowling. "It's only now that Mom's dead, you've finally decided to notice me. Where were you when I was six or eight or even ten years old, Dad?"

"I'll admit my job took a lot of time, Mallory, but—"

"Yeah, right." She made a crude sound.

"We can still be a family, Mallory. We can get to know each other, but not if we waste the time we have together fighting."

"Give it up, Dad. It's too late."

Sam felt sick. "It's never too late for a fresh start, Mally."

"Then why are you trying to make my life miserable!" She glared at him, her blue eyes too bright. "I'm not a slave to just obey rules I don't have any part in making up."

"We've discussed all this, Mallory," he said wearily.

"*You* discussed. You forced me to listen."

Sam gripped the wheel. He felt frustrated and overwhelmed by the responsibility of raising a teenage daughter alone. Even though Elaine had barely functioned as a human being for the past five years, Mallory had at least benefited from the illusion of having a mother. It had only been toward the end of Elaine's life that Sam had managed to put some distance between himself and the demands of his profession. God, maybe it *was* too late.

With a sigh, Sam decided that nothing he could say would reach Mallory right now. She stared sullenly out her side as he pulled into their driveway. Her hands lay, palms up, in her lap. On her wrist was a slim gold chain bracelet that Sam had given to Elaine one Valentine's Day. He wondered what Mallory would say—what she would do—if he reached over, took both her hands in his and told her how sorry he was that he'd put his job and ambition above his duties as a husband and father for too many years; that he wished he'd made more time when she was younger to be a presence in her life.

What he said was, "We have to stop this, Mallory."

She shrugged.

"I know it's a bad time for you. For us both. I wish I could make it hurt less."

This time there was no shrug. Just nothing.

"Mallory?"

Still sullenly silent, she took her hair in one hand, lifted it off her neck and dropped it back again, tucking a tawny strand behind one ear. Her gaze was fixed on the view in front of her.

"Can't we talk at all, Mallory? Is this the way it's going to be? What can I do to change things if I don't know what's wrong."

For one moment, she seemed frozen, then she turned to look at him in amazement. "What's wrong? Are you serious? What's *wrong?*" Her voice went up crazily. "My mother has just died, my father has finally noticed I'm alive and is acting like a freaking dictator. It's vacation, and I'm confined to my room like a prisoner or something, and you're wondering what's wrong?" She gave a short, humorless laugh. "Hey, nothing's wrong, Dad. Don't even think it. Everything's cool."

"I'm sorry your mother died. I wish I could have prevented it."

"Yeah, right."

"You don't believe me?"

She was looking through the side window again. "You're a doctor," she said woodenly. "You did everything you could."

Did I? God, did I? "She was in great pain, Mallory."

A small spasm came and went on her face, and Mallory shrugged. "So she was better off."

"I didn't say that, Mally."

"But you were thinking it. Everyone was."

Sam closed his eyes, sickened to hear the truth from his daughter. How could he comfort her? "You shouldn't blame people for trying to find something...something—"

"Something to make it not hurt so much?" she said, turning to look at him. "Like, 'Oh, Mallory, we feel *so-o-o* bad for you, but your mother's better off, honey.'" Her face crumpled like it had when she was six and hurt and couldn't hold back the tears. "Because she was a nutcase anyway! That's what they think, Dad. Not that she was better off because there was no more to be done for her cancer, but because she wasn't all there anymore. Because she hadn't been a real person for five years since she...since she...did it. But you can't say stuff like that, so they just tell her daughter and her husband to look at it as a blessing when she dies. Well, that's bullshit, too! It seems to me the whole world's full of people talking bullshit!"

Sam pulled into the garage and stopped. For a moment he sat, utterly bereft of words. "Your mother didn't have the mental capacity she did before the...accident, Mallory, but—"

"It was no accident, Dad!" Mallory said miserably. "She tried to kill herself."

For Sam, Elaine's act still triggered feelings of guilt and failure, but it hadn't been him or his wife who'd suffered when she'd tried to commit suicide, so much as their daughter. Sam reached out, but Mallory shied away from his touch. "I know you probably won't believe this, Mallory," he said wearily. "But I think your mother knew she'd made a huge mistake. I honestly think she regretted it. Even though she wasn't...herself, she certainly was aware of you as her daughter. She knew about all the things you did for her. She was always better when you were around. She loved you. She wouldn't want you to keep hurting this way."

With both hands on her face, her eyes swimming with tears, Mallory gazed at Sam, shaking her head mutely.

"It's true, Mally," Sam insisted, heartsick that she seemed to reject what he knew to be true.

"If she didn't want to hurt me, then why did she take those pills? How do you think I felt when my mother hated living so much that she chose to do something like that? She knew you weren't much of a father. She knew I didn't have anyone else. Didn't she realize I'd be left alone?"

Such pain and anger. Even childishly self-centered as she sounded, the truth in his daughter's words hurt like the slash of a scalpel. Sam was shamed by his own guilt.

Forget the dark legacy left to kids when a parent chose suicide. What about the one who was left to pick up the pieces? Sam scraped a hand over his face, knowing he'd been a sorry substitute for a parent then.

"I don't believe your mother was thinking very clearly at all when she…did that, Mallory. Certainly it had nothing to do with you."

Mallory sniffed, wiped at both eyes again, then sat looking down at her hands for a moment. "I don't think we're getting anywhere with this conversation, Dad," she said quietly. "You can try to make it seem okay, just like all those people at the funeral and everything, but it doesn't change anything, does it?"

She made a move to leave the car. With her hand on the door handle, she turned to look back at Sam. "I'm sorry I acted like that just now, you know, like…being rude and all. I shouldn't have left the house, I guess, but I get so…I don't know. It's awful being alone and bored and…you know—" she shrugged "—it's lonely."

Relieved at the change of subject, Sam managed a smile. "It's okay, Mally." He could definitely understand feeling lonely.

"Just having Mary to talk to doesn't really hack it, you know?"

Mary Morvant was the aging housekeeper who'd been with them since before Mallory was born. She was more like a relative than hired help, yet she had little patience with loud music and endless phone conversations. Sam reached over and stroked the crown of his daughter's head. "I'm sorry if I seemed hard on you, Mally. How about we call the restriction over and done with and you phone Jill and Rachel to come over? We'll send out for pizza."

After a moment, Mallory nodded. "Sure, Dad. Cool." She pushed the door open and got out. With a troubled look, Sam watched her hurry up the walk to the steps of the house.

For a moment after she was gone, Sam fought an urge to start the car and head back to the hospital. There were several patients there he could look in on. He had another surgery scheduled tomorrow morning. A thyroidectomy. Female, age forty-six, anxious and fearful that the tumor he'd discovered would be malignant. He could drop in, say a few calming words. The hours would pass in a blur until he'd be so tired that when he got home he'd fall into bed and fall asleep.

For years he'd immersed himself in the demands of a job where life-and-death issues reigned supreme. Personal problems—Elaine's illness, her suicide attempt, his daughter's needs, his affair with Kate Madison—had all been relegated to second place when weighed against the drama of his profession. That was the way he'd coped in the past.

And look at the consequences.

He sighed and rubbed both hands over his face. Slinking off to the hospital wouldn't cut it anymore. Mallory was going through a tough time, but he knew it wasn't too late for them as long as he worked at it, spent time with her, acted like a father. They would make it. What worried him more was Kate Madison.

He'd been distracted by thoughts of her all day and stunned by Leo's impossible offer to let her into the practice. How could he work with Kate? Spending all day every day around her now was not an option. Not with their history. Which now seemed a lifetime ago. It was hard to believe he'd once clung to the delusion that when the nightmare he'd been living had passed they might have a future together. He'd been a romantic fool in those days.

He got out of the car and slammed the door. And now

Leo expected him to smile and say "Welcome." No way. He couldn't do it. He wore a deep frown as he headed to the back of the Range Rover to get Mallory's bike. He couldn't imagine why Kate would want to practice in Bayou Blanc anyway. Conventional wisdom was that the only way any doctor would leave the rarefied medical atmosphere of the East Coast would be by force. And he couldn't imagine that applying to Kate. She was good; better than good. Lifting the bike out, he set it on the sidewalk and closed the tailgate. Maybe it was the divorce.

He had to admit to being curious. Leo had mentioned it at the time, but Sam had been caught up in Elaine's deteriorating health to the exclusion of almost everything else. Then he'd had the funeral to contend with. And Mallory's problems. Added to that, he'd felt overwhelmed, blindsided by fate, or maybe by God.

Using the remote, he closed the garage door and then, as he headed for the front steps, he turned to gaze at the end of the street where Cocodrie met Vermilion Lane. He'd known when he decided to relocate to Bayou Blanc that Kate had been raised in this neighborhood. He realized now that Kate would probably be living with her mother. Was her concern for Victoria genuine? Once he would never have thought something so unflattering about Kate, but that was before he'd experienced her vindictiveness firsthand. Remembering it brought a new scowl to his face. He took the steps at a fast clip. No, he didn't want the complication of Kate Madison. That part of his life was over and done with.

EIGHT

One of the good things about a small town, Kate thought as she tied the strings on her running shoes, was that a woman could go out safely after dark. She tossed her gym bag onto the seat and slammed the car door. She did some stretching exercises while studying the layout of Bayou Blanc's jogging track, an eight-foot-wide trail that meandered through a grove of live oaks. Bright spotlights were tucked in the limbs of the oaks, dramatizing the beauty and strength of the ancient trees, which, during the day, provided much-needed shade. Bending from her waist to touch the ground, she blessed whatever civic-minded group had sponsored the project.

Twenty minutes later, after only half her usual run, she felt as if she were breathing through a thick fog, thanks to the oppressive humidity. Collapsed on a bench beneath one of the oaks, her eyes closed, she huffed and puffed and fantasized about Boston's crisp, cool climate.

"That's no way to cool down."

Her eyes snapped open and she found herself looking at Sam Delacourt for the second time that day. In navy shorts and a gray T-shirt that clung to impressive biceps and a board-flat abdomen, he was soaked to the skin. And grinning. Instead of being done in by the heat and humidity, he simply seemed invigorated. Jogging in place and breathing hard, he was more virile than the law should allow.

Kate discovered she hadn't enough energy to get to her feet. "I'm not cooling down," she said, lifting her hair off her steamy neck. "I'm melting down."

Chuckling, Sam sat down on the bench beside her, giving off waves of heat and healthy masculinity. "I've often wondered whether half those folks who run the Boston Marathon could last an hour in the humidity down here."

"Hmm. And if the humidity didn't do them in, the heat would." She watched him remove a white sweatband and rake both hands through his hair, then quickly brought her gaze back to safer territory. She didn't want to find anything appealing about Sam. "Remember when they had the Olympics in Atlanta? Several of the favorites didn't win. I wondered whether they might have been sabotaged by the heat. Now I know."

He slanted her a sideways look. "Think of the alternative—sixty inches of snowfall."

"Not quite." She drank thirstily from a bottle of water. "But close. I remember one February blizzard when St. Luke's had to send a snowplow to get extra hands to man the E.R. There'd been an apartment-building fire, and they needed everybody who could possibly get there to help."

He nodded, a somber look on his face. "Fire in an apartment building. That would be a tough one."

"Yes."

"What made you choose Boston?"

"I wanted to be as far away from here as possible."

"As far away from *me* as possible, right?"

"Right. So… I think I'll give it another try." She stood, then began more stretching exercises. "I usually run about five miles. If I quit too soon, I'll never work back up."

Sam rose, too. "Kate, I know I'll probably never be able to explain why I—"

"You're so right." She jerked at a loose shoelace. "So don't bother to try." She finished tying it and then turned to look at him. "It's a sordid little episode in both our lives. I don't know about you, but I've put it behind me. We don't ever need to speak of it again."

"And you think that's possible?"

"It most certainly is for me."

He nodded to a pair of power-walking senior citizens huffing past. "I never meant to hurt you, Kate."

"Oh, pu-*leez*, Sam." She yanked at her socks and reached for her sweatband, lying on the bench.

"You think I set out to seduce you? You think I had it in my mind to start an affair with you the day we met at that conference?"

"Maybe not with me, Sam. But I think you were look-ing for a woman, yes. And almost any woman would do. Your wife was ill, you were frustrated and angry and horny. We met. We clicked. Boom. Only you conveniently forgot to mention Elaine and your daughter."

"I didn't forget them, not for a minute."

"Uh-huh."

He dropped his head back, clamping a hand behind his neck. "Mallory's a mess right now."

"Your daughter?"

"Yeah. She's mad at her mother for dying."

Kate turned away. Part of her wanted to take off at a dead run to escape the memories he was stirring up. An-other part wanted to hear about his life, his daughter. The part of her that had once fantasized about having a child with Sam. Incredible.

"I didn't know Elaine had died until today when Leo mentioned it," she said. "It must have been…difficult."

"She lingered a long time. In and out of remission… It was difficult for a child seeing that, living with it."

"Mallory's probably feeling what any normal teenager would, under the circumstances."

"Her feelings are complicated by Elaine's suicide attempt. She's angry and confused over that."

"I didn't know about that, either, until today."

"No?"

"No, I didn't," she replied, puzzled by something in his voice.

After subjecting her to a long look, he said, "You're right. Maybe pretending there never was anything between us is the best way to handle this."

"Good. Fine. But why do I feel as if I'm missing something, here? If so, why don't you fill me in?"

"Why don't *you* tell *me*, Kate?"

She gazed at him in growing irritation. "What are you getting at, Sam? What's with all the…these cryptic looks and remarks? If you're implying something, you'll have to come right out with it, because it beats me what it could be."

He seemed to come to a decision. "I admitted it was wrong to begin a relationship when I wasn't free. I never expected to feel the way I—" He shook his head. "But I came to my senses, Kate. Nobody forced my hand on that. I knew what we were doing was wrong and—"

"*We* were wrong? No, Sam, it was wrong for you, not me. Damn you!" She moved away, paced a few steps and walked back to him. "It happened for me the way it happens with most single women. I met a man and began a relationship. You were the one with a family. You were the one who decided to cheat. Maybe as time passed you managed to rewrite our history so that I now share the guilt and the consequences, but that's your fantasy, Sam, not mine."

"I've admitted I was wrong, Kate, but you definitely have to share the consequences. I can't overlook what you did afterward. Once you found out about Elaine, you knew how sick she was. Telling her about our...about what had happened between us was vindictive and hateful. You didn't hurt me by doing it nearly as much as you hurt her."

She was staring at him, her hands on her hips. "I don't know what the hell you're talking about, Sam," she said in a tone that vibrated with outrage. "I've never spoken a word to your wife. I've never even *seen* your wife."

His eyes locked with hers as if he were trying to decide whether or not to believe her. Except for his hands fisting at his sides, he didn't move a muscle. "She had a visitor that day. I was told— You were seen leaving our house."

"That would be the house on Prytania?"

"Yes."

"Well, it isn't possible. I've never even been near that house." She reached for a towel she'd left on the bench. "Somebody's lying."

Still staring hard at her, he said, "After that visit—it couldn't have been more than a couple of hours—she took a whole bottle of Valium and washed it down with Scotch."

Bending over, Kate dropped the towel into her gym bag, then zipped it up. The sound was like the scrape of nails on a blackboard. She straightened, and when she spoke, her voice teemed with emotions so turbulent, she could barely form the words. "Are you actually saying you believe I was so filled with hate and rage that I went to see your extremely ill wife and told her I'd been having an affair with you? That I, a physician sworn to hold all life sacred, deliberately set out to destroy a woman already living under a death sentence? Is that what you're saying, Sam?"

"You're saying you didn't."

"Is that a question?"

He looked away from her, focusing on a point beyond them. "I...don't know. It seemed—"

"You believed I would do something like that?"

He was shaking his head. "I didn't want to, but we'd just had that scene in the restaurant." He lifted a shoulder. "Who else?"

"I don't have a clue," she said bitterly. "It's for you to figure out, but it's plain you never doubted your source."

She was amazed at the tangle of emotions roiling inside her. She hadn't realized Sam Delacourt could possibly hurt her any more. If he could believe she was capable of such cruel behavior, what did that say about her own character? What kind of person was she that she chose men with so little substance they would believe that of her?

She recapped the water bottle with fingers that trembled and tossed it into the trash can nearby. Until she'd met Sam, she'd had little time for men in her life. Making it as a physician had been everything. She hadn't even realized how empty and barren her personal life had been until Sam opened those doors. Then it was as if all the missing parts of her very soul had suddenly been found, only for it to be shattered on the night he'd told her he already had a wife. A child. Another life. And that he would not be seeing her again.

Now he believed she had taken a woman's revenge by telling all to his dying wife.

"'Hell hath no fury.' Is that it, Sam?" She looked straight into his eyes.

They stood in sizzling silence for another moment. Then Sam said, "I think you can see that with everything that's happened between us, the last thing we need is to work together. I talked to Leo today. I guess he'd been thinking about retirement for a while, or at least he'd been thinking about cutting back on his hours. I told him I

wanted some time to sort this out, not telling him anything about our...past, of course. Frankly, I assumed that
after you and I had talked privately you'd see it wouldn't
work."

"Oh, you assumed that, did you?"

He sighed. "Listen, Kate, I don't know why you've suddenly got it in your head that you want to try your hand
at a practice that isn't even in the same universe as what
you left in Boston. You'd be bored here in a week. Hell, in
a day! The culture shock alone would be enough to drive
you nuts. It's not—"

"Wait a minute, Sam." She jammed her hands against
her hips. "Where in hell do you get off trying to tell me
what you think is best for me and my career? Leo made
me an offer, and I'm going to take him up on it. As for
boredom and culture shock, I'll handle it."

She swept up her gym bag and started toward her car.

Sam hurried after her, caught her arm, dropped it as
she yanked away. "You're still mad at me. Okay, I accept
that, but we have to come to an understanding on this,
Kate. If not tonight, then pretty soon."

She turned, her face a picture of amazed scorn. "'An
understanding'? Don't tell me. Let me guess what that
'understanding' will be. You'll keep hammering at Leo,
hoping to drive me someplace else where you won't have
to see me or be reminded of our 'past,' as you so delicately
put it. Well, I don't think so. You know what your problem is, Sam?" She jerked her car door open and tossed the
gym bag inside. "You're eaten up with guilt. You cheated
on your wife, and she found out somehow and reacted as
any desperately ill woman might have done. But you
couldn't assume the responsibility for anything so tragic,
so you've spent the years since our rotten romance ended
convincing yourself I was somehow responsible for
Elaine's decision to end it all."

Now behind the wheel, she turned the key with a vicious twist and gunned the BMW's motor to the max before buzzing the window down for one more shot. "You made your bed, Dr. Delacourt, so now you can sleep in it. Alone."

Turning up the stereo to ear-blasting volume, she drove off.

She was still fuming when she pulled into Victoria's driveway. Her ex-lover was convinced she was a vindictive bitch who'd tried to drive his sick wife to suicide. She made a short, humorless sound as she stopped her car. And to think she'd expected life to be kinder and gentler in the Deep South.

She reached for her gym bag, thinking that one thing was very clear: Sam was just as reluctant as she for them to work together. But it was also clear neither had any option at this point. She knew her own reasons, but she wasn't sure what motivated Sam. Why would he suddenly quit the fast track to medical stardom to practice in Bayou Blanc? Most patients with complicated medical problems headed for the city and to specialists in practices such as Sam had just abandoned.

She closed the car door and locked it. Sam's determination to keep her out of Leo's practice concerned her. Where else could she go where there would be no inquiry into her background or scrutiny of her performance at St. Luke's? Unless she screwed up again. No, she had to seize this chance, and she was counting on fewer crises in the clinic until she got over this bizarre period. With her gym bag slung over her shoulder, she climbed the front steps of her mother's house. Sam's hostility was troubling, but her own fear of failure was ten times more terrifying.

Before she reached the front door, it opened and Amber came out. "Hi, Kate. No need asking where you've been."

Eyeing Kate's damp T-shirt and glistening skin, she wrinkled her nose. "I never understood how you athletic types could stand all that sweat and effort. It must be ninety degrees out here."

"Amber. I thought you went back to New Orleans."

"I did, but I'm back. With Stephen, not Deke. I dropped in looking for you, but Victoria said you were out running." She motioned to the wicker chairs on the porch. "Let's sit over there. The fan's on overhead. You can cool off." Assuming Kate would follow, she went over and sat down. In a low tone, she asked, "What did you think about your mama?"

Kate dropped her gym bag on the floor. "I was as shocked as you knew I would be. And upset. Why didn't you tell me, Amber? Why didn't you call me sooner?"

Amber sighed. "I knew you'd be pissed. But blame it on Victoria, *chère.* She wouldn't let anyone tell you because of the divorce. She said you were going through a bad time and didn't need the added stress. Once the chemo was over she planned to let you know. She knew once you found out, you'd come straight home."

"What if her heart had given out, Amber? What if she'd had an extreme reaction to the chemo?" Kate got to her feet in agitation. "You shouldn't have paid any attention to such a ridiculous request. You should have called me."

"Well, I didn't because Victoria asked me not to. And you should leave it there. A person's privacy should be respected, Kate, even when it's your own mother. So save the lecture and the outrage until you think over what I'm saying."

Kate moved to the edge of the porch. Amber's suggestion was unnecessary. She'd spent a lot of time worrying over her mother since arriving in Bayou Blanc. So much for coming home seeking sanctuary. Everything seemed to be going downhill. With a sigh, she turned to face Amber. "Are you here for a few days? I don't remember you saying you'd be back until the Fais Do-Do Fest, but that's not for a couple of weeks, is it?"

"I hadn't counted on your visit. I want to spend some time with you. I have some commitments, but I think my staff can handle them. I've recorded a couple of TV spots the station can use for just this kind of thing." She gave a shrug and a blithe smile. "So, until the Fais Do-Do is over, we can catch up to our hearts' content."

"What does Deke have to say about you spending a couple of weeks away from him? I remember when you first married you laughed about him hardly letting you out of his sight. Have things changed?"

"Deke will never change. He'll be in and out, of course, but he's not going to be underfoot every minute, thank God."

"What about his broadcasts?"

"Oh, he can always broadcast from the local station."

Kate smiled. "Well, Bayou Blanc's nightlife can't compare with anything in New Orleans."

"Right." Amber made a sound as if exhaling smoke. "I figure a couple of days, maximum, and he'll be so bored he'll head on back." Her tone changed. "He'll expect Stephen to keep an eye on me."

Her teenage stepson as bodyguard? Maybe another time Kate would have risen to that—and to that edge in Amber's tone. Anger? Bitterness? Whatever, she wasn't up to figuring it out tonight. At this moment, she had her hands full wrestling with her own demons. "Leo will be glad to have you both."

"Yeah, he really loves Stephen."

"And you, Amber," she added dryly.

"I guess. Anyway, let's save lots of time for each other." Amber stood and moved to the steps. "Don't get all tied up with stuff, because we have a lot of catching up to do."

"Too late. I'm going to be filling in a bit for Leo at the practice."

"What! Why? No, Kate…c'mon."

"I decided I didn't like doing nothing."

"How do you know? You haven't tried it yet," Amber said in exasperation. Her gaze suddenly narrowed. "Did Daddy do a guilt trip on you over this?"

"You know Leo wouldn't do anything like that, Amber."

"Yes, he would. If he thought there was a chance in hell of getting you into his practice, he'd do or say anything short of blackmail. So if he thought of a way to strong-arm you into the clinic, he'd do it." She made a grumpy sound. "He's always liked you best."

Kate smiled. "Oh, sure."

"It's true." Amber's pretty mouth slanted in a pout. "You know when the boat caught fire and sank all those years ago? Well, I used to wonder as a kid whether somehow or other they got us mixed up, you and me. And Leo should be your dad and Victoria should be my mama."

It was a sign of Kate's unsettled state that Amber's remark sounded almost plausible. Indeed, Leo had loomed large in every major accomplishment in her life. And there had always been a special rapport shared by Victoria and Amber. Kate leaned against a pillar, still smiling. "I'm too tired to even begin to point out how absurd that is, Amber. We were six years old, not infants." She bent to pick up her gym bag. "I'd better go in and check on Mother."

Amber got halfway down the steps before stopping and turning back. "Wait a minute. I've got it! It's Sam Delacourt, right?"

"Sam Delacourt? What are you talking about?"

"He's part of Daddy's practice now, so that's why you've suddenly chucked the prestige and glamour of Boston for little ole Bayou Blanc, huh?"

Kate reached for the doorknob. "I didn't even know Sam was part of the practice until after Leo and I talked. That had nothing to do with my decision, Amber."

"Does anybody but me know the two of you have history?"

Kate sighed. "It's *ancient* history, Amber."

"Uh-huh. But the veggie wife is now dead."

Kate turned to see Amber's eyebrows wagging Groucho-style. "Why did I ever tell you about Sam?"

"Because in those days you told me everything, *chère*. And I told you everything. Almost."

"Well, I've certainly learned my lesson."

Amber was still chuckling when Kate opened the door and went inside.

NINE

Kate found her mother in the sunroom, smoking. "You just missed Amber," Victoria said, looking up from the book she was reading.

Kate dropped her gym bag on the floor. "I saw her on the porch as she was leaving. Mother, you shouldn't be smoking."

Victoria stubbed out her cigarette with a sigh and laid the book aside. Removing her glasses, she rubbed her eyes. "My vision just isn't what it used to be. It takes some of the pleasure out of reading when everything is a blur."

Resisting the urge to snatch the cigarettes from the table, Kate walked to the water pitcher. She drank half a glass, then said, "Maybe you need a new prescription. How long has it been?"

"A year or two, who knows?" Victoria shrugged. "You look a little upset. Didn't you have a good run?"

"Mother, we need to talk."

Victoria sighed. "Provided it's not about smoking or this awful cancer, then go right ahead. One of the nicest things about having you home for an indefinite stay is that we'll have time to catch up on what's been going on. Tell me about Robert. Did he marry that silly twit he was fooling around with? I hope you didn't let his infidelity bother you, Kate. Robert is the kind of man who is never going to be satisfied with what he has. He'll always be looking for greener pastures."

For a moment, Kate held the cold glass against her forehead. Victoria wasn't going to talk about her health, and Kate wasn't going to share her feelings about her failed marriage and boring divorce. Stalemate. The more things changed, the more they stayed the same.

"Mother, you probably won't believe this, but Robert's affair with Hillary couldn't have bothered me less. What bothered me was that I think Robert was right when he accused me of neglecting him. I didn't expect to have to coddle a husband, because, after all, I was wrapped up in a very demanding career when we married. But it turned out that intimacy is something I'm not very good at. And apparently he noticed and looked for it elsewhere."

"Oh, that's ridiculous! Is that what he said? Well, if you want my opinion, I think it sounds like an excuse for him to screw around. Men don't need much of a reason to sample anything or anyone who catches their eye."

"Did my father do that?"

Victoria looked startled. "John? What makes you ask that?"

"Your tone of voice, for one thing. You sounded as if you were speaking from personal experience."

"My goodness, girl, he's been dead for over thirty years."

"Yes, but did he?"

"Infidelity wasn't one of your father's sins."

"Then what were they, Mother? He mustn't have been perfect, because you would have spoken more about him as I was growing up. Do you realize I know hardly anything about my father? Actually, I feel closer to Leo than to Daddy." She gave a bewildered shake of her head, while inside, her heart was beating fast. "Do you know I don't even remember what I called him. Was it 'Daddy'? 'Dad'? Or 'Father'?"

Victoria put her glasses on and got to her feet—shakily,

it seemed to Kate. "Was this what you wanted to talk to me about? Goodness, I thought I was going to have to fend off questions about my health. This is almost a relief."

"Why? Because there's so little to tell, Mother?" Touching her forehead, Kate began pacing the room. "Everything's so vague about that day on the boat, but when I start thinking about it, I get...I feel..." She shook her head, frowning. "I don't know. Anxious or...fearful." She looked at Victoria, trying to smile. "Isn't that odd, Mama?"

Victoria's tone softened at Kate's use of the childhood name.

"You called John 'Daddy,' Kate." Victoria moved to a table and opened a family album. In it were pictures of Kate as a small child. One snapshot showed the three of them—Victoria, John and Kate—when Kate was about four years old. No one in the photo was smiling. "The reason your memories are vague is because you saw so little of him. He was a very busy man, ambitious. A workaholic, actually. He was here only on weekends and then spent much of his time on the phone or closed up in his study with the people he did business with."

"Were you happy?"

Victoria closed the album. "I should have gone out and gotten myself a job. I had the education and the intelligence. A woman shouldn't depend on her husband to define herself. If I was unhappy, it was my own fault."

"Why didn't you get a job?"

"John disapproved."

Again, Kate was feeling anxious and apprehensive. Why would talking like this bring on these feelings? Victoria, she noticed, was looking fragile and tired. Kate set her glass down and took a seat in the chair beside the one her mother had just vacated. "Come and sit down again,

Mother. You know I've always been curious about
Daddy, but it looks as if he's destined to remain a shadowy figure in my memory. Besides, I don't know why I
keep on trying to dig up childhood stuff. It can't mean
anything, can it?"

"No."

Kate smiled and patted the chair again. "And you were
right. It wasn't Daddy I wanted to talk about, it was you.
And your medical situation."

"The cancer." With a sigh, Victoria sat back down.
"You can say it out loud, Kate. I've learned to."

"I talked to Sam Delacourt about you today. I wanted
to look at your records, and he wouldn't give me access."

"I hope not."

"Mother, I want to see those records!"

Victoria reached over and put a hand on Kate's bare
knee. "I've already had this talk with Leo, Kate. Sam's an
excellent doctor. I couldn't have better care, believe me.
And try to accept this, darling. Sam isn't emotionally involved in this. You are. Leo is. Sam has been there for me
when I needed him, and yet I don't have to feel I'm taking
a toll on him personally as I would if it were you or Leo."
She sighed, patting Kate again. "Now, will you let me
handle this in my own way?"

Kate leaned back in the chair, resting her head against
the hard carving on the wood frame. "I guess I have to,
don't I?"

"You do."

For now. Kate straightened and looked at her mother.
"Can I at least examine you? My bag's in my room. It'll
only take a minute to run up and get it." She saw the
frown gathering on her mother's face and rushed on.
"Just BP and pulse and listening a bit to your chest, okay?
Cross my heart, that's all."

"Kate..."

"And maybe a quick peek at your medication."

"Kate!"

Backing away, Kate said softly, "I'll tell all about Robert and the tawdry blonde he dumped me for...."

She glimpsed the wry smile playing on Victoria's dry lips before turning to get her bag.

TEN

Kate spent a leisurely week before taking Leo up on his offer to enter the practice. If she decided to stay in Bayou Blanc, there were practical arrangements to be made, which kept her occupied for a while. Through an agent, she arranged to sublet the condo she was renting in Boston. She canceled memberships in health clubs and sent cards to friends to let them know where she was. She wrote lists for the time when she might want to make the break permanent. She made a few calls.

That accomplished, she began to feel restless. She was used to a grueling work schedule. Whiling away hours by the pool was boring. Rose Jenner, Victoria's longtime housekeeper, took good care of most of her needs, so there was little left for Kate to do except lunch with Amber and keep her mother company. That left too much time to obsess over whether or not she'd be able to handle practicing medicine again without unraveling in a crisis. A week of it was all she could take.

She arrived early that first day, planning to familiarize herself with the layout of Leo's office and get a feel for patient procedures, lab techniques, billing and the like. She went right to the source, Ruby Zeringue.

"It's about time you got here, Kate, yes." Ruby stood, hustled Kate down the hall to the coffee lounge. She poured each of them a wickedly strong chicory-flavored brew and leaned back against the counter, cupping the mug in both hands. Her black eyes gleamed mischievously. "What'd I tell you, darlin'? You come back at Fais Do-Do time and you take a chance gettin' hexed. Dr. Leo, he tells me you want to do a little practice work right here with us, hmm?"

"Temporarily, Ruby."

Ruby snorted. "We'll see about that. But first, we get you outfitted with what you need to see patients. Did Doctor tell you we've got an extra office? We just haven't found anybody we liked to occupy it." She grinned, her wiry curls bobbing. "Until now."

"Does each doctor have a particular nurse?" Kate asked.

Ruby's smile changed subtly. "Only Sam. You met Diane Crawford last week, yeah? He brought her with him from New Orleans, so don't make the mistake of asking her to assist."

Kate arched an eyebrow. "Got it."

"Cheryl's good and won't gripe even if she has to stay late. Jenny's got two little ones, so it'll be appreciated if you consider that when we're forced to see patients late."

"Does that happen often?"

"That we can't get away by five, five-thirty? More than it used to. Sam's bringing in new patients in droves, yeah. Folks in the habit of going to New Orleans are now comin' in here." She sipped at the hot black brew. "You're a godsend, *chère*. That Leo, he grinned all over hisself las' week when you tol' him you'd stay, uh-huh. And jus' wait. Now we got you, no way we gonna let you loose!"

Kate smiled into the coffee mug. After the anxiety of the past week and Sam's blunt disapproval, Ruby's words warmed her heart. But her satisfaction vanished at the sound of Sam's voice.

"I don't think you have to worry about that, Ruby."

Kate started and whipped her head around, almost

scalding herself as hot coffee sloshed over her fingers. He stood at the door, hands shoved into the pockets of his Dockers. His yellow pullover was bloodstained. He appeared rumpled and tired and a little too appealing.

"Oh, you been at the E.R. again, *chèr?*" Ruby was already pouring coffee for him. She passed it to him as Kate hastily turned on the faucet and rinsed her hand.

Sam took the cup. "A kid on a motorcycle forced off the road by a drunk in a pickup. Both of them wound up in the E.R. sometime after midnight."

Kate wiped at the coffee she'd splashed on the counter. "There's no regular trauma surgeon on call?"

Sam leaned against the door frame, his battered white Nikes crossed at the ankles. "The best—Martin Lee, but both patients were in critical condition, so Marty called me to handle the kid while he took the drunk."

"I thought you said there would be less excitement here than at St. Luke's."

"I said there would be fewer gunshot victims. We get plenty of drunk drivers, like anywhere else." He set his cup down. "Are you here to schmooze with Ruby or do you plan to see patients?"

"I'm here to see patients," Kate replied, giving him a tight smile. "But don't worry, I'll try to avoid getting in your way or stealing any of yours."

He glanced at Ruby. "I'm heading home. If there's an emergency, call me. Otherwise, I'll try to grab a nap after I clean up." He shifted his gaze to Kate, who was unable to read anything in the darkness of his eyes. "Kate can have Agnes Wainwright if she comes in today, Ruby." And with that, he walked out.

"Who's Agnes Wainwright?" Kate asked.

"A pain-in-the-patoot patient," Ruby murmured with a baffled look at Sam as he disappeared down the hall. "Makes up reasons to see the doctors. What in the name of all that's holy was that about, *chère?* Sam mad at you about something?''

Yeah, I remind him of past sins. "I suppose he's offended because Leo invited me into the practice without consulting him first," Kate said. "But I'm not going to let him drive me away, Ruby."

"He's just tired, that one," Ruby said with a worried look at the door. "Works too hard. Then his wife dyin' only a few months ago, that girl of his givin' him fits, and him tryin' to be mama and daddy to her now." She was shaking her head. "I don't want you to think it's anything personal, Kate, no. Sam isn't like that. He's one fine doctor, yes. A better man you wouldn't find anywhere." With a sigh, she moved to the sink and rinsed out her cup before turning to look at Kate. "He's tired, that's it, *chère.* Has to be."

By the end of that first day, Kate felt reasonably certain she would be able to handle whatever came up. Except for a few chronically ill patients, the people she saw suffered from a wide variety of minor aches and pains—everything from sinus infections to stomachaches. In fact, the high point of the day came when a teenage boy had to be sedated while she removed ingrown toenails from both his big toes. If she hadn't known how painful it was, his howls would have been funny.

Now Kate headed for the lounge, having seen her last patient of the day. Leo hadn't exaggerated when he'd said there was room in the practice for another doctor. Sam had shown up after lunch, although she'd been so busy she hadn't seen him other than to pass by him a couple of times in the hallway.

Diane Crawford was chatting with Cheryl in front of the microwave as Kate entered the lounge. She nodded pleasantly to both, but their conversation ended as Kate dumped the remains of the diet drink she hadn't found time to consume.

"This must seem very boring to you after five years in Boston," Diane said. Cheryl, a plain young woman with strikingly beautiful eyes, had a pleasant look on her face, but Diane's smile had a sharp edge.

"To tell the truth," Kate said, "I was so busy today, I didn't have time to be bored."

"You were busy, all right," Cheryl said. "Mondays are usually nonstop, but today was something else." She glanced at Diane. "Can you believe Ruby conned her into seeing Agnes Wainwright? But you must have worked a miracle, Dr. Madison," she added, dunking a tea bag, "because Agnes actually left happy."

"How does she usually leave?" Kate asked.

Cheryl rolled her eyes. "Mumbling under her breath about how doctors are like lawyers now—out for the almighty dollar."

Kate rinsed her glass and placed it in the dishwasher. "She's lonely and aging and in pain with chronic arthritis. I took an extra ten minutes to let her tell me all about it."

"Sam and Leo have both heard it a thousand times," Diane said coolly. "You probably won't be so sympathetic after you've been here awhile." She dropped a spoon into the sink with a clatter. "And speaking of that, how long do you plan on staying? I heard how Leo pressured you into filling in while we look for someone who's right for the practice. You simply have to stand up to him. With your mother's condition so uncertain right now, I'm sure you don't need this."

Kate turned to look at the nurse. "This may surprise you, but actually I do need this right now. I'm a physician. Physicians heal. Since you're Sam's nurse, you must know he's treating my mother. If I can't do that service for my mother, it actually gives me some sense of satisfaction to be able to treat other patients." Kate smiled. "Excuse me, I think I hear Ruby calling again."

She left the lounge but, thinking everyone else had gone, she defied Sam's orders and tried to sneak a look at her mother's file. Her attempt was foiled when, as she was combing through the M's for Madison, Ruby returned unexpectedly. Victoria's file was in Sam's personal keeping, Ruby informed her with a chiding look. Which meant that Diane Crawford had access and Kate didn't. She hated the nurse having even that small victory.

There'd been nothing subtle about the nurse's attitude in the lounge. Had Sam told Diane that he wasn't particularly pleased to have Kate here? As for Kate not being "right" for the practice, whether she decided to stay or not, she planned to make the nurse—and Sam—eat those words.

Stepping into late-summer sunshine, she felt she'd made a good decision by accepting Leo's invitation. Compared to the E.R. at St. Luke's, the stress level at the clinic was in the minus zone.

Of course she might have swapped one kind of stress for another. Working with Sam Delacourt wouldn't be a walk in the park. But neither would it require life-and-death decisions day in and day out, with no end ever in sight.

She glanced at her watch as she started her car. Not yet six and she was free for the evening. Incredible. Only one other car in the parking lot, but with the setting sun in her eyes, the driver was just a shape behind the wheel of a four-wheel drive. It wasn't Sam, who was taller and broader.

Several blocks later, the man was still behind her. She thought little of it until she turned off the main highway onto the less-traveled road that eventually connected with Vermilion Lane and saw him take the same turn.

Was he following her? She reached Vermilion and, glancing in the rearview mirror, she watched him do the same. She felt a sudden chill. A neighbor in Boston had been followed from her workplace to her condo, then attacked and raped after ducking inside her garage before the automatic door had closed completely. But this was Bayou Blanc, not inner-city Boston. Still, she didn't like the idea that she'd been followed all the way to Victoria's rather isolated neighborhood.

And he *was* following her. He was right on her tail and making no secret of it. At Victoria's house, she pulled into the driveway a little too recklessly and stopped abruptly. Now what? Deciding not to enter the garage, she reached for her car phone and got out with it pressed to her ear as if she were dialing for help, and started toward the door in a hurry.

"Whoa, Kate! Wait up!"

She looked back to see her would-be stalker getting rather awkwardly out of his vehicle. Not a rapist, she decided. He was obviously in no shape for it. One arm was in a sling and he limped slightly. Her panic fizzled entirely when he headed up the drive toward her, grinning. She knew that smile.

She was caught up in a hard, one-sided embrace, and when he turned her loose, she clapped her hand over her heart. "Nick Santana, I'm shaking like a leaf. You had me totally freaked out!"

He looked startled. "'Freaked out'? How?"

Kate slumped against her car. "I thought I was being followed by a rapist or something."

"What the hell kind of greeting is that for your old chemistry partner?"

She was smiling now, too. "You've forgotten we were expelled from Mr. Sturgis's class after that crazy idea you had to try something you'd read in *Soldier of Fortune* magazine."

"Yeah, well, it doesn't seem to have stunted your career." He stepped back, looking her over admiringly. "Jeez, you're looking good, Kate. It's about damn time you came home. I never knew what the hell Boston had that we don't have right here in New Orleans."

"Bayou Blanc isn't New Orleans, Nick."

"Close enough. Hell, you know what I mean."

Leaning against the door of her BMW, she studied him—black hair, near-black eyes and lean as a jungle cat. Lord, he was gorgeous. But Nick Santana had always been attractive. She could still see traces of the teenage boy who'd been Amber's steady boyfriend. Now, however, there was an uncompromising set to his mouth and a laser sharpness in his gaze that belied the notorious Santana grin. His years as a cop in New Orleans had marked him, but he was still stunning.

"How the hell are you, Kate?"

"I'm okay, Nick. How about you?"

He was nodding, his keen gaze intent on her. "Fine. Can't complain."

"Oh, really?" She glanced at the sling. "What happened?"

"Some shit went down on the job and I zigged when I should have zagged."

"How bad was it?"

"Took two slugs—one in this arm, the other low and inside. Donated a sizable chunk of one lung." He was propped against her car, his legs crossed at the ankles.

"Sounds as if you're lucky to be alive."

"Yeah, but my partner *wasn't* so lucky. A bullet nicked his heart and he died on the way to the E.R."

"Oh, Nick...I'm sorry."

"Yeah, it was tough." He looked down, studying the

seam in the driveway. "It was a drive-by and nobody saw a thing." He brought his gaze back to Kate. "A dozen people hanging out on the corner that night, and yet they didn't notice a car cruising by with somebody inside shooting at two cops."

"You have no suspects?"

"Suspects, but nothing solid. It's not a problem." He touched the sling. "Soon as I shed this thing, I'm going to be all over the city lookin' for those scumbags. No place in the Big Easy is gonna be dark enough or deep enough."

"You need to concentrate on getting well, Nick."

"I *am* getting well. What else can I do right now? But I concentrate on figuring out how to nail Joe's killers."

"Joe? Oh, not Joe Morales?"

"Yeah, two years behind us in high school. Joe was a helluva cop."

"I had a flat once on the causeway when it was raining cats and dogs," Kate said softly. "Joe stopped and changed it for me. He saved my life that day."

"Yeah, well…whoever did it is gonna pay."

She glanced beyond him to the sport-utility vehicle. "Should you be driving, Nick?"

"Sam says it's okay as long as I don't overdo. I get a little stir crazy with nothing to do but read or watch TV. I can't stomach talk radio. Ten minutes of Deke Russo trashing the department, and my blood pressure is off the stick. Hell, the high point of my week is my appointment with Sam."

She frowned. "I thought Sam was gone for the day."

"He was. I stopped Ruby as she was leaving. Some form for the insurance company."

"Oh." Which explained how Ruby had caught her red-handed, riffling through the patient files.

Nick glanced down the street. "I'm staying in the neighborhood. Did your mama mention it?"

"No, where? Have you bought a house?"

"In Vermilion Place? On my salary? Homicide detectives do okay at the NOPD, but not well enough to live here, darlin'. Besides, we have to reside in the city to work there. No, I'm at the old Yeager place until Sam pronounces me fit to work again."

"Claude and Émilie Yeager's house? Mother wrote me when they died, but I didn't hear what happened to the house."

"Nothing, yet. I mean, the heirs haven't decided—one of whom happens to be Cody's godfather. He insisted I stay there until I was on my feet again, since it was standing empty and—" he shrugged "—here we are."

"Cody. That's your son, isn't it?"

"Yeah. He's fourteen now."

She sighed. "Wow, time does fly, doesn't it? How's your wife? I don't think we ever met."

"Well, it's too late now. We split when Cody was eight. She didn't like the job, the hours or the pay scale."

"And Cody lives with you?"

"Only for the summer. His mother remarried—a lawyer—and moved to Houston." There was a bitter twist to his smile. "I don't see nearly as much of Cody as I'd like, so when I got the chance to stay here in Bayou Blanc and Cody was out of school, I figured it was a good opportunity to spend some time with him." He shifted, favoring his injured arm. "How's your mama, Kate? I see her sometimes getting her mail and we chat. She was looking so frail a couple of weeks ago that I even went so far as to mention it to Sam."

"She has cancer, Nick."

He was shaking his head. "I was afraid it was something serious. How is she?"

"She's finished her chemotherapy. We'll just have to wait and see."

"Tough for you," he said with sympathy. "And Amber. I remember how Victoria treated her almost like a second daughter."

"Speaking of Amber," Kate said. "Did you know she and Deke are the headliners for the Fais Do-Do Fest?"

"Yeah, I heard." He rubbed the back of his neck. "Actually, Leo invited me to the party."

"Party?"

"Oh, shit. Have I let the cat out of the bag?" He kicked at the seam in the concrete. "Forget I said that, will you?"

Kate groaned. "Amber's planning something in honor of my homecoming, right?"

Nick shrugged helplessly.

"She promised!" Kate wailed.

"Well…it's her thing, after all. Amber Lifestyles," he drawled, his mouth twisting again. "Social consultant in New Orleans for those who demand the very best."

"I don't know why I'm surprised," Kate said dryly. "As you say, it's her thing."

Nick looked beyond Kate to the roof of Amber's childhood home, just visible through the trees. "I remember when we were dating she used to spend hours redecorating houses in her head and planning menus for fancy parties. I knew even then I wasn't going to be able to give her the kind of life she dreamed of. But, hell, if I'd known she was going to parlay her fantasies into big business, I might have invested."

"She *has* done extremely well," Kate said, her tone soft as she recalled Nick and Amber as high-school sweethearts. They'd been a couple from the time both were in tenth grade. Nobody had been more surprised than Kate when Amber had broken off her long relationship with Nick only weeks after she and Kate were enrolled at SMU in Dallas. Nick had stayed behind, of necessity, and enrolled in a local college. One of several kids in a big working-class family, he'd been forced to live at home and work two jobs just to get a degree.

Kate remembered the letters and phone calls from Nick pouring in those first few months after Amber broke it off. They had stopped abruptly after he'd shown up one weekend, surprising Amber. He'd caused a ruckus by crashing a fraternity party. After pushing his way inside, he'd embarrassed Amber by decking the guy she'd come with. Kate didn't think Amber had seen Nick since.

"So, will you be there?" she asked.

He laughed shortly. "What do you think?"

"Maybe we could skip it together," Kate said, more than half serious.

After a moment, Nick sobered. "Could I ask you a question, Kate?"

"Sure, although I won't promise to answer it." She smiled.

"It's about Amber's marriage—her second one, I mean. I guess I understood when she dumped me and married that rich guy—Ethan somebody—after graduating from SMU. She divorced him, and that didn't surprise me, either. He was too old for her. But it beats the hell out of me what she ever saw in Deke Russo." Nick was shaking his head as if mystified. "I can't believe she married that jerk. Can you explain it?"

"You sound as if you know him."

"We've met, but we don't run in the same circles," Nick said dryly. Then, after a pause, he reminded, "You didn't answer my question."

"Who knows why two people are attracted, Nick."

"Meaning you don't like him, either."

"I didn't say that!"

His grin returned. "Still loyal and true. You haven't changed, Kate. Except to get more beautiful."

"Neither have you," she replied, wondering not for the

first time if Amber had ever regretted breaking up with a man as attractive and just plain nice as Nick Santana.

"Oh, yes, I have. The last time you saw me, I was still nuts about Amber. That's changed, thank God."

"I should hope so. That was—what?—twenty-something years ago. Lots of water under the bridge since then. For all of us. Marriage, divorce, career changes, kids…" She touched her temple. "Which reminds me…Stephen, Amber's stepson, is here. He's fifteen and he'll probably be glad to have somebody Cody's age nearby, so be sure and bring him along. Mother's probably already offered to let y'all use the pool. If not, you're more than welcome. Nobody uses it anymore."

"You never did," Nick said. "Are you still nervous around water?"

"I wish I could deny it, but, yes, I am. Silly, isn't it?"

"I don't know. Considering that accident when you were so young, well, I've seen worse phobias."

Kate gave him a rueful smile. "I always swear this is the summer I'm going to overcome it and learn to swim. But somehow I never do."

"I just figured out the reason you went to Boston." Nick's eyebrows lifted as if a light had come on. "It's so cold there, you knew you'd never have a chance to go swimming again."

"No, it was because I wouldn't have to tolerate any hot-shot homicide detectives giving me a hard time."

"Okay, if I can't get any sympathy, I'm outta here." Nick backed toward his vehicle, grinning.

Shaking her head, she called out, "You take care of yourself, you hear?"

Nick hooted. "Hear that, folks? A few days in God's country and she's talkin' Southern again."

"Don't you need to take a pill or something?"

Unfazed, he pulled the door open. "So, how long can you stay, Kate?"

"I really haven't made up my mind."

"Whoa! Now you *have* surprised me." He watched her replace the cell phone in the car and close the door. "I guess it was Victoria, huh? She must be thrilled. Having you back will probably do more for her than any treatment they could throw at her, chemo included."

"I wish it were that simple."

"Don't dismiss it, Doc. In my line of work, I've seen some things that defy science." He waited for a moment as she opened her purse and dropped her car keys inside. "I'm serious, Kate. You ought to stick around. It wouldn't only make your mama happy—Leo would be over the moon." He winked. "You know Amber always said he liked you best."

Kate propped her hands on her hips. "You and Amber! Leo adores his daughter. If she'd chosen medicine, he'd have her practicing with him. I just happened to share that with him."

"Did you ever try to tell Amber that when she was sixteen and couldn't pass chemistry, no matter how hard we coached her?"

"Well, she's overcome it. She's now the quintessential nineties woman. She juggles her career, her marriage, motherhood, and she's in the public eye constantly, both as Amber Lifestyles and as the wife of a celebrity. I still can't even throw a dinner party without help."

"As I said, loyal and true to the end."

Kate chuckled. "I think I hear my mom calling me."

"Uh-huh. Now, if you were really smart, you'd join up with Leo and Sam and forget all about Boston."

"Well, that's a plan all right."

She could see she'd surprised him. "You're actually considering it?"

"Why wouldn't I?"

"Yeah, why? Leo's getting on now, bound to be thinking of retirement. And if that happens, Sam will need help. They'd both probably kill to have someone with your credentials, Doc. Leo hasn't taken any new patients in a while. So for me, it was either Dr. Delacourt or drive across the causeway with a dicey lung and a broken wing. Hey, it was a no-brainer. Sam's tops."

"So I hear," Kate said. Nick's eyebrows arched upward, but she was spared from having to explain when a teenage boy called to him from across the street.

"You've got a phone call, Dad!"

Looking at the boy, Kate thought he could have been Nick about twenty years ago. "That would be Cody, I presume," she said, settling her purse strap on her shoulder.

"Yeah." Nick lifted a hand to acknowledge the boy before turning back to Kate. "It's great to have you back in Bayou Blanc, Kate. There are a lot worse places. Take it from me."

ELEVEN

A few days later, Victoria was again in the sunroom when Kate came in at the end of the day. She hesitated, then walked into the room. "How are you feeling today, Mother?" Victoria still refused to confide in Kate about her illness, and Kate was still hurt over it.

"Fine. I'm just fine." Victoria marked a place in the magazine she was reading and set it aside. *Southern Accents*, Kate noted, heading for the bar. The contents were devoted to gorgeous, upscale homes and lifestyles to match. Kate was suddenly reminded of Victoria's visit to Boston a couple of years before the divorce. Her mother had toured Kate's house with a look of pained tolerance, comparing it, no doubt, to Amber's exquisite showplace in the Garden District.

Kate reached for a bottle of Merlot. "How about something cool to drink, Mother?"

"No, I have some lemonade here. Thanks."

"You don't mind if I have a glass of wine?" She paused in the act of pouring the Merlot into cranberry crystal.

"No, of course not. But don't get too comfortable."

Kate replaced the bottle and took a sip of the wine. "Why? What's up?"

"Amber called a while ago."

"Oh, really?"

Kate carried her wineglass across the room. She took a sip before settling into the love seat with a sigh.

"She'd like you to come over for a drink."

"Oh, okay."

"Deke's there."

Some of Kate's pleasure ebbed. "Will you come with me?" Victoria spent too much time alone in the house. If it weren't for Leo, she'd hardly see anyone. Kate thought she needed to get out more.

Victoria removed her glasses. "I don't think so. Not tonight, anyway. You go on without me. It's been nice having you to myself, but you and Amber have hardly spent any time together."

"If Deke's there, we still won't," Kate said with a wry twist of her mouth. "Whenever we've seen each other in the five years they've been married, he's acted as if I'm a bad influence." She stared into her wine. "It's almost as if he's afraid we'll get into mischief or something if he doesn't hang around and keep us straight. So silly."

Victoria was gazing through the French doors to the courtyard. "You've never liked Deke, have you?"

"You're the second person who's asked me that lately, Mother. I don't really know him, so I'm...neutral."

"Who else asked you? Not Leo."

"No, it was Nick. Nick Santana."

"The man she should have married."

Kate was astonished. She couldn't recall Victoria expressing any regret years ago when Amber broke it off with Nick. "It's a little late for that, don't you think?"

"Unfortunately." Victoria slipped her glasses into a tapestry case and stood. "You'd better freshen up and walk on over. They probably saw you drive up. I'll tell Rose to delay dinner until you get back."

She followed Kate to the stairs before asking, "How did it go today? Are you settling in?"

"So far, so good." With Sam out of the office, Kate had had time to work without distraction. It hadn't taken long for her to discover one of the advantages of working in a small-town practice. The great frustration in trauma care was the anonymity of patients. There was seldom any patient history unless a family member or close associate was available, so she had often worked in the dark. But in Leo's clinic, there was time to think and rethink. God forbid she'd make another mistake and screw up this chance to rebuild her career and her confidence.

She'd decided she never wanted to return to Boston. Before leaving the clinic today, she'd called Maureen Reynolds and instructed her to take the last offer Robert's lawyer had made for the settlement on the sale of the house. In effect, she'd burned all her bridges. Whether Sam Delacourt proved a distraction or not, Kate was practicing medicine in Bayou Blanc for the duration.

But settling in? She'd have to wait until she and Sam had worked awhile in close proximity before she could answer that. At least her fragile defenses were still intact.

A few minutes later, she was making her way across the grounds that separated her mother's house from Leo's sprawling Creole cottage. From habit, she headed for the patio instead of the front of the house. Light poured from the undraped windows of the family room, where sounds from a stereo blasted rock music. She stepped up to the French doors and heard Deke Russo's distinctive voice. Kate couldn't make out the words, but she heard the anger. She stood for a moment, debating. Did she want this tonight?

But Amber had spotted her. Kate put on a smile and turned the doorknob as Amber crushed out her cigarette and headed toward her, hands out.

"Kate! At last! We were wonderin' if you forgot how to get here, *chère*." She threw her arms around Kate and hugged her before stepping back. In a quick once-over, Amber's green eyes took in Kate's haircut, casual sundress, skimpy sandals and still-trim shape. "You look fabulous, Kate. Doesn't she, Deke? Didn't I tell you? They say trauma burns a person out before they're forty, but obviously it's a damn lie. Just look at you, darlin'."

"Hi, Amber." Kate leaned forward and kissed her cheek. "You're looking fabulous yourself. As always." She glanced beyond Amber to where Deke stood at the bar watching them with an odd smile on his face. "Hello, Deke. How are you?"

Lifting his glass, he inclined his head. "I'm good, Kate. I hear you've joined Leo's practice. Big adjustment from the hallowed Ivy League halls you just left, right?"

"It's different." She turned, flashed a smile at the teenage boy who sat on a barstool across the room. "Hi, Stephen."

"Hi."

"Wow, I'm not sure I would have recognized you. You've grown about a foot, but I guess you hear that a lot, don't you?"

"I guess."

Deke swore suddenly. "Turn that noise down, Stephen! We can't hear ourselves think."

Stephen shot his father a sullen look, but he complied, punching a button on the stereo system and cutting off the music. Amber's laugh was brittle in the sudden silence. "What can I get you, Kate?" she asked, hurrying to the bar. "Wine? Gin and tonic?"

"Wine, please. Not much, though. I've had one already with Mother."

Amber waved a hand at an impressive array of bottles. "What's your pleasure?"

"Merlot if you have it."

"Sure do." She scanned the wine rack and pulled out a bottle. "This one's excellent. I used it for a dinner party with the mayor and some officials of the Vieux Carré just last week."

Deke rolled his eyes. "Oh, Christ, here we go again."

Color rose into Amber's cheeks. Rushing a little, she began twisting the corkscrew. Kate moved closer. "The mayor, huh? I met him a few years before he was elected. He was a state senator then. He seems like an interesting person."

"He's an idiot," Deke said.

"Deke," Amber said softly, her smile strained.

"Hey, I call it the way I see it, Amber. Besides, we're among friends, aren't we?" He finished his drink and set the empty glass on the bar. "Kate's almost family. Right, Kate?"

"Knock it off, Dad," Stephen said in a low, tense tone.

"What? First my wife and now my kid. Fix me another one, sugar, and this time put some booze in it." He gave his empty glass a shove down the bar, and Amber scrambled to rescue it a split second before it crashed.

Stephen hunched his shoulders and rammed his hands into his pockets. "I'm outta here," he said in disgust, and left the room.

Deke laughed. "Kid's been away from his laptop for nearly ten minutes now. Gotta go get a cyber fix."

"He's no crazier about computers than the average fifteen-year-old, Deke," Amber said with a determined smile. "You know how kids are today, Kate. They're into computer games and the Internet and all that in a big way. But Deke thinks Stephen should be outside shooting baskets."

Deke made a disgusted sound. "Like he'd know the difference between a basketball and a volleyball."

Kate turned at a sound in the hall. With relief she watched Leo enter the room. "Kate. I didn't know you'd arrived." He came toward her and gave her a hug. "Did you get a drink?" He turned to Amber. "Amber, fix Kate whatever she wants."

"Merlot, Daddy. It's coming up."

Leo glanced around the room. "Where's Stephen?"

"He got pissed and left," Deke said.

Leo smiled wearily. "I missed the fireworks, huh?"

"You didn't miss much," Amber said, handing Kate her wine. "Stephen's so touchy lately."

"Comes with the territory," Leo said, taking a seat. Kate watched him ease onto the sofa. His color was off and deep lines bracketed his mouth. She wondered if he could be ill. First her mother, now Leo. It couldn't be. Not both of them!

"Are you feeling okay, Leo?" She took a seat beside him. "You look tired."

"I'm fine, darlin'. Better than fine, after this week." He looked at Deke and Amber. "It was our lucky day when Kate decided to leave Boston. I actually left around mid-day today. Played a few holes of golf with Bert Landry."

"How many?" Kate asked, wondering when Leo had had a physical. On Monday, whether he liked it or not, she was going to examine him.

He fumbled for a cigar in his shirt pocket. "Enough to lose twenty bucks to Bert."

"Maybe that's why you look tired," Amber said, studying him with a worried look. "It was over ninety degrees today, Daddy. You shouldn't play when it's that hot."

"We played after it cooled down. Which didn't seem to help my game one iota," he grumbled, stroking the cigar. "Thanks to Kate, I ought to improve now that I can play with some regularity."

"Maybe you should schedule a physical, Leo," Kate said. "And cut back your hours even more."

Amber looked alarmed. "There isn't something you aren't telling us about, is there, Daddy?"

"Whoa, both of you!" Leo snipped the end from his cigar. "Quit worrying. I'm fine."

"I wish you wouldn't smoke, Daddy."

"Nag, nag, nag." Deke rapped impatiently on the bar to hurry Amber with his fresh drink. "What is it with you women? A man wants to play golf in the heat, he doesn't want to hear a lot of nagging. He chooses to smoke a cigar, that's his business, too." Amber looked distressed by his belligerence, but he seemed not to notice. "It's only the cigar stink you're objecting to, anyway, Amber. You're obviously not concerned about the health hazard with the amount of cigarettes you smoke."

"Deke..." Amber looked at him in pained dismay.

"Oops. Am I embarrassing the perfect little hostess?"

Deke Russo was clearly drunk, Kate decided. Was it the alcohol or was it in character for him to be offensive and rude? Amber's oblique remarks about her husband made more sense now.

She turned decisively to Amber. "So, tell me about Amber Lifestyles," she said. "And while you're at it, you can give me some tips. I'm hopelessly left-brained about such things."

Amber beamed. "I love it, Kate. I can't believe I'm making a living out of something that's so much fun to do."

"Mother says you're *the* social consultant in New Orleans," Kate said, smiling. "You must be so proud."

"*Proud's* hardly the word, right, Amber?" Deke refused to be ignored. He swallowed more of his drink, then emphasized his point by setting his glass down with a thunk. "She's so caught up in that goddamned business that I have to remind her now and then that her own home has to be her top priority."

"I don't neglect my home, Deke," she said quietly.

"I also have to remind her how she got there."

Kate glanced at Amber, who was studying the pattern

of her designer napkin. "Talent and hard work, right, Amber?"

"It wasn't easy."

Deke watched Amber with an odd smile. "But the right social connections helped a tiny bit—am I not right, darlin'?"

"It always helps to know the right people."

He gave a derisive snort. "Yeah, and the TV spot was pretty nice, too, huh?"

"Television helped increase my celebrity."

"Increase your celebrity? Goddamn right. In the end, that's what made you. The right connections and television exposure. And I'm the man who opened those doors, right, baby? Without that boost, you'd still be scribbling fancy place cards and arranging flowers on the tables of the rich and famous in New Orleans. Instead of that—" he paused to take another healthy gulp "—you're rich and famous." He grinned at them. "Business in the Big Easy. Is this a great town or what?"

"You haven't touched your wine, Kate." Amber glanced at Kate's glass.

Kate tasted it obediently, then conjured up a bright smile. "So, what kind of act are you two planning for the Fais Do-Do next week?"

"Deke is the one with the experience," Amber said, wiping up a small spill on the bar. "He's been working on the routine."

Kate looked at Deke, hoping to find something to talk about that would be more fun to him than taking potshots at his wife. "Is there much difference between a live audience and working on radio?"

He smiled tightly. "You haven't been listening to those left-wing radicals, have you, Kate?"

She gave a blank look. "I guess not, since I don't know what you're talking about."

"I got a bunch of liberals trying to circulate the rumor that my audience is dwindling. Which is a goddamn lie, right, Amber?"

Amber crossed the room and offered Kate and Leo each a cocktail napkin. In the corner, tiny stars circling a sun and moon had been painstakingly painted. Amber's artwork, no doubt.

"I didn't hear you, babe," Deke prompted.

"Your audience is as loyal as ever, Deke," Amber murmured.

"And as strong as ever."

Leo spoke from a cloud of cigar smoke. "It'll be something watching Amber perform again. Kate, too bad the two of you can't share the stage like you did when you were in that play—what was it?"

"I want to forget it," Kate said dryly. "All I recall was my fear and Amber's total lack of it. I swear if we hadn't had to hold hands to do that tap-dance number, I would have collapsed."

"'The Good Ship Lollipop,'" Amber reminded, smiling.

"It was horrible," Kate said, shuddering.

"It was a showstopper," Leo countered with fatherly pride. "But Kate's right. She was miserable onstage and Amber was in her element."

"That was so many years ago," Kate said, thinking back. "Mother had our costumes made. Remember, Amber? Mine was yellow sequins and yours was pink. We looked like two Easter eggs."

"It was an Easter play!" Amber cried, laughing. "I still have the home movie Daddy shot of it."

Kate groaned. "Oh, please, say it isn't so."

Deke settled on a barstool with a fresh drink. "What is this, Reminisce-Over-Stupid-Kid-Tricks Night?"

"Sorry," Kate said, still smiling. "You'd have to have been there, I guess."

Later, thinking back, Kate didn't know why she'd said what she did next. Maybe she'd simply wanted to rile Deke and had sensed that mentioning Nick Santana would do it. She turned back to Amber. "Speaking of old times, guess who I bumped into a couple of days ago?"

"Who?"

"Nick Santana. He's one of Sam's new patients."

"Nick?" Amber seemed to freeze.

"Small world, huh?"

"Apparently." Amber busily adjusted the blooms in an arrangement on the bar.

"He's living here temporarily, he says. He was wounded a few weeks ago in New Orleans. I'm surprised you didn't hear about it. His partner was killed." Kate glanced at Deke. "Surely something like that would interest your listeners, Deke."

Deke was watching Amber. "Yeah, it came up. A couple of dumb cops blundered into the wrong neighborhood. Blew their asses away."

"Not quite," Kate said evenly. "Nick survived, although a bullet collapsed one lung and broke a bone in his left arm. And I wouldn't characterize Nick Santana as a dumb cop, either. He's a detective with the NOPD, but he's also licensed to practise law. He just chose to enforce it instead."

"Well, shit. Maybe he'll be nominated Man of the Year."

Kate shrugged. "I don't know about that, but Cop of the Year sounds plausible."

Deke propped a foot on a rung of the adjacent barstool. "I hope he's left-handed."

"Deke!" Amber said, softly chiding.

Shoving his glass aside, he got up from the barstool.

"What? You don't like anybody bad-mouthing your old high-school sweetheart, sugar?"

"Deke, that was so long ago. We were kids."

"Yeah? Well, you don't act like a kid when his name comes up. You act like the prom was last night."

"I don't! I never mention his name. It's always you."

Leo stirred from his seat on the couch. "Well, I think Deedy's just about ready with dinner. Kate—"

But Deke was not to be sidetracked. He looked at Kate. "Did he tell you he dropped out of sight after the shooting when rumors started flying about him and his partner being on the take? Both of them were supposed to get it that night, according to my sources."

"It sounds as if you know quite a bit about what happened," Kate observed.

"I make it my business to know what goes on in the Big Easy."

"Who was it that wanted them killed?"

"Uh, uh, uh…" Deke's eyes gleamed as he held up one finger. "That would be telling."

"I'm sure Nick would be interested in any information you may have that could shed some light on the investigation," Kate said.

"I'm sure he would," Deke replied with a spiteful grin. "But we in the media have to be careful about revealing our sources. I start blabbing everything I know, and soon I won't have any sources."

Leo struggled to his feet. "Well, all this is very interesting, but it still doesn't change the fact that Deedy has dinner on the table. How about it, folks?"

"Just one more thing." Deke reached over the bar for the whiskey decanter. Forgetting the ice, he poured bourbon straight into his glass. "You didn't happen to mention to Amber that Nick Santana was a patient at the clinic, did you, Leo?"

"I don't believe I did, no," Leo said, touching his temple with a shaky hand.

"No, he didn't," Amber said firmly. She reached for a cigarette.

"Are you okay, Leo?" Kate moved quickly to his side. She shot Deke a quelling glance. The hostility the guy stirred up had to be disturbing to Leo. And Deke's rudeness to Amber had to distress him even more.

"I'm fine." Leo gave her a strained smile. "Just hungry, I guess. Are you going to join us, Katy-girl?" he asked with a hopeful look.

"I can't, Leo. I promised Mama."

"Oh, don't leave, Kate." Amber stubbed out her cigarette and hurried over.

"Rose is holding dinner," Kate said. "I really should go."

"Well, let's drink a toast first. It's just so good to have you back." Amber's eyes, meeting Kate's, were too bright and filled with...what? Pain? Humiliation? And her hands, when they touched Kate's, were cold.

Their wineglasses pinged as they met. "Cheers," Kate said softly. "It's good to be home."

"Yes." Amber's lips trembled, but her chin went up and she took a hasty sip. "To better days."

TWELVE

Stephen went straight to his room to change clothes. He'd never have chosen the stuff he had on, but Amber had asked, and he could never refuse Amber. He'd been polite just now only because Amber had asked him to. He was in Bayou Blanc only because of Amber. Angrily he shrugged into an oversize T-shirt and cutoffs and on his way out, he kicked the pants and pullover into the corner. Then he left the house, slamming the front door, not giving a damn if they heard him and got pissed.

Not they, but *him*. Deke. His dad. Ha.

He never thought of Deke as his dad anymore. When he thought about him at all lately, it was as The Asshole. A bona fide, grade-A, top-of-the-line asshole.

Nobody but an asshole would behave the way his old man did. Jeez, what would Amber's friend think? Deke had had a few drinks, yeah, but Stephen knew tons of people who drank—a lot—and they didn't turn into stupid loudmouths. They didn't become rude, crude and just plain mean—well—assholes. What was it with Deke? He had a beautiful wife and a great job. People looked up to him for the simple reason that they didn't know him. They only knew the guy they listened to on talk radio— New Orleans' right-wing guru.

He was king of the hill there, the voice of conservatism and family values, the champion of the ordinary man, the last true believer in the American Way—which, to his old man's way of thinking, was the right to own a shitload of deadly weapons and to tote them around in plain sight if you wanted to.

God, it was enough to make you puke.

Stephen thought he might be able to tolerate most of that, but what he couldn't tolerate—what was beginning to get to him in a way that he didn't know if he could stand much longer—was Deke's treatment of Amber.

He crammed his hands into his pockets and kicked at a fallen pinecone. If only he were a little older, or taller and stronger, he'd show Deke a thing or two when he started in on Amber. She didn't deserve the kind of treatment she got from him. Deke was her husband, for Chrissake. He didn't know another family where the guy acted like Deke. At least he didn't think he did, but how could you tell these days? He sure as hell didn't dare let on what really went on at their house—behind closed doors. He stepped off the curb to cross the street. And he'd bet Amber would die before she talked about it.

"Hey, watch out!" a guy called out.

"Oh, noooo…!" cried a girl's voice.

Spotting the two bikers too late, Stephen scrambled backward, but still the front wheel rammed into his thigh. He fell against the curb and landed on his back with bone-jarring force. The girl biker had swerved hard but lost the battle to stay upright. She went sailing over the handlebars, catching herself with both hands.

"Aw, shit!" Her companion dismounted and hurried to help her up. "Are you okay, Mallory? Aw, man, look at your hands. They're all scraped." He turned to Stephen in a fury. "Look what you did, you jerk! You walk around with your head up yours and innocent people get hurt. You're supposed to look where you're going."

"Hey, man, I'm sorry." Stephen winced, getting to his feet. His elbow was stinging and his thigh was throbbing.

He looked apologetically at the girl. "Are you hurt? I just didn't see y'all," he explained, feeling embarrassed and stupid.

"You didn't see us because you didn't look, buddy." The kid's expression changed to anxious concern as he turned back to the girl. "C'mon, Mallory, let's go inside and see about your hands. My dad's home and he's pretty good with a first-aid kit."

"I'm okay, Cody. It's mostly dirt and stuff." Gingerly she brushed road grit from her hands, then dusted off the seat of her pants. As she did so, she looked over at Stephen. "Are you all right? That was a solid hit."

"It's nothing," he lied, carefully balancing his weight on one leg. "It was my own fault, stepping out into the street like that." He gave a wry grin. "Good thing you two weren't on a couple of Harley hogs."

Her smile gave her face a soft, pretty look. But there was curiosity in the way she was studying him. "You look familiar. Have we met somewhere before?"

"Naw, you're probably thinking of Deke Russo."

Her expression lit up. "Yeah, that's it! Gosh, you really look like him. You must be related."

"Yeah."

"How?"

"My father."

Mallory watched him bend over and pick up her bicycle. "So your mother must be Amber Russo."

"She's married to my dad, but she's not my mother."

"She's so cool. I try to do those things she demonstrates on TV, but my stuff never looks like hers." Her blue eyes widened. "Hey, do you live here now? Gosh, is Amber Lifestyles gonna be my neighbor?"

"We're just visiting. Leo Castille is my stepgrandfather."

"Dr. Leo? My dad practices with him. Sam Delacourt—have you met him? Hey, isn't this cool, Cody?"

"Yeah, I guess."

Stephen straightened the cocked seat on her bike. "I don't know your dad. We don't get across the lake too much."

Mallory glanced at Cody. "The Fais Do-Do Fest, Cody. Remember I told you Deke Russo and Amber are the guest hosts this year? Because Amber used to live in Bayou Blanc." She grinned at Stephen again. "But I'd never guessed she used to live in this neighborhood. Dad and I only moved in a few months ago. That's why I didn't make the connection."

Stephen tested the bike, moving it back and forth. "Do you live close by? I'll take your bike home for you."

"Well…sure. Great. My house is just a couple—"

"You can leave it here," Cody said gruffly, indicating the driveway just across the street. "I'll keep it in our garage until tomorrow, then I'll take it over to your house, Mallory."

"Okay," she said, then turned back to Stephen, "I'm Mallory Delacourt, and this is Cody Santana."

Cody's scowl eased a little as he nodded.

"Stephen Russo."

"Come inside with us," Mallory invited with a smile that made refusal next to impossible. "No matter what you say, that's a nasty bruise. Cody's dad can take a look, right, Cody?"

"Sure, I guess. After he checks out your hands."

"I'm okay," Stephen insisted.

"Me, too," Mallory insisted with an exasperated look at Cody. "But come inside and have a Coke or something. Neighbors should get to know each other, right?"

"If you say so," Stephen said, smiling.

"And you can tell me how Amber made that gorgeous

pyramid with lemons and cranberries and magnolia leaves that was featured in *New Orleans Magazine*. Mine kept leaning sideways. I finally gave it up." With wary looks at each other, both males fell into step, one on each side of her. Mallory chattered on.

Nick recognized the kid the instant he walked into the kitchen. He'd never seen Deke Russo's son, but with Kate's information fresh in his mind and the boy's remarkable resemblance to Deke, he couldn't be anybody else.

"Hi, Dad." Cody pulled a chair away from the table for Mallory. "Mallory took a header on the bike a few minutes ago and skinned her hands. She says they're okay, but—"

"They *are* okay, Cody," Mallory said, refusing to sit. "Besides, your dad's not a doctor. I can go home if I need a doctor."

"He's a cop," Cody argued. "They know about these things."

"Why don't I just take a look?" Nick glanced at the Russo kid. "You must be Deke Russo's son." Nick put out his hand. "I'm Nick Santana."

"Stephen," the boy muttered. He shook hands, meeting Nick's gaze for only a split second.

"Heard y'all were in town," Nick said. The kid was going to have to work on the social graces if he wanted to follow his old man's career path. "Here, Mallory. Have a seat so I can check out the damage."

"My dad got shot on duty," Cody explained as Nick found a comfortable place for his injured arm. "That's why his arm's in a sling."

Stephen cleared his throat, looking anywhere but at Nick. "Tough."

"Cody, get that kit from the cabinet above the coffeepot. It has some cotton balls and some antiseptic spray."

"It's really nothing, Mr. Santana," Mallory insisted. "Just a few scratches. Besides, Stephen's leg is worse."

Nick glanced at the bruise just above Stephen's knee. "He'll be my second patient." He waited for her to sit down, then picked up her hands as Cody set the kit on the table. "So, is everybody ready for the Fais Do-Do?"

Cody went to the fridge and took out some cans of soda. "I would be if you'd float me a small loan, Dad," he said with a sly grin.

"And maybe I'd consider it if the lawn had been mowed and the weed-eating finished when I got home from the doctor's office today." Nick bent closer to study Mallory's right palm. "Hand me a cotton ball, Cody. And wet it slightly, will you?"

Cody complied, then tossed a canned drink to Stephen. "I was gonna break out the mower later today when it wasn't so hot."

"It'll be dark in about thirty minutes." Nick gingerly cleansed the scrape. "You must work fast."

"I'll do it tomorrow morning, Dad. No joke. Early."

Nick examined Mallory's left hand. "You'll have to if you want to go to the fest with money in your pocket."

Stephen popped the top on his soda. "You wouldn't miss much," he said in a surly tone.

Nick glanced at him before reaching for a clean cotton ball. "Oh, I don't know. Your dad and stepmom make quite a team. The two of them onstage should be entertaining."

"How did you know she was his stepmom?" Cody asked. His gaze left Mallory's palm to zero in on Nick's face. "I mean, how did you know Amber Lifestyles wasn't his real mother?"

Nick tossed the cotton ball and positioned both of Mallory's hands, palms up, on the table. "Stay right there for just a second, honey." He took a small can of antiseptic spray, shook it, then sprayed a light film on her palms. "Okay, that ought to fix you up. But you probably won't be able to ride your bike for a day or so."

"No big deal," she said. "Stephen, show him your leg."

"I'm fine, Mr. Santana," Stephen insisted, keeping his injury out of sight. "Honest. I'll clean it up when I get back to my grandpa's house."

Nick nodded, understanding. Except under extreme duress, no self-respecting kid would allow a girl to observe while his war wounds were tended.

"So how'd you know that about the Russos, Dad?" Cody asked again.

Nick snapped the first-aid box shut. "What is this? You studying interrogation techniques, Cody?"

Cody looked sheepish. "Well, you just never mentioned you knew them, that's all."

Stephen set his soda can on the table. "He might not know them personally, but he can't help but know about Deke Russo." He glanced at the arm Nick favored, then looked directly at him. "Are you the Nick Santana from the NOPD who got shot a while back? Your partner was killed?"

"Yeah, that was me."

"My dad really kicked up a fuss over that, didn't he?"

"He did."

"I'm sorry about that."

Nick smiled. "You aren't responsible for what your dad says on his talk show, Steve."

"But he's been pretty hard on a lot of people in the police department."

Nick shrugged, winced when it hurt, and settled back. "It's a free country. He can say what he pleases. I'd be the last person to deprive a man of his right to speak his mind."

"Yeah, well…" Stephen stared at his drink can, turning

it around and around. "I just don't always agree with him, even if we are related."

Related. Nick gave him a curious look. Could it be that Russo's relationship with his kid wasn't as close as his audience in Radioland assumed? Wouldn't that be a shocker? Still, Nick was hardly the man to criticize when it came to parental concerns. He hadn't exactly been a model father. If it hadn't been for the bullet that had put Nick out of commission, he wouldn't be spending the summer with Cody. At least Russo lived with his kid, was there for him. That was more than Nick had been able to do for Cody. He glanced over at his son, who, along with Mallory, was all ears.

"You didn't answer yet, Dad," Cody said. "How'd you know?"

Nick sighed. "Kate Madison told me," he said, shoving the first-aid box into Cody's hands. "Here. Put this back where you got it, son."

"Who's Kate Madison?" Cody asked.

"Kate's an old friend I ran into at Sam's office today. She's been practicing medicine in Boston, but she's decided to come back home. She's going to be practicing with Sam and Leo."

Mallory set her drink carefully on the table. Her face had gone pale and she was frowning. "Did you say Kate Madison?"

"Yeah. Do you know her?"

"And she's going to be practicing with my dad?" Her voice was rising with distress.

"I think so, Mallory. I could be wrong."

She was shaking her head. "It can't be the same person I used to know. That was when we were in New Orleans. I mean, Madison's a pretty common name, isn't it?"

Cody shrugged. "I guess."

"You can see for yourself soon enough," Stephen said.

"Her mom lives next door to Grandpa Leo, and that's where she lives. At least that's what I think she said."

Mallory looked at him. "You talked to her?"

"I met her at the house. She and Amber used to be best friends."

Mallory stood abruptly. "I don't believe this."

Cody's drink paused halfway to his mouth. He lowered the can, looking at her intently. "What's the matter, Mal? Even if it's the same person you know, what difference does it make?"

"I've gotta go." Snatching up her drink, Mallory took it to the sink and dropped it with a clatter. Without another word, she was out the door.

Cody started after her. "Wait, Mallory! What's—"

"Let her go, son." Nick put his hand on Cody's arm.

After a second, Cody turned back to his dad and Stephen with a bewildered look. "Would somebody tell me what that was all about? Who's Kate Madison?"

Stephen shrugged. "I don't know. She's just someone who's coming into Grandpa Leo's practice. She seemed okay to me."

"She is okay," Nick said, his gaze thoughtful as he watched Mallory disappear in a wild dash across the back patio. He hadn't run in the same circles as Kate and Amber in years, but he still trusted his instincts. Kate Madison had been a good person then, and it would surprise him to discover she'd changed. Still, Mallory's reaction was intriguing. That is, if the Kate Madison she knew and his former school chum were one and the same.

"Daddy, it's not true, is it? You aren't going to let Kate Madison into your practice, are you?"

Sam looked up as his daughter rushed into his office. She was pale and had a smudge beneath one eye as if she'd been crying. Frowning with concern, he got up from his desk and pushed the door closed before he spoke. "What's the matter, Mallory? You've been crying." He glanced down at her hands and made a sound, reaching for them. "You've hurt yourself! How? What happened?"

She jerked her hands away. "It's nothing. It happened yesterday. I fell on my bike." She crossed to the other side of his office, well out of his reach. "Where were you last night, Daddy?"

"I got home from the hospital late, Mallory. There was an emergency."

"I waited and waited because I needed to talk to you."

"I'm sorry, honey, but you were asleep when I looked in on you. Why? What's wrong?"

"It's about Kate Madison."

"Kate? What about her?"

"Daddy, is Kate Madison here or not?"

He was shaking his head, still surprised by her abrupt appearance. She rarely came to his office. Now she was almost trembling as she stood waiting for an answer. "How do you know Kate? What is this?"

Mallory stamped her foot. "I know her, Daddy! Just answer me. Is she going to be working here?"

"Yes, she's—"

Her face suddenly dissolved into a look of utter despair. "O-o-o-hhh…no-o, Dad-deee…" she wailed, staring at him in disbelief.

"Mallory, what on earth—"

She stared at him tearfully. She put a hand to her trembling lips, shaking her head. Her eyes were wide with distress. Sam took a step toward her, but she threw out a hand to hold him off. "No, Daddy. Don't try t-to t-treat me like a b-baby now. It won't work." Suddenly she flopped onto the couch and covered her face with her hands. "Oh, you can't do this, Daddy!"

"Do what, Mallory?" Sam stared at his daughter, dumbfounded. "What's wrong, for God's sake!"

Mallory lifted her head, shaking it slowly and looking as if her world was ending. Sam felt a cold dread but rejected his suspicions. He told himself there was no way Mallory could know about his affair with Kate. She'd only been nine years old then. He was suddenly terrified inside.

He went to the couch and sat down beside her. He touched her hair, pushing it back from her tearstained cheek. "Mallory, what's this all about, honey? Why do you have a problem with Kate Madison being a part of the practice?"

"You *know*, Daddy," she countered, her voice coming out in a childish squeak.

"No, I don't know, Mallory. So tell me."

She turned away, lifting her chin defiantly. "She's the one who made Mama try to kill herself. I hate her!"

It was like a blow square to his chest. He hadn't had a clue that she'd suspected anything. God, what had she conjured up in her imagination back then? Keeping his tone even, he asked carefully, "What makes you think that, Mallory?"

She turned away, refusing to look at him. "I just know it."

"What do you think Kate Madison did that would matter so much to your mother?"

"She was trying to make you fall in love with her and leave us."

Sam swallowed hard. "You can't know something like that, Mallory. You've never met Kate or spoken to her, have you?"

"No, but... Is it true?"

They exchanged long looks, hers abject and questioning, his concerned and fearful. "We knew each other then,

Mallory. We worked out of the same hospital. She was busy with her internship and I was on the staff, so naturally we knew each other. But Kate didn't try to make me fall in love with her. If there was gossip, I wasn't aware of it. How did you pick this up? Who told you?"

"Just somebody," Mallory said, refusing to look at him. "I don't remember who."

"Was it your mother, Mallory? Did your mom say something?"

She sprang up from the couch. "No! What does it matter who told me? I heard it, that's all. What matters is who told Mama, isn't it? And it hurt her so bad, she didn't want to live anymore!" She turned from him, covering her face with her hands again. This time, Sam didn't allow her to push him away. He caught her and pulled her into his arms. He rocked her through a storm of tears, worried that he wouldn't find the words to comfort her, scared that she would press him for details. But he couldn't lie, and then she'd be even more devastated than she seemed right now.

"I don't think it's right for her to come b-back and mess up our l-lives again, Daddy," Mallory said brokenly.

Sam rubbed her shoulders, then gave her another comforting squeeze before turning to get a box of tissues from his desk. He passed them to her. "Kate didn't mess up our lives, Mally. She was not responsible for your mother's cancer."

"She didn't try to get you to leave us and be with her?"

"Absolutely not, honey." He watched her wipe her face and blow her nose. "I want you to believe that, Mallory. I swear it's true."

"Really?"

"Really. You shouldn't believe everything you hear. How would you like it if you were judged by someone who'd never spoken a word to you?"

"But is she going to be working with you, Daddy?"

"For a while, yes. She's known Dr. Leo ever since she was a little girl, and he's very happy to have her in the practice. Kate has super credentials, Mally. And I'm sure that once you meet her, you'll see she's a decent human being."

Mallory sniffed and took fresh tissues from the box. "Do I have to meet her?"

"Not today. Not until you want to." He tipped up her face and smiled at her. "But sooner or later, if you keep popping in like this, you're bound to run into her."

"Then I'm staying away." She tossed the tissues into his trash can on her way to the door. Once there, she paused, drew a deep breath and smoothed her hair, tucking it behind both ears. Then she pulled the door open.

"Oh!" she said, startled to find Diane Crawford on the other side.

"Hi, Mallory," Diane said, giving her a quick, keen look.

"Uh, hello, Diane," Mallory said self-consciously.

Diane smiled, puzzled and openly curious. "What's wrong, sweetie?"

"Nothing," Mallory mumbled breathlessly, glancing back at Sam as if he might reveal the truth. He moved to her side reassuringly.

"Mallory was just leaving."

"I've hardly seen you at all since we moved the office to Bayou Blanc," Diane said, still smiling. "How do you like it here? Have you made lots of new friends?"

"One or two."

"Well, it takes time, doesn't it?"

"I guess." Mallory stood miserably between both adults. Then, noticing Ruby at the end of the hall, she started toward the older nurse.

Diane's courtesy was wearing thin. "Give me a call

sometime, Mallory. We'll stop in at Coffee Galore and I'll treat you to a cappuccino. Of course, it probably won't taste anything like the ones we got in New Orleans, but that was then and this is now, hmm?"

"Uh-huh." Over her shoulder, she gave Sam one last look. "Bye, Daddy."

"Bye, honey."

They watched her scurry down the hall to the reception area where Ruby welcomed her with a warm hug.

"She's been crying, Sam. What's wrong?" Diane asked. "Is there anything I can do?"

"I don't think so, Diane. This is one I'll have to handle on my own." Sam's troubled gaze was still on his daughter. "But thanks anyway."

Later, while most of the clinic staff was at lunch, Sam had been sitting at his desk, thinking, when he suddenly got up and headed down the hall looking for Kate. He found her alone in the snack room making herself a cup of tea. He watched her dunk the tiny bag in a cup a few times. "Isn't it too hot to drink that stuff?"

She expertly squeezed the excess liquid from the bag before tossing it into the trash. Lifting the cup, she took a dainty sip. "Is it too hot for you to drink that sludge you call coffee?"

"That's different." He poured himself some to prove his point. "Coffee's a tradition in Louisiana. Hot tea's a fad."

"Another 'tradition' is fried alligator, and I don't eat that, either. Besides, tea is kinder and gentler to my nervous system than coffee."

He propped a hip against the counter, watching her. "What do you have to be nervous about?"

"The usual." She grabbed a napkin and started to leave. "I have a life, therefore I have concerns. Why add an acid stomach to complicate things?"

"Wait." He moved to stop her. "Drink tea if you like. I didn't come in here for that. I came to ask you something."

She paused with her hands cupped around the warm drink. "What?"

He was shaking his head. "The damnedest thing. I'm not sure whether you have a clue about it or not. I sure didn't." He gave a shrug. "You could have knocked me over with a feather. I mean, she was just a kid. She only—"

"Sam, I have three patients waiting. If you could get to the point…"

He set his coffee on the counter. "It's Mallory. She came to see me…here at my office."

"And?"

"She was upset, almost hysterical."

Kate frowned. "Why? What happened?"

"She knows about us."

"'Us'? There's nothing to know about us, unless you mean that we'll be practicing together."

"That, too. She wasn't happy to find out that you're going to join the practice."

"Well, what do you expect? You hate it, too, and you haven't exactly kept your thoughts about it a secret. Naturally she's influenced by what you think. You're her father."

"A pretty clueless one, it seems," he said, suddenly fixing his gaze thoughtfully on his feet. "I'm learning more and more lately how little I actually know about my daughter and what she's thinking."

"If that's the extent of your worries, Sam, relax. Nobody knows what teenagers are thinking. Their thought processes are one of the great mysteries of life—if you'll permit an observation from a childless female," she added dryly.

That brought his gaze up. "Have you ever regretted not having children?"

"What does that have to do with anything?" Kate asked as they stepped into the hall.

After a brief silence, he said, "Nothing."

"So, if this conversation isn't about any yearnings I may or may not have about motherhood, what's on your mind?"

He was shaking his head, wondering how the conversation had strayed into that territory. "As I said, it's Mallory." His attention was caught by Ruby coming down the corridor. "Look, would you come into my office for a minute? This is a little too private to discuss here."

"Dr. Sam! Kate!" Ruby hurried toward them. "We've got two patients brought in by Bayou Blanc PD. One's Pammy LaRue. She's bruised and scratched up a little, but not too bad. Other one's Janine Baptiste. She's bleeding, you wouldn't believe. Janine wouldn't go to the hospital, so the chief said they could both come here, save her the embarrassment."

"'Embarrassment'? What's the problem?" Sam asked.

"Janine. Her husband roughed her up real bad before Pammy got there."

Sam ushered Kate ahead of him. "Okay, Ruby. Get Diane to assist. Which one do you want, Kate?"

"I'll take the friend." Anything except another battered woman. Charlene Miller was still too fresh in her mind. The deceased Charlene Miller.

"Pamela LaRue is a rookie on the PD," Ruby explained, walking beside them. "That crazy Remo beaned her with a broom handle. I suppose we should be glad it's summertime. Otherwise it could have been an iron poker."

"Who is Remo?" Kate asked.

"Remo Baptiste, Janine's no-good husband. And Diane's gone to lunch, Sam." Ruby snatched latex gloves from a dispenser and handed both Sam and Kate a pair.

"Can you assist, Ruby?" he asked.

"On anything short of brain surgery," she quipped. "Kate won't need help with Pammy. The lump is swollen, but it'll be okay. This time."

"What happened?" Kate asked.

"Remo was beating up on Janine and Pammy took the call. Didn't have her partner with her, Jimmy Jakes. Said he was having lunch at Belle Rose Diner. Ha! Anyway, Pammy couldn't get 'em separated, then Remo just went a little crazy."

"Batterers do," Kate said grimly. She stopped to put on the gloves. "A cop with more experience would have hesitated getting into a heated domestic quarrel."

"Maybe, but Pammy has a lot to prove to the men at the station." Ruby's expression revealed her disgust. "She's the chief's token female. Which probably explains why they sent her alone on a domestic call, hoping she'd find herself in a situation she couldn't handle without help from a man."

"Ruby…" Sam said in a warning tone.

Ruby gave an innocent shrug. "Would I lie?" She handed him a file. "We've got a big chart on Janine."

Sam sighed, taking the chart with a grim look. Kate knew the feeling. Another battered woman, too bullied and humiliated to let the world know her husband controlled her with his fists and worse. She turned the doorknob and went into the examining room to deal with Bayou Blanc PD's token female.

At first glance Pamela LaRue appeared too small and slight to meet the physical standards at any police academy. Kate put out a hand. "Hi, I'm Kate Madison." As the young woman shook hands, Kate studied her. Her dark hair was cut in a short, sassy style that was easily main-tained. However, just now her bangs were standing on end and she held a bloodstained bandage against her temple. Her face was pretty and heart-shaped, but her best asset was her beautiful green eyes. In her uniform, she was immaculate—as spiffy as any hotshot recruit, except for the jagged tear separating the sleeve from the shoulder seam of her shirt.

Kate smiled. "You look like it's been one of those days."

Pamela's smile was pained as she lowered the bandage. "You could say that."

Kate parted the hair on the young woman's temple to get a look. "That's your cue to say, 'You should see the other guy.'"

"Yeah." She winced as Kate probed gently. "Maybe you should."

"Inflicted some pain, hmm?"

"Not as much as he deserved." She blinked as Kate examined her pupils. "I've never had my clothes ripped off before. At least, not under these circumstances."

"No concussion, but I'd take it easy for a day or two." Kate cleaned the head wound, then bandaged it. She turned next to Pamela's arm and gingerly lifted what was left of her sleeve to take a look. "That's a deep scratch he gave you, and you're going to have a nasty bruise. That must have been some skirmish."

Pamela shuddered. "The guy was crazy. Insane."

"Well, batterers are."

"It's one of the worst things I have to deal with in my job."

"Hmm." Kate cleaned and prepared the scraped skin for a bandage. "And very dangerous. Batterers are very unpredictable."

"You're telling me. My sister was a battered wife. She never knew what to expect from one day to the next.

From one *hour* to the next. Finally we persuaded her to get help."

"One of the lucky ones."

"Right." Pamela watched as Kate secured the bandage on her arm. "I went to school with Janine Baptiste, and that's why I thought I could respond to the call without backup, that Remo wouldn't risk assaulting someone he knew." She laughed harshly. "Shows what a dope I am."

"You'll know better next time." Kate tossed the soiled gauze into the trash, then stripped off her gloves. With her back to the young rookie, she began washing her hands.

"The hardest thing was seeing her little girl," Pamela went on. "She was huddled in a corner in their bedroom. It baffles me why people do this in front of their children, Dr. Madison. That little girl was terrified. And she had such a look on her face. I saw it with my sister's kids, which was one of the reasons she finally got out. You just can't understand if you've never..."

As Kate went through the motions of washing up, she raised her eyes to the mirror above the sink. Pamela LaRue's voice seemed to recede, as if coming through an echo chamber. Then it ceased altogether, and in the mirror Kate's image shifted into something else. She was seeing another bedroom, another terrified little girl huddled in the corner. She actually felt the child's terror. She froze, hearing the rage in the man's voice as he reared back to deliver another blow. She trembled with fear for the woman, who cringed, her hands out in a futile defensive plea.

"Dr. Madison?"

Kate wasn't sure how long she'd been staring at herself when Officer LaRue's voice finally penetrated. Kate's heart was thudding, her fingers clenched on the faucets at the sink. Hot water gushed from the spigot, steaming up the mirror, obliterating the mirage—or whatever it had been.

"Dr. Madison…"

For a moment as she'd hallucinated—which was what she'd been doing as she'd gazed into the mirror—that bedroom had been oddly familiar. And the people in it…

"Dr. Madison, are you all right?"

Kate shut off the water abruptly and ripped a paper towel from the holder on the wall. "How did you persuade your sister to get help?" she asked. When she turned, Pamela was looking at her curiously.

"I didn't. I couldn't," Pamela said, slipping down from the table. Using surgical tape, she closed the ripped seam of her shirt, then began rebuttoning and tucking the tails into her waistband. "It was Howard, her bastard of a husband. He beat her up once too often, broke her arm and gave her a concussion. She was in the hospital six days. Until then, they'd been able to keep Howard's rages from his employer. He was an accountant."

The policewoman's voice was filled with disgust as she began gathering her gear. "You'd never guess from his appearance, meek and mild, Yuppie glasses—yuck—that he was as mean as a junkyard dog. But this time there was no way to explain away a broken arm and a concussion, so the hospital called the cops, and Howard's employer got wind of it."

Pamela's gun was holstered in a shiny black leather apparatus that looked ludicrously bulky on her small waist, but she fastened it into position with all the confidence of a veteran.

"You're not going back to work, I hope," Kate said with concern. Cautioning a patient was instinctive, even though she was still quaking inside from the episode at the mirror.

Pamela smiled. "Not to pull the rest of my shift, no,"

she said. "But before I go home and put my feet up, I'm going to the station to see that Remo Baptiste is charged and has at least one night in jail to think over what he's done. Not that it will matter, if Janine won't press charges." She put out her hand. "Thanks, Dr. Madison. I hope when we meet again, it'll be under better circumstances."

"Ditto to that." Kate took her hand. "And, please, call me Kate."

"Kate." Pamela picked up a small leather notebook. "Can't forget this. I still have to file that arrest report. Jimmy, my partner, took Remo in, but I want to be sure all the i's are dotted and the t's crossed."

"Take care, now," Kate said.

"I will." At the door, Pamela LaRue turned back to look at Kate. "Incidentally, if you'd like more information about spousal abuse—you know, in case you want to refer a patient or anything like that—call me at the station. I've got some really good stuff."

"Thanks. I'll do that."

Pamela smiled. "Okay, I'm outta here."

It wasn't over. Oh, God, it hadn't ended when she left St. Luke's.

Kate sank down on the physician's stool and closed her eyes. Maybe she was possessed. But that was ridiculous. She didn't believe in the occult. Then again, why else would she be seeing these crazy things? And they seemed so real. For a moment there—when Pamela LaRue must have thought she was going off the deep end—Kate had actually felt as if she knew those people. That poor woman. The little girl. The man. But that was nuts. Impossible! She had never personally witnessed a violent attack on a person. All the battered patients she'd treated had been strangers. So what did it mean? What was happening?

A quick knock on the door interrupted her frantic thoughts. Ruby stuck her head in. "You ready for the next patient, darlin'?"

Kate managed to smile at Ruby as she reached out to take the patient's chart. Get a grip, she told herself. You're a doctor. Act like one.

THIRTEEN

Amber surveyed her father's large family room with a critical eye. Preparations were complete. Tasteful touches were tucked here and there in the house—everything personally chosen by Amber, everything unique and appealing and in keeping with her reputation.

She went over to a side table where several trays of hors d'oeuvres, dips and tiny finger sandwiches sat ready to be strategically placed for the expected thirty or forty guests. She'd hired two women who worked for a good caterer in Bayou Blanc to help prepare the food, but everything had been supervised by Amber, of course. She felt tired but pleased. One thing she did well was throw a good party. She wanted this one to be perfect because it was Kate's welcome-home.

She was rearranging flowers sculpted from various veggies when Stephen came in from the patio. "I finally found what was shorting out the patio lights, Amber," he said. "Grandpa Leo probably damaged the wire while he was trimming the hedge. I fixed it with electrical tape."

Amber touched his cheek and gave him a smile. "Thanks, honey. It's a good thing you knew what to look for. It's too late to call a repairman, and we both know Daddy and Deke aren't too handy around the house."

"Aw, it was nothing."

She gave his arm a little squeeze. "It was, too, something. What if you hadn't fixed it? We would have had people on the patio stumbling all over themselves in the dark. Can't have that."

"Is there anything else you need?" Stephen asked.

"Not right now, sugar. You go on up and change into that great-looking shirt I laid out for you and the jeans hanging beside it. I pity any teenage girls who show up tonight, because you're gonna look so incredibly gorgeous, you'll cause a riot."

A flush darkened his boyishly handsome face. "I don't care about teenage girls."

Amber smiled as if they shared a secret, then chose a fat grape frosted with sugar and popped it into her mouth. "Which just makes you that much more irresistible to them, Stevie."

Stephen dismissed that notion with a shrug of his shoulders. "I may not stick around after things really get going. Is that okay?"

"Stephen…"

"Nobody'll miss me."

"I will, darlin'." Her lips came together in a little pout. "Besides, what'll you do? You don't know anybody."

He wiped one hand on his jeans and helped himself to a shrimp on a fancy toothpick. "I met a couple of kids a few days ago."

Amber took a shrimp, too. "Who?"

"Mallory Delacourt, for one."

She paused, looking at him. "Sam Delacourt's daughter?"

"Yeah. She's just a kid, but—"

"Well, I had a boyfriend when I was her age."

He shrugged. "She was with Cody Santana."

"Santana. Oh, Stephen, tell me he's not who I think he is."

"Yeah, Nick Santana's his dad." He watched her carefully wrap the uneaten shrimp in a napkin.

"You know what Deke would say if he found out you were talking to anybody even remotely connected to Nick Santana, Stephen."

"The same thing he'll say when Nick shows up for the party, I guess."

"What? Nick's coming here? Tonight?"

"That's what he said. Grandpa Leo probably invited him."

No wonder her father had been so shaken when Nick's name was mentioned the night Kate came over for drinks. He'd already invited him to the party. "How do you know all this?"

"I told you. I met Mallory and Cody. I was in their house. Nick was there. He's an okay guy, Amber."

"Omigod." Amber put both hands to her cheeks.

"Forget about Deke. What can he do?"

"You know what he can do, Stephen."

"What? Take it out on you because he knows that's the only way he can keep me in line."

"But Nick Santana…" She shook her head, dreading the inevitable. Suddenly she thought of something else. "Where was this, Stephen? Not anywhere close by?"

"Cody's a couple of doors down. I think Nick said somebody named Yeager used to live there. Mallory's house is on Vermilion, one street over."

"I can't believe this," she murmured. "Nick Santana practically on our doorstep."

"What's the big deal, Amber? Deke can't dictate who comes and goes in everybody's life. If Grandpa Leo wants to invite Nick over, he can," Stephen said in a low, furious tone. "And he can't dictate who can be my friends, either. He may think he's the king of the world, but he's not."

"This is going to be awful, Stephen. And that's the reason you're cutting out early, isn't it? You don't want to be around if Deke starts to get ugly."

"Can you blame me? And you know it's gonna happen. Haven't you noticed how nice it's been for the past three days because he's been too busy to cross the lake and bug us? There must be something really big distracting him, because there's no way he'd let you stay here this long without him."

"Maybe tonight will be different."

"It won't be different, Amber. Every night's the same."

"Shh." Amber put her finger to her lips. "He'll hear you, Stephen, and the party will be ruined before it even starts."

"I wish he didn't ever have to be at your parties. I don't know why you don't kick him out. The things he does—"

"Don't, Stevie." She leaned closer, letting her hair brush his cheek as she squeezed his arm again. "Let's don't talk about that tonight."

Stephen's chest heaved with frustration and anger. Amber was so sweet. He hated that she had to cope with Deke's moods. And his temper. He just wished there was something he could do. He turned a little, filling his senses with her essence. Her hair was so soft, and she smelled so good. He hated being only fifteen. It was like his hands were tied. The world wasn't set up for guys to do anything important before they turned eighteen. And that seemed a million years away.

They stood united in their shared hostility when suddenly there was a loud crash. From the back of the house, Deke was swearing furiously.

"Damn it, Amber! Where the hell did you put my pocket calendar? I can't find shit in here!"

"Yadda, yadda, yadda," Stephen muttered. "The fun begins."

"Your calendar's on top of the armoire," Amber called back.

"This stupid lamp fell off the goddamn table!"

"I'm on my way. Just a minute." Hastily she tossed the used napkin and gave the room a last once-over.

"Sounds like he's in good shape already," Stephen said. He grabbed a handful of nuts from a silver bowl and followed her out of the den. "I'm gonna be polite tonight, Amber, but I'm not sticking around to watch him make an ass of himself. And us."

"Amber!"

"I'm coming, Deke!" He hadn't bothered to close the door to the bedroom they shared when they visited Leo. Her father's door, she noticed with relief, was closed. Hopefully he'd missed Deke's outburst. His temper had been simmering when he'd arrived an hour before, because he'd been drinking, of course. Before stepping in, she paused and took a deep breath, bracing herself to face yet another of his tantrums.

Deke stood in disgust over the remains of a broken lamp on the floor. "Oh, no..." she breathed. The lamp was a French antique, treasured and beautiful, which had belonged to her mother. A crystal tumbler and spilled ice lay on the sodden carpet. There was a strong whiskey smell. For a moment she fought blind fury, but when she spoke, her tone was even.

"What happened?" she asked, bending to pick up the pieces.

"It's your fault," Deke snapped, yanking the cord from the wall socket. "I was looking for my calendar. I've told you a thousand times to leave my things alone."

"Your calendar was never there, Deke," she said quietly. She began picking broken glass from the carpet. She would need a towel to blot the remains of his drink. "It was on the vanity in the bathroom. I was afraid it would be damaged by the moisture, so I put it on your armoire."

He went over and snatched it from the tall dresser. "Why do you second-guess everything I do, Amber?

Can't I put my goddamn calendar where I want it? Or don't I have any rights here in your old man's house?"

She continued cleaning up after him. "You know that isn't true, Deke. Daddy has always welcomed you here."

"Bullshit."

She glanced up at him, her hands full of broken glass. "You're obviously upset. Has something else happened at the station?"

"You mean something other than that prick Dick Rogers taking program control away from me?" He was almost snarling. "Something besides having that bastard decide I need some hotshot woman as a cohost because he thinks the show needs more balance?"

My God, they were bringing in a woman on "Talk the Right Way." Nothing would be more intolerable from Deke's point of view. And whoever the woman was, she must have a death wish. Or she simply didn't know what she was getting into. Deke could be a devil when crossed. When threatened, he could be downright dangerous. Amber couldn't think of any safe response. When he was like this, the least wrong word and he'd go off like a rocket.

"What? Suddenly you're speechless?"

She dropped the glass into a trash can. "Uh, when is this going to take effect?"

"Never—if I have anything to say about it. I've still got clout with my audience, and that's power, baby. They won't stand for any feminist crap on 'Talk the Right Way.' Dick Rogers will get more than he bargained for when he starts monkeying around in my territory." Deke had picked up his glass from where it lay on the carpet. Without bothering to wipe it clean, he refilled it from a bottle inside the armoire, sans ice.

"'Balance'!" He spat out the word as if it were a live bug. "We don't need balance from the female element.

Hell, they're on the verge of taking over as it is. Men have to fight to hold on to the power nowadays. That's the line my audience wants to hear and it's made my show the hottest talk in town. I say if it ain't broke, don't fix it. Dick Rogers is an idiot."

"I'm sure you'll work it out." Amber stood, carefully brushing glass particles from her hands.

"That's what I need to hear," he said, sneering. "A really well-thought-out analysis of my problem."

"I believe in you, Deke," she lied—anything to calm him down enough to face their guests.

"In spite of our troubles?"

A warning bell sounded in her head. When he dropped his voice like that, she never knew what would come next. "What do you mean?" she asked cautiously.

"You. Me. Our 'relationship,' to use a term so popular nowadays."

"Well, maybe we both need to try harder in our relationship."

"This isn't a 'relationship,' Amber. Relationships are like revolving doors—you go in, you go out. There's no permanence. No, what we've got here is a marriage. A forever thing. You know—you and me till death do us part."

Whatever. Amber knew better than to say one word right now. Silence was always best when Deke got like this.

"Work harder, you say?" His smile was dangerously bland. "You want to enlarge on the way you think we can overcome our troubles, then? Maybe more and better flower arrangements, hmm? Or how about an extra fork or two beside our plates? Hell, we only have about four now. Or maybe we could weave our own cloth together at night, whaddaya say?"

"Deke, this is ridiculous. I wasn't suggesting that—"

"You can suggest until hell freezes over, Amber, but I know what you really want."

She kept doggedly silent, knowing what was coming.

"You want a fucking divorce. But you don't want the consequences, right? Which would be the trashing of your precious public image. And I *would* trash it, sweetheart. Don't doubt it for a minute." He assumed a thoughtful look, tapping the calendar case against his chin. "Now, how would it look if the public suddenly found out that the woman who invented Amber Lifestyles was not what she appeared? What if her own personal lifestyle wasn't all graciousness and charm? What if she cheated on her husband? What if she had other nasty secrets, hmm? By the way, where's my boy?"

"Deke, you know I've never been unfaithful. You know I—"

"What I know is this. You want out, Amber. Just like my other fair-weather friends. Times get a little rough, they desert like rats on a sinking ship." His head jutted forward belligerently. "Come on, you can say it, Amber. Say it! You want out."

Yes, she cried frantically in her head. *Yes, yes, yes!* She wanted out. God, how she wanted out. And in going, she'd like to scream to the world all the things she'd kept bottled up for so long. The man who proudly spouted his love for traditional family values and law and order was a bully at home. The spokesman for a large segment of New Orleans talk-radio junkies was a mean-spirited snake. He was criminally cruel to his wife and his own son. He had dark secrets his followers would be horrified to know.

"Cat got your tongue again?"

She shook her head mutely, forcing her eyes down, because to look at him might reveal unspeakable things. But she was through lying to herself and the world. He was right about her wanting out. She just had to choose the proper time.

"Guess what else I found out today," he said in a soft tone.

"Deke, our guests will be here in just a few minutes."

"Screw our guests." He moved until he was so close she could feel the power of him. Her heart was beating like a drum, but she didn't turn. "I found out where your old friend Nick Santana is staying. Come on, guess where?"

"And deprive you of a good punch line?"

He grinned. "Getting a little feisty, aren't you, baby?"

She glanced at her watch. "I've only got a few minutes to get dressed, Deke."

"Your high-school sweetheart is right here on this very street. Is that a helluva coincidence or what?"

"Dad mentioned seeing him out getting the paper one morning," she said quietly. She couldn't deny knowing it. He'd never believe her. But she couldn't tell him that Stephen was her source. When Deke was in a jealous rage, no one was safe—not even his own son. "He said Nick's still pretty weak."

"Poor baby."

"I haven't seen him." At least that was the truth.

"Because you don't have a death wish, right?"

"Because I don't have any interest in seeing him, Deke," she lied with cool dignity, her eyes still straight ahead. Could he tell her heart was almost beating out of her chest?

"He's freeloading from one of the Yeager heirs, did you know that? Or did you think he'd amassed such a fortune in drug money and graft that he was able to buy the place?"

She drew in a breath and faced him. "Deke, this is not the time to discuss Nick."

His temper suddenly snapped and he lunged for her. She scrambled backward, but he was too quick. He grabbed her wrist. "Do you think I'm an idiot, Amber? That prick is right across the street. Across the street! And you've wangled it so you can be here at the same time."

He was hurting her, but she knew from experience not to show pain. "You won't believe me, but I didn't know Nick was in Bayou Blanc when I came home. I'm here because Kate's back. I wanted to spend some time with her because it's been so long since we've been able to see each other."

"Well, guess what, darlin'?" Deke smiled, loosened his grip on her wrist and brought it up to his lips for a kiss. "You'd better visit your precious Kate in a hurry because after the festival your sweet little ass is going back to my house where it belongs."

Did he think that was a major news flash? She'd been lucky to get away from him for a few days. And from the moment she'd learned Nick was recuperating here, she'd also known her days in Bayou Blanc were numbered.

At the sound of the doorbell, he let her go. "As for fantasizing about a divorce, just remember this. You push it, you're going to pay and pay big-time, Amber."

He tucked the calendar inside his jacket before scooping up his cell phone. "Now, I think you're right, for once. Our guests are here. But since you're not dressed yet, I'll go down and make nice."

With her fists clenched, she watched him walk out of the bedroom. He was like a powder keg, and she was always the lighted match that set him off. Tonight his jealousy had taken the form of bravado and threats, and he'd kept it between the two of them—so far. With a sigh, she turned and headed for the closet. Discovering Nick living so close by, on top of the setbacks at the station, had been too much for him.

Quickly selecting a dress from the closet, she hurried into the bathroom, dragging her T-shirt over her head as she walked, tossing it at the hamper in disgust. Tonight they were going to appear to be a normal couple if it killed her. Because Kate would be watching.

And Nick would be there.

FOURTEEN

To her surprise, Kate was enjoying the party. It felt good to put her misgivings out of her mind, even if it was only for one night. Although she'd been busy at the clinic, since experiencing the weird flashback in front of Pamela LaRue, she hadn't been able to set aside her worries that her life was somehow unraveling.

She took a flute of champagne from a silver tray when a waiter glided by. Apparently it had been Victoria's task to produce Kate once the festivities were under way, and having a hand in the surprise had put a tiny spot of color in Victoria's cheeks. That alone made the occasion worthwhile to Kate. And thanks to Nick, Kate wasn't utterly unprepared. She might not have been surprised when a houseful of guests had shouted "welcome home!" but she was genuinely touched. She hadn't realized so many people in Bayou Blanc would be glad to see her.

"Come on, you can tell me. Were you really surprised?"

The champagne in her glass sloshed a bit as she whirled to meet Sam Delacourt's dark eyes. Taking the napkin he offered, she dabbed at her fingers. "Why? Didn't I look surprised?"

"Overly."

"Oh, no. Really?"

"Somebody let it slip, huh?"

She laughed. "Nick Santana. And he was so apologetic.

He made me swear not to tell Amber. But I'm glad he did." She indicated her outfit with a wave of her hand—a lime-green tube-shaped sundress that clung softly to her breasts and hips. "Otherwise I might have shown up in a T-shirt and my jogging shorts."

For a moment she saw something in his eyes that made her want to look away. But his comment was not about her or her appearance. "Speaking of Nick, I thought he might be here."

"He was undecided."

"I gather the two of you are longtime friends?"

"Once upon a time, yes. Good friends. In high school." She sipped at her champagne.

Sam's gaze drifted to Deke Russo across the room. New Orleans' right-wing guru was drunk. In the time Sam had been here—and he'd arrived late after delivering a baby—Deke had knocked back several stiff whiskeys. His distinctive voice easily carried to where they stood. The subject was politics, and he seemed to have an enthralled audience.

"Actually, it was Amber who was close to Nick," Kate said. "They were a couple until we graduated."

"I'll bet that's something Deke's audience doesn't know," Sam said. "He was pretty hard on Nick when he was shot. Every broadcast was laced with innuendo and unfounded rumors. He hammered on it for weeks. I wonder what it would do to his credibility if his fans knew Russo's wife and Nick Santana had once been close?"

Kate shrugged. "You know how people are. Some of them would be shocked, others would overlook it or rationalize it somehow."

"You're probably right. Actually, if you can get beyond his personality, he's not totally off-the-wall on some issues. As for others…" Sam waggled his hand.

"I wouldn't know. I haven't tuned him in since I've been back. Are you saying you're one of his fans?"

"No, but I listen occasionally. Anything to pass the twenty boring minutes commuting across the causeway bridge. He preaches responsibility and the virtues of working hard, of getting a good education. He's big on family values and law and order, which of course hardly anybody opposes. He's extremely traditional. I don't think any variation in lifestyles would get his seal of approval."

Kate rolled her eyes. "That doesn't surprise me."

He chuckled. "Something tells me you won't be joining his fan club."

"I hardly know him, to tell the truth."

"That surprises me. You and Amber are so close."

"We used to be, but not so much after I left." Kate's gaze, too, went to the Russos. Deke's arm was draped possessively over Amber's shoulder while he waved the other, punching the air to make each point. He was smiling and so was Amber. But something about their body language struck Kate as wrong. Studying Amber, Kate asked in a thoughtful tone, "Does she look happy to you?"

Sam followed her gaze. "How does 'happy' look? She's smiling, he's smiling."

"Which means exactly nothing. Serial killers smile."

"Whoa." Sam's eyebrows rose. "We've jumped from bigot to serial killer. Should we check to see if he's carrying?"

"It wouldn't surprise me if he had a concealed weapon on him. That's one of his trademarks, too," she said. "Trumpeting every citizen's right to own a gun."

"I don't think Deke Russo is alone there, Kate," Sam said dryly. "It's in the Constitution."

"A typical male response," Kate replied. She turned

and set her empty glass on a tray. "Why do men want everybody to have a gun? To hear them tell it, it's right up there with the expectation of having a chicken in every pot. If Deke really valued families and personal responsibility, he'd try to do something about AK-47s and Uzis, which are almost as common in our culture as personal computers."

She glanced up to find Sam watching her with amusement. "I'd forgotten how passionate you can be about things," he said, allowing his gaze to rove over her face.

She felt herself flush, but fortunately the lighting wasn't strong where they were standing. "If you'd seen as much carnage as I have when guns are in the hands of the wrong people, you'd agree that they ought to be banned."

"It'll never happen, Kate."

She gave Deke Russo a dark look. "Not as long as people like him stay on the airways."

"It's still a free country."

She realized she sounded irrational and, worse, emotional. To a man like Sam, that destroyed her credibility. "I'm going outside. I need some fresh air."

"To cool off?" His lips tilted as he fought a smile.

She laughed. "Yeah, to cool off. You knew you pushed a button when you mentioned guns."

"Who, me?" Grinning, he reached around her to open the door onto the patio.

"Hey, what's this about guns?" Deke interrupted before Kate could step outside. "Hell, there I was across the room talking about the governor and gambling when the really interesting stuff is going down without me. So...Kate, you thinking about getting a little piece for protection? Good idea, since you don't have a man to look out for you now."

"Wrong on two counts, Deke," she said coolly. "I don't need a gun *or* a man for protection."

Deke gave Sam a men-only smirk. "You hear that, Sam? Kate's been brainwashed up in Boston where the liberals love to trash the American Way." He looked at Amber, still close by his side. "Don't you be getting any bright ideas from your girlfriend," he told her, wagging a finger in her face. "You hear me, sugar?"

Amber avoided a reply by smiling tightly, then pretending to catch the eye of the bartender.

"I'll try not to corrupt her," Kate said smoothly.

Deke's smile stayed in place, but his eyes danced with a challenge. "Do your damnedest, Katy-did. My woman's incorruptible."

"We were just headed outside," Sam said, grasping Kate's elbow.

"Yes." Kate gladly let herself be ushered outside as Amber escaped to handle the problem at the bar. Two encounters with Amber's husband since she'd been back home were enough to cement Kate's dislike of him. How could Amber live with such an overbearing man?

"I ought to take him up on his dare," she told Sam, fuming. "The man's a jerk! That stupid stuff about needing a man to protect me. And patronizing Amber like that. Ugh!"

"I wouldn't look for ways to antagonize him if I were you, Kate." Sam had turned back, frowning as he watched Deke weave a path across the room to the bar. The man had his cellular phone to his ear and was talking while gesturing to the bartender for another drink. "He's drunk tonight, but I have a feeling that Deke Russo's dangerous whether he's drunk *or* sober. Steer clear of him."

Amber was alone in the kitchen rummaging in the pantry when Deke caught her elbow in a bruising grip and turned her to face him. "Where's Stephen?"

"What? I don't know." She tried to break his hold on her arm. "Deke, you're hurting me. Please."

He released her impatiently. "I sent somebody across the lake to run an errand for me. Now I get a call saying he never showed. I need Stephen."

She frowned. "You want him to drive across the lake? Deke, he only has his learner's permit. I don't think—"

"Is he in his room?"

"I don't know. Deke! Wait!" She made a grab for him, but he headed toward the front hall yelling Stephen's name. She was grateful that most of the guests were on the patio. With the music coming from the stereo system and the sounds of a lively party, they probably hadn't heard Deke—yet. She knew if he kept drinking tonight, he was going to embarrass her. At this rate, she didn't know how much longer she'd be able to keep their problems private.

She hurried after him. "He wouldn't have gone far without telling me," she said breathlessly. "Whatever you need, can it really not wait?"

He ignored her question. "What the hell did you mean, letting him go anywhere tonight? Any other time he'd be up in his room plugged into his earphones or tagging along behind you, making sheep's eyes."

"Let me see if I can find him," she said, forcing calm into her voice. "Why don't you wait for me here? Or in the breezeway off the garage." She went to the kitchen door and nearly sagged in relief when he actually followed her outside. If he continued to rant and rave, they wouldn't be overheard here.

Deke stopped at the wrought-iron gate off the breezeway. "Where the hell did he go?" he demanded, rattling the gate when the latch failed to release.

She hovered, afraid to touch him for fear it would be

the spark that set him off. "He's with some friends, I think."

"Friends? Like who? He doesn't know anybody."

"He met Sam Delacourt's daughter a couple of days ago. He mentioned something about seeing her tonight. I'll call over there." She managed a placating smile, backing toward the door.

"This bugs the shit out of me, Amber. I have a deal pending, and it's big. Really big. If it sours because I had to phone around the whole goddamn neighborhood to find my kid when I needed him, I'm gonna be pissed."

"What if he's stopped by a policeman, Deke? What if he has an accident? Can't it wait until morning? He's—"

She winced as he caught her upper arm. "I guess you didn't hear me, Amber." He pulled her up close until just her toes touched the ground. "You do not question me when I say I need my kid to drive across the causeway. You don't question me if I say he's gonna drive to fucking Canada, Amber!"

She closed her eyes, biting her lip against pain and fury as he squeezed. How dare he! He knew she had a houseful of guests. Tomorrow... Yes, tomorrow, she was going to do something! She was tired of—

"That's twice in one day I've had to remind you that the rules don't change just because you're in your daddy's house. You hear me, Amber?" He gave her a little shake for emphasis.

"I'll call," she gasped, turning her face from him. "I'll find him."

"You sure as hell will if you know what's good for you."

Suddenly Stephen was at the gate on the breezeway. "Let her go, Dad!" he cried, fumbling at the latch.

Deke didn't move. He smiled, keeping his gaze on Amber. "Hello-o-o... It's Prince Charming come to save you, sweetheart."

"Deke was looking for you, Stephen." Amber's voice came out thin and breathless.

Finally freeing the latch, Stephen pushed the gate open. He rushed over, making a grab at Deke's arm. "Turn her loose, Dad! I mean it. You're hurting her."

Deke glanced at him. "Listen to this. The kid's finally gettin' some balls."

"Yeah. It's about time someone in this family did."

Nick Santana stood at the gate. Deke and Amber gaped as he shouldered past it, his gaze locked on Deke. "Is manhandling women the way you get pumped up, Russo?"

Deke dropped Amber's arm, his expression almost comical with surprise. "What the hell are you doing here, Santana?"

"I was invited."

Deke turned back to Amber, who was shaking her head in desperate denial. "You told me you hadn't talked to him, Amber!"

"I haven't, Deke. I swear it. Daddy sees him at the clinic. It must—"

"What difference does it make how I got here?" Nick demanded in disgust. "It looks like I arrived just in time to save your ass from a very public scandal."

"What the hell are you talking about?"

"Battering is against the law, Russo." Nick glanced at Amber's arm. "I arrest people for that."

"I'm okay." Amber ceased rubbing herself and locked both arms around her midriff.

"Sure you are," Nick said, his disgust still evident.

"Wait a minute." Deke bristled as he faced Nick. "Are you threatening me, Santana?"

"Call it what you please, Russo. You had your wife in a

vise grip when I walked up just now. Anybody could see you were hurting her."

Deke stared at him with belligerence, then, without turning, he gave a curt nod of his head. "Stephen, get lost."

The boy stared at him. "I thought you needed me for something."

"I changed my mind." Deke's gaze was still on Nick. "Don't go too far."

Stephen backed away reluctantly, still concerned about Amber. "You want to go inside and put an ice pack on your arm, Amber?"

She closed her eyes thinking of the spectacle that would create. "Go, Stephen. Please."

Deke took a step, his fists clenched. "You having trouble with your hearing, boy!"

Stephen put up both hands. "I heard you. I'm going."

When the gate closed behind the boy, Deke spoke to Amber. "Now. Back to business. Was I hurting you, Amber?" he asked in a very soft tone. "Were you in pain?"

Her head barely moved in denial. "No."

Deke looked at Nick. "You hear that?"

"I heard it."

"Me and my wife were having a private conversation."

"I can see why you'd want to keep a conversation like that private," Nick drawled, then looked deliberately at Amber, who ducked her head. "Makes me wonder what else goes on behind closed doors in the Russo household."

"As if I care a flying fuck what you think," Deke snarled.

"Whoa, is this the family-values, right-thinking guru talking dirty?" Nick was shaking his head. "What would your admiring public say?"

"Get the hell away from here, Santana."

Nick grinned. "Not before I pay my respects to the host, who invited me. And then I've gotta welcome my old friend Kate back home."

"You're going to regret this, Santana."

"You know where to find me." Nick lifted his arm and thumped the cast. "I won't have this on forever."

Amber made a small sound. "Nick…"

Nick looked toward the opposite end of the breezeway, where the glow of hidden lights illuminated the path that led to the rear of the house and the patio. Sounds were muted, but clearly the party wasn't over. "This is still the way to the patio, isn't it, Amber?" he asked, unable to resist a final shot at Russo. He'd had free access to Amber's patio for more years than the talk-show king had been married to her.

"Yes," she replied, sounding as if he'd asked the way to a funeral.

At the end of the breezeway, just before heading for the action, Nick turned back and, looking at Deke Russo, used his thumb and forefinger like a gun and pretended to pull the trigger.

"Gotcha."

FIFTEEN

Kate moved with Sam to the edge of the patio and drew in a cleansing breath, glad to escape the smoke and noise of the party. Straight ahead, a huge full moon shone through the moss-draped limbs of a giant live oak. Tiny white lights had been strung in the crepe myrtles dotting the yard. The citrusy scent of sweet olive drifted wraith-like in the night air. She picked a sprig of the tiny waxy flower and twirled it beneath her nose.

"Do you know the reason sweet olive was always planted in cemeteries in Louisiana?"

Sam shrugged. "Because it doesn't lose its leaves in the winter?"

"No, to mask the smell of death in summer. Its unique fragrance is activated in full sun."

"Ugh."

"Right. In August all those tombs situated above ground presented a problem."

As they strolled, Kate wondered why she was out here with him. When she'd decided to join the practice—however temporarily—she'd promised herself their relationship would be strictly professional. That didn't include intimate walks in the moonlight.

In a shadowy corner, water trickled from a small fishpond. As they neared it, a bullfrog croaked, then plunged in. Kate rubbed her naked arms briskly, warding off a mosquito.

"Welcome home from Louisiana's state bird," Sam said dryly when she slapped at her arm.

"Amber thinks of everything, but not even she can keep the bugs away," Kate replied.

"Maybe not, but those fans she rigged up out here do a pretty good job of blowing them away. The woman thinks of everything."

"Everything to make life gracious and good," Kate said. "That's what Amber Lifestyles is all about."

"Yeah, the woman's a marvel." Sam tossed a leaf into the fishpond. "But I didn't come out here with you to chat about Amber."

"Do we have to chat at all?"

"I think at the least we have to be professional about this situation, Kate. Here, let's sit down." He brushed at the brick ledge around the pond and waited for her to sit. "I've been trying to get a word with you ever since we were interrupted in my office."

She laid her tiny shoulder purse between them. "When Pamela LaRue and the battered wife came in."

"Yeah."

"And Mallory. Who knows about our affair."

"She suspects. I'm not about to confirm or deny it." He sat bent forward with his elbows on his knees, dangling his drink between them. "Not to her or anyone."

"Including yourself?"

He jiggled the ice in his glass, then straightened and finished his drink. He placed the glass beside him and looked directly at her. "I owe you an apology. About believing that you would have gone to Elaine and told her about us after we broke up."

"Yeah, that was pretty low."

"Thinking you could be responsible for a human being taking their own life. I wish I could come up with some reason that would make it seem less..."

"Rotten?"

He cleared his throat.

"Reprehensible? Unfair? How about incomprehensible? Considering that you'd known me—intimately—for six months, Sam."

"Yeah, I guess I was—"

"Feeling guilty and looking for someone else to blame?"

He drew a deep breath. "Come on, Kate. I'm trying to—"

"Relieve your conscience."

"No!"

"Yes, Sam. What I said when you stunned me with that incredible accusation still goes. Your wife had been sick for a long time. You were tired, bored and horny. You wanted distraction and the exhilaration that comes from an extramarital affair. Well, you got all that and more...because apparently someone *did* tell Elaine. So what's the problem? I'm not going to make trouble for you." She laughed shortly. "If you want absolution, it has to come from somebody bigger than me. But if you want to apologize, okay, I accept that. If you want me to say I forgive you, that's a bit much."

He stood. "I should have known we couldn't have a reasonable discussion about this. I told you already that I didn't mean to hurt you. I didn't know I'd actually—" He turned his face quickly away. "I was in love with you, Kate."

She rolled her eyes. "You would have been in love with anybody then, Sam. Don't confuse love with lust. I promise you, I don't." She stood then, brushing off the back of her skirt. "As for Mallory, I'll be the soul of propriety when we meet. There's no reason for her to worry that I'll get my hooks into you again."

When he started to say something, she interrupted him.

"Look, you said she knew about us and was upset. Ten-to-one she suspects the same thing you did—that I some-how had a hand in her mom's suicide. Although I'm not a mother, I'm female and I've been a teenager. Adolescent emotions run as wild as adolescent hormones. Mallory's all set to hate me, and nothing you can do is going to make one iota of difference. Seems to me you have no choice but to ride it out. Meantime, we'll all just have to try to rock along together for a while." She reached for her purse and looped the spaghetti strap over her shoul-der. "My mother's dying and Leo's looking pretty frail, so I'm afraid you're stuck with me. For now."

Amber stood in a shadowy corner concealed among the leaves of a huge split-leaf philodendron and watched the byplay between Kate and Sam. They might have been alone in the world, they were so wrapped up in each other. And they didn't look particularly friendly. They looked...intense. Emotional. Which was unlike Kate. Am-ber used to wonder what it would take to rattle Kate. She'd never known anybody so buttoned up. But now...well, Kate could say whatever she pleased, but there was definitely something still unresolved from that affair five years ago. Amber gave it a month, tops, and they'd be sleeping together again.

With her finger on her lips and her eyes narrowed in speculation, Amber studied Sam Delacourt. She had to hand it to Kate; she had good taste. He didn't look like a doctor. With that face and his smooth, dark tan and a body to die for, he looked more like a male model. No, that was too bland. He looked like...an athlete—not one who got all pumped up on steroids, but the sort that was naturally male and beautifully put together. She'd bet he was a dynamite lover. Lucky Kate.

Amber plucked dejectedly at a leaf. What was it about

Kate that good things just fell into her lap? Amber had seen it all her life. No matter how hard Amber tried, Kate always got the best grades. She had the most friends, the sharpest clothes, even the best career. People respected doctors—never mind that Leo had practically handed Kate's medical degree to her. She would have been a dope to screw up with Leo there to encourage her. Then he'd smoothed her path to med school. If the truth were known, he'd probably fixed up that job in Boston for her, too. Which was just about the most prestigious place anybody would want to be in the medical profession today.

No. Screwing up had always been Amber's department. While Leo just loved everything Kate did, Amber was a disappointment to him. He didn't have to say it; she just knew it. Parents could never hide things like that. Nobody ever thought to look at Amber's life and see that she'd never had a mother and Kate did. Oh, she knew Kate's daddy had died the same day that Caroline Castille had drowned, but it wasn't the same. A mother was more important than a father. Especially when your father preferred your best friend to his own daughter.

She threw the crushed leaf away. But that was all due to change now. Her own star was rising at last. She was Amber Lifestyles, damn it. She had it all—a fabulous career, fame and fortune, a gorgeous home. She was a mother, too, in a manner of speaking, and she had a handsome, famous husband. The icing on the cake was the cushy contract from Maison Belle. She was going to make *beaucoup* money. Yes, she had really made it. And in spite of truly overwhelming odds. Unconsciously she rubbed her upper arms through the silk sleeves of her tunic. If the world only knew.

When she thought how close Deke had been coming lately to ruining everything, she could easily kill him. Naturally, he'd hauled out tonight after that scene in the breezeway. He could never face up to the havoc he created. Of course he'd be back in the wee hours apologizing for losing his temper and manhandling her. He'd expect her to forget all those hateful things he'd said.

It was the drinking that was going to do him in. He just lost it when he got drunk. Which was probably how he'd gotten mixed up in that other stuff he was always worrying about. And losing control in front of Nick, of all people, was pushing his luck. She hadn't been lying when she'd said she never saw or talked to Nick now, but it was only human nature to keep an eye on somebody who'd been your first love, wasn't it? Especially when you lived in the same town. And at the NOPD, Nick had a reputation for being tenacious, tough and smart. In that way, he hadn't changed that much from the person she'd dated in high school. So losing control in front of Nick Santana had been stupid.

She slipped her hand into a pocket for her cigarettes. Everything she'd created could go down the drain if Deke didn't get a grip. Her career and his, their whole personae were based on a traditional philosophy of marriage and family. The husband was the protector and keeper of the cave. The wife was his "helpmeet"—God, she hated that term. Kids were obedient and respectful. If the world—or Nick—started looking too closely, everything could be jeopardized.

Deke was an idiot. She didn't know what had possessed her not to see through him in the beginning. But for Nick Santana to see it...

She looked around surreptitiously before tapping out a cigarette and quickly lighting up. She inhaled deeply, tilting her head to blow the smoke into the huge philodendron. It really bothered her from an entirely different perspective that Nick had witnessed the scene in the breezeway tonight. Until then, only Stephen had ever actually seen the reality. Sometimes she thought Victoria suspected, but now Nick knew their dirty little secret.

"Is it okay for the hostess to take a break?"

Amber's heart jumped into her throat. "Nick. I thought you must have gone home."

"You mean you hoped I'd gone home."

He stepped away from the light coming through the windows and moved into the close, shadowed space beside her. She smelled his aftershave and was transported to the night when they'd gone all the way for the first time. She remembered that Kate had slept over with her that night and was waiting when she got home. Of course Kate had known instantly that something had happened, but Amber had gleefully blabbed the whole thing anyway; bragged about it, since she knew Kate would never tell. Kate was too uptight, too straitlaced. But Nick had been a great lover and Amber just couldn't help herself.

That night had been only the beginning. For the next two years, they'd screwed like rabbits—couldn't get enough of each other. There'd been consequences, too, but Amber had taken care of it. She looked into Nick's dark features now and tried to visualize what his child might have looked like. She would never know. Two abortions had nixed that. She hadn't told him. She knew Nick wouldn't have been any more reasonable about that kind of thing than Kate, who'd wrung her hands and worried enough about it for the three of them.

"I never wish my guests elsewhere when I give a party," she said, savoring her reaction to Nick. Her heart was actually racing. It was a delicious feeling—something she hadn't experienced in a long time. Maybe Deke wasn't too far off base, sensing that Nick was a threat.

"Good, because I had a couple of concerns."

She looked at him through a cloud of smoke. "What kind of concerns?"

"How about letting me take a look at your arm."

"Forget it, Nick."

"He was hurting you, Amber. Your face was white. You were ready to cry."

"Over the situation, not because I was in pain."

"I saw what I saw, Amber."

"It was my fault. He was irritated by something I said. I knew better, I just wasn't thinking. It was nothing."

"That answers my question right there," he said, turning away with a look of disgust.

"What? What question? I don't know what you're talking about."

"Cops hear it all the time from battered wives. Are you thinking it's your fault? That you shouldn't have made him mad? That you knew you'd push his buttons when you...whatever." He moved his hand. "You fill in the blanks, Amber. There are about a dozen ways a battered wife 'provokes' a violent husband, and it's bullshit to assume responsibility for his behavior."

"I'm not a—" She looked around, afraid someone would overhear.

"Battered wife?"

"Will you be quiet, for God's sake! I have guests. I don't want..." She took a deep breath. "That's not how it is with Deke and me."

Her denials met with silence from Nick.

"You misunderstood what you think you saw, Nick."

"Have it your way," he said after a minute. "But I meant it when I told him he was pushing his luck. He needs to know he can be arrested, Amber. Otherwise he'll just get worse. He won't stop at squeezing your arm black-and-blue. He'll start punching next—if he hasn't already crossed that line."

"I can take care of myself."

His eyes narrowed. "*Has* he crossed that line?"

She sighed, dropped her cigarette and crushed it beneath her sandal. "Don't get mixed up in this, Nick. He's already got it in for you because we used to be together. I hate to think what he'd do if he thought I had any personal contact with you."

"Is that why he tried to smear my name when I got shot?"

"It didn't help that we were once friends."

"You think he had something to do with it?"

"The shooting? No!" She shook her head. "He's... He has a lot of faults, but he wouldn't do something like that. No way."

Nick was staring at her. "And stop saying we were 'together,' or that we used to be 'friends.' We were lovers, Amber. We were once so hot for each other we couldn't be in the same room without wanting to tear each other's clothes off."

"We were kids, Nick. Everybody acts like that when they first discover sex."

"Don't you believe it, babe."

She looked away from him. "Well, it was a long time ago. So many years, I don't want to count 'em."

"I don't know why. You still look good to me. Beautiful, in fact."

A smile touched her lips. "You've held up pretty well, yourself."

Nick had been boyishly handsome at eighteen. Now those good looks had matured. He was broad in the shoulders; taller, too. But some things were still the same. His eyes, and that straight-on way of looking right at you. As if he could see what you were thinking. Being a cop suited him.

"Yeah. Well." He put a hand on her shoulder and squeezed it briefly. "Just remember what I told you. You don't have to put up with it if he crosses the line, Amber.

You've got a fabulous career. You blow the whistle on Deke, and he's the one who'll go down. You'll be a hero with countless women. You wouldn't believe how many."

"One of the maids is coming this way." Amber smoothed her hands down the front of her tunic, fluffed her hair, then straightened her shoulders. "I've got to go, Nick."

He took a step back, his dark eyes as unreadable as ever. "Sure. I'll have a word with Leo and then I'm outta here."

Victoria hadn't missed the exchange between Amber and Nick. In fact, she'd stood watch, sitting on an iron bench tucked away on the patio, in case Deke should appear and find his wife talking to a man he hated. There was no certainty he wouldn't embarrass them all, considering the way he'd been drinking lately. Victoria didn't want a scene tonight—for Amber's sake as well as Kate's.

After Amber went back inside, Victoria's attention moved to Kate and Sam Delacourt in intense conversation at the fishpond. Something about their body language and Kate's face as she looked at Sam struck Victoria as being more than casual. She thought back with a frown, trying to recall whether Kate had some past connection with Sam, but nothing came to mind.

Not that Kate was ever in the habit of confiding the secrets of her relationships to her mother. Why would she, when their own relationship was so flawed? Somehow, she and Kate never saw things in the same way. It had been a constant battle when Kate was a teenager. The move to Boston had widened the gulf between them. Kate would have been stunned to know how deeply her mother missed her. Victoria had nearly died of loneliness. But, thank God, she did have Leo.

She closed her eyes momentarily, realizing she was tired. And too warm. The mosquitoes were beginning to annoy her. She'd pushed herself tonight, but she would have gone much further and pushed harder to show Kate how much she valued having her back home again. She got up from the bench and went inside, weaving a slow path through the thinning guests. Hopefully the front room would be deserted. She caught Leo's eye, as he chatted at the bar with Nick, knowing he would follow her. No words were necessary between them; hadn't been for—oh, she couldn't remember how many years. She glanced at the antique clock on the mantel as she sank onto the sofa. A few minutes' rest and she'd walk home.

"Want some company?" Leo asked.

She nodded, patting the space on the sofa beside her. As she watched her old friend, she resisted the evidence of her own eyes. He'd been looking every day of his age lately. Something deep inside her hated that. Once, Leo could have risen at five in the morning, done three surgeries before ten, handled a full roster of patients at his office, then played nine holes of golf. For that matter, she'd once been his equal in stamina. Once.

"You look tired," she said.

"Look who's talking." He sat, settling beside her with easy familiarity. Had they been alone, he would have taken her hand. Now he simply sat close, his thigh touching hers. Like her, he grew weary of meaningless party talk, but unlike her he could put up with it longer.

Victoria smiled, rubbing at the tight muscles in her neck. "I wanted a few moments to myself. Amber throws a fabulous party, but the noise began to seem too much after a while."

His look became concerned. "You're taking the vitamins, aren't you? They'll help with the fatigue."

"Leo, Leo...not now." She patted his hand, and he

turned his palm up and gave hers an affectionate squeeze. She'd always loved his hands—long-fingered, strong, beautifully male in shape; perfectly designed for his life's work. She rested her head against the back of the sofa. "All I ask is just one brief evening without being reminded of this god-awful disease."

"I know, darling. I'm sorry."

They sat quietly listening to the sounds of the party. Outside, a car's headlights reflected off the polished panes of the tall windows. In the distance, a vehicle backfired.

"Nice to have Kate home, hmm?"

Without looking, she knew he was smiling. "More than you know."

"Nice to have her working with me at last, too."

"What about Sam?" Victoria asked, recalling her earlier thought. "Is he as pleased as you?"

"He will be as soon as he sees how well she fits in," Leo replied.

"Meaning he has some doubt."

"He'll get over it."

"Do you think they have some history, Leo?"

"They knew each other while Kate was interning. Other than that…" He shrugged. "Why? Has Kate said anything?"

"No, and she wouldn't. At least, not to me."

Leo caught the sad note in her voice. "It's early yet, Vicky. She could have chosen any number of places to practice when she left Boston. She came home. She chose to move in with you. Accept that and enjoy it. Don't question it."

After a moment, she asked, "Do you think everything's okay with her?"

He looked at her. "Did you hear anything I just said?"

"I heard, Leo, but there's just something.…"

"It's understandable that a trauma specialist would want a change of pace after five years."

"You didn't answer the question, Leo."

He gave her hand a little shake. "Don't borrow trouble, Vicky."

She held his gaze, knowing he would understand her thoughts. "But if anything *is* wrong, you'll stand by her? You'll do what it takes to help her see it through? Promise me, Leo."

"I don't like the way this conversation is going, Victoria. You don't need to worry about Kate. She's strong, she's smart, she's capable of solving her own problems. She's enough like you that I don't worry about her, not for a second."

"Promise me anyway, Leo."

He sighed. "I promise, for what it's worth, Vicky."

She nodded. "Thank you."

Leo stared at the objects on the coffee table in front of them. A crystal bird came from his honeymoon trip to Ireland with Caroline. A tiny framed photo of the two of them stood beside it. That day seemed a hundred years ago. Another photo captured Amber and Kate as giggly ten-year-olds. He remembered the day Victoria had snapped it as if it were yesterday. "It upsets me when you talk like this," he said.

"I'm sorry. I don't like to burden you more than—" She stopped when he put a finger on her lips.

"Nothing you do could ever burden me, Vicky." Without thinking, he took her hand, fragile and frail now, and felt the deep fear that always came when he was reminded of her illness.

She was shaking her head. "But our children, Leo…"

"They're not children now, Vicky. They're adults."

"Maybe so, but we're still parents, and I have a feeling neither one of them is happy."

Leo gazed through the windows at the dark street. "You noticed the way Deke was drinking tonight."

"Yes. If he has so little control when there's a houseful of guests, it makes me shudder to think how he might act when there's no one around."

"Surely Stephen would alert us if—"

Suddenly the front door burst open and Stephen shouted, "Somebody come quick! Cody's hurt bad!" He almost missed Leo and Victoria as he dashed into the house.

Leo rose hastily. "What's the matter, son?"

"You gotta do something, Dr. Leo. It's Cody. He's been shot!"

"Shot!"

"Oh, my God." Victoria stood.

Leo caught the boy's arm. "Where is he?"

"At the house. Mallory's calling 911, but he needs help right now, Dr. Leo."

"Calm down, boy. Victoria, go get Sam and Kate. Tell them to follow us on over to the Yeagers' house. Get Nick, too."

Victoria was already headed toward the den. Some of the guests had overheard and were now murmuring among themselves. Amber jerked the patio door open and called for Sam and Kate.

"What is it?" Kate asked, looking first at Amber, then at her mother.

"Kate, there's been an accident," Victoria said calmly. "Leo wants you and Sam to hurry over to the Yeagers'."

"What kind of accident?" Nick pushed past Amber as Kate and Sam hurried toward the front door.

"Kate, you go ahead," Sam ordered. "I'll get my bag. It's in my car."

"Okay."

By now the crowd had moved through the den toward

the front door. When Nick saw Stephen, he charged over to the boy. "What's wrong, damn it!"

"I'm sorry, Nick." Stephen was crying now, and trembling all over. "We were l-looking at your g-gun and—"

"Ah, God…no. No!" Nick turned, making for the foyer. At the front door, he dashed out and took the short steps leading off the porch in one leap and hit the ground running. His heart pounded with a terror so profound he couldn't think. His gun. Cody. His son. No!

Leo and Kate reached the house together. Leo was huffing and puffing and pressing a hand to his chest as they burst through the front door. "Mallory!" he called. "Where are you?"

"In here!" The girl's voice came from the rear of the house. "In the den. Come quick!"

Kate rushed past Leo, who stopped, resting against the wall. Vaguely, she remembered having been inside the house before, but it had been years ago. The hall took a right turn into the kitchen and family room, as she recalled. She hurried past the open door of a powder room. Her heart lurched at the sight of a blood-soaked towel on the sink.

"Mallory Delacourt!" she called. "Talk to me. Where are you?"

"In here. Somebody help Cody, please."

Following the sound of her voice, Kate crossed the kitchen to get to the breakfast nook. Blood was everywhere. A teenage boy lay on the floor. Nick's son. A girl knelt beside him trying valiantly to stanch the blood from a neck wound.

"Please help me to do the right thing now," Kate prayed, dropping to her knees beside the girl. A handgun lay on the floor beside them, blue-black, shiny, hideous. Deadly.

"Thank heavens you're here," Mallory said, her eyes

wild with fear. "I've been trying to put pressure—that's right, isn't it? I got all the tea towels from the drawer, but—"

"Let me see," Kate said, tearing her eyes away from the gun. A buzzing had started in her head. Lights flashed. She forced back the bile rising in her throat. How many times had she played this scene?

She lifted the folded towel and gazed at the wound. Blood welled out of a gaping hole. No time to probe for the bullet. First, try to slow the deadly flow of the boy's blood. With her fingers, she explored the wound, then withdrew to clamp a fresh towel passed to her by Mallory. She stared at her hands, bloodstained and shaking. A dizzying wave washed over her.

God, please, don't let this happen again. Where was Sam?

"Thank God you're here," Leo said, squatting beside her. "We're woefully short on experience with gunshot wounds."

"We're going to need an ambulance, and quick," Kate said.

Beneath her fingers, she felt the flutter of the boy's pulse, very faint and slowing.

"I called 911," Mallory said. "They're on the way."

"Good girl," Leo said, touching her arm gently. "Why don't you stand over there and give Kate room to work."

"Okay."

"How bad is it!" Nick yelled. He squatted down and cradled Cody's head in his hands. There was terror in his eyes as he looked at Kate. "Don't let him die, Kate."

Leo lifted the boy's lids, then met Kate's eyes gravely. "Fixed and dilated, Kate. It's bad," he murmured.

"I...I..." Kate closed her eyes. "I can't do this."

Had she said the words out loud? Or had she only thought them? Kate looked at her hands. What was the next step? She couldn't let this boy die. Not Nick's son.

"Hold on, boy," Leo said, checking the boy's pulse.

Nick kissed the top of Cody's head. "Cody, son, it's Dad. You're going to be okay."

"He needs an airway," Kate said, fighting panic.

But she was paralyzed. Helpless. Frozen.

"What is it?"

Sam's voice. He was beside her now. His tone was sharp. Insistent. Suspicious. She felt a relief so overwhelming, she almost fainted. He had his bag open. He pulled something out, but there was a bright spot in her vision and she couldn't tell what it was. The buzz in her head was a thunderous roar now.

"Here," she said, moving aside and making room for him. She fumbled for Sam's hand and brought it to the folded towel directly over the wound. "You take over," she said, meeting his puzzled glance for a split second. Then she stumbled to her feet and pushed past him, brushing against Leo, seeking the way out of the house by the back door. Gasping, she ran through it, then across the patio, around the corner of the huge house. She fell to her knees and vomited.

SIXTEEN

Stephen sat on a hard hospital chair in the waiting room, his arms resting on his knees as he rotated a squashed cola can in his hands. Inside, about a million emotions were all jumbled together, he felt like he'd been kicked in the stomach. He had almost killed somebody. Cody, a kid he liked. A friend. All because they were fooling around with that stupid gun and it went off. He knew guns, damn it. Some of his earliest memories were of Deke fondling his weapons, taking them apart and making Stephen watch while he put them together again; then going to the firing range and having to shoot round after round after round until he could hit the target to suit his old man with whichever gun from his collection he wanted to show off to the guys that day.

And now he'd almost killed Cody.

If it hadn't been for Mallory knowing what to do, Cody would be dead.

There was going to be a death anyway, he thought with dark humor. Deke was going to kill him for screwing up. What the hell. He deserved it.

"Stephen? Stephen Russo?"

He stared first at feet and legs in cop-uniform pants—pressed and neat but becoming a female shape as his gaze moved upward. He looked at her belt with a gun and radio and other cop stuff on it, past her breasts in a shirt that had pockets and flaps and a nameplate. Pamela LaRue.

Then on up to her face. She was looking pretty seriously at him. Well, yeah. Shooting somebody was a serious thing.

"I'm Officer LaRue," she said. Her voice was nice— husky and low and almost like it had a smile in it. "I need to ask you some questions."

"Okay. I mean, yes, ma'am."

"I know you told the EMTs what happened, and the officers who came to the scene have your statement, but you were pretty upset. I thought you might have recalled more details since then."

"Like what?"

She sat down beside him and rested a little notebook, just like they had on "N.Y.P.D. Blue," on her knee. She had a pen in her right hand. She clicked it, ready to write.

"Do I need a lawyer?" he asked.

She looked at him. "Why would you need a lawyer, Stephen? You told the EMTs and the officers at the scene that Cody was shot accidentally. Do you want to change your statement?"

"No, ma'am. It was definitely an accident."

She smiled. She was pretty when she smiled. "Then I don't think you need a lawyer."

"I knew it was stupid to even look at that gun, but Cody said it was a Ruger and I knew it wasn't. It was a Smith & Wesson .38 revolver."

"How did you know that?"

"My... Deke taught me a lot about guns."

"Your father?"

"Yeah. He's a big supporter of the second amendment. You know, the right of every citizen to own a weapon?"

"The second amendment. Right. So you recognized the gun as a Smith & Wesson?"

"Yeah. They look a lot like Rugers, but it wasn't a

Ruger. A lot of cops carry a Smith & Wesson. You just point it and fire."

"And is that what you did? You just picked it up and pointed it and it fired?"

"No. You think I'm crazy? Cody had it out, but I wanted to put it back into Nick's holster. Jeez, I knew Nick would have a fit if he thought Cody had even touched his weapon, let alone taken it out. Anybody would. But Cody insisted on proving that it was a Ruger. I knew that gun fired fast, especially if it had a hair trigger. I also figured Nick, being a cop and all, might have his gun at the ready, so to speak."

"What do you mean, 'at the ready'?"

"Like loaded with a bullet in the chamber, you know. And sure enough, it was. Loaded, I mean, but with only five bullets. The chamber was empty for safety's sake, I guess. Still, I knew you could pull the trigger and the gun would skip that empty chamber and fire. The empty chamber's for if you, like, drop it, so it won't go off and shoot your foot."

"Then how did it go off, Stephen?"

"Well, Cody was handling it pretty carelessly. So I'm, like, trying to get him to put the gun back. He sort of laughed and raised it high, trying to keep it out of my reach. Mallory was sitting there all this time. I could just imagine the shit if something happened to her." He winced, making a face. "'Scuse me, ma'am. So I shoved her out of the way. She said later I knocked her down, but I was really nervous. Man, that big sucker in Cody's hands like that and him waving it around, not realizing— You know what I mean?"

"How did it go off, Stephen?" she repeated.

Stephen spread his hands in misery and his eyes teared up. "It was my fault, ma'am. It was me reaching for it that caused it. I said, 'Give it to me, Cody. I'm putting it back

where it belongs.' And he didn't object or anything. He
started to hand it right over like you would a knife, when
you don't point it at the person you're handing it to, you
know what I mean?"

"I know," Pamela said softly.

"He turned it around, passed it over to me, but in the
transfer somehow the trigger got touched. It just went off.
Boom! It sounded like an atom bomb."

"What did you do then?"

"Mallory." He swallowed hard. "It was Mallory. She
was great. She screamed, then she grabbed a towel from
somewhere and pressed it against the hole in Cody's...
Cody's...th-throat." He rubbed his eyes, remembering.
"Mallory called 911, then yelled at me to get her dad. So
that's what I did."

Pamela made a final note on the pad, clicked her pen
and slipped it into her shirt pocket. She touched his knee,
then stood, tucking the pad into her pants. "Thanks, Stephen. I think that'll take care of it, at least for now."

"My dad's gonna kill me."

"It was an accident, Stephen. He might be upset, but if
he's as familiar with guns as you say, he understands that
accidents happen. Especially when a weapon is in the
hands of an inexperienced person. In this case, Cody."

Stephen shook his head. "No, he won't understand.
You don't know him. He's really gonna kill me."

She touched him again, on the shoulder. "I'm going to
talk to Nick now. Will you be okay?"

"Nick." His shoulders drooped even lower. "He'll
think I'm a dumb-ass, too."

"Nick has seen many gunshot accidents in his line of
work. Just sit tight for now."

"Okay, I guess." He looked across the room to where
Amber and Nick stood talking. "My—Amber's over
there. She said she's called Deke and he's on his way."

"Then I'll see you later."

Pamela headed across the room to talk to Nick, who appeared to be in deep conversation with Amber Russo. They were old friends, high-school friends. Nick had mentioned it when the celebrity promotions had first appeared for the town's Fais Do-Do. Looking at them together now, Pamela noticed a sort of familiar intimacy in their manner.

She had met Nick about two months ago while waiting in line at a convenience-store checkout. Seeing her uniform, he'd struck up a conversation in the way fellow police officers do. Later, to her surprise, he'd called her and asked her out. In spite of the fact that she told herself Nick Santana was in Bayou Blanc only until he was well again, that he'd be back in New Orleans as fast as humanly possible, she had fallen for him as if she'd been a teenager and he was the quarterback on the football team.

Drawing close, she could see that he was still shaken by Cody's narrow escape. He was grim faced and his dark hair was wild and unruly. He looked as if he needed a hug, and she had a very uncoplike urge to slip her arms around his waist and give him one. Maybe later.

"Nick, I'll need to ask a few questions."

He turned and, for an instant, it seemed he almost didn't recognize her. She knew shock did that sometimes, but she still felt a little pang.

"Pam. Okay." He nodded, then rubbed a hand over his face. "Uh, Amber, this is Pamela LaRue, Officer Pamela LaRue of the Bayou Blanc PD. Pam, Amber Russo."

"Hi," Amber said.

"Hello, Ms. Russo. You're Stephen's mother, right?" She wasn't like anybody's mother Pamela knew. She was too exotic looking, like one of the famed Creole beauties of New Orleans's past.

"I'm Stephen's stepmother."

"Oh. Well, I was just talking to him, and he's feeling upset and guilty over what happened. I thought you might want to try to put his mind at ease while I take Nick's statement."

Nick clamped a hand on the back of his neck. "If we're passing guilt around, I'm the one to yell at. It was my gun."

"It was no one's fault, Nick," Amber said, giving his arm a small shake.

"If I hadn't had the gun in the house, it wouldn't have happened."

"You're a cop," Pamela said. "Where else would your service weapon be if not at home?"

"Locked away somewhere." He was staring ahead stonily.

"Come on, Nick." Pamela had never seen this side of him. In spite of his close call in New Orleans, he'd remained almost arrogantly confident. According to his peers at the NOPD, he was a highly intelligent, street-smart detective with a conviction rate that was the envy of every cop in Homicide.

"Anyway," Pamela continued, turning to Amber, "Stephen is worrying, especially about his father. He thinks he's in for it when his dad finds out."

Amber sighed. Ignoring Pamela, she said to Nick, "I've told him these things happen and he shouldn't blame himself, but he's sensitive—far more than most fifteen-year-old boys. He'll beat up on himself forever on this, wait and see."

"Actually, almost anyone would obsess over something like this, Ms. Russo." For some reason, Pamela felt compelled to defend the boy. His stepmother was saying the right words, but there was something missing. "In fact, Stephen didn't pull the trigger. Cody did that himself."

"He shot himself?" Nick asked sharply. "How do you know?"

"According to Stephen's statement, that's what happened, Nick."

"Jesus." Nick turned away.

Pamela blinked with confusion before it dawned on her what he thought. "Nick, Cody didn't pull the trigger on purpose. That's not what I meant. The gun went off as he was passing it over to Stephen to put it back in your holster." She touched his shoulder, and with a cant of her chin indicated the chairs a few feet away. "Come on, let's sit down over there so I can finish this statement and you can get some rest."

"I won't get any rest tonight."

"I know you don't want to leave Cody, but you can find a quiet place out of the traffic."

"This is good, Nick." Amber brought her hands together prayerlike, beneath her chin. "If she's right about the details, it'll make it a lot easier to explain to Deke."

"Your stepson has experienced a trauma tonight, Ms. Russo," Pamela said. "It's Stephen who needs careful handling, not his father." She took out her notebook and gave Nick a direct look. "About that statement, Nick."

"Yeah, okay." He touched Amber's arm before angling his head toward the chair where Stephen was waiting. "Talk to Stephen, Amber. Tell him it's okay. My fault, not his."

"Nick. You worry too much." Then, as she was turning away, she said, "It was Chief Escavez who took my statement. Deke has some clout with the department. You might want to wait and talk to him." With a smile meant strictly for Nick, Amber left to go to her stepson.

Nick and Pam watched in silence as she sat down beside Stephen. "Do you want to give the chief your statement?" Pamela asked quietly.

"No."

"He's around, Nick. Talking to Sam, I think. Just say the word."

"No."

Her eyes were still on Stephen. "The distress that boy's feeling is very real," she said. She was human enough to feel unsettled by Amber Russo's snub. "I hope Amber won't just dismiss his feelings. He needs reassurance now."

"You want some coffee?" Nick asked after a minute. He picked up a foam cup resting on the window ledge. "There's a pot over by the nurses' station."

"This can wait until tomorrow if you say the word, Nick." She looked closely at his face. "How are you doing? Are you okay?"

"As okay as a man can be who nearly lost his son because of his own stupidity. And no need to wait until tomorrow. Nothing's going to change." He left her and went to get some coffee. Pam shook her head when he raised his eyebrows to ask again if she wanted any, then he followed her as she walked across to chairs and a settee in a small alcove.

"Sit, Nick."

He dropped like a stone, splashing some of the coffee on his hand. Swearing, he set it aside and fished his handkerchief out of his pocket to wipe his hand. He leaned back, bumping his head wearily against the wall. "Ask away."

She studied him in silence for a moment before starting. "Where was the gun?"

"In the kitchen pantry on a shelf where all he had to do was open the door and pick it up."

"Is that where you usually keep it?"

"No. I have a locked cabinet, but this time...I forgot."

"Why?"

"I was cleaning it tonight, killing time." He laughed grimly, shaking his head.

"What is it?"

"There was this party going on across the street at Leo's house. Amber was throwing it to welcome Kate Madison home. I was invited, but I didn't plan to go."

"You changed your mind?"

"I'm used to cramming every hour of every day with work. While this healed—" he touched a spot on his chest "—I've had more time on my hands than ever in my life. Tonight I was just bored. Restless."

As Pamela scribbled in her notebook, she wondered if there was a message on her voice mail at home. She seldom worked the late shift and Nick knew that. Had he called, hoping to find her in and available? Or had he wanted to go to that party?

"Kate Madison is an old friend, too?"

He looked at her. "Yeah."

"You mentioned once that you and Amber were acquainted. I just wondered if Kate was the attraction at the party."

He glanced at her notebook. "How are you going to record the answer to that in your notes, Pam?"

She was out of line and he was right to call her on it. "So, did you just toss a loaded .38 on a pantry shelf alongside the chips and canned veggies so you could spend two more minutes at a party across the street?"

"That's the question I've been asking myself since it happened."

"Nick…"

He stood with a growl. "Look, I've already admitted I was stupid. I put the gun in the pantry, never dreaming Cody would even see it. And if he did see it, he knew not to pick it up. Not to touch it." Nick made a vicious swipe with his hand. "Ever! For any reason!"

"But he did."

Nick raked his fingers through his hair. "Yeah, he did."

She released a sigh. "It happens, Nick. Boys and guns."

"Not to me. Not to Cody."

"A moment's carelessness." Pam shrugged. "You aren't the first, you won't be the last."

"Get over it, huh?"

"I didn't say that. And I wasn't dismissing your breach of responsibility. Your son was seriously hurt, but quick thinking by that young girl and a party full of physicians saved his life. You're lucky. Dwell on that if you want to obsess over something tonight." She flicked the cover of her notebook closed and stood. "Like other police officers, I've had to give some unlucky parents a far different message."

She turned to leave, but Nick stopped her with a hand on her arm. "Look, Pam...I'm sorry. If I seem short or distracted or something, it's because I can't believe this has happened. Again. I mean, somebody close to me getting shot. I was really shaken when my partner was killed. Move that bullet a hair to the left and it would have been me. So I had a lot of time lying in the hospital to ask what I would have left behind. What memories would my son have about me? They probably wouldn't be about the precious few times I took him to the Superdome for a game, you can bet on that. More likely he'd remember the god-awful fights Lisa and I had before we finally split. Or maybe all the times I promised to show up at his school events and didn't. Or maybe those fishing trips we planned that never panned out."

"Nick..." She touched his arm. "Cody had a close call. You have a right to be shaken, but you don't need to beat up on yourself this way."

"I've been divorced five years, but I haven't been a decent father to Cody for a lot longer than that. I had a major wake-up call the night Joe Morales died on the street. Later, lying in the hospital, I swore if Lisa would let me have Cody for the summer while I got back on my feet, I'd change that. And she did. And it's been good, Pam. I got a second chance." He rubbed a hand over his face. "If I'd lost him tonight…"

"But you didn't lose him, Nick. He's going to be okay." Pam wanted to touch him, comfort him in some way. Glancing behind her, she saw that Amber was watching them.

Nick reached for his coffee cup and sat back down. His hand was unsteady, but he managed to swallow, then grimaced. "Coffee's gotta be left over from last week."

Pam could see that he was embarrassed. She stepped closer, blocking him from curious eyes, and put her hand on his shoulder.

"Have you called Lisa?" she asked, rubbing his tense muscles.

"She's a teacher. She's enrolled in a summer course at Rice University in Houston. I waited to call her until Cody was out of surgery and Sam said he'd be okay."

"She must have been terribly upset."

"She'll be here by morning, and I bet she'll want to take him away from me."

"Maybe not, unless Cody wants to leave. I'm betting he chooses to stay the rest of the summer with you."

She felt the shudder that ran through Nick. "I won't make any demands if he'll just be okay."

SEVENTEEN

Kate stood before a dark window on the surgical floor near the elevators, well away from Cody Santana's family and friends. Her hands were wrapped around hot coffee in a foam cup, but nothing could warm the chill in her soul. Nick's son would survive, no thanks to her.

The surgery had lasted more than two hours. Kate had stayed in the background, avoiding Sam's eye while he briefed the anxious group afterward. The bullet had entered just beneath Cody's collarbone, plowed upward and nicked his carotid artery. Two units of blood furnished by Nick had replaced some of the astonishing amount he'd lost. Usually the clavicle healed quickly in young healthy boys, and Cody would probably be out of the hospital within three days. Thank God.

Relief was palpable. Sam openly credited his daughter for her quick, unpanicked thinking. To Kate, he said nothing.

She was devastated. No matter what Sam might say, it couldn't compare to what she thought herself. She had hoped—prayed—that she'd left behind whatever demon had been riding her in Boston. But, the demon was still with her, and on top of her professional collapse, she was unraveling emotionally. She'd hoped the comfort and familiarity of being in Bayou Blanc would work a miracle, but she should have been warned by the episode in her office with Pamela LaRue. Instead of a miracle, she'd almost brought about a tragedy.

"Dr. Madison?"

Kate turned from the wide, black void and looked into the anxious eyes of Sam Delacourt's daughter. "Yes?"

"I just wanted to say thank you."

"'Thank you'?"

Mallory waved a hand vaguely. "Back at Cody's house. I was so scared, and when you came, you knew just what to do. Before Daddy got there, I mean. And you were so calm. I was never so glad to see anybody in my life."

"Looks can be deceiving," Kate said. She'd looked calm? How could that be?

"Well, I just wanted to thank you."

Kate shook her head. "There's nothing to thank me for, Mallory."

"I hear you're practicing with my dad now."

"Yes." *Although now he has the goods to force me out.*

Kate set her cup on a nearby table. "You're the real hero tonight, Mallory. By not panicking, you were able to keep Cody's bleeding under control until help arrived."

Mallory dismissed that with a shrug. "You just learn a few things when your dad's a doctor. I knew to put pressure on a wound that's bleeding a lot."

"Well, you definitely did the right thing. And I'm sure Cody will want to thank you as soon as he's able."

Mallory chewed her lip for a moment, looking out the window. "How long have you known my dad?"

"How long?"

"Yeah, how long? I know y'all knew each other before now."

"He was on the staff at the hospital in New Orleans when I was an intern," Kate said, choosing her words carefully.

"But were you friends?"

Kate decided this was not a time for complete honesty. She hoped the look on her face wouldn't give her away. "If you decide to go into the field of medicine, Mallory, you'll soon discover that the term 'friendship' could never describe the relationship between interns and doctors. Interns are pretty low on the totem pole in a hospital. I was one of many who worked with your dad." Before Mallory could sort through her words, Kate asked, "Are you interested in a career in medicine?"

"Like becoming a doctor, you mean? I've thought about it."

"You have a great role model in your dad, but I don't suppose it's necessary to tell you that," Kate said.

Mallory's face lit up. "I'd never had a chance to see my dad in action before. He was really cool, wasn't he?"

"Yes, really cool," Kate said. *And thank God one of us was.*

"You know what, Mallory? You should tell him that. Even dads love to get a sincere compliment—especially from their kids."

"You think so?"

"I do." Kate smiled. "And you just might mention that you're thinking of following in his footsteps, too."

Both turned at the ping of the nearby elevator. When the doors slid open, Deke Russo stepped out and turned toward them. From the scowl on his face and the way he searched the corridor, he hadn't come out of kindness. Kate sighed, wishing she'd left ten minutes ago as she'd planned.

Deke stopped short when he spotted Kate and Mallory. "Where the hell are they?"

"Who?"

"Amber. Stephen."

"In the ICU waiting room. They're—"

"How's the kid?"

"Cody's going to be okay."

She realized he expected her to walk along with him, and for Amber's and Stephen's sakes, she did. She was certain that in Deke's present frame of mind, his wife and son would receive the brunt of his anger. Maybe she could help.

Kate indicated the double doors at the end of the hall. "Everyone's in there. Sam said—"

"How the hell did this happen? I've taught that kid how to handle firearms." He shot Mallory a hard look. "Whose idea was it to fool with the gun?"

Beside them, Mallory skipped a little, trying to keep up. "Cody said his dad had a Ruger and took it out to prove it. Stephen tried to stop him. Honest. Anyway, it just went off."

"Goddamn! He knows better than to touch another man's weapon. He'd better have a good story lined up, because I'm royally pissed about this."

"It was an accident, Deke. Stephen feels terrible, but he wasn't—"

"He only feels terrible right now. When I get through with him, he's gonna feel a lot worse."

They'd reached the doors leading to the waiting room. Stephen was already feeling guilty and scared. The last thing he needed was his own father ranting and raving at him in public.

When Deke started to push through the doors, Kate stepped in front of him.

"Deke, let Mallory go inside and tell Amber you're here." She gave the girl a nod, and Mallory scooted off. "The police are in there taking statements from Stephen and Nick Santana. There's bound to be publicity, but—"

"That son of a bitch! Probably playing the macho cop with his guns laying around so any kid can pick 'em up and shoot 'em. That's negligence. And I'm gonna have his ass for it!"

"Then maybe you'll rethink your position on handguns in general," Kate said, suddenly out of patience. Did the man ever have a thought for anything except himself? "Your radio show is a forum where you could do some good, Deke. Now that a near tragedy has occurred close to home, you can see how devastating guns are in the wrong hands."

He stared at her, his outstretched arm still holding the door open. "I'm not believing this! We got a case of a stupid cop letting his kid play with his service weapon, and you want to remove all the handguns from everybody else." He released the door to point a finger at her. "Let me tell you something, Kate. It's not guns that kill people—it's people who kill people."

She sighed. "That's such a tired cliché, Deke."

"Yeah, well, here's another one. Take away the people's guns and the only ones'll have them are criminals! I guess you disagree with that, too! Sheesh!" He was shaking his head. "What makes these sayings stick in people's minds, Kate, is that they're true. You liberals don't like to admit that."

The door was suddenly pushed open from the other side, and a huge man wearing a Stetson hat and snakeskin boots nearly ran over them. Deke's scowl changed instantly to a smile. "Chief Escavez!" He stuck out his hand. "Glad to see you, Chief. I'm here to see what's going on with my boy. I'm real sorry to hear there's been an accident. Have you talked to him yet?"

"Hello, Deke." Waylon Escavez pumped Russo's hand with real enthusiasm, his grin stretching his big drooping mustache even wider. "About time you showed up. We got some excitement, all right. Your boy about snuffed out the offspring of that Noo Awlins cop. But he's tough like his daddy, seems like. Gonna pull through."

Deke put a friendly hand on the chief's shoulder. "You aren't thinking of filing any charges against Stephen, now, are you?"

"Naw. I been lookin' over Santana's statement, taken by my girl, Pamela. Any charges get filed, it'd probably be against him." Escavez scratched the side of his head, cocking his Stetson at an angle. "Had a couple of cases in other states used that argument. Negligence. I'll get Pamela to look it up. You might want to think about it."

He seemed to notice Kate then. "Ma'am. You'll be the new doc down at Leo's clinic, am I right?"

"Kate Madison." She held out her hand.

"Dr. Madison." He pumped her hand warmly. "Welcome to Bayou Blanc. I know your mama, but I wasn't hired for the job here until after you'd gone on to Boston, wasn't it?"

"That's right, Boston."

"Good to have you back. Yes sirree." He was nodding, smiling, approval all over his red face. Hypertension, she diagnosed mentally. Eighty pounds overweight and borderline diabetic. She'd bet his cholesterol level was off the stick, too.

"Here's Amber," she said to Deke, glancing beyond the chief.

She watched as Amber approached. She seemed tense to Kate. Any normal married couple would embrace at a time like this, wouldn't they? Their son had accidentally shot another boy who'd narrowly escaped death. But there was no reassuring hug from either party.

"The chief's been filling me in, honeybun. Looks like Stephen's got himself in a bind tonight." His voice was quiet, but Kate heard the steel. Amber did, too, from the look on her face. She gave Chief Escavez a nervous smile.

"He didn't actually pull the trigger, did he, Chief? Stephen was trying to put the gun away. Cody shot himself."

"Uh-huh. That's what I was just telling Deke, here, Miz Russo." He reached into his pocket for his car keys. "I tell you what, folks. Y'all just hang around here for a while, since you're concerned about the Santana boy, and come on into my office in a day or two if you decide you want to file any charges against his daddy."

"Charges against Nick?"

Amber spoke without thinking. Deke's smile could have cut through steel with the look he shot her. "Thanks, Chief, we'll do that."

With a wave, Chief Escavez left them. All eyes followed him as he shuffled down the hall and turned into the elevator alcove. The instant the elevator pinged, Deke motioned to Stephen, still huddled in a chair against the wall, and hissed, "Get over here, boy!"

Amber put a tentative hand on his arm. "Deke, can't it wait until we get home?"

"Why?" He glanced at Kate. "We're all family, aren't we?"

Stephen obeyed, his eyes locked on his father. When he reached Deke, he held himself straight, like a recruit before a hard first sergeant. Kate realized she was holding her breath. If Deke said half the ugly things he'd threatened to when he got off the elevator, the boy would be crushed.

"Hey, Dad."

"What the fuck did you do now?" Deke growled.

"Deke..." Amber's voice went high with anxiety as she quickly panned the room.

"I'll handle this, Amber!" he snarled back.

"Leave her alone," Stephen said quietly. "I'm the one who screwed up. Cody was transferring the gun to me to put it away and it went off. It was a Smith & Wesson .38. He didn't realize what a hair trigger it had."

Kate was amazed at the boy's composure. Deke's temper was ticking like a time bomb, and Stephen, of all people, must know what would happen if he blew.

Deke's face was tight with rage. "You know better than to touch a firearm belonging to somebody else!"

"People are looking, Deke," Kate warned. He'd been recognized, and people in the room were turning to watch. He might ignore Amber's pleas, but she guessed he'd rather the rest of the world not be exposed to one of his tantrums. To make matters worse, Nick was headed their way.

"If you want to yell at somebody, maybe it should be me," Nick said.

His remark was like a red flag to Deke.

"Don't worry, you'll be next." Deke was snarling again. "Leaving a weapon lying right out in the open where a bunch of kids can pick it up is criminal. You're lucky your boy's not dead tonight."

It was a sure shot. Nick's jaw flexed. "I am that. And I've told Stephen it's not his fault."

"Goddamn right it's not his fault, except for being in the wrong place at the wrong time. According to the chief, your kid pulled the trigger himself."

"It was both of us," Stephen insisted. He looked at Amber. "Can't we go somewhere else to talk about this?"

"You want to run to Leo so he'll coddle you like your stepmama here, don't you?" Deke's sneer included both his wife and his son.

"You're browbeating the wrong people, Russo," Nick said. "I've admitted the buck stops here. It was my house, my gun and my responsibility to have it locked up. You want to threaten anybody, try me."

Deke's lip curled. "Don't think they'll be empty threats,

either, Santana. I've already discussed the grounds for a lawsuit against you."

Beyond the nurses' station, the door leading to ICU opened suddenly and Sam came out, still in his surgical greens. He started toward them, but Nick reached him before he'd taken half-a-dozen strides. "I just released Cody from ICU, Nick. He's on his way to a room. See the nurses for the number, but give them about twenty minutes." Sam clamped a hand on his shoulder. "And don't worry. Your boy's going to be fine."

Kate left the hospital and headed directly to the jogging track. She simply couldn't go home and face another nightmare—not on top of everything else tonight—and running was the only way she knew to cope with the emotions roiling inside her. There was release to be found in pushing her body to a punishing pace, and she yearned for it.

Thunder rumbled in the distance, but she ignored it. The smell of rain was in the air, but so far it was holding off. Using her car phone, she called Victoria to let her know she wouldn't be home for another hour or so and to update her about Cody. She didn't say she was going for a late-night run.

She locked her gym bag in her car, taking nothing except a bottle of water and a towel to the track. A little more daunting than the threat of a storm was the near desertion of the area. Only two cars were parked in the space reserved for vehicles. Two people jogged side by side beneath the security light on the opposite curve of the track, and she saw one other woman. She'd have to wrap it up when they did.

After some stretches and a deep, cleansing breath, she set out. The hospital was in her head—the sounds, the smells, the urgency, the anxiety. Grimly she picked up speed, seeking to outrun the nightmare of the past few hours. With every thud of her Nikes, she worked to push fear into another place and to keep her life from unraveling for one more hour.

Twenty minutes later a stitch in her side forced her to slow down at the far end of the track. She looked around and saw that only one car was left in the space next to her own. Jogging in place, she felt the first raindrops, and with her face uplifted, closed her eyes. A mistake. Instantly, the scene with Cody materialized—the boy in a pool of his own blood, the gun, her faltering hands, Sam's sharp, suspicious look.

Forgetting safety precautions, she started to run again to escape the images. Rain was now falling steadily. She was drenched in seconds, her hair plastered to her head, her shoes splashing in the puddles. Then a bolt of lightning came so close, she literally felt the crackle of electricity. She picked up her pace, realizing she was as far away from her car as it was possible to be on the track. She tried to recall how close she was to one of the track's small wooden shelters.

Suddenly a figure loomed out of the rain and an arm came out to stop her. Her heart pounded with fear as she struggled to stay on her feet.

"What the hell do you think you're doing?" Sam yelled. "Are you crazy!"

She stared into his face in confusion. He was the last person she would have expected out here tonight.

Cursing, he caught her arm and half dragged, half carried her to a rest shelter. She pulled free of his hold and stumbled to the bench.

"Are you trying to get yourself killed by lightning?"

She pushed her hair from her face with both hands to look at him. Her teeth were chattering, but she managed to ask, "What are you d-doing out here?"

"Looking for you. What else?" He removed a nylon windbreaker and handed it to her. "Here, put this on. You're soaked." He paced a few feet, then turned. "If you weren't concerned about the storm, what about the fact you're out here alone?" He waved an arm. "Anything could happen. Jesus! What's the matter with you, Kate?"

She made no move to put the jacket on. "I got caught in the rain. I didn't realize—"

"You saw the lightning. You saw the place was deserted. You think you have a charmed life, for God's sake?"

"It wasn't deserted. There were...people."

"Who wisely left at the first drop of rain."

He stood facing her with his back to the lighted track behind him, so she couldn't read his face.

"How did you know I was out here?" she asked.

"I knew when you freaked over Cody you'd be upset." He plowed a hand through his own damp hair, sending droplets flying. "When you're upset, you like to run. It was a no-brainer."

Both of them tensed when the world lit up with dazzling white light, then exploded with another earsplitting boom. "Even in a thunderstorm?" she asked wryly.

"Yeah, even in a thunderstorm." He took the jacket from her, shook the rain from it and draped it over her shoulders. "You should take that wet shirt off because we're going to be stuck here until the worst of the lightning passes. I'm not making a run for the car through those trees and taking a chance on making Mallory an orphan."

He was right. She was chilled and miserable now that she'd cooled down from the run. What had she been thinking to get herself into a mess like this?

"So are you taking off the shirt or are you going to sit there and shiver?"

"Turn around."

"No problem." Sam went to the front of the shelter and stood looking out with one arm propped on the rough-cut timber. The rain pelted down in sheets with no indication of slacking off. Wind whistled around the walls of the shelter. Lightning kept the sky lit up, and thunder was so constant that it made conversation virtually impossible.

Kate pulled her T-shirt over her head and draped it, dripping, over the bench against the side wall. Quickly she slipped her arms into the jacket and was instantly enveloped in the essence of Sam. She had a crazy impulse to bury her face in the soft nylon. There had been a connection between Sam and her five years ago that had promised something wonderful. Nothing in her life today was wonderful, and she was suddenly filled with a need so desperate it frightened her.

She rose abruptly. Thinking that way was certain disaster. She went to the opposite side of the shelter, as far away from Sam as possible, and watched the fury of the storm. He spoke in a lull between crashes of thunder.

"What happened with Cody before I got there?"

"Your daughter had applied pressure to the wound. I took over, probed for the bullet, but it wasn't—"

"I'm not talking about that, Kate. You panicked. I want to know why."

She was glad there was no light for him to see her face. "Fatigue, I guess. Guns and violence. Another young victim, and this time I knew him."

He turned to look at her. "Has this happened before?"

With her head bent, she rubbed at her forehead before facing him. "Look, Sam, I can't deny I'm upset over what happened tonight. But I don't want to try and explain it right now. I've handled dozens of gunshot victims in the past five years—maybe hundreds. I've never failed to do what was necessary. And besides, you were there, and we

both know there's no medical situation you can't handle."
If there was sarcasm in her tone, she didn't care.

"You're saying that if I hadn't been there, you would
have done the job you were trained for?"

I'm saying I don't know. I don't know. I don't know. But she
managed to reply calmly. "I've admitted I wanted a
change from trauma care, which is why I'm here and not
at St. Luke's."

"You looked like hell staring at Cody's blood on your
hands. I've seen that look on the faces of first-year interns.
Next thing, they're passed out on the floor. Or they run
for the nearest can to throw up. Some don't show up the
day after, and then we hear they've decided medicine
isn't for them."

"Is that what you think happened?"

"Hell, I don't know. That's what I'm asking you. Fortunately I was there, and yes, I can handle a gunshot
wound. I'm just wondering what would've happened if I
hadn't been there."

"I would have managed." *Somehow.*

"Would you?" He was watching her narrowly.

"Is this why you came looking for me? To tell me I
don't measure up?"

"It's my business when you endanger the life of a patient." He had to raise his voice to be heard over a deafening crash of thunder.

"Okay! All right! But was that the real reason you came
looking for me tonight?"

"I was worried about you, damn it! You ran like the demons of hell were after you when you should have stuck
with me to see that we'd done everything we could for
Cody. Then, at the hospital, you looked ready to break
into a million pieces when I came out of the O.R. with a
report on that boy."

"I wasn't the only one. Everyone was worried."

"Admit it, Kate. There's something wrong in your life or you'd never have returned to Bayou Blanc."

"My mother is dying of cancer!"

"A fact that you didn't even know until you got here. And you've just been through a divorce. Life's tough. But I'm talking about your professional life."

"I've got to go," she muttered, reaching for her wet T-shirt. She balled it up, ready to leave. "Mother will be worried."

Sam grabbed her arm and she started past him. "Stonewalling won't work, Kate. You may as well tell me what's going on."

"I don't have to tell you anything!" She jerked her arm to free herself.

"So there *is* something."

"Let me go!" She strained toward the front of the shelter.

Instead of turning her loose, he reached for her other arm, forcing her to look at him. "You aren't going out there, Kate. I'm not letting you get struck by lightning just because you're angry and scared."

She jerked her chin up to look at him. "That's ridiculous!"

"Is it?"

The storm still raged as she stared at him. Wind whistled around the sturdy shed. Debris swirled outside, propelled by gale-like gusts lashing rain against the outside walls. But inside, suddenly, neither of them dared move. Flickering lightning gave her a glimpse of his face and her heart began to pound. He looked hard, determined. His gaze fell to her lips. She felt the flex of his hands, as if he were reacquainting himself with the feel of her. With a thrill, she realized that it wasn't anger motivating him now.

"You're already angry, so what do I have to lose?" he

muttered, pulling her close. And before she could say a word to stop him, he was kissing her.

For a second, she was so stunned she did nothing. His arms were suddenly around her, holding her hard against him as his mouth opened wide on hers. She was instantly aware of the familiar fit of his body to hers, of the smell of him, the taste of him. It seemed incredible that five years had passed since she'd felt the exquisite pleasure of kissing Sam Delacourt.

His mouth was hot and hungry and demanding. He pushed his leg between hers and pressed against her. Searing need exploded in her with all the fury of the storm raging outside. And, oh, Lord, it felt good. So good.

She moaned as he found her breasts, naked and tight, beneath the nylon of his jacket. He pushed the jacket off and flung it away, then bent to taste her, making a sound deep in his throat. With his hot mouth on her breast, she dropped her head forward to kiss his hair, to run her fingers through it, caressing his ears, the angle of his jaw— touching, touching, in an orgy of sensation.

"Sam—"

"Don't talk. Not now. Just tell me you're ready, sweetheart."

"Yes..."

A vague caution hovered at the edge of Sam's mind, but he pushed it away. He stood with his arms tightly around Kate, savoring the feel of her, wet and warm and ready. Ruled by lust now, he was caught in a whirlwind that rivaled the storm itself. He had to have this woman again. Drawing a deep breath, he shuddered as he removed their clothes and buried himself deep inside her.

Kate was grateful for the darkness. The storm had moved on, though it still rained, keeping them trapped in the shed. The other insanity had passed, too. Sam was again standing at the front of the shed, braced by one arm. She could barely see the outline of his profile, but she saw enough to know he felt as stunned as she by what had just happened. And as grim.

Desperate to get away, she had her shorts on, damp and clinging unpleasantly to her skin. She stood, her shoes squishing on her feet without her soaked socks.

"I don't know how to explain that," he said suddenly, his gaze still fixed straight ahead.

She zipped up his jacket. "Shit happens."

He turned. "Kate—"

She grabbed her sodden T-shirt. "The lightning's passed. I'll see you tomorrow." Before he could stop her, she'd slipped past him to make a mad dash for her car.

EIGHTEEN

Kate drove all the way home in a slow drizzle without allowing herself to think. After letting herself inside Victoria's house as silently as she could, she dropped her gym bag on the floor and went immediately to the cabinet where her mother kept a meager bar. Her life was spiraling out of control. Tonight she'd come close to tragedy with Cody. She seemed to have lost her way as a physician. Her mother was dying and she could only stand by helplessly. And if all of that wasn't enough, she'd had sex with Sam Delacourt.

"Kate?"

Oh, no. She didn't want to talk to her mother—not tonight. Victoria had always possessed a shrewdness where Kate was concerned. She'd be able to tell.

"Mother." Without opening the cabinet, Kate turned instead to the refrigerator and opened it. She took out orange juice and held it up. "Want something to drink?"

"You're soaked, Kate!" Victoria moved closer, taking in her bedraggled state with a frown. "Shorts? Surely you haven't been running. Not in this weather."

"I'm afraid I have, and you don't have to bother with the lecture. I've learned my lesson. I'm soaked and I'm tired and I'm calling myself all kinds of fool for doing it."

"Whose jacket is that?"

"Sam Delacourt's."

Her mother was watching her narrowly. "Sam was at the track, too?"

Kate opened the orange-juice carton. "Now there're two crazies in Leo's clinic."

"Go upstairs and change into something dry before you make yourself sick, Kate." Shaking her head, Victoria reached over and took the carton, returning it to the fridge. "I'll make us both some tea and bring it up. Then you can tell me how it happens that you don't have anything on under that jacket."

Kate wasn't about to touch that one, feeling the way she did at this moment. She swept up her gym bag and high-tailed it out of the kitchen. Taking the stairs at a run, she rushed into her room and flung Sam's jacket into the corner, kicked her Nikes aside, and began peeling off the sodden shorts, stopping midway to remove her panties from one of her pockets. She'd been so desperate to get away from Sam she was lucky she'd managed to get decent enough to come home.

In the bathroom she stepped into a warm shower, hoping to wash away the smell of him on her skin. And the taste of him on her tongue. And the feel of him inside her. Covering her face, she let the spray pound her until sounds from the bedroom told her that Victoria was there with some motherly notion of helping.

It was going to take more than tea to fix Kate's problem.

She toweled off and put on a thick terry-cloth robe, wrapped a towel turban-style around her wet head, took a deep breath, and left the bathroom.

Her mother had placed the tea tray on a small piecrust table and was sitting beside it in a rocking chair. In the soft glow of the lamp, her face was a pale oval, almost ghostly. She wore a ruffled cap, but it was slightly askew, so that a part of her smooth scalp was exposed. Kate felt a tightening in her throat. She'd so seldom seen her mother look vulnerable.

"It's the middle of the night, Mother. You should be in bed, not in here coddling me."

"I'm where I want to be, Kate. Besides, I was awake reading when I heard you come in."

"I hope you weren't waiting up."

"Not really."

"You have something to help you sleep, don't you?"

"I don't need much sleep anymore." She watched Kate pull the towel from her head and rub at her damp hair. "Tell me why you felt you had to run in this weather and so late, Kate."

"I was...tense. Running helps."

"Tense about what?"

Kate was glad to hide behind the towel. "The change of jobs, I suppose. Adjusting to being back home again, becoming accustomed to a new work environment." *Cody's accident. My meltdown. Sam's suspicions. Sam, period.* Still holding the towel, she motioned to the tray. "Don't wait for me. Have your tea."

"You, too. It'll relax you. It's a blend of herbs or something. Amber's idea. She picked it up for me in that natural-foods store near her neighborhood. Tastes like steeped rope, but don't tell her I said so. I added whiskey to yours."

Kate blinked. "You added whiskey?"

"You look as though you could use something stronger than plain tea."

Kate dropped the towel and finger-combed her hair, tucking the sides behind her ears. Her mother had set the scene for a kind of intimacy that had never existed between them. As a girl, Kate had wished for that bond—longed for it at one time—but she wasn't sure she was ready for it now. Spiked tea was another matter.

"Sit down, Kate. You'll ruin the beneficial effect of the whiskey, pacing like that."

Kate let out a short, helpless laugh. She took a seat on the edge of an ottoman at the foot of her bed.

"I saw you with Sam tonight."

"At the track?"

"No, no. At Amber's party." Victoria dropped a sugar cube into her tea and began stirring it with a small silver spoon. "I thought the two of you looked…what word can I use? *Intense.* I told Leo that I couldn't remember whether you knew Sam before going to Boston. Leo said you did."

"He was on staff at Tulane when I was an intern."

"Five years ago."

"Yes."

"He called here tonight and asked for you."

Kate brought the teacup to her lips. "He shouldn't have bothered you, Mother."

"Whyever not? You live here. Can't you have a phone call?"

"At such a late hour? No. Only if it's an emergency."

"Perhaps he thought it was." She looked pointedly at the jacket thrown in the corner. "I assume he found you at the track."

"Yes."

"Then I recalled the way you both looked tonight at the party."

"Forget it. There's nothing there, Mother."

"Wishful thinking on my part," Victoria said, studying the contents of her teacup. "Sam has been very good to me since…this." She touched the scarf on her head with one hand.

"Sam is very good. I can see why you feel confident in his care."

"I would feel confident in *your* care, too, Kate. But I

don't want you to have to cope with the—" she waved a hand "—the unpleasantness of it."

Kate felt her lips quivering. She was surprised by how much she longed to remove the barriers between them.

"Coping with the reality of illness is my job, Mother. What have I ever done to make you think I wouldn't want to do whatever I'm able to do to help you?"

Her mother looked stricken. "That's not what I meant, Kate. I just want you to be with me, not have to...do all that." She shuddered delicately. "It's awful. I hate it."

Kate had never thought of her mother as simply needing her. "I could do both, Mother," she said quietly.

"Yes, I know. But I don't want you to."

Draining the last of the tea, Kate rose and moved to the window. Pulling the curtain aside, she saw that the rain had stopped. Catercorner across the street, the Yeager place was dark. Nick would be at the hospital watching over Cody. Would Sam go back? Would he go home? Would he be wondering—as she was—what the hell had happened tonight?

Victoria placed her teacup in its saucer and set it on the tray. "Our relationship has never been comfortable, has it, Kate?" When Kate failed to reply, she went on. "I have friends who talk every day on the phone to their daughters—even though they might live hundreds of miles away. One friend can't buy a piece of furniture or select a trinket without consulting her daughter first. Another actually senses when her daughter is troubled." Victoria met Kate's gaze with a look of sadness. "I don't know what causes that sort of empathy with a child, but I think I know when that opportunity was lost to us."

Kate frowned. "When?"

"The day your father died. The day Caroline Castille drowned. I always felt it was my fault."

Kate's hand fell, and the curtains came together, enclos-

ing them in the room where Kate had filled countless
hours wondering what had happened on that boat. Iron-
ically, it seemed her mother was ready to talk about it tonight, just when Kate was on emotional overload.

"I didn't want to go that day," Victoria said in a soft
voice. "But your father was determined. It was I who persuaded him to invite Leo and Caroline. They were good
friends, good company. I would have them as a buffer between John and me, and, of course, you would have Amber to play with. I didn't want to be alone with him."

"You didn't want to be alone with your husband?"

"He was...difficult."

"In what way?"

Victoria sighed, smoothing the tiny napkin over her
knee. "To tell the truth, Deke Russo reminds me of him."

Deke? That drunken, insensitive bully? Kate sank again
onto the ottoman, shaken by the image.

"After the accident, I felt so guilty. And overwhelmed.
I wanted to withdraw from everything, but that wasn't
possible. You were fatherless, Amber was motherless.
She— Well, somehow she seemed to need me more. You
were strong. Self-reliant. Smart. It wasn't a conscious
thing. I—It just...happened. I told myself that at least
each of you had half a mother."

Kate hadn't expected to hear anything like this. So
many of the half-formed impressions of her childhood
suddenly settled into place. Amber's easy relationship
with her mother had always contrasted strongly with her
own "uncomfortable" one, to use Victoria's word. It
made Kate uncomfortable now, coming too late. She
didn't know what to say.

She got up and went to the tea tray to begin tidying up.
"The accident wasn't your fault, Mother."

"Oh, no?" Victoria smiled ruefully. "If I hadn't asked
the Castilles, Caroline would be alive today. Leo would

have a full life. Amber would have a loving mother. You wouldn't be plagued with nightmares."

"Everyone has a nightmare now and then."

"Not like yours. When you were a little girl, the nightmares would come if you were particularly frightened or threatened. It was as if you were in danger of drowning again." Victoria reached out to touch one of Kate's hands. "What is making you afraid now, Kate?"

Kate gazed at the frail hand covering hers. Her mother's hands had always been beautiful, pampered and elegant. Kate's were less so, the nails filed short and kept unpolished as was practical for a physician. She remembered as a child going regularly with Victoria—and Amber—to a salon where her mother had a standing appointment for a manicure. Kate realized she hadn't had a manicure since she'd last accompanied her mother to that salon.

"It's late," Kate said, and reached for the tray. "I'll take this down to the kitchen while you get back to bed."

Victoria's hand on her arm stopped her. "Leo called me from the hospital tonight."

"After Cody came out of surgery?" Kate managed a smile. "Then you know it's Sam we have to thank for saving his life. You made a good choice there, Mother. He's the best, all right."

"This is not about Sam. Leo was concerned about you."

"I'm okay, Mother."

"Leo didn't seem to think so. What happened at Nick's house when you got there and saw Cody?"

Kate's first thought was to spare her mother more worry. In the time Victoria had left, what was the point? But something in her expression made Kate change her mind. She set the tray back and moved away, wrapping her arms around herself. "Are you sure you want to hear this tonight, Mother?"

"I want to hear whatever it is that's wrong, Kate. How can I help if you won't tell me anything? And even if I can't help, anything that makes you unhappy concerns me."

"I can understand that," Kate said, giving her mother a sidelong look, "because I feel exactly the same way about being shut out of your illness."

"Are you angling for a quid pro quo?" Victoria asked with a wry smile.

"Such as?"

"Such as, if I let you in on the grisly details of my situation, you'll tell me why you left St. Luke's so abruptly without any apparent plan to return?"

Kate laughed. "You should have been a lawyer, Mother."

Victoria nodded complacently. "I've often thought so myself."

Kate sighed. "I didn't choose to leave St. Luke's. I didn't have a choice in the matter." At Victoria's perplexed look, she added, "I'm afraid the way things stand now, I'm not going to be practicing medicine much longer, Mother. Not at St. Luke's or anywhere else."

"What an incredible statement. Whyever not?"

"I didn't just decide to take a sabbatical," Kate said, wearily running a hand over her still-damp hair. "It was strongly suggested that I leave. In fact, my employment is suspended until further notice. Whatever that means," she added on bitterly.

"How did all this come about?" Victoria asked.

"I'd been having trouble coping with the stress of trauma care lately. A couple of times, the...anxiety that I felt interfered with patient care, especially if the patient was a child. Or—and I know this sounds odd—a battered woman. It was terrifying, losing control without understanding why."

Kate turned her hands up, shaking her head. "Now, after tonight and what happened with Cody, I'm not sure I won't panic again and jeopardize a patient."

"Is that what happened tonight? You panicked?"

"What did Leo tell you?"

"Just that something seemed to go wrong."

"I'd hoped in the excitement he hadn't noticed."

"He said you were doing everything you should, when suddenly you just seemed to shut down."

Kate frowned, looking beyond Victoria. "It was as if I was transported to another place, another time. As Cody lay there, I suddenly began getting these crazy images. Blood, panic, a roaring sound. It was scary as hell. Cody's life was draining away and I was in the twilight zone. I couldn't remember what to do. What if Sam and Leo hadn't been there?"

"But they were." Victoria sat for a moment, occupied with her own thoughts. Watching her, Kate felt oddly relieved by sharing the burden with her mother. At this late date maybe there was no need for restraint between them anymore. It was sad that it had taken upheaval in both their lives to bring down the old barriers.

"Did this begin during your divorce?" Victoria asked.

"More or less."

"Stress, Kate. It could happen to anyone."

"A trauma specialist can't afford the luxury of giving in to stress, Mother," Kate said. "And neither can a small-town physician."

After a moment, she added in a distant voice, "It's happening here, now. I thought I'd put it behind me when I left Boston, but I was wrong. It's a terrible feeling, Mother. I sense the presence of...evil." She looked straight at Victoria. "What can it be?"

Victoria's hand was unsteady as it went to her head. "A person's subconscious is a mysterious thing, Kate. You've had a lot on your plate—divorce, the incidents at St. Luke's, your suspension. Once you've had a chance to settle in here and get a new perspective, it'll pass. You'll see."

Kate smiled sadly. "I hope you're right."

"What specifically was the reason for your suspension?"

"I made two wrong decisions during my shift. I treated a battered woman earlier and for some reason, I've just never learned to be objective with those patients. Something about her…oh, I don't know. I was…shaken. Right on the heels of that, a little boy died. A stupid accident with a gun. It was very similar to what happened tonight with Cody. I was actually in tears. Another trauma specialist had to force me to call time on the boy. It was horribly unprofessional. Then, before I'd pulled myself together, a man having a heart attack was admitted and I delayed too long in administering a certain medication. He died." She picked at a thread on the cuff of her bathrobe, not wanting to see her mother's face. "Then, on top of all that, the battered woman died upstairs in O.R."

"My God, with so many crises in a few hours, anyone would be affected, Kate."

Kate was shaking her head. "That's just not an option in this specialty, Mother."

"And so in hindsight, what could you have done differently?"

"I'm not sure. The boy was hopeless from the moment we got him. As for the man who died, I honestly think it was a judgment call. The battered woman was bleeding and shocky before she got there. Her pregnancy was a complication." Kate shrugged. "Who knows?"

"Then put it all behind you, Kate." Her mother spoke earnestly, but Kate was back at St. Luke's seeing Charlene Miller's little girl.

"She had a little girl."

"What?"

"The battered woman, Charlene Miller. She had a child with her, a six-year-old. Lindy was her name. I could tell it was nothing new to Lindy to see her mother bruised and bleeding because of a man. She looked so hopeless. Her eyes were too old for her years." Kate shifted her gaze to Victoria. "Something about her really got to me that day."

"What happened to the man?"

"I don't know. I'm sure he was arrested. He'll probably be charged with manslaughter, but given a minimum jail sentence. Most likely he'll be out in a few years, battering another woman."

Victoria's thoughts seemed to drift for a moment as she rocked slowly and silently in the chair. "Quitting won't solve anything, Kate."

Kate said nothing, but moved to pick up the tray again. Before she lifted it, Victoria gripped her arm, giving it a stern shake. "Don't give in to this, Kate. You can crawl into a corner and waste a lot of time conjecturing and feeling sorry for yourself, but you won't get any answers that way, and you won't get beyond it, either. Better to spend it doing what you are trained to do."

"I'm not sure I'll have any choice if Sam has anything to say about it. He wasn't eager to have me in the practice in the first place, and tonight I handed him the weapon to push me out."

"Then don't give him the satisfaction," Victoria said. "Get back in there and fight, girl!"

"I may have no choice, especially now that Leo's aware I have a problem, too."

"Leo will not allow you to leave. He's too happy to have you in the practice."

"Who needs a doctor who freaks out when things get sticky?"

"The practice needs you. This is just a bad patch. It'll pass." Victoria rose from the rocking chair, looking more fragile than ever. But there was a light in her eye that Kate hadn't seen in a long time. "Go. Take that tray down, then come on back to bed and try to get some rest. Situations that seem desperate in the middle of the night always look better in the morning."

As Kate picked up the tray, Victoria walked over to the bed and transferred the two pillow shams to the ottoman, then turned down the duvet and sheets to an inviting angle. Kate watched the room take on a familiar look. Victoria plumped the bed pillows, smoothed the wrinkles from everything and, last of all, turned on the reading lamp.

When Kate had been a teenager, and later in college, home for a visit, Victoria had always performed this ritual. But never with Kate looking on. It was done before she got home for the night. Or when she was in the bath or talking on the phone or watching television or plugged into earphones, lost in the latest rock tunes.

Now, with the room and Kate's bed fixed to her satisfaction, Victoria came to the door, and to Kate's further surprise, gave her a hug, heedless of the delicate china cups that rattled on the tray. "Don't worry about your place in Leo's clinic, Kate," she said, patting Kate's cheek. "I'll leave it to you to bring Sam Delacourt around."

Kate did her best to fight off the nightmares that night, but they came anyway. New, sharper images flashed before her flinching eyelids. Cody lying in a pool of blood. Sam's face etched in shadow, unsmiling. Deke Russo with teeth bared, smiling like an alligator.

She came awake with a start, sensing herself so close to

an abyss, she was afraid nothing could save her.
Breathing hard and tangled in sweat-soaked sheets, she
pulled her knees up to her chin and buried her face in her
hands. How many chances would she get before she fell
to her destruction?

and save the baby, but another that of her wished now
had arisen.

She heard Deke tray before the saw it. As it turned into
the driveway, she stubbed out another cigarette and hur-

NINETEEN

Amber was too keyed up to go to bed. She smoked as she paced. Every time a car passed on the street, she tensed, thinking it might be Deke. In the foyer, the big clock struck 2:00 a.m.—more than four hours since he'd left the hospital, heading for the police department with Waylon Escavez to be certain that he, Deke, would have a hand spinning the story to the media. When the newspaper came out tomorrow morning, the article would state clearly that Cody was responsible for shooting himself. Deke wasn't taking any chances on bad publicity over this. Amber stubbed out her cigarette in a small ashtray and went to the window for the tenth time in as many minutes.

She watched the lights of a passing car reflecting off the wet streets and thought of Nick. Deke had made certain she hadn't stayed behind at the hospital. He was capable of ignoring the fact that they owed Nick the courtesy of showing concern after Cody's accident by staying nearby. But Deke was giving her no chance to rekindle anything with her high-school sweetheart.

Amber sighed, leaning her forehead against the cool pane. Deke would be impossible to live with until they'd finished their engagement at the festival and were back in New Orleans, where the chances of running into Nick were slim to none. She was tempted to simply cancel out and save the hassle, but another part of her wanted to see Nick again.

She heard Deke's car before she saw it. As it turned into the driveway, she stubbed out another cigarette and left the living room. A car door slammed, and he walked the short distance between the flagstone breezeway and the back door. He made no effort to be quiet, but when he saw her, his eyes widened in mock surprise.

"Yo, look at this. You waiting up for me, baby?" He was wearing a different shirt from the one he'd had on when he left the hospital, so she knew instantly that he'd been somewhere else after leaving Escavez. For a moment she was furious. Not because she cared if he was unfaithful. But if the media caught him with another woman, it would ruin him and tarnish her own image.

"I was concerned about Stephen and what the chief decided to do about it," she said evenly. "Is everything all right?"

"Didn't I tell you it would be?" He had the tails of his shirt in both hands now, pulling it free of his pants. "Where's the kid?"

"Stephen? He's in his room, hopefully asleep. But he didn't settle down after we left until he'd called the hospital to see that Cody was really okay. He spoke to Nick."

"He did or you did?"

"Stephen did, Deke. Don't you think I know not to initiate a call to a man you hate?"

"That bastard." Muttering, he went to the bar and poured himself a straight shot. After tossing it back, he pointed to her, still holding the glass. "I don't want Stephen over there again, even when the kid comes home from the hospital, you hear me? I've gotta get back to the city tomorrow for a couple of days, but I don't want to hear that either of you has been within fifty yards of Santana's place."

"We won't go, don't worry." Amber turned for fear he'd read the look in her eyes. Freedom for a couple of days!

"I'm not worried, darlin'," he said, smiling suddenly. Now that he'd laid down the law, he allowed himself to feel the warmth of the whiskey. "I've got that bastard right where I want him this time. He won't take a chance on pissing me off."

"What do you mean?"

Deke snapped off the overhead light and nudged her toward the hall leading to their bedroom. As he passed the bar, he snagged the whiskey bottle. He took off the cap, holding it in his teeth and talking around it as he poured himself another drink. "He's got himself in some serious shit by not securing that weapon. A kid's been shot, never mind that it's his own. He'll lay low now, waiting to see if I'm serious about pushing it."

"And are you?" Amber asked. She almost trembled with the need to slap the satisfied smirk off his face.

He replaced the cap and draped his arm around her neck. "Hell, yes. Wait and see."

"Deke, are you sure you want to do this?"

"Why? You want to plead for mercy for him?"

With her stomach fluttering, she said, "Forget this is Nick Santana, Deke. No matter who it was, I'd want you to consider how he must feel."

"Well, I'm listening, honeybun."

"I'd just ask you to remember that his partner was killed a few months ago and he was shot up pretty bad himself then. Now his son has come close to dying from his own negligence, and no one's more aware of that than Nick. On top of everything else, he's scared his ex-wife's going to try to take Cody away from him. Don't you think all that's punishment enough? Why would you want to add to his misery?"

"Because he's trash! He's crap!" Deke removed his arm abruptly and shoved the bedroom door open. "He came from sorry-ass people on the wrong side of the tracks, but he's reinvented himself into some kind of folk hero. It galls me to see folks buying into it. You, of all people, ought to want him exposed for the scum he is. You didn't dump him because he was such a nice guy with a bright future, did you, sugar? Hell, no. You dumped him because he wasn't good enough for Leo Castille's daughter."

"That's not true! We were just kids, Deke. We broke up for the reasons most kids do. We outgrew each other."

"Ha! If he'd been Kate's brother with a trust fund from his dead daddy, I'll bet you'd have been singing another tune."

"You make me sound like a snob, Deke."

"You *are* a snob, Amber," he said, giving a disgusting snort.

She could see there was no reasoning with him tonight. "We need to get to bed. It's almost 3:00 a.m." She opened a drawer to look for a nightgown.

"He's got that sorry-ass law degree he makes sure everybody knows about—only he's above practicing like other lawyers. Instead, he sucks his way up the ladder at the NOPD." He poured himself another drink.

"Do you need to set the alarm?" Amber asked, slipping her robe off. She realized he was looking at her bruised arms, and hastily pulled the robe back on.

"Fuck the alarm! I'm talking, here, so why are you trying to change the subject?"

"You've explained your position, Deke. You're not going to cut Nick any slack. Okay. Now let's go to bed. Please."

He was looking at her. "How do you know what's going on between him and his ex-wife?"

"I don't, for heaven's sake! I've never seen his ex-wife. I don't even know her name. He only mentioned it as a possibility. He was...worried about it, Deke. The way people do when they're very upset."

"And when they've got a very friendly shoulder to cry on."

"He wasn't crying on my shoulder." She reached for a bottle of lotion just to have something to do with her hands. As she rubbed her palms together, she said, "Actually, the person who seemed the most concerned about Nick was that policewoman. Pamela something-or-other."

"Jealous?" One of Deke's eyebrows went up.

Amber took in a slow, deep breath, determined not to let him know he'd hit a nerve. "We have truly exhausted this subject, Deke," she said, grabbing a pillow. "I can't take any more tonight. And if you can't leave it alone, I'm going to sleep on the couch. It's late. I'm tired."

She got all the way to the foot of the bed before he caught her, bringing her around with a vicious yank. She winced with pain as he gripped the bruised flesh of her upper arms. He gave her a little shake, forcing her to look at him.

"You can't take any more?" he repeated, smiling coldly. "You think you can flirt half the night with a bastard like Santana and then pick a fight so you'll have an excuse not to sleep with me?"

"Deke, you're hurting me."

"I don't give a shit! You act like a slut, you deserve a little pain!"

"You're drunk, Deke. Let me go." She strained away from him, trying to dislodge his hold on her arms.

"She's not a slut! You let her go!" Stephen stood in the doorway in his boxer shorts, his eyes the same blazing blue as his father's. He was barefoot and naked from the

waist up, a slim, adolescent replica of Deke. He held a
portable phone in his hand. "You see this? You let her go
or I'm dialing 911. And if you think you can stop me before I can get the number, think again, Dad. You're drunk.
I'm not. I can outrun you even if I'm not big enough to
overpower you." He waved the phone in front of him like
a matador waving a cape. "Come on, you miserable,
stinking shithead!"

Out of sheer astonishment, Deke let Amber go. "Stephen," she murmured, hurrying to him. Taking his arm,
she hustled him out of the bedroom and closed the door.
There was a crash as Deke threw something at the door.
His drink, she guessed.

"One less for him to guzzle tonight, the jerk," Stephen
said with disgust.

Amber pulled him down the hallway, not slowing until
they reached the den. "Hang on to the phone in case he
decides to take you up on that challenge," she said, unconsciously stroking her arms.

"Are you okay?" he asked, studying her with concern.
He made a sharp sound when he saw the bruises on her
arm. "Too bad it wasn't him instead of Cody I nearly
killed tonight."

"You shouldn't say that, Stephen."

"Is there anything you can do? Put ice on it or something?"

"No. I'll be all right. And thanks for stepping in. Although you were taking a big risk."

"Naw, no risk. When he saw I had the phone, he knew
he'd been outmaneuvered. He doesn't want the publicity,
Amber."

"I know, but I was afraid he was beyond thinking rationally." She gave a deep sigh.

"I can't figure out why he keeps doing it. Someday

you're bound to report it, and then the jig's up. Everybody'll know him for the creep he is."

"He's sick." Amber sank down on the sofa. "Sometimes I think *I'm* sick for putting up with it this long." She reached up and pulled him down to sit beside her. "I don't think I *could* put up with it if it weren't for you, Stephen."

He studied her face with anxious eyes. "I worry about when I might not be around. He could kill you, Amber. People like him walk a pretty narrow line. One tantrum too many and he might cross that line."

"But not while you're here." She slipped her arm around his waist and leaned her head against his young shoulder. "I love you, Stephen."

Pale gray light was filtering through the long windows of the den when Deke touched her on the arm. She came awake with a start, her heart jumping in her chest. "What…"

"Shh. It's just me, baby."

"Deke…no, I don't—"

"It's okay, sweetheart." His hand moved toward her face, and she angled away in alarm. "Ah, don't, baby." He touched her, a soft feathering of his fingers on her cheek. "Come back to bed with me, darlin'. I don't know what makes me lose my temper like that. God, I never want to hurt you. You're everything to me. I'm sorry. You know I'm sorry, don't you, sweetheart?"

She scooted to the corner of the couch, watching him warily.

"Ah, Jesus, I hate it when you look at me like that. I'm sorry, baby. You believe me, don't you?" He reached for her. "Come on, let's be together in bed where we belong. I won't do anything—I'll just put my arms around you."

She whimpered as his hands gripped her bruised arms.

"Oh, shit, did that hurt? Damn." He bent and kissed the dark streaks. "I was drunk, baby. It was the booze, you know? I won't do it again, swear to God. This is the last time."

He was pulling her up. With his arm around her waist, he urged her for the second time that night toward their bedroom. He kissed her temple. "I love you, Amber."

She sighed with dull acceptance. "If you hurt me again, Deke, Stephen is going to kill you."

TWENTY

"We need to talk, Kate."

Sam stood at the door of Kate's office. She punched the button on her recorder and laid it on the open chart in front of her. Sam had been in surgery all morning and Leo wasn't feeling well. Since arriving at the clinic at 8:00 a.m., she'd seen more than a dozen patients, and the afternoon promised to be just as hectic. She'd skipped lunch to get the charts caught up. She was hungry and irritable and uptight.

"Can't it wait? I need to finish these charts."

"They can wait. This can't." He came inside and closed the door behind him.

Kate folded her hands on top of the file. She'd spent the weekend rehearsing ways to discuss their encounter Friday night. As much as she wished it, it wasn't something they could pretend hadn't happened. She watched him take a seat in the chair opposite her desk and cock his ankle over his knee. His white jacket fell open, revealing a wine-colored pullover and khaki pants. He sat slightly forward, folding his hands over one foot. She turned her eyes to the window rather than look at him. "Okay, you're here. Talk."

"We need to discuss what happened so we can decide where we go from here."

"We had sex—that's what happened. It was a mistake." She shrugged, looking at her folded hands. "The storm, the...thing with Cody, stress overload. We could both probably name several reasons we got carried away." She looked at him then. "It happened, but it won't happen again."

"I don't know about you, but nothing like that's ever happened to me before."

"You've never been in a situation where things just spiraled out of control?" Her tone was skeptical.

"Things, yes. Sex, no." His dark eyes were watchful. "Is this some kind of coping mechanism you picked up in Boston?"

"That sounds as if you're saying it was mostly me," Kate said, feeling her temper rise. "I don't recall you voicing any caution at the time."

"To tell the truth, I gave up thinking straight about the time you peeled off that T-shirt."

She stared at him in outrage. "I took my shirt off because it was wet! And you suggested it, damn it!"

"Did I say otherwise?"

"You insinuated—"

"No, I stated that for me, caution went the way of the wind the minute you took off your shirt."

She stood and walked to the window. "What is the point of this conversation, Sam?"

"I'm wondering why, Kate. Unlike you, I don't dismiss something I found so mind-blowing as meaningless. We aren't reckless people, either of us. We were in a public place Friday night, storm or no. Anybody could have—"

"No. By then, the track was totally deserted." With her back to him, she adjusted the blinds to see outside. "And it was raining cats and dogs. Nobody was going to see."

"Can you honestly say you thought about that at the time?"

She was silent, embarrassed because it was true. Behind

her, she heard the sound of his indrawn breath. "I'm sorry" he muttered. "But hell, Kate…"

She watched a pregnant woman with a toddler making her way across the parking lot. "I wish I could explain what happened. I've spent most of the weekend worrying about it, and I'm no closer to figuring it out than I was ten minutes after we… After it was over."

She turned to look at him. "What I said earlier about stress is true. Maybe not for you, but for me. I was in a state over what had happened with Cody. Looking back, the whole evening's pretty much a blur. I did go to the track to try to cope, just as you said. Then you showed up, the storm was raging—" She shrugged. "It was an emotional moment that ended in a very human way. We were consenting adults, no one was hurt by what happened, so I vote for putting it behind us."

"'Consenting adults.'"

"At the time, yes. But I think we're both agreed the last thing we want is to get involved that way again."

"Are you on the Pill?"

She sighed and shoved her hands into her pockets. "No. But I'm not worried about that."

"Why not?"

"It's a very remote possibility. I've got bigger things to worry about and—"

"A pregnancy wouldn't be a big thing to you?"

"I didn't say that."

"You'd tell me if the 'remote possibility' became a reality, wouldn't you?"

She met his eyes. "Of course."

"Swear to God?"

She laughed and tucked a strand of hair behind her ear. "Trust me."

Sam leaned back in his chair, looking at her. He was silent for so long, she frowned. "What?"

He seemed bemused. "Every now and then I remember why I fell in love with you."

She felt her heart take a flying leap. A part of her wanted to ask why, yearned for details, longed to believe him. Dismissing that as foolishness, she said, "Knock it off, Sam. We went there, did that. We're at different places in our lives now. Let's leave the past where it belongs."

"Then how about talking about the recent past?"

"As in…"

"What happened with Cody."

"What's to talk about? I've had some…difficulty lately, but I'm working on it."

He was nodding, as if sorting through her words. "Before we got…distracted the other night with other things, you mentioned wanting a change from trauma care. I know it's a difficult specialty. Burnout's common. Is that what happened? Or is it something else?"

"I've told you—"

He put up a hand to stop her. "I know what you told me, but I know what I saw. I'd be stupid if I didn't have some concerns. What if you unraveled while treating a patient here in the clinic? Not only would you be exposed in a legal sense, but Leo and I would be, too."

He wasn't going to let it go. He was going to keep on until he convinced Leo she wasn't worth the hassle. And yet, how could she trust him with the truth? It was going to sound weird. *She* was going to sound weird.

With a resigned sigh, she sat down at her desk. "I'm telling you this in confidence, Sam. Since you aren't going to give me a minute's peace and—" she put up a hand when he started to speak "—and since I can see your point about the clinic's liability, if I try to explain, maybe you'll back off a little."

"I'm listening," he said.

"I'm sure it's just stress. You mentioned burnout. It's the most logical explanation. I think—"

"*What* could be stress? *What* could be burnout? Don't beat around the bush, Kate. Spit it out."

"Look, do you mind? This is difficult. I'm trying to tell you, but in my own way."

"Okay."

"For a while I've been having these...these...uh, sort of...moments when I see...things." She found a spot on the desk and polished it industriously with one finger. "They come and go, but mostly they seem to occur while I'm treating patients who have suffered truly serious injury."

"What comes and goes? What sorts of moments?"

She jumped up. "I'm trying to tell you! It's...not easy," she added defensively.

This time he waited in silence.

"Flashbacks," she said. "I've been seeing bits and pieces of some kind of...incident, and the best way I can describe it is...like a flashback of a previous experience. Or something. I don't know what or why. But they come over me suddenly, I never expect them, and I can't seem to do anything to control them. They're like a movie in slow motion with distorted sound. Except the pictures are all disjointed. They don't make any sense."

She sank back into her chair and, lowering her head, rubbed her temples wearily. Then she lifted her gaze to his. "You mentioned burnout, and you're right. It is common in trauma medicine. I might be having something like posttraumatic stress syndrome. It's very scary." She glanced up at him, ready to jump all over him if he dared to dismiss what she was telling him. But he was listening intently.

"Go on," he said.

"Well, if it's PTSS, that would mean that I'm flashing

back to traumatizing events, right? But if that's the case, why don't I recognize what I'm seeing? Because it's not any specific E.R. trauma I've ever experienced. I mean, I see blood and lights and guns. I feel panic and hear a rushing, roaring sound—and people screaming."

"Wow."

"Yeah, wow." Suddenly she gave a self-conscious laugh. "Listen to me. You'll think I've really gone off the deep end." She shrugged. "As I said, the whole thing is pretty...unsettling. For a doctor." Her smile faded as her eyes strayed to the window. There was no need to get specific about that last day at St. Luke's. Or to mention the hallucination when she'd treated Pamela LaRue.

Sam was sitting forward now. "And this happens only when you're dealing with patients?"

"Mostly in high-stress times, such as with...with Cody." Kate sighed and pinched the bridge of her nose. "If you don't count the nightmares."

"You have nightmares, too?"

"I'm all screwed up, right?"

"Are the nightmares like the daytime flashbacks?"

She shrugged. "Pretty much. So now can you see why I haven't tried to explain?"

"It could be posttraumatic stress. From what you've described, the experience sounds a lot like what goes on in the emergency room." He rubbed the side of his cheek thoughtfully. "Except for the noise—the roaring, rushing sound. You say nothing you've experienced is similar to the events you see when you flash back?"

"Not really."

"What about repressed memory?"

"What about it?"

"Could some trauma you've repressed be trying to surface?"

She wasn't going to tell him about her obsession with

the boating accident so long ago. As it was, she'd revealed far more than she intended to. "That's enough about my hang-ups," she said with an embarrassed laugh.

"Just one more thought," Sam said, leaning back. "I've had patients who were Vietnam vets. Without exception, they benefited from counseling. Have you considered that?"

"Are you suggesting I need a psychiatrist?" What a dope she'd been to tell him. She'd just given Sam enough rope to hang her with.

"I'm not suggesting anything, Kate. It was a random thought. But now that I have a better understanding of what's going on, at least I can be prepared to deal with it…if it should happen again."

"It's not going to happen again."

"I hope you're right."

She worried in the days that followed about what Sam might do now that he knew about the flashbacks. It still amazed her that she'd told him. Once started, she'd just seemed to spill it all out. Leo would have been the logical person to tell. Never Sam. But time passed and he did nothing.

The one bright spot was that Cody broke all records getting well.

"It's amazing how that boy has bounced back," Amber said, watching as Cody paddled on a float in Victoria's pool while Mallory circled him like a playful otter. "It was only three days and he was out of the hospital."

"Four, if you don't count the night he went in." Nick sat forward, elbows on his knees, holding a can of beer. "Another twenty-four hours and they were going to have to use restraints to keep him in that bed."

"He's young and healthy," Kate said. "If we could dis-till the essence of that, we'd cut hospital stays in half."

"Speaking of distilling, who needs another beer?" Amber, in funky sunglasses, reclined on a chaise with her drink balanced on her tummy. One knee was raised, showing her long legs to advantage in a black French-cut bikini. A white mesh coverup protected her arms and shoulders, which she'd confided to Kate were prone to freckling if she got too much sun.

"Look out, Mallory!" Nick started up from his chair as the float tilted and almost dumped Cody. "He can't get his dressing wet."

"Aw, she knows that. She's okay." Stephen sat nearby, dangling his legs in the water.

"Why don't you go in, Stephen?" Kate suggested. He'd been sitting for a long time with the grown-ups and must be getting bored.

"I'm okay."

"I'm okay, you're okay, we're all okay," Amber said, smiling and wagging her empty beer can. "Beer, please, Stephen. I'm dry, honey."

"Maybe you better not have any more," Stephen said, frowning.

Amber rolled her eyes. "He's afraid Deke will show up and find us all having a good time without him."

"Well, you are on vacation, after all," Kate said.

"Yeah, and it's great! Although…" Amber put a finger to her lips and glanced at Nick who'd moved to the edge of the pool. "Don't tell anyone—we're not supposed to be within a mile of Nick."

Kate frowned. "Why not?"

"Deke said so."

"But why?" Kate was still bewildered.

Amber batted her eyelashes. "The green-eyed monster."

"Deke's jealous of Nick?"

"Big-time."

Kate's gaze moved to Nick, who was now skirting the edge of the pool, anxiously watching his son. "Does he have reason, Amber?"

"Not yet."

Kate looked at her. "'Not yet'?"

"Stephen, I'd like another beer, please," Amber said, this time in a firmer tone. "And so would Nick."

Stephen gave Nick a surly look. "Is that right?"

"Stephen…" Amber said.

"I'm fine," Nick told her, lifting his beer slightly.

"You've had enough, Amber," the boy said. "No kidding."

Amber drew a deep breath, rising from the chaise. The cover-up started to slip from one shoulder, and she quickly pulled it back. "The men in my family like to give orders."

"Deke's gonna be here soon so y'all can rehearse the performance for Saturday night," Stephen said. "What if he shows up early?"

Amber gave Kate a what-did-I-tell-you look.

"I'm serious, Amber," Stephen said, intercepting the look.

"Oh, all right. I have to go potty anyway."

"There's iced tea and lemonade," Kate said, rising to go with her. Amber *had* had enough. "I'll get it."

Nick looked up. "Need any help there?" His eyes were on Amber, weaving slightly now that she was on her feet.

"Whoooo-eee!" Giggling, Amber clutched at Kate's arm. "The world's ju-ussst a li-it-tle bit unstable, if you know what I mean."

Nick started forward, but Stephen moved to intercept him.

"If she needs help, I'll do it," the boy said.

Nick put out a hand. "No problem."

"We can manage," Kate said. She slipped an arm

around Amber's waist and guided her across the patio. "A little too much beer and heat. Brings on dehydration. Come on, Amber. Let's get you inside where it's cool. You might want to lie down awhile."

"Sober up before the big bad wolf comes back, huh?"

Kate opened the French doors. "The sobering-up part is right."

It was cool and quiet inside. Amber headed unsteadily to the small powder room just off the kitchen. After a minute or two, she came out, then headed for the sofa. Dropping with a sigh, she flopped back and closed her eyes. "Whoa! The world is really spinning."

"Lemonade coming up." Kate poured the beverage over ice in a tall container.

"Typical Kate," Amber muttered, her arm over her eyes. "Always the responsible one, and me always the screw-up. Have you ever screwed up, Kate?"

"Yes." Kate snapped on a plastic lid and poked a straw into the top.

"Liar, liar, pants on fire."

Kate walked to the sofa. "Here. You don't have to get up. The cup's sealed, so you can drink it through the straw." As Amber took it, the wide sleeve of the cover-up fell away revealing the bruises on her upper arm. Kate waited until she'd finished the lemonade, then took the container. "Better?"

"I'll let you know when I'm back from Disneyland."

Kate reached for a cotton throw and covered her, then sat beside her on the sofa. Amber's eyes were closed, but Kate sensed the tension in her. She lifted Amber's arm and gently traced an ugly purple mark just above her elbow. "What happened, Amber?"

"Uh-oh. Lecture time, right?"

"No lecture, just concern. How'd you get this?"

"Fell in the shower."

"Try to be a little more original," Kate said dryly.

"Heard that one before, huh?"

"These bruises are recent and they're deep."

"Some men don't know their own strength." Amber freed her arm and pulled her sleeves down to her wrists. Her mouth twisted. "Deke gets carried away sometimes."

"How often is 'sometimes,' Amber? Tell me what's going on, here."

Amber managed a low, bitter laugh. "Nothing that you can help, Kate. Deke's hardly the teddy bear his fans like to think he is, but he's not a complete Neanderthal. He knows when he crosses the line. We understand each other."

"Those bruises tell me he's crossed the line, Amber. I just wonder how often. These situations don't get better—they tend to get worse."

"I'm tired, Kate. Don't nag. Let me rest for a little bit. I've gotta be together before *he* gets back. We'll talk later."

"Promise?"

"Cross my...heart..."

She was out. Kate sat without moving for a moment. For some reason, her own heart was racing. She was shocked by Amber's predicament, but uncertain why it felt so threatening to her. With slightly unsteady hands, she tucked the throw snugly around Amber, then stood. Oddly, she thought of Charlene Miller. But there could be no comparison of Amber with a woman like Charlene, she told herself.

She was on her way back to the kitchen when she sensed movement in the hall. Turning, she saw her mother and realized Victoria must have heard everything. For a moment their gazes locked, then Victoria turned and walked back down the hall.

TWENTY-ONE

After a week of intermittent rain, Saturday dawned bright, beautiful and hot, as was usual for Bayou Blanc's summer Fais Do-Do Festival. Kate found herself looking forward to it. She'd been unable to talk her mother into venturing out, even for a little while, and the prospect of going alone wasn't as much fun. But Amber had promised to try to find an hour to stroll around with her, provided Deke was satisfied with their rehearsal.

Kate arrived about 4:00 p.m. and was immediately caught up in the sounds and smells and carnival atmosphere. Off-key calliope music blared amid the squeals and shouts of kids of all ages twirling, zipping, spinning and dipping on gravity-defying rides.

Meandering through the crowd, she gawked at freak shows and resisted hucksters offering every imaginable tacky carnival memento. The food booths, though, set apart a Louisiana festival from all others. There were dozens along the perimeter of the fairgrounds, and crowds were ten deep in front of each, waiting for crayfish tails, fried alligator on a stick, turtle soup, fried softshell crabs, boiled crabs, shrimp in a dozen varieties, oysters raw and fried, gumbo as-you-like-it. Nobody left Bayou Blanc's Fais Do-Do hungry.

Kate strolled past the entertainment area looking for Amber, whose performance with Deke was scheduled for later that night. Until then, the crowd would be entertained by a variety of talent, local and imported. Nothing was too hokey for the fun-loving crowd. At a refreshment booth near the outdoor stage, she spotted Amber chatting with Nick Santana. So much for Deke's order to stay away from Nick.

"Hi, Amber. Nick."

"Kate! You made it, *chère*." Amber gave her a hug. "Nick and I were just reminiscing about the time we ate a ton of junk at the food booths and decided to ride the Zephyr. Then we panicked and the operator had to make an emergency stop so I could get off and upchuck."

"You panicked, I didn't," Nick said, smiling.

Kate grinned. "I remember that night. We were in eighth grade. But I would have thought you'd want to forget."

"Only the sickie part," Amber said, giving Nick a sultry look. She was already in costume—a bloodred, low-cut gypsy blouse with a full, gathered skirt in a splashy print cinched at the waist with a black cummerbund. Large gold hoop earrings dangled nearly to her shoulders. She might have been from another century.

Kate looked around curiously for Deke. "Where's the king of talk?"

Amber lifted her hair from her neck and fanned herself with one hand. "Gone to find another guy to work the electronics for our act. He didn't like the way the original soundman was doing things, so phfft! He's out."

Kate glanced at her watch. "He's cutting it pretty close, isn't he?"

"I tried to tell him that." Amber shrugged. "He wasn't in the mood for advice."

Was he ever? Kate turned to Nick. "Is Cody here?"

Nick scanned the crowd clustered at the foot of the stage where a rock band was performing. "Over there. With Mallory and Stephen. He begged to come, but as soon as Amber's act is over, I'm taking him home. I checked with Sam about bringing him at all, considering the heat and the excitement, but he said let him do what he wanted within reason."

"I agree, so long as he doesn't overdo. He's bound to be stir-crazy by now."

"I'll say. It's been like trying to keep a mustang in a pen since he got home from the hospital, but, lucky for Cody, Mallory and Stephen have been great about keeping him entertained."

Amber grabbed Kate's arm. "Look, Kate, there's Sam!"

Forcing herself to turn casually, Kate spotted him easily. He was with Diane Crawford, who looked nothing like she did at the clinic. In a short shift of bright yellow that bared her tanned arms and long legs, she looked smart and sexy. She, not Sam, saw Kate and Amber, but she looked straight through them before snagging his arm and steering him in the opposite direction.

Amber snickered and lapsed into her Cajun persona. "*Mais non,* look at that. Nurse Ratched has got herself one fine date for the Fais Do-Do, *chère.* And she isn't planning to share, no."

"Behave yourself, Amber." Kate turned away from the sight of Diane clinging to Sam as if she couldn't walk without help. "I haven't sampled any of the food yet. Who's hungry?"

"Me," Nick said. "And the kids. Tell you what. I'll go get something and bring it back here." Nick signaled Cody. "The jambalaya's best at the last booth. And the Cajun kabobs are a big hit at the booth next to it. Why don't I pick up enough for all of us? Amber, can you fix it so we can eat backstage where they've got tables and chairs set up with fans?"

"Leave it to me. How about it, Kate?"

"Sure. Let me give you some money." She reached into

the pocket of her khaki shorts, but Nick stopped her. "I'll get it." He waved away her objection, already heading toward the kids.

"He's such a nice guy," Kate said, watching him drape an arm around Cody's shoulders. Mallory and Stephen fell into step beside them, heading for the food booths.

"He's better than nice, Kate."

Kate turned and caught the look on Amber's face. "What are you doing, Amber? Somebody's bound to mention that Nick was here, and then what? Do you think it's worth it?"

Amber's smile became a little tight. "Shouldn't you be worrying about your own love life, Kate? Diane Crawford looked pretty territorial hanging on to Sam like that."

"She's his nurse. They're close. What Sam and I had was over five years ago. We don't—"

She turned as Amber put her finger to her lips and gestured behind her. Sam.

"Where's Diane," she asked casually.

"Diane? I have no idea. I only saw her for a minute or two. I just wondered if you wanted some company while you waited for Amber's act to begin."

Shrugging, Kate gave in to the inevitable.

"Tired?" Sam asked, watching Kate rub her forehead wearily.

"A little." They were both nursing beers at a table reserved for VIPs, compliments of the festival management, thanks to Amber. A fan stirred the hot night air, while bursts of laughter from the audience punctuated snippets of Deke and Amber's dialogue onstage.

"I can't believe I'm still here," Kate said, looking over the rowdy spectators. "I wouldn't do this for anybody except Amber."

Her gaze wandered to the two on stage. It amazed Kate to see them radiating charm and humor. Only minutes before, they'd had a heated, knock-down-drag-out argument. Returning from his quest to find a new soundman, Deke had nearly gone up in flames when the first person he'd spotted was Nick Santana. If he and Amber hadn't been obligated to do the headliner act, Kate suspected that Deke would have grabbed Amber then and there and hauled her off to New Orleans. The way the man talked to his wife was appalling. Not for the first time, Kate wondered why Amber put up with it. The act was half over, but it had lost much of its appeal for Kate.

"She's very good up there," Sam said, watching Amber captivate the crowd.

"According to Amber, they've done quite a bit of entertaining as a couple since Amber Lifestyles took off." Kate watched Amber walk seductively across the stage, one hand on her hip, smiling at the audience. She turned with a flash of long legs and began singing. The crowd went wild—shouts and whistles came from every direction. It was part of the act for Deke to stop her with one of his zingers, but the crowd hissed and booed him unmercifully, killing his line.

Chanting began from the front rows. "Amber! Amber! We want Amber!"

Kate watched him struggle to regain control of the audience, but in vain. Amber, intoxicated with her success, played shamelessly to the cheering throng.

"Uh-oh," Kate murmured. "I bet Deke didn't count on being upstaged by the little woman."

"Then he shouldn't have written a skit that showcased her talents rather than his own," Sam said. "She looks great, her timing's flawless, the crowd's in the palm of her hand and she's one of Bayou Blanc's own. He's second banana tonight whether he likes it or not."

"This is not a good thing, Sam, believe me."

"Enough about them." Sam shoved his chair back. "Let's go get another beer. The act's winding down anyway, and I don't think I want to be around to hear him tell her how pissed he is that she was such a big success."

"You may have a point," Kate murmured, wincing as someone at the back of the crowd again heckled Deke, burying another punch line.

Sam caught her hand and pulled her out of her chair. "I've seen enough. How about a ride on the Ferris wheel?"

Kate sighed, looking at the Ferris wheel across the way. Her first kiss had been on the Ferris wheel when she was fourteen years old. She wondered how it would feel to be kissed by Sam while hanging high above the world.

She became flustered when he suddenly slipped his arm around her shoulders and gave her an affectionate hug. Kate responded instantly. Ever since that night in the rain, she'd been trying to deny she felt anything for Sam except some natural leftover emotion from their previously intimate relationship. But with his impulsive hug, she had an equally impulsive desire to lean her head against his shoulder and forget the pain they'd also shared in that relationship. It would be nice to give herself over to a few hours of plain, uncomplicated pleasure. Unfortunately, nothing with Sam could ever be uncomplicated.

They strolled past a booth selling small stuffed alligators. Was she interested? he asked with a silent lift of his eyebrows. She laughed. "Don't even think it!"

He gave her another squeeze, then his smile changed. "About Diane Crawford..."

"Where is she, anyway?"

"I told you I have no idea. She was with a couple of friends when I arrived with Mallory and Stephen. You know how kids are—they don't want to be caught dead with a parent. They took off, Diane didn't. You misinterpreted what you saw."

"It's none of my business if you're involved with your nurse," she said stiffly.

"People who work together shouldn't get involved personally," Sam said. "It usually spells disaster."

"I definitely won't disagree with that."

"I didn't finish," Sam said. "There are exceptions."

"You can't mean you and me. We did that, and it was definitely a disaster."

"Because I was a married man. If I'd been single then, we'd be married now, Kate. To each other."

While she was still thinking what to say to that, he took her arm and steered her back into the crowd. "I never got around to eating," he said, tucking her against his side. "I hear the alligator kabobs are great."

TWENTY-TWO

"Can I catch a ride, Kate? Deke is on a rampage, and would you believe he just walked off and left me to find a way home?" Amber shoved her curly hair away from her face, sending the large gold hoops in her ears swinging crazily. Without waiting for permission, she opened the door of Kate's car and got in, sighing as she settled back.

"What happened?" With a glance into the rearview mirror, Kate pulled into the line of cars leaving the fairgrounds. Sam had driven off a few minutes earlier with Mallory and Stephen.

"He's drunk and jealous and I'm fed up. I've just about had it, Kate." Digging into her bag, she pulled out a pack of cigarettes. Kate noticed her hands were a little shaky, but smoking wasn't something she could tolerate, no matter how needy the smoker.

"Don't light that, Amber. You know I hate it."

Amber rolled her eyes. "You never change, Kate."

"If Mother's cancer and Leo's cigar addiction aren't enough to make you quit, I'm not wasting any energy giving you the facts. So, did Deke catch you flirting with Nick?"

"No, but apparently plenty of people were willing to fill him in on what he missed." She tapped the unlit cigarette on her thigh. "What really ticked him off was the act. He's just green with envy because I was a big hit tonight."

"He wrote the skit. If you'd flubbed it, he'd be angry over that, too, wouldn't he?"

"Obviously you expect him to be logical. Forget that. He was forced to just stand by like one of the props, and it was more than he could take."

"It wasn't quite that bad," Kate said.

Amber's smile was wicked. "From Deke's point of view? Oh, yeah, it was."

"I hope he doesn't do anything rash," Kate replied with some concern. She glanced at Amber. "Do you think he might?"

"Who the hell knows? Maybe." She stared out the side window, no longer smiling. "That is, if he decides to come home at all. He could be out all night. Not that I care anymore."

"He seemed to be drinking quite a bit before you even got onstage, which could be why his performance wasn't up to par. But should he be out in that condition, Amber? What if he's stopped on a DUI? Worse yet, what if he's the cause of an accident and somebody else is hurt?"

"All of which would spell disaster for both of us professionally," Amber said bitterly. "I've warned him a dozen times, but you can't tell him anything. You've been around him lately. You see how he is."

Kate slowed at a caution light. "Has he ever considered A.A.?"

"And let the world know the king of talk has a drinking problem?" Amber snorted in disgust. "You must be kidding."

Kate shook her head. "I don't know what to say, Amber."

"What's to say?" Amber propped her elbow on the window frame and leaned her head into her hand. "I made a big mistake when I married him, Kate. What I have to do now is figure out how to undo that mistake without undoing my career. I've built my reputation by successfully juggling everything that's out there for today's woman—marriage, home, family and career. To get a divorce, I'd have to reveal a lot of shit that makes it all a sham."

Kate looked at her with sympathy. "Sometimes we don't have any choices left."

"Yes, but so far it's just *my* dirty little secret. A divorce tells the whole world I've screwed up again."

As Kate signaled to turn in at Leo's house, Amber said, "You know what, Kate? I don't think I'm up to dealing with Deke tonight if he should show up. He's drunk and pissed off. Anything can happen when he's like that. Do you think I could stay with you and Victoria?"

Without hesitation, Kate passed Leo's house and headed for Victoria's driveway. "You don't even have to ask. You know you're always welcome."

Kate wasn't surprised to find Victoria awake in the family room when they went inside. She was often sleepless at night, prowling around to cope with constant pain. Most of the time she refused narcotics, claiming that in the time she had left she'd rather be lucid than drugged. Kate had given up trying to manage her mother's illness her way. In truth, had Victoria been a patient without any personal ties to her, Kate would have had no choice but to allow her to call the shots.

"Hi, Victoria." Amber smiled, completely masking the unhappiness she'd displayed a few minutes before. "Kate invited me to stay over tonight. Hope that's okay."

"Of course. Take the middle bedroom." Victoria eased into a chair, then looked from one to the other. "You two look grim. What's happened?"

Still smiling, Amber spread both hands. "Does something have to happen before I can spend the night with my best friend?" She looked at Kate. "Just like old times, huh, *chère?* Victoria takes one look at us and the old radar goes up. You'd think we were—"

Closing her eyes, Victoria silenced Amber with a raised hand. "Where's Deke?"

Amber sighed. "Who knows? Who cares?"

"If I know him," Victoria said dryly, "when he comes home, he will expect to find you waiting for him, Amber."

"So he'll be in for a little surprise for a change." Amber flopped down on the sofa. "I don't have to ask his permission, Victoria."

"Oh? Since when?" She glanced at the phone. "You'd better phone Leo and tell him you're here. Otherwise Deke's likely to make an uncomfortable scene when he does get in."

"Good idea," said Kate, unsurprised by Victoria's insight. She was beginning to think her mother was aware of far more about Amber's situation than anyone guessed.

"And if he tries to force his way in," Victoria added, "I'll phone Nick. He's more than a match for Deke."

Kate went to the bar to break out a bottle of wine. It was going to be a long night.

Kate was awake early the next morning. Before going to bed, all three women had waited tensely, expecting an enraged Deke to show up any moment. From what Kate had observed, Deke seemed capable of more than simply ranting and raving at Amber when he was unhappy. Kate suspected he would see his wife's defiance as a direct challenge to his authority and control. Although he didn't show up, Kate never relaxed completely.

Amber had decided he must have gone back to New Orleans. Victoria had retired first, reluctantly agreeing to take something for pain. Amber had coped by drinking steadily until she'd fallen asleep on the sofa. Kate was last, finally going to bed to wrestle with a bewildering mix of emotions. Bayou Blanc was to have been her refuge while she sorted out the mess her life was in after fleeing Boston. Instead she'd found her mother terminally ill, her best friend in deep marital trouble, her ex-lover in her life again, and, most disturbing of all, the strange flashbacks were still plaguing her.

She had welcomed the morning and time to get up.

After dressing in shorts and a T-shirt, she went downstairs, noticing on her way to the kitchen that Amber was no longer on the sofa in the family room. Considering her own restlessness during the night, it surprised Kate that she hadn't heard Amber when she'd climbed the stairs and headed into the bedroom.

Kate started the coffee, then went outdoors to get the morning paper. It was a gorgeous summer day, sunny and not yet hot. Overhead the sky was a brilliant blue and the trees were alive with bird sounds. The air was already fragrant with sweet olive. She breathed in deeply with pleasure as she walked to the edge of the lawn and picked up the paper.

Across the way at the Yeagers' house, Nick Santana was out getting his paper, too. She waved, then decided to stroll a bit farther along the sidewalk.

No fence separated the boundary between Leo's house and Victoria's. She plucked a creamy white gardenia from a bush her mother had planted years ago and savored the fragrance. As she stood twirling the flower beneath her nose, her gaze wandered over the familiar grounds. But her reverie ended abruptly at the sight of Deke's big Mercedes parked in Leo's driveway. Which meant he hadn't gone to New Orleans, after all. On the off chance that he might be awake and stirring, Kate stuck to the sidewalk. A conversation with Deke Russo before breakfast was guaranteed to spoil a nice morning.

She was almost directly behind the Mercedes when she

realized someone was seated inside. One look told her the driver seemed to be sleeping, slouched low behind the wheel. Too drunk to make it inside, she thought with disgust. That would explain why Deke hadn't ripped the neighborhood apart looking for Amber.

With a sort of morbid curiosity, she ventured a little closer. Something about the way he was sitting seemed…wrong. Her eyes narrowed, then a wild leap of understanding sent her stumbling to the car. She fumbled frantically to open the door, then recoiled in shock. Her hand flew to her mouth and she choked back a strangled sound. She'd been wrong. Deke Russo wasn't sleeping; he was dead.

TWENTY-THREE

For a moment, Kate was rigid with horror. It was one thing to preside over the death of a gunshot victim in the controlled environment of the E.R. It was another to chance upon the dead husband of a best friend. Even as she resisted the evidence of her eyes, details were imprinted upon her mind. Gaping wound in his head. Blood and bits of brain matter spattered on the dash and door. One eye destroyed, the other blank and open. Gun in his slack fingers on the console.

Kate covered her mouth with one hand and fought the bitter rise of gall in her throat. She wanted to turn and run, to start the day over again without the obscenity of violent death. As she stood transfixed, a blue jay in a tall cypress gave a harsh cry. The sound seemed to start up her heart again and she was able to breathe. And move.

Knowing it was unnecessary, she felt for a pulse on his carotid artery. There was none. The bullet had entered his right temple and exited the back of his head slightly to the left of center. Surprisingly, there wasn't much blood except for the spattered dash and driver's door. She frowned at that, but she was too rattled to do more than note it. Stepping back, she looked at the blood on her trembling fingers and wished for something to wipe it off.

"What the hell!"

Nick Santana was at her shoulder. And then he was shouldering past her to get to the body. Moving in, he did what Kate had done, pressing two fingers against Deke's neck, seeking a pulse. He straightened. "Guess the ole right wing'll have to find a new guru. The king is definitely dead."

"Yes."

Nick wiped blood from his fingers with a handkerchief and passed it over to her, his eyes still on Deke. "We'd better call Bayou Blanc's finest."

"Yes."

Something in her voice made him look at her. "Shit! You're white as a ghost. You okay, Kate?"

"I'm okay. It's just…" She met his eyes. "So…close."

"Yeah. Where's Amber?"

"At… With Victoria. She spent the night with us."

"How about Stephen?"

Kate drew a deep breath. "Inside with Leo, I guess."

Nick looked toward Leo's garage. "Used to be a phone at Leo's workbench when we were kids. Is it still there?"

"What about that one?" She pointed to the cell phone in Deke's car. "Can't we use that?"

"Better not. It's a crime scene. Any violent death is." Before Nick could stop her, Kate leaned gingerly into the car, avoiding contact with Deke's body, and plucked the garage-door opener from the sun visor and activated it. Nick hurried inside as the door rolled up, grabbed the phone near the workbench and dialed 911. She heard him giving brief details in a clipped, no-nonsense voice. Breaking that connection, he dialed again, turning to face her as someone picked up.

"Yeah, hey, Sam. Nick. We've got Deke Russo in his car in Leo's driveway, shot in the head with the weapon beside him." He paused, listening, then looked at Deke. "Yeah, looks like suicide. Gun's still in his hand. I've called the cops, but I thought you'd like to be nearby when I tell Leo." He paused again. "No, but Kate's here."

Another pause. "Yeah, she found him a few minutes ago. I was out early, saw her open the car door.... No, she's with Victoria. Spent the night with Kate and her mama.... Yeah, no problem."

"He's on his way," Nick said after hanging up. "One of us needs to get Amber. It'll be better for Amber if she sees him without a bunch of people watching, don't you think?"

Kate put her hand to her head, still not quite able to shake her disbelief. *Deke, dead! Suicide? No way!*

"Come on, Kate. You've been around people shot in the head before. We need to tell his family. Now."

"Deke would never commit suicide," she declared, staring at the corpse.

"You can never second-guess these things," Nick said, moving backward toward Leo's house. "So, you want to tell Amber?"

"Amber. Ah, yes. I guess so."

He was already at the side door, between the breezeway and the garage. He pushed the bell. "Don't fool around, Kate. Tell her if she wants to see him before the cops, to get here fast."

"Right."

Kate started off across the lawn, but after only a few steps, she found herself picking up speed. And then she was running, pushed by the urgency of her errand and the horror that was filling her chest. Thank God Nick had been close by. He'd been surprised, but he'd quickly controlled his emotions. It had been Nick the homicide detective who'd taken charge, she realized.

Her hands were still shaking as she opened the door and slipped into the house. At the stairs in the foyer, she hesitated and looked up to find Victoria standing with one hand on the newel post at the top of the stairs.

"Mother." She started up. "Is Amber awake?"

"I believe I heard her in the bathroom a few minutes ago," Victoria said, studying her as she climbed the stairs. "What's wrong, Kate?"

Kate touched Victoria's hand. "Why don't you go down and pour yourself some coffee? I'll be there in a second."

"First, tell me what's wrong. Your hands are trembling."

"There's been a terrible accident, Mother. I need to talk to Amber."

Victoria glanced toward the bedroom Amber always used. "What kind of accident?"

Kate dropped her voice. "Please, Mother."

Amber appeared at the bedroom door, her hairbrush in one hand. "What's going on?"

She looked like a breath of fresh air in a yellow T-shirt and white shorts, Kate thought. The night before, Kate had left the clothes out for her, knowing she'd want clean things in the morning.

"Amber, there's been an accident. It's Deke." Now that she was facing her childhood friend, the words Kate had said to countless family members in the E.R. seemed utterly inadequate.

"What kind of accident?" Amber asked.

"He's... We found... Deke is...dead, Amber."

With the hairbrush clutched in both hands pressed to her breasts, Amber came forward. "Was it a car accident?"

"No, he's in his car, but—"

"But what, Kate?" Amber looked at her, waiting.

"We've called the police, but we didn't know— Do you feel up to going out there?"

Amber shook her head with impatience. "You're not making sense, Kate! You said Deke's dead, right?"

"Yes. I'm so sorry, Amber. He—"

Still shaking her head, Amber said, "But he didn't have an accident in his car? He's outside? Where?"

"In Leo's driveway. In the front yard."

"God." Amber dropped the brush and started down the stairs.

"Wait! Amber, I need to—" Kate rushed behind her, caught her as she reached the bottom of the stairs. "Please, wait a minute. Before you go... There's something you need to know about the way he died, Amber."

"'The way he died'?" Amber looked at her with confusion but without tears. Or anything else Kate might have expected. As Kate stared into Amber's gypsy-green eyes, she realized that she herself had reacted more emotionally to seeing Deke dead.

Shock, Kate told herself. *A natural human reaction that often masked terrible inner turmoil.* The textbook explanation scrolled across Kate's mind even as she sought a way to soften what would surely penetrate Amber's defenses.

"It's bad, Amber. I found him. I was out getting the paper and I saw his car. He was inside, and something about the way he was sitting made me go a bit closer to have a look."

Amber was nodding. Waiting.

"I opened the door, and I saw that he was...not alive."

"He was dead? In his car?" Amber looked bewildered. "How? Was it a heart attack? Did you check to be sure? Did you get Daddy to come out and—"

"I could see it was too late for that. He...he didn't have a heart attack. He was... It was a gun."

"'A gun'?" Amber's face was a study in astonishment. Then, after a moment, she said, "He has a gun in his glove compartment. He's a nut about carrying one for protection. I told him someday somebody was going to shoot him with his own gun." She looked at Victoria for confirmation. "Didn't I, Victoria? Victoria's heard me tell him that many times. People think guns are gonna protect them against criminals, but more often than not they get shot with their own weapons when criminals manage to overpower them. He's a crack shot, but what does that matter when you're drunk? He *was* drunk, we know that. I mean, when he left the festival he was already pretty bombed, and you can believe he didn't stop afterward. So now you're saying he's…h-he's…d-dead…and…and…"

"Hush, darling. Hush, now." Victoria put her arms around Amber as she broke into tears. "It's all right. You're going to be all right now." Murmuring softly, Victoria stroked her hair, meeting Kate's eyes with a look of such sadness that Kate felt her own eyes growing moist.

"Do…do you want to go out there, Amber?" she asked. "By now Nick has probably told Leo and Stephen."

Amber pulled back to look at Kate. "Nick? Nick's out there?"

"Yes."

Using her fingers, Amber wiped the tears from her eyes. "I'm okay. I can do this." She started toward the front of the house.

"Wait, Amber." At the door Kate put her hand over Amber's to stop her. "There's one more thing. We don't know, of course. We can't tell, but it looks as if… Nick thinks he…"

Behind them, Victoria stirred and gave an impatient sound. "Say it, Kate, for heaven's sake!"

Kate caught Amber's hand and squeezed it. "No one turned Deke's gun on him, Amber. It doesn't look like someone else did this. Deke shot himself."

TWENTY-FOUR

On the morning Deke Russo's body was discovered, Pamela LaRue was on her way to work, almost forty-five minutes early for the seven o'clock shift. When the call came through on the radio she recognized the address as being near where Nick and Cody were staying for the summer. Instead of turning right at the intersection as she left her neighborhood, she turned left. She called dispatch only as she approached Vermilion Lane. It paid to be one jump ahead of Escavez, who might have directed her elsewhere if she wasn't within spitting distance of the scene.

Pamela couldn't remember when she didn't want to be a cop. Her father had retired from the police force in Baton Rouge after thirty years, the last twenty spent as a homicide detective. Her mother had been a police dispatcher throughout Pamela's teen years. Although she'd wanted to apply to the police academy fresh out of high school, her parents had persuaded her to get a degree first, which she'd done at LSU. By the time she'd graduated, her folks were living in Bayou Blanc, and she'd applied there.

She was convinced it wasn't her excellent credentials that had won her the job, but her sex. Chief Escavez wouldn't have hired her, except at the time there were federal funds provided to small towns for increasing the number of cops on the street and Uncle Sam tended to look critically at the composition of police departments, gender-wise. She was the only woman in the previously all-male, blatantly chauvinistic Bayou Blanc Police Department. And she'd been trying to prove herself worthy of the job ever since. She was resigned to paying her dues as a rookie, but she longed to be assigned to the detective division.

Fat chance of that happening, she thought, scanning the curb for the address. At least, not as long as Howard Sloan was in charge.

Sloan was Escavez's flunky. He'd been handpicked and trained to dance to the chief's tune. Anytime Escavez was out of town, Sloan sat in as acting chief. Sloan had asked her out several times when she'd first hired on, but there was something about him that made her uncomfortable. Then he'd become downright nasty after she'd begun dating Nick.

Pamela pulled up to the curb in front of Leo Castille's house. As she got out of her car, she counted nine people clustered near a very large black Mercedes. The group was familiar. She saw at a glance that it was largely comprised of the same people who'd kept vigil in the hospital with Nick when Cody had been hurt. As she approached, she glimpsed the body in the open door of the Mercedes.

Nick greeted her. "Pam. You caught the call?"

"I was in the vicinity," she lied. She nodded at Sam Delacourt and Kate Madison, then looked behind them at Mallory and Cody. They stood well back, big-eyed with curiosity. Slightly apart from the group were Amber and Stephen Russo. Flanking them on either side were Victoria Madison and Leo Castille. She hoped she'd get a chance to question everyone, but that job would no doubt go to Howard Sloan.

Turning her attention once more to Deke's body, she addressed Nick. "What happened?"

"Appears to be suicide," Nick said. "Kate and I found

him a few minutes ago. We didn't realize he was dead, but once the car door was opened, well... You can see for yourself."

"What time was that, exactly?" Pamela asked, forcing herself not to dwell on the fact that Nick and Kate had been together at 6:00 a.m.

"Not long," Kate Madison said. "As Nick says, a few minutes."

"How long is a few minutes?" Pamela asked.

Nick looked at his watch. "Six...six-ten. I'm guessing. I wasn't thinking about the time."

"Why not, Nick? You're a professional."

"Not when I'm looking at the body of someone I know, Pam."

Pamela drew a breath. "Who opened the door?"

"I did," Kate replied.

Pamela studied the body, slumped sideways behind the wheel. It did indeed look like suicide, but you could never tell. One good thing—he hadn't been pulled out of the car, thus contaminating the evidence further.

The proper procedure in apparent suicides was clear. Pamela didn't have her father's years of experience, but she could hear him now. *"Never assume. In an apparent suicide—emphasis on the* apparent—*always treat the crime scene as if someone other than the victim pulled the trigger."*

She turned to Kate Madison. "Did you touch anything?"

"I checked to see if I could find a pulse. I couldn't. Sam did the same when he got here." Sam Delacourt nodded in agreement.

"Me, too," Nick said. "It was strictly a formality, Pam. Anybody could see he was dead and had been for quite a while. Look for yourself. Oh, Kate used the garage remote stuck in the visor. We called 911 from the garage phone."

"Why?"

"Why what?" he asked, not understanding.

"Why was anything touched? Why couldn't you have used the phone in the house?"

"I actually grabbed the remote without thinking, Pamela," Kate said. "I'm sorry."

Pamela nodded after a quick look at Nick, then stepped a little closer to examine the car's interior. The gun still lay in Russo's slack fingers. It should go into a bag, and Russo's hands should be bagged, too, she thought, wishing for a crime-scene kit. The interior and exterior of the Mercedes should be carefully dusted for prints, especially the doors. She had nothing in her car except her radio and her lunch. Whoever Escavez sent should have what they needed, but it was the last hour of the midnight shift. Anybody getting the call would be tired and irritable. Possibly sloppy. In the two years she'd been a part of BBPD, she'd seen some very poor detective work, especially on this shift. God, she wished the chief would let her collect the evidence.

However, until her colleagues got here...

Pamela turned away from the body and pulled her notebook from a leather holder anchored on her belt before glancing up to locate Amber Russo. The widow stood well back from the car, dry-eyed and silent. Stephen stood close beside her, blank-faced. Both were pale.

"I'd like to talk to you for a moment, Ms. Russo," Pamela said in a gentle tone.

"Amber. Call me Amber."

"Amber." Pamela nodded with a sympathetic smile. "First, I'm sorry for your loss."

"Thank you."

"Was there anything about your husband's behavior lately that suggested he was contemplating suicide?"

"Can't this wait?" Nick asked with a frown. "Jesus,

Pam, she's hardly had a chance to take it all in. She needs a minute."

With her eyes still on Amber, Pamela asked, "Do you need some time? Would you like to wait awhile?"

Amber managed a ghost of a smile for Nick. "I'm okay. Really." She met Pamela's gaze. "And, no, I didn't have a clue Deke was thinking of suicide."

"Was there a note?"

When Amber shook her head, Pamela glanced around the group and got the same reaction. No note.

"When did you see your husband last?"

Amber looked at Kate, as if for confirmation. "Last night after the performance, which was about eleven-thirty. Right, Kate? We finished and Deke wanted to party on. I didn't, so I got a ride with Kate and then decided to spend the night at her house."

"Was that unusual?"

"Kate's been living in Boston. But when we were kids we frequently slept over at each other's house."

"I meant was it unusual for you to spend the night away from your husband when the two of you were staying at your father's home?"

"I suppose so."

"Then why last night? Did something happen?"

"He was drunk."

"And was that unusual?"

"No, he's often drunk." Amber rubbed her forehead with one finger. "Or I guess I should speak in the past tense now, huh? He *was* often drunk."

"And you preferred sleeping away from him when he was drunk?"

Amber gave a short laugh. "Would you like sleeping with a drunk?"

Pamela made a notation. "Did Mr. Russo have any serious problems? Anything that would push him to this extreme?"

"His ratings were down."

Pamela realized Nick was listening as intently to Amber's replies as she. "His show was in trouble?"

Amber shrugged. "Not enough that it would have been cancelled, but Deke resented the things they were doing, like throwing out ideas when he felt he knew what worked and what didn't. But they said it needed, you know, sort of a jump start. They brought in a woman, which did not sit well with Deke."

"A woman?" Pamela looked up from the notebook. "Would Mr. Russo resent input from a woman?"

"Absolutely. If you knew him, you wouldn't even ask that question."

"Did he dislike women?"

"Amber—" There was caution in Nick's tone as he moved to stand beside her. Pamela had a thought that he wanted to take the widow's hand, but he settled for simply standing close beside her. Protectively. As if some kind of unspoken communication existed between them. "These questions should wait until Amber has had a chance to absorb the shock of Deke's death, Pamela," he said.

Pamela. She wasn't Pam anymore. Was Nick letting her know whose side he was on in this one? Why? she wondered, studying his expression.

She turned to Amber. "One last question," she said, ignoring Nick's grim look. "Are you surprised your husband committed suicide?"

"Yes," Amber said flatly. "Stunned. It's a total shock."

"Why?"

Nick made a sound. "You said one question, Pamela."

Amber touched his arm. "It's okay, Nick." To Pamela, she said, "Deke was simply too egotistical to think of ending his own life. He didn't think any show of which he was the star could fail. If nothing else, he would stay alive simply to prove he was right and the station was wrong."

Nick took Amber's hand and squeezed it in an attempt to silence her, but she was too caught up in bitterness to heed him. "You want the truth, Officer LaRue? Deke enjoyed making my life hell too much to shoot himself."

"Okay, that's it." Nick moved to lead her toward the house, but she shook him off. "What's the point of pretending now, Nick? Everything will be out in the open once the publicity breaks. He couldn't run into a tree," she said bitterly. "No, not Deke. He had to go and kill himself."

"Take her inside, Leo," Nick ordered curtly.

Even as Leo moved toward Amber, Kate was beside her, slipping an arm around her and urging her toward the door. But Pamela knew she might not get another chance to ask one last question.

"Ms. Russo!" she called.

Amber paused, looking back at Pamela. "Yes?"

"Since you're convinced he wouldn't shoot himself, can you think of anyone who would want to murder him?"

She didn't expect an answer and she didn't get one.

The EMTs arrived with lights flashing but no siren. As the unit pulled up to the curb behind Pamela's car, a squad car from the BBPD screeched to a stop. Chief Escavez climbed out and adjusted his Stetson, then ponderously made his way up the driveway. Trailing him was Howard Sloan. A slight, short man whose sparse brown hair was slicked flat against his skull with styling gel, he made an almost-comical contrast with Waylon Escavez's bulk and height.

"What've we got here, missy?" Escavez demanded of

Pamela. Pushing back his hat, he frowned at Deke Russo's remains.

"An apparent suicide, Chief." Pamela tucked her notebook into her belt. "Mr. Russo was discovered between six and 6:10 a.m. by Dr. Madison and Mr. Santana. They both report finding him dead then. Dr. Delacourt arrived a few minutes later."

Escavez glanced around, settling his gaze on Sam. "You agree with that, Sam?"

"He's definitely dead, Chief."

"Well, hell, I can see that. I'm askin' for something official before we let the EMTs take him to the morgue."

Pamela edged back into the chief's line of vision. "We would need the coroner for that, Chief. I know Dr. Delacourt is a physician, but officially—"

Escavez gave her a fierce look. "Are you sayin' Sam Delacourt doesn't know a dead man when he sees one?"

"No, sir. But he can't categorically state that it was a suicide. Sir."

"Why the hell not? He's layin' there with his brains splattered all over the place and…the gun's in his hand. Looks like suicide to me."

"Excuse me, sir. But shouldn't we wait until we've collected some evidence before we make that determination?"

"Are you tryin' to tell me how to handle a suicide, missy?"

"No, sir, but—"

"But, hell!" Escavez moved closer to the body, bent a little to scrutinize what was left of Deke's skull, then straightened with a harrumph. "From where I stand, looks like a self-inflicted gunshot from the .38 he's got in his hand. What d'you think, Howard?"

Howard Sloan nodded. "Suicide, without a doubt."

Escavez turned to Pamela. "You got a problem with that, missy?"

"It *appears* to be suicide, sir," she said evenly.

Escavez turned to the EMTs who stood nearby awaiting permission to remove the body. "Take 'im, boys."

"Just a minute, Chief." Nick stepped forward. "Officer LaRue is right. Even in an apparent suicide, it's standard procedure to bag the victim's hands and the gun, then dust for fingerprints. You can never tell what questions might arise later in cases like this. I would also suggest you impound the vehicle."

Escavez's black eyes narrowed. "I don't recall askin' for your suggestions, Santana. You might be the homicide hotshot in Noo Awlins, but here in Bayou Blanc, you're a private citizen, no more, no less. I don't need advice from you. Any damn fool can see Deke Russo blew his own brains out."

Pamela took a deep breath. "Excuse me, Chief, but I questioned Amber Russo, and she firmly stated that her husband gave no hint that he was contemplating suicide. Furthermore, she didn't believe he would take his own life."

Escavez's glare intensified. "You're saying somebody killed the man?"

Pamela ground her teeth in vexation. "No, sir. I'm saying we shouldn't assume he committed suicide until we've carefully considered the evidence."

Escavez grunted and scratched the side of his head as he viewed Deke's corpse sourly. "I guess there was no note or nothin'...."

"No, sir," Pamela replied.

After a moment, the chief swore, then turned to Sloan. "Howard, go call the goddamned coroner. We got a bunch of amateur detectives here don't believe the evidence of their own eyes."

"We don't have to listen to them, Chief," Sloan said, giving Nick Santana a sullen look.

"No, I know that." The chief straightened his hat and pulled in his gut a little, standing tall. "Which'll make it that much more satisfyin' when it turns out we was right after all."

Another half hour passed before the coroner arrived. While they waited, Escavez directed Pamela to help Sloan examine the crime scene. Sure enough, the half hour before and after shift change had rendered the force short-handed, which gave him little choice. Howard Sloan grudgingly popped the trunk of the chief's vehicle and withdrew an evidence kit. The chief himself had taken charge of the gun, slipping it into a resealable plastic bag.

Nick stood at the front passenger door of the Mercedes, watching as Pamela snapped rubber bands around Deke's wrists to secure the paperbags covering his hands. She'd donned surgical gloves at the outset, but Sloan worked with bare hands, collecting residue from the floor mats. Pamela worked meticulously, writing everything down in her notebook. So far, Nick hadn't seen Sloan write anything down. Not only was the guy a jerk, but he was stupid. No matter how good a detective was, memory was never reliable at a crime scene, much less when and if the case ever came to court.

Stephen walked over to Nick. He avoided looking at his father to ask, "What's gonna happen next?"

Nick turned and drew Stephen away from the grisly sight. He'd already tried to coax the boy inside with Amber, but Stephen stubbornly insisted on watching the whole process. "It depends on the chief, Stephen. If I were investigating, I'd do just as Pamela did—ask questions of the family, then move to close associates, business and personal. The point being to remove any doubt that it was suicide."

Stephen's mouth twisted. "Amber's right. No matter how it looks, he was too much of an asshole to kill himself."

Frowning, Nick dropped his tone after glancing toward the cops working the scene. "Did Deke have enemies, Stephen?"

"Are you kidding?"

"Forget his radio audience. Anybody in the public eye attracts a certain number of people with opposing views. I'm talking about someone who might actually want to see him dead."

"Besides me?" Stephen answered bitterly. "Too many to count."

"Careful, son." Nick shifted to conceal Stephen from Pamela's shrewd gaze. "I understand you're upset, but your dad's death isn't officially a suicide yet. You want to watch what you say. Careless remarks can lead to complications." He gave the boy a direct look. "Understand?"

Stephen's gaze fell and he kicked at a pebble. "Yeah, whatever."

At a flash, they both turned to see Pamela photographing the body with a Polaroid camera. Howard Sloan had moved to the rear of the Mercedes, examining the open trunk. The two EMTs stood talking to each other. Squawking noise came from the radio in the ambulance, as well as from the chief's police unit.

Nick turned back to the boy. "About his enemies, can you name specific people?"

Stephen picked at a spot on his thumbnail. "Naw, no names. He was into a lot of shit, but he liked to play his cards close to his chest. He liked keeping secrets."

Name a few, Nick wanted to say, but he glanced up to find Pamela listening and decided there would be a better time to get details. "Why don't you go inside and see if Amber needs anything," he told the boy. With his eyes still on Pamela, he squeezed Stephen's shoulder. "We'll talk more later, okay?"

Pamela watched Nick wrap up his conversation with Deke's son and send the boy into the house. Setting the camera on the hood of the Mercedes, she walked over to Nick. "For a kid who's just lost his father, Stephen seems pretty cool, doesn't he?"

Nick reached for his sunglasses hooked in the neck of his T-shirt. "You can never tell what people are feeling when they've just lost a family member. You know that, Pamela."

"I'm getting the impression that this was a very dysfunctional family."

Nick shrugged. "Just as we don't know what people are feeling, we shouldn't put too much stock in what they say while they're still in shock."

"The widow definitely didn't mince words." Pamela patted the notebook in her pocket. She knew she was pushing, but she'd bet Nick had gotten an earful from the boy. "Was Stephen that candid?"

"He had some questions about what happens next."

"Translated, that means you're not going to repeat anything he told you." She kept her eyes level, steady. "Have you turned in your shield, Nick?"

"You heard Escavez. My homicide experience is not required here."

"So you thought you'd dust off your law degree instead."

Nick looked harassed and irritable. "Look, Pamela, I've known these people a long time. Stephen may seem unemotional on the surface, but his father has just been found dead. No matter how it looks, he's shocked and bewildered that Deke's gone. I just cautioned him about speaking out without thinking."

"What were you afraid he'd say?"

"Nothing particularly earth-shattering, Pam, but it just seemed best not to give 'Barney Fife' any bright ideas. Is that so off-the-wall?"

"Come on, Nick. It looked as if you were coaching a witness."

"Coaching a witness? The kid's father is the victim, Pamela. If he's spouting off while he's still in shock, he could find himself having to answer a load of unnecessary questions. I was just trying to head that off." Nick reached for his baseball cap, resettling it on his head. "Hell, it's bad enough that the kid—and Amber—are having to go through something like this. We were pretty close once, Amber and I. If I can help them avoid a bump or two along the way, then I'm happy to do it."

"I hope that doesn't include tampering with evidence."

"'Tampering with evidence'? Come on, Pam! What are you talking about?"

"You've already admitted opening the door—"

"That was Kate, not me."

"Then using the garage remote to—"

"That was Kate, too. But I stand by her. She acted without thinking, just as she said." He adjusted his cap again. "It happens, Pam. Especially when you know the victim."

"Maybe. I suppose I'm just a little surprised that you seem to have forgotten basic crime-scene procedures, Nick."

He stood for a minute looking away, his hand clamped on the back of his neck. "Well, I guess you'll just have to think whatever you please, Pamela. I've been as honest as I know how. Discuss your suspicions with Escavez, because even though I know you're bucking for a promotion, you can't seriously want to confer with 'Barney Fife' on something as serious as this." His face behind the shield of his sunglasses was hard. "I'm not a practicing attorney, but when cops begin looking for ways to intimidate and misuse power, then I'm prepared to dust off that degree you mentioned, if that's what it takes to protect people I care about."

"And that's it, isn't it, Nick? You still care about her."

"Even if I did, it shouldn't make one iota of difference to the way she's treated, Pam. Don't you see that?" He was silent for a moment before turning away. "I'm outta here."

TWENTY-FIVE

Kate spotted Sam as she made the sixth lap on the jogging track that night. He was propped against the trunk of a big cypress. As always, the sight of him brought a rush of confusing emotions. After the day she'd been through with Amber, she wasn't sure she could cope with Sam, too. By the time she reached the small shed where she'd left her gym bag, he'd pushed away from the tree and was headed toward her.

Huffing and puffing, she unzipped the bag to get her water bottle. "You obviously aren't dressed for jogging," she said, glancing at his jeans and white pullover.

"Guilty." He reached for her towel while she drank thirstily, then handed it over and watched as she dampened it to cool herself off. "And after everything that happened today, I'm surprised you have the energy to run."

"We can run, but we can't hide," she muttered, her face buried.

He nodded, as if understanding. "Did seeing Deke get to you?"

She gazed beyond him to the joggers strung out along the track. By telling him about the flashbacks, she'd given him reason to think that. What surprised her was how much she wanted to believe that Sam could be trusted with her confidences. Why she'd think that, when he'd trampled on her heart once before, she didn't know.

"Do you know anything about repressed memory, Sam?"

"Not much. Only what I've read."

"Do you believe an experience can be buried so deeply in a person's subconscious they could actually have no memory of it?"

"I think it's probably possible," he said. "Especially if it's something extremely frightening or traumatic. But it's more uncommon than we're led to believe by pop psychologists today."

"'Probably possible,'" she murmured.

"Just my opinion," he said with a shrug. "Why? Are we talking about the flashbacks?"

"Forget it." She bent her knee and locked her hand around her ankle. "I get a lot of nutty ideas when I run."

"Psychologists differ about repressed memory, if I recall."

"Uh-huh."

"With good reason. When so-called repressed memory is retrieved, and it's detrimental, it can be the ruination of a person's reputation."

"I'm not thinking of anybody's reputation except my own."

"So where do you think the incident happened?"

"What incident?"

He grinned, catching her towel as it slid off her shoulders. "The one with the gun, the lights, the screams and the rushing, roaring sounds."

She took the towel from him and draped it around her neck. "Sounds like a movie I saw once. A very bad movie."

"I recognize stonewalling when I see it."

"It was just a thought. Really."

Taking her gym bag, he began walking back to her car. "How's Amber?" he asked.

"Coping." At the car, she braced both hands against the top and stretched the hamstring muscles in her calves.

Sam lounged against the car, watching her. "How about Stephen?"

"The same. Both are...dazed."

"How about you?"

"I'm dazed, too. I still can't believe it."

"Who's making funeral arrangements and the like?"

She gave him a quick sideways glance. "One guess."

"Best friend Kate."

"Leo seems too shocked, and I don't think Amber should have to cope with all the details, considering. Although when the funeral's over, she might regret leaving me in charge." Kate bent over and touched the ground with the tips of her fingers, revealing the curve of her buttocks, unaware of the heat in Sam's gaze. "The wake is tomorrow night, and I'm no expert in taste and style—just ask my mother."

"What can it require other than flowers and a place to hold the service?"

"A big place. The guy's a celebrity, after all."

"Sounds as if you have everything under control."

"I hope you're right. I just don't want anyone expecting an Amber Lifestyles occasion."

"You sell yourself short, Kate. You have as much taste and style as any woman I know."

Kate removed the sweatband from her forehead and ran the fingers of both hands through her hair before tucking it behind her ears. "What are you doing out here tonight, Sam?"

"Looking for you."

Without taking the gym bag from him, she unzipped it and felt around inside, looking for her car keys. "Why?"

"Victoria isn't comfortable knowing you're out here alone."

She gave him a startled look. "My mother called you?"

"Is that so surprising? She's your mother and she worries."

Kate shook her head. "I'm sorry you had to bother. I should have guessed she was feeling unsettled about Deke. I don't think Mother liked him any more than I did. But she clucked over Amber today like a hen with one chick."

"For a guy with such an adoring public, Deke sure seemed to generate a lot of dislike in his personal relationships. Think about it. You, Victoria, Leo, Nick, his wife. Even his kid."

"And those are only the people we know," Kate said dryly.

"Yeah. Makes you wonder about the ones we don't know."

Using the remote on her key chain, Kate unlocked her BMW. But she didn't get in. "Are you thinking murder and not suicide?"

"Are you?"

"You first."

He scratched his chin thoughtfully. "On the surface, it appears to be suicide. And we'll know after the autopsy whether he was drunk or not. If he was, and he was passed out, I suppose somebody could have shot him and made it look like suicide. I saw contact powder burns, so the gun was very close when the trigger was pulled." After a moment, he added, "Hard to see anybody sitting still for something like that."

"But it's even harder to imagine Deke Russo shooting himself."

Sam reached out and brushed at a strand of hair on her cheek. "What do you say we drop the subject of Deke Russo for now?"

Ignoring the leap of her pulse, she took her gym bag

from him and opened the rear door. "Suits me." She tossed the bag onto the seat and slammed the door.

Instead of letting her get into the car, he stopped her with a hand on the door. "Where are you headed now?"

She glanced down at herself with a laugh. "To the shower, Sam."

"Can I come, too?"

"No!"

He was chuckling softly. "Okay, then how about you showering first while I wait and then we'll go out for dinner? And before you say no, wouldn't you like to get away from everything, even if it's just for a few hours?"

"I should stay close in case Amber needs me. Or my mother. Or Stephen."

"Okay, we'll go to my house. I'll call my housekeeper and have her fix something. When you're done, walk over. You'll be two minutes from Amber and your mother."

Holding on to the ends of the towel draped around her neck, she looked at him. The last time they'd been alone together—right here on the track—he'd taken her to the moon and back. It had turned her emotions upside down at a time when she needed all her wits about her. She thought they'd agreed not to start anything. "What's going on, Sam?"

"I wish I knew. When I figure it out, I'll let you know."

"I'm not having sex with you again."

He cupped her chin in his hand and looked straight into her eyes. "Maybe not tonight, Kate. But you will. And the next time, it'll be because it's right and we both want it." He dropped his hand. "So, how about dinner?"

"This is crazy," she muttered.

"Not crazy. Just inevitable." He opened the car door. "Now go. I'll be right behind you."

TWENTY-SIX

"Do you remember my mama's funeral?"

Amber's question drew Kate's attention from the list in front of her. She couldn't see Amber's face. She was standing at the French doors with her back to Kate, looking into the backyard. It was just dusk, and the yard was alive with evening sounds. Kate was trying to finalize details for Deke's funeral, set for tomorrow morning. But first there was the wake tonight in New Orleans.

"Caroline's funeral? Not really." Kate marked her place at an item on the list. There were a hundred details to be worked out in planning a funeral, she'd discovered.

"It rained that day," Amber murmured.

"Hmm. The truth is, I don't even remember the service for my own father. They were back-to-back, weren't they?"

"No. Mama's was at ten in the morning and your daddy's was at two in the afternoon."

Check music. Kate made a little mark beside the notation. "I hope 'Amazing Grace' is okay for the music at the funeral, Amber. Stephen liked it. Can you think of anything else you'd prefer?"

Amber stared at a tiny green lizard hiding in a hanging fern. "It doesn't seem right that it rained on the day when my mama was buried and the weather is gorgeous for Deke, does it?"

"I wouldn't count on sunny skies tomorrow," Kate

said. She put down her pen and stretched her arms and shoulders. "It rains nearly every day in August."

"Afternoon thundershowers," Amber said, and pulled the cord that controlled the draperies. "By then Deke's service will be over and everyone'll be gone, remembering what a nice occasion it was and how many beautiful flowers there were and what lovely things were said by his friends." She turned to look at Kate. "It's a good thing no one expects the widow and the kid to do a eulogy, isn't it? That'd be sure to turn the event on its ear."

Kate stood without replying. With Deke dead, the bitterness in Amber swirled dangerously close to the surface. As Deke's widow, she would be the focus of hundreds of curious eyes. His suicide had become a major media event, and the sharks were out in force. Kate was holding her breath, hoping Amber would manage to get through the wake and funeral before her emotions overwhelmed her.

Carrying her notes, Kate crossed the room to an alcove beside Leo's bar. "It'll soon be time for us to leave for the wake," she said, putting the notebook in a slot for paperwork. "We both need to start dressing."

"I don't suppose I could skip it," Amber muttered.

"You suppose right. Come on, I'll help you choose something, then I'll run over and check on Victoria. She insists she's able to do this tonight."

On the way down the hall, as they passed Leo's office, Stephen emerged. "I heard you, Amber," he said, his stormy eyes so like Deke's. "We don't have to do anything just because people expect it. Screw the funeral." He followed Amber and Kate into the bedroom. "We can just move away from here, go someplace like California where nobody ever heard of Deke and start a new life."

Dropping onto the bed, Amber bent her head and rubbed her temples wearily. "Hush, Stephen. Kate's right. We have to do the expected thing. We can't run away. Besides, my career is here." Her shoulders sagged suddenly as she added bitterly, "That is, if this latest caper of Deke's hasn't destroyed everything I've worked for."

Kate sighed. "She wasn't serious, Stephen."

Stephen went down on his haunches in front of Amber, catching her hand. His eyes roved over her face anxiously. "Are you sure, Amber? We're free now. We can do as we please."

His hair had fallen onto his forehead. Smiling faintly, Amber reached out and threaded her fingers through it, pushing it back from his face. "Free at last. It feels good, doesn't it?"

He shrugged. "I guess. So long as nobody expects me to look sad or cry or anything. I don't feel like that," he added fiercely. "Do you?"

She was stroking his shoulder now, her gaze unfocused, as if searching inside herself to answer his question. "I don't know what I feel, Stephen. Dazed, sure. But mostly relieved, you know? So, no tears from me, either."

"Amber," Kate murmured, giving her a chiding look.

Stephen looked up at her. "It's okay, Kate. If we pretended to be grieving, it'd be a lie. My dad put Amber through a lot, and it was tough for me to just sit back and watch it." He turned to look at Amber with naked adoration. "I was just waiting for the right time when both of us could get away from him."

"Shh." Amber put a finger to his lips. "I shouldn't be talking about Deke this way to you, Stephen. He's your father, after all. Let's agree to put everything behind us from this day on. Forevermore. Okay?"

He nodded. "Sounds good to me."

She gave his shoulder a little pat. "Now, go get changed. I brought your dark blue suit, the one you wore

the night Deke received the award from that gun club."
She shot Kate an impish look. "They honored him for
helping push the concealed-weapon legislation."

Stephen hesitated for a second, then stood, grinning.
"Yeah, right. Good choice, Amber."

Kate was shaking her head when the door closed behind Stephen. "Come on, Amber. I know you're both angry as hell at him, but you're an adult, he's a kid. Think of
how he might remember this in years to come."

"Like you remember your father's funeral?"

Kate frowned. "I don't have much early memory at all,
I can't deny that. If I did, I don't think I'd like to recall it in
any disrespectful light."

"That's because John Madison wasn't a jerk."

"As I said, I just don't recall anything. When we were
kids, you were always the one who conjured up pictures
of the time when we both had two parents. No matter
how hard I tried, I never managed to get beyond the haz-
iest recollections."

"And it didn't do you any harm, right?"

Maybe. Maybe not. With Amber's emotions balanced
so delicately, now was not the time for Kate to admit to
having some pretty strange memory associations lately.
"There's a difference between no memory and bad memory, Amber."

Amber heaved a sigh as she kicked off her sandals.
"Okay, Mother. I'll behave. At least until the festivities
are over."

Festivities? Giving up, Kate realized that arguing with
Amber when she was in a mood was a useless exercise.
"You need to choose something to wear tonight, Amber,"
she suggested, opting to change the subject.

"Whatever." Getting to her feet, Amber caught the tail
end of her shirt and pulled it over her head.

Kate selected a plum-colored linen dress from several hanging in the closet. "How about this?"

"Great."

Kate turned in time to see a large bruise discoloring Amber's midriff as she donned an ivory satin slip. Kate moved closer, catching Amber's arm before she could lower it. "My God, how on earth did you get such a vicious bruise?" With a touch to her shoulder, Kate tried to turn her toward the lamp to get a better look, but Amber quickly covered the injury.

"It's nothing. Don't worry about it, Kate. Especially now."

"A blow like that could have fractured a rib," Kate said, fighting a sick, uneasy feeling. "Did Deke do this?"

"Didn't we have this conversation a few days ago, Kate?"

"You downplayed it then, Amber. Now there's no need. Deke was habitually violent, wasn't he?"

"What difference does it make? He never will be again."

"Only because he's dead!" Kate exclaimed.

Amber yanked open a drawer. "Yes. Thank you, Jesus."

This time it was Kate who sat on the bed. "I guess there was more than a shouting match the other night."

"I told you he was on a rampage. I tried to avoid him when I realized how pissed he was, but he cornered me in the dressing room. Fortunately the thing was soundproof," she said, "because he was yelling bloody murder and shaking me enough to make my teeth rattle. Then he just tossed me across that place like a rag doll. I crashed into something—a trunk, I think—which is how I got hurt. He'd really lost it. I couldn't catch my breath at first. Then when I did, I knew better than to do or say anything.

I mean, I didn't move a muscle, Kate. He's really a bastard once he gets pumped up on that shit."

"Pumped up? Do you think he was using drugs, too?"

Amber rooted in the drawer for panty hose. "I think so, but it was hardly the time to ask."

Heedless of Kate's shock, Amber went to the bed and sat down with the panty hose. "The problem was, he was really steamed over finding Nick...'sniffing around me' was the way Deke put it. Which wouldn't have happened if he hadn't acted like a jerk and fired the soundman and then had to leave to find another one. He brings it all on himself, Kate. He's such a jerk. I lied to you before. He broke my collarbone once, can you believe that? You just can't imagine what it's like to live with someone who's out of control most of the time."

Kate was still trying to take it all in. "That blow could have done more damage than just knock the breath out of you, Amber. You're lucky you don't have a concussion from being slammed into the wall.'"

Amber stood. "I *was* a little dazed, but frankly I'm used to it."

"You're 'used to it'?"

"What can I say?" Amber shrugged. "I speak in the past tense now. The bastard's dead. And good riddance," she added, taking the dress from its hanger. "The good news is that this time I won't have to listen to one of his whining, begging, disgusting apologies where he vows with tears in his eyes that he'll never do it again. The asshole!"

She unzipped the dress and stepped into it as Kate watched. "He was always contrite after being violent?"

"Very. For what it was worth. Which was nothing."

"Do you think that's why he...ended it all?" Kate asked, still trying to fit the picture of a violent, abusive Deke beside her own picture of Amber—bright, ambitious, creative. The image didn't fit the victims of domestic abuse she'd attended at St. Luke's.

"If you mean," Amber said, stepping into plum leather Ferragamo pumps, "do I think he could have been so distraught with guilt that suicide was the only answer, then hell, no. But who am I to argue with the facts? You saw for yourself. He was sitting in his car with the gun in his hand. What else is there to think?"

The doorbell rang as Kate was leaving to get dressed herself. Thinking it would be more people bearing food—as was the way in Bayou Blanc when a death occurred—she opened the door to find Sam Delacourt and Nick Santana.

Nick was darkly handsome in sober navy blue, his male appeal undiminished by the sling cradling his left arm. She gave him a friendly smile, then faced Sam, tall and heart-stopping in stern gray. What was it about this man that sent her senses into a tailspin?

Today there'd been no time to be distracted by thoughts of Sam and where they were headed. Just as he'd promised, Sam had made no attempt to touch her last night, but he'd plied her with wine and dinner and charm—a combination almost as lethal as sex. Kate's head had been spinning when at midnight he'd walked her across Vermilion Lane to Victoria's house. Too much wine, or too much Sam Delacourt?

She forced herself to turn her gaze to Nick as he spoke. "Hi, Kate. Sam and I thought we'd check to see if you might need a couple of escorts for the drive across the lake."

Kate touched her head helplessly. "Can you believe I haven't even thought about transportation?" She tucked a strand of hair behind one ear. "But now that you mention it, I'm not sure Amber should drive. Or Leo. Which means we'll have five people in my car." She sighed. "It would probably be better if we split up." She moved to let them inside. "Let's see what Amber says."

"We don't need anybody to drive us. I can do it."

All heads turned at Stephen's sullen remark. The challenge was directed to the two men, Kate realized. "I've driven across the lake for my dad a lot," he added with a look that dared anyone to argue. "If Amber needs anybody to drive her, it'll be me."

Kate smiled at him. "I'm sure you're perfectly capable, Stephen. But under the circumstances, don't you think it would be better if someone who's not a family member helps us out tonight?"

Before the boy could reply, Nick said, "No sense taking a chance on getting a ticket, Stephen."

Without saying it outright, Nick was reminding the boy that he didn't yet have his license. Stephen plunged his hands deep in his pockets, still scowling. "Who's going to know?"

"These folks, just to name two," Sam muttered with a glance toward the street where two figures were getting out of a police car.

"Oh, no," Kate murmured, watching the chief of police making his way up the sidewalk, his big cowboy boots eating up the distance. Beside him, Pamela LaRue was forced to take very long strides to keep up. Kate's uneasy feeling was suddenly full-blown anxiety. There couldn't be any positive reason for the chief's visit at this moment.

"Evening, all." Chief Escavez tipped his Stetson at Kate, then nodded to the others with almost-courtly politeness. Pamela stood slightly back, as if not quite comfortable. In one hand she held papers rolled into a cylinder.

"Looks like my timing was on the money," the chief said. "Getting ready for the wake, are you?"

"It's scheduled for seven, Chief," Kate said, glancing at her watch. "We're going to have to get going soon."

"I don't think this is a social call, Kate," Nick said, lounging against the porch railing.

"What's up, Chief?" Sam asked. "Kate's right. The family's ready to leave for New Orleans. Unless you have something significant—"

"What's going on?" Amber appeared suddenly, looking sharply around the circle of faces and settling on Nick's. "I didn't know you were here, Nick. Did you come with these people?"

"He came with Sam, Amber," Kate murmured, taking her hand. It was cold, and she could feel her slight trembling. "We really can't be late for the wake, Chief Escavez," she added, hoping he wouldn't upset Amber more.

"I understand. And I'm not going to hold you up any longer than necessary, but I think you'll want to hear this." Escavez cleared his throat, and without looking at Pamela, held out his big hand. "You got that report, missy?"

"Yes, sir." Pamela put the rolled-up papers into his palm. "Forensics," she said in response to Nick's silent inquiry. He moved from the railing to stand protectively behind Amber.

Escavez fished his reading glasses from his pocket and tipped his head to focus on the words. "Since we had a lot of differing opinion here yesterday morning over the question of Deke Russo's death, I thought you all would be interested to know that Forensics found something odd when they got that Mercedes in the lab and put the light on it."

"Light?" Amber murmured.

The chief peered at her over his glasses. "Lama Light, they call it. It's a gizmo shines special blue light on surfaces where they suspect there might be bloodstains. Now, when looking at it with the naked eye, you don't see a thing. But anywhere there's been blood spilled, it shows up under that light clear as day." He paused, letting his gaze rove over the group.

Amber wrapped her arms around herself. "What does all this mean to us, Chief?" she asked.

"Well, Ms. Russo, it turns out there was a helluva lot of blood in that car which wasn't visible to the naked eye." He found a paragraph summarizing the findings. "Says here it appears the victim's blood was all over the place and that a common household spray cleaner was used to soak it down, then it was mopped up with paper towels. The light showed it was all over the dash and the passenger seat and the console. Some on the floor carpet, too."

He looked up, studying the faces of his audience. "It figures, logically speaking, that Deke couldn't very well have mopped his own blood up, right? So we have to assume somebody else was in that car." He removed his reading glasses and tucked them back into his pocket. "Leaving us with the question—did that person find Deke dead and just wipe up because he likes things all nice and tidy? Odd thing, any way you look at it."

Nick pounced. "He? You think it was a man?"

Escavez took his time replying. "I don't think anything yet, Detective. That was just a figure of speech." He bumped the rolled paper against his thigh a few times, studying Nick. "Why, you got something you'd like to share with us?"

"No," Nick said.

"You get anything, you'll let me know, okay?" Escavez handed the report back to Pamela.

"Wait a minute, Chief." Amber looked confused. "You say somebody else was in the car? I thought—does this mean somebody helped Deke kill himself?"

"Well, now…" Escavez scratched the side of his head as if in thought. "I suppose that's one way to look at it, Ms. Russo. But the fact is, I believe your husband was flat-out murdered."

"'Murdered.'" Amber's lips barely moved.

"Well, g'night, ladies and gentlemen. Time enough to discuss all this tomorrow. After the funeral." He tipped his hat. "I'll just head on out now, so y'all can get to that wake."

TWENTY-SEVEN

Nick was so furious, he didn't give a thought to the engine noise of his SUV as he gunned it through the small, quietly sleeping neighborhood. When he reached the modest house nestled behind two pretty magnolia trees, he jammed his foot on the brake, taking satisfaction from the loud squeal of the tortured tires. Almost before the vehicle stopped, he was out of it, slamming the door hard, heedless of sleeping neighbors. As he stormed up the driveway, a dog at a nearby house began barking.

Without slowing his pace, he pulled at the knot of his tie to loosen it, then jerked it off and crammed it into the pocket of his suit jacket. Swearing at the inconvenience of doing everything with one hand, he leaped over the porch steps and stalked to the front door.

He punched the doorbell, then waited, glaring at the floor. Midnight or not, he was here to get some answers. Ten seconds later, he ground the button again, using his thumb. Another brief wait and he buzzed a third time. Now a light came on somewhere in the back of the house. He lifted his head and stared straight into the security hole.

The lock gave and the chain rattled as it was removed. The door was opened cautiously.

"Nick?" Pamela stared at him, obviously surprised and only half awake. "What—"

Too incensed to wait for an invitation, he pushed his

way inside, closing the door with the flat of his hand, then faced her angrily. "What the hell was that all about tonight, Pamela?"

She was holding on to the sides of her silk kimono, groping for the belt. In spite of her efforts, Nick glimpsed the sleek ivory flesh of one thigh. It struck him that Pamela slept nude. He didn't want to know that right now.

"Do you realize what time it is?" she asked, knotting the belt.

"Midnight," he snapped. "Ten after. And I just got back from a wake, otherwise I'd have been over here before to get some answers."

"Answers? What's wrong with you, Nick? I've never seen you like this."

"Then take a look, darlin', because this is how I get when I'm pissed." He paced away from her before turning back irately. "That was the most disgusting, inconsiderate display of power I've ever witnessed, Pamela. And where I come from, I've seen some real power shit."

"Would you calm down, please? I assume you have a problem with Chief Escavez's investigative techniques, Nick, but barging into my house in the middle of the night ranting and raving like a crazy person won't change anything. Besides, I just do what I'm told. You know that." Pamela turned a lamp on and flooded the modest living room with light. She was still clutching the kimono at her breasts, looking tousled and soft—except for the firm set of her pretty mouth—and nothing like the all-business cop who'd stood at Waylon Escavez's side a few hours ago.

"Sorry," he muttered. "I know it's late, but—"

"I know, you've been to a wake," she said dryly. Resisting the urge to roll her eyes, she turned and motioned him to follow. "I'll make us some coffee. Maybe it'll settle you down some."

"You don't have to do that," Nick said, his irritation fading. It was Escavez he was ticked at, not Pamela. He watched her stride down the narrow hall, tugging primly at the kimono to make sure it covered her butt. Nevertheless, she made an enticing picture from the rear, Nick noted reluctantly. Was it only a couple of weeks ago that he and Pamela had come very close to having a full-blown affair? But now Amber was in his life again. Not for the first time, he conceded that his irritation with Pamela was somehow tangled up with his confusion over his feelings for Amber.

"I guess I can go to the station tomorrow morning and we can talk there," he told her.

"No, we couldn't talk there." Pam pushed through swing half-doors that led into the kitchen. Close on her heels, Nick had to move quickly to keep from being smacked in the face. "How would it look if the chief saw you chatting me up after that scene you're so pissed over?"

"Then you agree he was out of line?"

"Did you hear me say that?"

"Pamela, Escavez rolled over the feelings of those people in some heavy-handed attempt to— Hell, I don't know what he was trying to do. Get the most dramatic impact when he delivered his big announcement? Add panic to their turmoil, maybe? If he was just there to tell them it wasn't suicide, it could have waited until after the funeral."

She held the decanter under the faucet and filled it with water. "Waylon Escavez doesn't tell me why he does anything," she said.

"He enjoyed that little stunt, Pamela," Nick said, pacing to the door and back again. "And it proved nothing."

"Maybe he just wanted to see their reaction."

Nick stopped, eyeing her narrowly. It dawned on him

with sudden clarity what had been at the edge of his mind all along. "Escavez thinks he knows who killed Deke, doesn't he?"

She poured the water into the pot, slid the decanter into place and flipped the switch on. Turning, she leaned back against the counter and looked at him. "Even if I knew the answer to that, it'd mean my job if I discussed it with you."

"That's what it was all about," Nick said. "In a homicide, any detective looks first at close family members." He glanced at Pamela. "Who's the favorite, Amber or Stephen?"

She was shaking her head, but Nick had warmed to his theory now. "Leo? Does he think it was Leo? What's the motive?"

"The coffee's almost ready."

"Forget the damn coffee!" Nick pulled a chair away from the table and urged her into it. He took a seat opposite her. "Pam, he's on the wrong track. You've got to tell him that. As long as Escavez concentrates on the family, the real killer is getting a pass. Deke Russo had enemies you wouldn't believe. He had his hand in a lot of pies. Plus, the guy was half nuts. You only had to listen to him—I mean, really listen through the whole program for a few days—to know that. I'm not just talking, here. I've been a target of his, so I know. When that incident happened with me and my partner, Deke tried to destroy me professionally and personally. I've learned since then that Russo had a network of connections that reaches into drugs, porn and prostitution. If he was murdered, tell Escavez to look there before turning the lives of his widow and kid upside down."

"If you had all this information, Nick, why have you been sitting on it? Is there an ongoing investigation at the NOPD?"

"No, and you're looking at my reason for sitting on it."
He lifted his arm with the cast. "I planned to wait until I
got rid of this before taking on something this big. Everything I know I've put together since I got hit. Until I was a
hundred-percent fit, I wasn't going to make the mistake
of underestimating somebody like Russo."

"Well, now you won't have to. He's dead, problem
solved." Pamela got up to pour two coffees.

"What's that supposed to mean?"

She faced him. "A lot of what you've said gives you a
motive to kill him, Nick."

He rose, moving away with irritation. "Be serious,
Pam. I didn't kill him."

"Really? I can think of two ways it would be beneficial.
You'd get rid of a vindictive enemy, and his wife would
be a free woman. No messy divorce, no long-drawn-out
legal battles over their joint property."

His eyes were suddenly hot with outrage. "That's
bullshit and you know it."

"You're in love with her, Nick. I think you always have
been." With a sigh, she dumped her coffee into the sink.
"Oh, forget that. I don't think you killed Deke Russo."
She waited until he raised his eyes to hers. "But somebody did. And we both heard Amber and Stephen when
it first happened. They were both very bitter. So instead of
blindly defending them, maybe you'd better take a more
objective look at reasons they might have for wanting to
be rid of him."

Nick could feel denial radiating from him in waves. It
was tough hearing Pamela saying things he'd been thinking privately. Since the moment he'd examined the crime
scene, he'd been busy denying his instincts. It had been no
surprise to learn Deke was murdered.

He looked at Pam. "So you're going to ignore what I

just told you? The guy had a secret life. He was into some deep shit."

"I'm ignoring nothing. I'll certainly pass that on to the chief."

"But you still favor Amber and Stephen as suspects?"

"I tend to favor the statistics in these cases."

"And you've had such vast experience," he said, resorting to sarcasm because he resented her insight.

Pamela crossed her arms defensively over her breasts and said nothing. But her small chin went up a notch.

"I can see I'm wasting my time here," he snapped. But as much as Nick hated to admit it, he had nothing to link Deke's murder to anybody else, either—not even a gut hunch. Picking up the coffee she'd poured for him, he dumped it into the sink, then shoved his chair neatly back into place at the table. He stopped at the swing doors and looked back at her. "We're expecting Escavez to be as good as his word, Pamela. Nobody in the family's talking to him until after the funeral."

"In the family," she repeated quietly. "Does that include you?"

"Just tell him what I said."

"Good night, Nick."

Amber's prediction about the weather proved true. There wasn't a cloud in the sky that hot August morning in Lafayette Cemetery. In spite of the fact that heat radiating from the sea of ancient whitewashed tombs drove the temperature beyond a bearable level, a host of fans and celebrity watchers lined up six deep outside the iron gates of the cemetery to pay homage to the king of talk.

Victoria, pale and near collapse, had been persuaded to stay in the air-conditioned limousine while the brief graveside ceremony was completed. Leo stood stoically beside Amber and Stephen, but Kate sensed that only willpower kept him on his feet. Fortunately, Nick was there to prop up both Leo and Amber. On this third day after Deke's death, they were all feeling the strain. Kate breathed a sigh of relief at the priest's final words.

As the mourners broke up, she slipped quietly from her place beside Leo and headed for the shade of an old oak tree several yards away. It would be a few minutes before Amber could leave. Kate knew funerals weren't supposed to be fun, but Deke's was one she'd never forget. People outside the gates carried signs and sang songs in his memory. Who in the world *were* those people? Fans? The curious? The morbid? Yearning for it all to be over, she sat down on an iron bench beneath the tree. It seemed like forever since she'd had a moment to herself.

Today was no different. She watched Waylon Escavez heading her way. With Howard Sloan and Pamela LaRue at his side, the chief had kept well back from family and friends in the cemetery. Now that the service was over, he apparently saw no reason not to get down to business.

In deference to the occasion, he'd donned a Western-style jacket over his shirt and jeans and added a bolo tie. "Interesting send-off, wouldn't you say, Doc?" he remarked, studying the crowd at the gate.

"Apparently Deke was known and loved by a lot of people."

"Maybe so, but there was definitely one person who didn't love him." Escavez glanced at the bench. "Mind if I join you?"

Shifting a little to make room, Kate crossed her legs. Escavez took no notice of her body language.

"So you've definitely decided he was murdered?" Kate said, cutting to the chase.

"I thought I'd made that point last night."

She looked at him. "Do you have any suspects?"

"Plenty," he replied, his gaze skimming Deke's fans

and then resting on the people lingering near the casket. "Too many."

"Really?"

"Deke Russo was one of those characters who polarize people as well as opinion, Doc. A man like that makes as many enemies as friends."

"That must complicate your job."

He chuckled. "Yes, ma'am, it surely does." Shifting, he crossed a boot over one knee. "I understand you and Amber have been friends since childhood."

"Yes." Her amusement faded.

"What can you tell me about her marriage, Doc?"

"Very little. I've only seen Amber twice in three years."

"I'm told she's been staying here in her daddy's house lately. And since that's right next door to your mama's place, y'all must have spent a good bit of time together recently."

"I'm at the clinic most of the day, Chief Escavez."

"You're saying you haven't been able to grab a little time to catch up?" He stroked his big mustache. "Now I find that hard to understand, Dr. Madison. Two girls raised almost as close as sisters not talking together about what's important in your lives. What's gone down since you were last together. How your love life is going. You know, girl talk."

She gave him a cool look. "Was there something specific you wanted to ask me, Chief?"

He picked up his hat and ran a finger around the brim. "Was there trouble in the Russos' marriage, Dr. Madison?"

After a cautious pause, Kate said, "They had the same ups and downs as any married couple."

"Did Amber know he sometimes fooled around?"

Kate frowned. "Deke was unfaithful? No, I don't... She never told me that." *Not in so many words.*

"What about drugs?"

"*He's really a bastard when he gets pumped up on that shit.*" Amber's words came back to her clearly. "What kind of drugs?" she asked, again with caution.

"Cocaine," Escavez said.

"You've seen the autopsy report?"

"Yes, ma'am. I have."

She shook her head. "I really didn't know Deke at all, Chief. Amber and I were much closer before they were married. So I'm afraid I can't help you there."

"You weren't close, but you knew they had 'ups and downs.' What kind of ups and downs?"

Kate's gaze strayed across the tombs to Amber, standing close to Nick, her dark head and his almost touching. Her hand, Kate noticed, clutched his arm. Nick looked up suddenly and saw Kate with Escavez. He said a word to Sam, who immediately started toward Kate.

"He... Deke didn't seem to give her enough credit for her achievements," Kate said. "It took talent and brains and energy to make Amber Lifestyles into the success it is today. Deke tended to underrate her efforts."

"And she resented that."

"Anyone would. But if you're thinking she resented it enough to murder him, you're reaching. In my opinion."

"Well, that's why I'm talking to you, Doc. To get your opinion."

Kate stood suddenly. "I'm really uncomfortable with this conversation, Chief. I don't like talking about a friend this way."

"I understand. And I admire your loyalty." He, too, was on his feet now. "But if you'd refused to talk to me, I would have been forced to ask you to come to my office, where things are a lot less—" he glanced around at the tombs and the thinning crowd with a sardonic smile "—friendly."

"Excuse me. They're ready to leave." Kate started toward Sam, trying not to rush. Even though she had nothing to hide, something about Escavez's questions sent all her instincts on red alert. It seemed clear that in the chief's mind, Amber was a suspect.

Sam saw her face and shot an accusatory look at Escavez. On her behalf? Kate wondered as he took her hand in his and squeezed it. It gave her the heady feeling that Sam might feel protective toward her. "They're waiting for us at the limousine, Kate."

His greeting to Escavez was curt. "Chief. How's it going?"

"I'm getting warm, Sam. Very warm. Me and the doc here managed to find a little shade."

Sam grasped Kate's elbow to urge her along the path. "I thought the plan was to hold off questioning the family until after the funeral."

"I don't consider Dr. Madison to be family, Sam," the chief said, falling into step with them.

"Leo and Amber might argue otherwise." Lifting his hand, Sam signaled to Nick. "We're holding up the show, Kate. Chief, you know where to find us."

Escavez stopped at the limo and watched as Sam assisted Kate inside. Pulling out his sunglasses, he slipped them on, then bent down to peer at the occupants. "Y'all be careful crossing that long bridge home, you hear?"

"What was that all about?" Leo asked as the driver of the limousine negotiated carefully through the crowd outside the gates.

"He thinks one of us killed Deke," Amber said, breaking the seal on a new pack of cigarettes.

"Don't light that in here," Kate warned. Then she bent her head, rubbing at a pain between her eyes. "Sorry, but

I don't think I can stand to breathe smoke all the way back to the north shore."

"I wasn't going to light it," Amber said, pulling a cigarette out of the pack. "I just want to hold it. It's comforting," she said defensively when Nick smiled and winked at her.

"Are you serious?" Stephen asked, looking back at the squad car following them. "He thinks one of us killed Dad? Who?"

"Me." Amber tugged at the skirt of her designer suit and returned Nick's smile.

"Get serious," Stephen said, watching the look they exchanged with resentment.

"I am serious." Amber twirled the cigarette between her fingers like a baton. She'd been the star of the drill team in high school, and one look at Nick assured her he remembered it. "Isn't that what he wanted when he cornered you under that tree just now, Kate? I bet he wanted to know where I was when Deke was shot."

"Don't be ridiculous," Victoria snapped. "He can't suspect you."

Leo reached over from the opposite seat and patted Amber's knee. "Vicky's right, honey. I think you're overreacting."

Amber held the cigarette against her lips, almost salivating over it. She looked directly at Kate. "Did he ask that, Kate? Did he ask about my alibi?"

"No, he didn't. His questions were pretty general."

"Such as?" Nick prompted.

"Did I know any particulars about…personal stuff. Which I didn't, so I wasn't much help."

"You know a lot," Amber said.

"I really don't."

"That was just a preliminary skirmish," Nick said after a moment. "He's just getting started."

* * *

Waylon Escavez arrived at Leo's house within an hour of the funeral with his sidekick, Howard Sloan, and Pamela LaRue as driver. Only Sloan was allowed to assist the chief in Amber's interrogation. Sizing up the situation, Nick declared himself Amber's attorney before Escavez could bar him from the room as he'd barred Kate. Now, as Kate watched from her perch on the edge of the fishpond, Nick prowled the room, disapproval on his features and in the set of his shoulders. But he might have been the family cat for all the notice Escavez took of him. Still, Kate felt some sense of relief that Amber wasn't alone at the chief's mercy.

"You look worried."

Kate started at the sound of Pamela's voice. The officer had materialized from the shadows of the huge split-leaf philodendron at the edge of the patio. As always, she was rigidly correct in uniform and manner. It amazed Kate that the gun holstered at her waist didn't look more ludicrous, considering the woman's petite size. Instead, it simply looked dangerous.

"Do I?"

"Uh-huh." With a hitch at the sharp crease in her pants, Pamela sat beside Kate on the stone ledge and turned her gaze to the ongoing drama in Leo's den. "Are you worried about your friend?"

"Amber? Of course. She's barely home from her husband's funeral. Any wife would be very vulnerable at a time like this."

"And Amber more than most, wouldn't you say?" Pamela's gaze was still fixed on the people inside.

"'More than most'? Why?"

Pamela looked at Kate. "I keep wondering how I'd feel if I were married to an abusive man and he was suddenly killed."

"Is that an assumption or do you know for a fact that Deke was abusive?"

"A little of both, I guess. On the morning Deke's body was discovered, I heard bits and pieces of Amber's conversation to Nick and you. I heard a woman so angry and so bitter, I began to wonder about her marriage. I did a little checking. In the past two years, she's made four visits to the emergency room at a hospital in New Orleans— once for a sprained wrist, once for head trauma, once for a sprained knee and once for a broken collarbone." Pamela watched Kate carefully. "She fell in the shower. She stumbled and fell down the stairs. She had an accident in her car, but, she didn't file an accident report. She's very clumsy, your friend Amber," Pamela added, gazing once more through the polished panes. "Did you notice that tendency when the two of you were growing up?"

"No."

"Why am I not surprised?"

"I've already told Escavez that Amber and I drifted apart after I moved to Boston."

"And you had no idea that Amber was a battered wife?"

Kate raked her hair back from her face and realized her heart was racing. "I don't like that term."

"Why? Is there a better way to describe a woman who's beaten and brutalized by the man who's vowed to love and honor her till death do them part?"

Without warning, lights began to pop in Kate's mind. A loud rushing sound roared in her ears, and images began flashing like snapshots. She squeezed her eyes shut and fought to block the sensations, but like film spinning out from an endless reel, the images kept scrolling, scrolling.... Two people—no, three, four. Screams. Violence. Gunshots! She bit back an outcry. Now water, so much water. She was going to fall into that cold, cold sea.

Kate threw a hand out, startled as she encountered real water.

"Kate? Are you all right?"

The fishpond, Kate realized. There was a splash as a panicked fish broke the surface. But now the rushing sound was receding. Blinking frantically, she brought Pamela's concerned face into focus. "What?"

"Gosh, you almost joined the goldfish. Was it a dizzy spell? Are you okay?"

"Yes. I mean..." Kate touched her forehead, turning away. Pamela LaRue saw too much. "It's been a long day."

"Three long days."

"I'm just... I'm tired."

"Are you sure you're okay, Kate? You looked so... You looked the way you did in your office when we talked about my sister's abuse."

"Yes. I mean, you're right. Spousal abuse, violence against kids, women... It's always upset me."

"And you don't know why?"

"No."

"Maybe you should try and figure it out."

"Maybe."

"You knew about Amber, didn't you?"

"No!"

"Kate."

Clearly Pamela didn't believe her. Kate covered her eyes with a shaking hand. "She said she could handle it. That she and Deke understood each other, that she knew how far to go before...before..."

"Before he got violent."

"Yes."

"And you didn't intervene? Didn't suggest anything to help her? You're a doctor. After five years in the E.R., you knew the signs. She was your best friend."

"No!" Denial came out of Kate in a wail. "I didn't want to believe it! I still can't believe it! She's too smart, too successful to let herself be victimized by anyone."

"It happens—smart women, stupid women, rich ones, poor ones, young or old. The battered know no social or economic bounds."

"Maybe I should have done something," Kate whispered, wringing her hands. "But I was just so appalled that it could happen to Amber."

Pamela reached over and touched her. "You're not alone in thinking that way. Abused women are incredibly successful at hiding it. They cover up, they lie, they go to elaborate extremes to keep from revealing what happens behind closed doors. Besides, given a little more time, you probably *would* have intervened. You've been home less than a month."

Kate wouldn't be consoled. "I kept denying the evidence in front of my eyes. I couldn't—wouldn't—let myself recognize the signs when it was Amber."

Neither spoke for a minute or two. Pamela looked away while Kate struggled to collect herself. The detective's gaze again strayed toward the undraped den where Amber was on her feet in animated conversation with Waylon Escavez.

"I saw them perform at the Fais Do-Do," Pamela said. "There was a kind of electricity between them. They were so good together. The crowd especially loved Amber."

"I know." Kate wiped surreptitiously at her eyes, surprised to discover she'd been crying.

"She sure did steal the show, didn't she?"

"Yes."

Pamela glanced at Kate's face. "Deke didn't strike me as the type of guy who was happy playing second fiddle onstage to anybody, not even his wife."

"He wrote the script."

316 Karen Young

"Did he? Well, anyway, I just happened to bump into some people who were around that night—stagehands, a couple of security guys, some of the cleanup crew. I was told that after the show Deke and Amber had a major row. It happened inside the eighteen-wheeler they were using as a dressing room."

"People always gossip about celebrities."

Pamela had her notebook out now, squinting to read it in what light there was. "You said, according to my notes, that Amber rode home from the Fais Do-Do with you."

"She did."

"My notes say she didn't even stop at her father's house."

"Yes."

"Your house is a two-story structure."

"My mother's house."

"Is your room on the second floor?"

"Why? Am I a suspect?" Kate asked dryly, beginning to feel more in control.

Pamela gave a tiny smile. "No, but these questions are necessary. Better to get them from me than from the chief."

"Amen to that," Kate said.

"Where is the guest bedroom, the room Amber used?"

"Upstairs."

"Near your room?"

"Yes."

"What time did y'all go to bed?"

"It was after midnight."

"Amber, too?"

"After midnight, too."

"Exactly when, Kate?"

"I'm not sure. We had some wine. We were talking. As you say, Amber was keyed up after the performance."

"Was she drunk?"

"No!"

"Was Deke drunk when you saw him last?"

Kate sighed. "He was well on the way."

"When *did* you see him last?"

"It was during the performance. They were still on-stage when Sam and I decided to stroll around. About an hour later, when Amber asked to ride home with me, Deke wasn't with her."

"Your mother was at home?"

"Yes, she was still awake. She suggested that Amber call Leo so he could let Deke know where she was when he came in."

"Did you see Amber after you went to bed?"

"No."

"So you can't really be sure that she never left your house from, say, midnight to 3:00 a.m.?"

"I *am* sure!"

"You actually saw her."

"I was sleeping, Pamela. We all were. But—"

"Somebody wasn't, Kate." Pamela picked up her note-book and slipped it into her pocket. "Somebody crept onto the grounds of Leo Castille's house, saw Deke Russo drunk and disoriented in his car, maybe even passed out, put the gun in his hand and pulled the trigger."

"It wasn't Amber."

"But you don't know that, Kate."

"It wasn't Amber," she repeated.

Pamela stood. "I hope you're right."

TWENTY-EIGHT

"The coroner puts the time of Deke's death in the early hours of Sunday morning, Ms. Russo." Escavez stroked his mustache slowly. "Where were you between midnight and 3:00 a.m.?"

"Sleeping at Kate's house. Ask her and Victoria. They'll tell you it's true."

"Uh-huh." The chief pulled a ballpoint pen from his pocket and spent a moment studying a yellow notepad before asking, "How long have you known about your husband's infidelities?"

After a quick glance at Nick, Amber focused on her hands. "I don't recall exactly. In the past year he didn't try very hard to pretend that he was happy being married to me, but I never saw him with another woman and he never told me anybody's name."

"But you knew he had other women?"

"I... Yes."

"That must have been difficult," Escavez said, watching her closely.

"Not so much difficult as risky. I thought he was taking a big chance, considering he'd built his reputation at 'Talk the Right Way' as an advocate of conservative family values and all that."

"Looked bad for you, too, didn't it, Ms. Russo?"

"It's embarrassing when your husband cheats on you. I won't deny that."

"What I meant was, you being the woman who created Amber Lifestyles, telling folks in New Orleans how to live graciously and with—how d'you say—panache. If your own lifestyle turned out to be a sham, it'd look bad, wouldn't it? Might hurt your image and undermine future plans. Stands to reason it would hurt you financially as well as personally and professionally."

"We had some discussion about that," Amber conceded. Rising from her chair, she moved to the French doors and stood looking out. "Deke was drinking too much. I think when a person has a drinking problem they behave in ways they wouldn't if they didn't. Have a problem, I mean. He always meant to get a handle on his drinking. At least, that's what he said."

"Then, when he started with the cocaine, you really must have been out of patience with him."

"I wasn't sure he was taking cocaine. He always denied it."

Howard Sloan spoke up. "You must have known he was taking something, Ms. Russo. When he came home drunk and incoherent, what'd you think?"

"I thought he was sick."

"Really?" Not bothering to conceal his disbelief, Sloan added, "By 'sick,' do you mean you consider alcoholism or drug addiction an illness?"

"Yes."

"And you didn't threaten to leave him if he didn't get a grip?"

"No."

Sloan glanced at the chief as if seeking permission, then asked, "How did you feel about your husband's taste in videos?"

"What?" Amber looked confused.

"Come on, Ms. Russo. We got a search warrant. We found his collection of flesh movies."

"'Flesh movies'?"

"Porn. Pornography. He was into some heavy stuff, moviewise."

Amber barely concealed a shudder. "I don't know anything about that."

Nick pushed away from the bar. "What does this have to do with Deke's murder?"

That brought a resentful look from Sloan. "It's got everything to do with it if she killed the guy so he couldn't screw up her *lifestyle*." He snickered. "How would it look if the public discovered that Deke Russo, right-wing bigshot, was leading a double life? The guy was doing everything he was preaching against to his radio audience. And here's his wife telling everybody how to make their lives pleasant and beautiful while her own life is pretty sordid."

"My life was not sordid!" Amber cried. "I didn't act like Deke and I'm not responsible for the choices he made."

Nick turned to the chief. "I think that's enough for now. If there's to be further questioning of my client, call me to set up a time and place. No more invading the privacy of her family. No more dropping in without notice for little 'chats.'"

Escavez looked at Amber. "That the way you feel about it, Ms. Russo? You don't want to answer any more questions?"

"Not tonight. I'm tired."

Escavez stood. "Okay, we'll respect that. For now." He handed the yellow notepad over to Sloan. "Where's our driver?"

"I'm here," Pamela said, moving away from the French doors where she'd been standing, watching.

"Where you been, missy? You should have been in here. Might have learned something."

"I was outside with Kate Madison."

The chief sent a sharp look in the direction of the patio. "Where's she at now?"

"She went home a few minutes ago. It's been a long day for these people, Chief."

Escavez put his hat on and nodded to Amber. "We'll be heading on out now, Ms. Russo. Tell your daddy I'll want to see him tomorrow to ask a few questions." He glanced at Nick. "That is, if your *lawyer* doesn't have any objection."

Amber looked worried. "This has been upsetting to my dad, Chief. Maybe—"

Nick silenced her with a look. "If you want to question Leo, call me to set up a time, Chief."

Both men headed for the front door, Howard Sloan hurrying forward to open it for Escavez. Pausing at the threshold, the chief looked back. "One more thing, Ms. Russo."

"Only one," Nick warned.

"On the night his daddy was murdered, where did your stepson sleep?"

"Stephen?" Amber put a hand to her throat. "Here. In his room."

"You were a guest in Victoria Madison's house."

"Yes."

He glanced at the roofline of Victoria's house, barely visible through the trees. "And yet you can say for a fact that the boy was here?"

"Yes!"

"And Leo will be able to back you up?"

Nick pulled Amber back from the threshold. "You can ask him that yourself, Chief."

"I hear you, counselor." He touched his hat again. "Good night, y'all."

With a faintly regretful look, Pamela brushed past Nick

and Amber, following the two ranking officers. She closed the door quietly behind her.

"Oh, that was horrible!" Rushing forward, Amber turned the bolt and flipped the switch that doused the light on the front porch. Without turning, she wrapped her arms around herself and pressed her forehead to the locked door. "What am I going to do, Nick?" she murmured in terror. "They think I killed him!"

Nick restricted himself to one quick touch on her shoulder. She'd just returned from her husband's funeral. "They're full of shit. Don't worry."

She was shaking her head in denial. "I brought it on myself. I said all those nasty things that morning. I made it sound as if I was glad he was dead. Why should they believe me?"

"Deke was hated by a ton of people. You're simply first on the chief's list. Not because you're his prime suspect," he added when she turned to look at him in dismay. "In a homicide, it's routine to look first at the victim's spouse. When they find nothing, they'll move on."

She gave a smothered moan. "Yeah, right. But you heard him. If it's not me, then they'll start in on Stephen."

"And they won't find any evidence against Stephen, either."

She searched his face anxiously. "Do you really believe that?"

He wanted to touch her hair, pull her close. "I really believe it. Trust me, Amber."

With a small cry, she closed the distance between them and threw her arms around him, bringing her body flush against his. He'd stripped his tie away hours ago and his shirt was open two or three buttons down. With her lips pressed to the hollow there, she whispered, "Nick, hold me, please. What would I do without you?"

Nick resisted, only allowing himself to grip her arms.

She'd been through a hell of a lot since Sunday, he told himself. It was stress causing her to do this. But God, how he wanted—

"Nick…" Rising up, she ground her hips against him and opened her mouth on his throat. The effect on Nick was like holding a torch to gasoline. He groaned when he felt the warmth of her kisses on his jaw, his chin. Then her lips were touching his.

"Kiss me, Nick."

Giving in, he put his arms around her and claimed her with a deep thrust of his tongue, releasing violent and ancient hunger. His hands swept low to pull her tightly against his hardness. She moved feverishly against him, whimpering. Impatiently, he pulled her shirttail from her waistband and plunged his hands inside, seeking her breasts. And with the kiss still unbroken, he backed her against the door, where he could exert more pressure, reacquaint himself with the pleasure of tasting and touching the first woman he'd ever loved.

Amber arched against him, threw her head back to give him access to her breasts, shifted to help when he fumbled to pull up her short skirt. She was chanting his name now, breathing it against his ear, his cheek, his mouth. With a groan, he pressed his forehead against hers.

He was wild to touch her, all concern for propriety lost now. Imagining the feel of her, hot and wet for him, he ran one hand up her thigh and rejoiced when he realized he was stroking sleek, naked skin. She was wearing nylons with a sexy garter belt. Nothing else. He plunged his fingers into her and sought her mouth again in a wild kiss to stifle her cry.

He wanted her now. Here. On the floor of her daddy's house, right at the front door. He stroked her with his fingers, savoring her moans. Her wild, uneven breathing was echoed in his own chest, which heaved with the force

of his lust. The intensity of her arms around his neck was
infinitely satisfying. Her frantic need had him a heartbeat
away from coming, but he wanted to be inside her when
it happened. He wanted—

"Amber! Where are you?"

Tearing her mouth from Nick's, she was able only to
stare, dazed and confused.

"It's Stephen," Nick said.

"No!" she said, wild with frustration.

"Yes." His hands were already moving to straighten
her skirt, to pull her top together. "Quick, go to your bedroom."

"Amber!" Stephen called again. He was a second away
from finding them.

"He m-must have come in the b-back way," she stam-
mered, still disoriented.

"I know. You need to hightail it out of here, Amber.
Go." Nick gave her a little shove toward the hall.

"But what—"

"I'll tell him something. Move!"

But Amber wasn't fast enough. Stephen was at the
archway now. Quick suspicion flared in his eyes as he
saw them. "What's going on, Amber? What's he doing?"

"He's just leaving, Stephen."

But one look at her wild hair and disordered clothing
and he knew. His fists balled at his sides. He turned on
Nick in outrage. "You keep your hands off her, damn
you!" he cried, his voice vibrating with fury. "Tell him,
Amber. Tell him!"

"Oh, Stephen." Amber was shaking her head.

Coolly, Nick put a hand up, palm out. "Amber's exhausted, Stephen. Escavez just left. She was heading for
bed."

"Oh, yeah? And you were going to give her some help
there, I guess."

"I was just on my way out."

Stephen's mouth curled. "You think I'm an idiot? I can see what was happening. You were making a move on her. What kind of prick are you? She's just been to a funeral, man."

Keeping to the shadows in the hall, Amber said, "It wasn't the way it looked, Stephen. Nick was— I was upset and he—"

"He was offering sympathy?" Stephen sneered. "I don't think so. I think he was in your pants, Amber."

"That's enough, Stephen." Nick's tone had cowed hardened criminals, but Stephen was beyond reason.

"You have no right!" he yelled.

Nick put up a hand. "Okay, son, I—"

"I'm not your son, so don't call me that! And I can say what I please around here. You're nobody to us. Amber has me and Leo. She doesn't need you. So get the hell out of this house!" Stephen literally vibrated with fury. "And keep your damn hands off Amber!"

Nick felt like some kind of pervert as he crossed the street and headed home. The boy was right. He had no business coming on to Amber like that. Especially now. Her husband had been murdered, and the funeral was barely over. Worse yet, Waylon Escavez was on her case, and regardless of Nick's reassuring words, he had a feeling the chief was convinced that Amber had killed Deke. Any way he looked at it, he'd been out of line. As her lawyer, he shouldn't touch her. As a decent human being, he should respect her situation right now. But Jesus, when she'd put her little pink tongue on his neck, he'd lost it. He'd been fantasizing about her ever since he'd moved a block away from her daddy's house. No sense lying to himself about it, but he hadn't intended to do anything.

Then he'd felt her, warm and soft and wrapped around him as snug as white on rice....

Hard again, he jogged up the driveway and around to the side door. If Stephen hadn't walked in right then, he just might have pulled her down and screwed her on the floor—with Leo due to walk in from his visit with Victoria at any minute. Nick shoved the back door open with a muttered curse. He should be thanking Stephen.

With Deke gone, the kid probably saw himself as Amber's protector. And he was playing his role to the hilt. A couple of times in the past few days, Nick had noticed Stephen watching him with an odd look on his face. Definitely unfriendly. Resentful, almost. As if Nick were...trespassing. Yeah, that was it. Trespassing. Hell, the kid acted more like a...a lover than a son.

"That you, Dad?"

"Yeah." Stopping at the fridge, Nick opened it and took out a long-necked beer. As he turned, Cody came in from the den with a pizza box in one hand and a canned soda in the other. "Everything okay with Miss Amber and the cops?"

"Escavez just left." He glanced at the pizza. "You got any of that left?"

"Sure." Flipping the cover, Cody revealed a couple of pieces of a pepperoni pizza. "Help yourself. Me and Stephen bought two, but this is all we've got left. I can always order another one."

"Naw, not necessary." Nick bit into a wedge.

"So how did it go with Escavez?" the boy asked. "Stephen was really antsy about him being there. He kept wanting to go check on Amber." Cody set his drink on the table and straddled a chair. "He thinks Escavez likes Amber for the murder, Dad, and he's really worried."

"No doubt Escavez is treating her like a suspect, son.

That's why I felt she should have some legal representation when he questioned her."

"Gosh, Dad, do you think she did it?"

"No." Nick wiped his fingers on a paper towel and picked up his bottle of beer. Cody's face was thoughtful as he rolled his drink can back and forth between his palms.

"Something on your mind, son?"

Cody raised his eyes to Nick. "If you really think Amber didn't do it, they'll have to start looking for somebody else, won't they?"

"Uh-huh, and Deke made a lot of enemies, so I don't expect this investigation to wrap up as quick as we'd all like. It'll take time to follow up every lead. Some cases drag out for years," Nick said. "I've had a few like that myself."

"On TV I've heard them give figures that show most people who're murdered are killed by somebody they know."

Nick finished his beer and got up to drop the bottle into the trash compactor. Then he leaned against the counter. "Depends on the type of murder, Cody. There's killing and there's killing. Generally speaking, most homicides are not just random acts perpetrated against strangers."

"As in, say, armed robbery," the boy said.

"Yeah."

"Or shootings by some guy who goes nuts and blows away a post office?"

Nick smiled. "This is an odd conversation, son. Is there a point you wanted to make?"

"I was just thinking about something Stephen said."

"Oh?"

"Yeah, well..." Cody rubbed some of the condensation from his drink can. "You remember the night I got shot?"

Nick's gaze went to the bandage on his son's neck. Al-

though reduced in size now, a dressing was still necessary. Every time Nick looked at it, it was a reminder of the
terror of seeing Cody on the floor, bleeding, and fearing
that he was about to lose his son.

"Yeah, I remember that night."

"Well, I never told you this, but Stephen said some stuff
that has sort of come back to me since Deke died and all. I
pretty much forgot about it until now. I mean, I didn't
even believe it when he said it. You know how people say
stuff and it's just bull—baloney?"

"What kind of stuff, Cody?"

"Well, we were talking about guns and I was saying
that cops don't really have all that many chances to use
their weapons. You've told me that before, Dad. I said
cops have to have them because they never know when
the time will come they might have to shoot. So Stephen
was looking at your gun, and he said there had been some
times lately when if he'd had a gun in his hand he would
have used it. He would have 'blown 'em away.'"

"Did he name any names?"

"When I asked him who he'd like to shoot, he said his
dad." Cody crumpled the drink can with one hand, adding, "It's funny, Stephen never called him his dad. He always said 'my old man' or 'the asshole.'" Cody watched
Nick anxiously, as if in repeating Stephen's words, he
might be violating an unwritten adolescent code of silence.

"Sounds like just tough talk, Cody. I wouldn't worry
about it."

Cody nodded with relief. "Yeah, that's what I thought.
Nobody would seriously consider shooting their own
dad, huh?"

"Well, it happens, but I can't see Stephen doing it."

"One more thing, Dad." He closed the empty pizza

box. "Would I have to testify about what Stephen said if Chief Escavez asks me?"

"He won't ask you." *Even if hell freezes over.*

"Great. 'Cause I sure didn't want to say anything that might look bad for Stephen. I like him."

"Me, too, Cody."

Cody stood. "So who could it be?" He stuffed his trash into the compactor and leaned against the kitchen counter, facing Nick. "I just thought of something, Dad. We're here across the lake from New Orleans because everybody says the Big Easy's a very violent place. And yet in poky little Bayou Blanc there's a murderer loose on the streets." He grinned at Nick. "Weird, huh?"

Victoria stood at a window where a tiny slice of the street in front of Leo's property was visible through a dense planting of azaleas. Waylon Escavez's police car was still parked in front of the house. She was shocked by the man's gall. Scores of people hated Deke Russo, and yet he'd singled out Amber as a prime suspect.

"I'm concerned, Leo." She turned from the window. "Escavez is absolutely overstepping his bounds! Coming around plying us all with questions, leaping to conclusions that have no basis in fact, insinuating Amber would murder her husband. It's preposterous, Leo!" Reaching up, she touched her turban. "What can we do?"

"I don't know, Vicky." Leo watched her move from table to desk in the sunroom, touching objects here and there, straightening, shifting, brushing at a speck of dust. "But working yourself up into a state won't do anybody any good," he said. "Kate has her hands full trying to be there for Amber. If you collapse, there'll be two loved ones for her to worry about."

With a sigh, Victoria sank onto an antique love seat.

"Nobody could possibly believe Amber would shoot Deke, could they, Leo?"

"Maybe no one close to Amber, but the police have to consider all possibilities."

She looked at him. "And what about you, Leo? You know she wouldn't do such a thing, don't you?"

He smiled sadly. "I do know."

She clasped her hands in her lap. "Do you have any ideas about who did it?"

He spread his hands. "Deke was a man with secrets. There are almost as many suspects as there were fans."

"That's just my point, Leo! Why must he concentrate on Amber?"

"Let Nick worry about that. You and I are in over our heads trying to second-guess someone like Escavez." He patted his pocket and came up with a cigar. Fondling it, unlit, he let his gaze wander in the direction of his house. "I need to get back, Vicky. Kate will want to get home, and I don't want Amber and Stephen to be alone. Besides, you're exhausted. You need to rest."

"Yes." Victoria smoothed the soft fabric of her caftan over her knees and managed a smile. "And you're right about Nick. He's more than a match for Escavez. I'm overreacting. I'm a great trial to you, Leo. I know it, but…" She put a hand to her cheek, vulnerable suddenly. "Life is so…fragile, isn't it?"

"Sometimes. But relationships aren't, Vicky. Look at us."

From the love seat, she studied his face. "How can you say that, Leo? Look at what I've put you through all these years."

With a smile, he pocketed the cigar and went over to her. Settling beside her on the love seat, he took her hand. "Thirty-three years of friendship, comfort and companionship, thirty-three years of sharing our daughters' ups and downs, of making my life infinitely richer. That's what you've put me through all these years, Vicky, and I've loved every minute of it."

She touched his face, stroked the line of his jaw, traced the still-firm cleft in his chin. "I've been thinking about the past a good bit lately."

"Don't. It's dead and buried."

"Maybe for you. Not for me. Kate's return has brought it all back again."

"Kate's going to be fine. So is Amber."

"I wish I had your faith."

He brushed a kiss on her forehead. "I'd give you more than faith if you'd just say the word."

She was smiling now. "Same old line. Don't you ever get tired of repeating it?"

"No."

"I can't, my darling," she said, her smile fading. "You know why."

"It doesn't matter anymore," he said fiercely. "It never did, to me."

"I know." She brought their joined hands to her lips for a kiss. "And I will always love you for that."

TWENTY-NINE

"Hi. Got a minute?"

Sam was already in her office as Kate pulled her gaze from the open window and swiveled around. Without rising, she waved at a chair. "Sure, have a seat."

She watched him close the door and move to the chair opposite her desk. He was carrying a patient's chart. Gesturing toward the window, he said, "You've been sitting there studying the view for the last fifteen minutes. Am I interrupting landscaping ideas for the parking lot?" His smile was slightly off center. "If so, we can talk later."

Kate's smile was faint and fleeting. "Just thinking."

"Uh-huh."

When she didn't reply, the amusement faded from his eyes. "Worried about Amber?"

"And my mother. And Leo. And Stephen." *And me.*

He grimaced sympathetically. "I guess you got more than you bargained for when you decided to come home, didn't you?"

"That's just one of the thoughts you interrupted." With a wry expression, she laced her fingers together and rested them on the charts in front of her—the charts she hadn't yet touched. Between Amber's situation, her mother's obvious weakening condition and her own unraveling as a physician, Kate had been wondering if returning to Bayou Blanc might actually have accelerated her downfall.

"How's Victoria taking all this?" Sam asked.

"She's worried about Amber because they seem to have picked her as the prime suspect in Deke's murder. Not that I consider her concern unusual. She's always been protective of Amber. I think she's worried about the toll it's taking on Leo, too. By the way, has he had a good physical lately? I thought he seemed tired at the funeral." She studied her fingers momentarily. "I know that's normal, considering the circumstances, but his color was off and he seemed a little unsteady at the graveside. Did you notice?"

"I did, as a matter of fact. I mentioned it and he actually promised to come in and submit to a few tests. However—" Sam flashed a grin "—as of ten minutes ago, according to Ruby, he hadn't made good on that promise."

Kate aimed a glance at the stack of folders. "Not that we need to be drumming up more business, but Leo's special. And he tends to neglect himself. Incidentally, are you as swamped as I am?"

"What's the problem? Leo wasn't completely honest about the workload when he was selling the idea of a partnership?"

She smiled. "I don't think he realized the popularity of the clinic. He's been treating a ton of patients so long, he thinks this is normal."

"But still nothing like the constant stream of patients in an E.R., right?"

"I'll say. So I'm not complaining."

Still, if she'd been able to avoid coming to the clinic today, she would have done so. Not because of the workload, but because she was still shaken by the latest flashbacks and would have preferred not to place herself in a situation where she might make some ghastly error and cause harm to an unsuspecting patient. But Leo was staying at home with Amber and Stephen for the rest of the week, and there was no way Sam alone could handle the patients. Fortunately, nothing today had triggered a reaction that zapped her into the twilight zone.

With a suddenly grave look, Sam leaned forward, his elbows on his knees. "Kate, I—"

He was interrupted when the door was opened abruptly by Diane Crawford. Her cold glance went first to Kate before settling on Sam. "There are a couple of charts on your desk you need to review before you leave tonight, Sam."

Sam exchanged an irritated look with Kate, but his reply to his nurse was courteous. "Okay, I'll take care of it, Diane."

Diane made a point of glancing at her watch. "I'll wait if you think you'll get to them within, say, five or ten minutes."

"I don't think I'll make it. But it's not a problem. Kate and I still have some things to wrap up here before we can leave. You go on."

"Well, if you're sure…"

"I'm sure. Good night, Diane."

After only an instant's hesitation, she closed the door with a firm snap. Sam's gaze remained on the chart in his hand until the nurse's footsteps had faded. No matter how hard Kate tried, there was no way she could warm up to Sam's nurse.

"What things do we have to 'wrap up'?" she asked as the silence stretched a little too long.

"This." He seemed to hesitate, still studying the chart. Then he put it on the desk and pushed it across to her.

Kate's heart jumped when she read the name: Madison, Victoria Delahoussaye. Her gaze flew to his.

He nodded. "She had some tests last week and the results came in Friday. She asked me to wait until after the festival to tell you."

Kate looked at the chart, still unopened in front of her. It was thick and well used, grim evidence of a very sick patient. Without looking at Sam, she swiveled in her chair again and fixed her gaze on the crepe-myrtle trees in the distance. "Just tell me, Sam. I don't think I want to wade through all the details to get to the bottom line."

"It's not good, Kate."

"I knew that." She watched several sparrows pecking busily at something on the sidewalk.

"Victoria agreed to an aggressive program of chemotherapy, and it was tough. Some patients tolerate nuclear medicine better than others, but for her, it turned out to be particularly difficult. Which makes me regret even more that it didn't succeed. The cancer has spread."

When Kate was a little girl, she'd learned that she could cope with scary things by taking herself to another place in her mind. It was a good way to hold reality at bay, but still hear and think and comprehend. As Sam talked, explaining in familiar medical jargon what was happening to Victoria and the exact treatment protocol, Kate stood on an imaginary seashore and listened not to her mother's death sentence, but to the quiet rush of the tide. She saw small seabirds on the sandy shore. She watched gulls swoop in graceful arcs down to the bright surface before lifting off again in graceful flight.

When he was done, she asked, "How much time does she have?"

"Kate…" She heard the dismay in his voice. Telling a family member that a loved one was going to die was never easy. She'd been in his place too many times.

"I want to know, Sam."

She heard him shift in his chair, heard the weary sigh. "These things are impossible to predict, you know that."

There were only crepe myrtles outside her window now. No seagulls, no sandpipers. She swiveled back, facing him. "At least she gave you permission to tell me. That's something."

"She's reaching out, Kate. I knew she would."

"Did you?" Kate made a tent of her hands, covering her trembling lips. She had to swallow hard before words would come. "You've been through this before, Sam. What can I do to make things easier for her?"

"You've done it, Kate. You came home to Bayou Blanc, and you chose to live in the same house. You share your life with her. I don't think she expected that. I think she's made peace with her situation, and your being here has a lot to do with that."

"Peace." Kate gave a short laugh, dropping her hands to her desk. "I'm glad one of us has it."

"Something else was bothering you before I came in. What is it, Kate?"

The tears she'd managed to hold back sprang to her eyes. She bent quickly, fumbling for her bag and car keys in a lower drawer. "I have to go, Sam. Mother will be waiting." When she stood, Sam had moved around until he was almost touching her. Not looking at his face, she concentrated on the bottom button of his polo shirt.

"Is it the flashbacks? Has it happened again?"

She thought of denying it, then sighed and closed her eyes.

"It did happen again," he said, taking both her hands. "When? Today? Last night?"

"Last night, at Leo's house. Right in front of Pamela LaRue. One minute we were talking normally, and the next, well... She must have thought I was nuts."

"She's a cop. She's seen everything." With a hand on her shoulder, he gently forced her to sit on the edge of her desk. Taking her bag and keys, he tossed them down beside her, then dragged a chair in front of her and sat.

"Okay, let's have it. And I promise, if I think you're nuts, I'll tell you so, flat out."

She managed a grim smile. What difference did it make if she told him? Maybe the telling would help her sort out some of the mystery of what was happening. Not because she was convinced that Sam had any particular expertise in this area, but he was the only person who knew what was happening to her. She certainly couldn't burden her mother now. And Leo had his hands full with Amber.

She pushed her hair back from her face and took the plunge. "I was outside on the patio last night because no one was allowed to be with Amber while she was being questioned by the chief. Leo was with Mother. Pamela LaRue appeared. We were chatting, and of course the subject was Deke Russo."

Sam remained quiet, listening.

"At least, that seemed to be the subject, but looking back, I wonder now if Pamela was on a fishing expedition. She had uncovered some pretty nasty things about Amber and Deke's marriage. And as we talked about it, Sam, just out of the blue I suddenly heard the rushing sound, and, well you know the rest."

Sam reached for her hands and held them fast. "It's not so surprising that your emotions sort of short-circuited, is it? Amber's your oldest friend, and her husband was murdered. Death does bizarre things to our equilibrium."

She hadn't realized she was trembling until she felt his hands on her arms moving slowly up and down, warm and reassuring. With a strangled murmur, Kate felt fatigue and bewilderment threaten to overcome her. She released a shaky laugh. "This is r-ridiculous," she said, looking at him with both hands pressed to her mouth.

"Ah, you need a hug, sweetheart." Sam stood and wrapped his arms around her. He didn't seem to notice that she didn't melt into the embrace; that her hands were balled between them, her body tense. But she was thinking how good it would feel to just let go and allow herself the luxury of letting someone else be strong. And how risky. This man could not be trusted. Could he?

Tucking her head beneath his chin, he spoke thoughtfully. "Let's analyze, okay? There has to be a common thread, here. Something that pushes a button, so to speak. Something that triggers buried memory."

His deep voice vibrating beneath her ear was all too seductive. What could be the harm in allowing herself the solace of human contact? It didn't have to mean lifetime commitment. With a sigh, she slipped her arms around his waist and allowed her body to press flush against his. She could hear the solid beat of his heart, smell the fading scent of his cologne, feel the hard strength in his thighs. After a moment, she realized they were both swaying gently. She would be happy, she thought, to stay here a long, long time.

"It isn't stress, Sam."

"No? You sound certain."

"I am. I know it's...more than stress." Pulling away from him—with reluctance, she admitted to herself—she began slipping her lab coat off to hang it on a coat-tree near the door.

"I know because, as you suggested, I've pieced together a sort of common thread." She looked back at him. "Pamela had seen it happen to me once before, here in the clinic. Remember when she came in with a battered wife—Janine Baptiste? Pamela had been mauled by Janine's husband. You treated Janine that day."

"Yeah. She'd really been roughed up."

"All of a sudden, as I was at the sink, the same scenes I saw last night materialized in the mirror. I was really shaken because I'd hoped moving away and leaving the E.R. and all the stress would mean the end of...that. Then, last night, I almost toppled into the fishpond. Pamela thought I was going to faint." She met his gaze directly. "The common thread is violence. And I seem most vulnerable if it's women or children." She studied her hands. "When I see a woman who's been abused, it just unravels me."

"Wait a minute. How, exactly, how does this relate to Amber and Deke? You're not saying they had an abusive relationship?"

"Yes."

"How do you know that?"

"Amber told me herself. I actually saw the evidence before she admitted it, but I was too thick to put it together."

"Jesus, how bad was it?"

"I'm not sure. A few days before their performance, she had a bruise on her forearm—'defensive marks' we used to call them in the E.R., when victims put up their arms and hands to try to ward off blows from their assailants. But Amber downplayed it, so I didn't push it. I'm still amazed that I was so...blind. Then, on the night Deke was killed, he really hurt her."

"How? In what way?" Sam was pacing now, displaying a decent man's outrage.

"She said he actually picked her up and tossed her across the room. It seems we were right that night when we guessed he wouldn't like being second banana."

"She told you all this?"

"Yes, when she asked for a ride home. She said she was fed up and that she wasn't going to put up with it anymore."

"Whew." Sam stopped with his hands propped on his hips. "That could sound pretty bad for Amber if you were ever questioned. She wouldn't be the first woman to get fed up and kill her abuser."

"I *have* been questioned. That's what Pamela wanted to

talk about last night. She knows, Sam. She dug up hospital reports that would horrify Amber if they were made public. They would also damage her career. Amber's set to sign a fabulous contract with a department-store chain."

Sam sat on the edge of her desk, looking thoughtful. "Did Pamela say she thinks Amber shot him?"

"Not in so many words, but it's the next logical step, once she uncovers all the reasons Amber might want him out of her life. And she's a very shrewd detective, Sam. Last night she was distracted by my flashback. So at least for now, she just has part of the picture. But she's not done. You mark my words."

"Are you worried about what she might find out?"

"Should I be? In your opinion?" she added, searching his face carefully.

"You're asking if I think Amber killed him."

"I... Yes."

He shrugged. "From what you've told me, I think it's plausible."

"'Plausible.'" She looked sad. "And that's what I'm afraid a lot of people will think."

"And you don't?"

She moved thoughtfully to her desk to pick up her bag and car keys. "You'll think I'm biased, but no, I don't believe that Amber shot Deke. I think she had reason to, and I think any affection in their marriage had long since died. I also think she was bitterly angry. She was frantically trying to figure out how to dump him without destroying everything she'd worked for."

"You just built a convincing case from circumstantial evidence," Sam said.

"I know. But she didn't do it."

"Are you sure this isn't your own guilt talking?"

"I feel guilty, all right, but I still say no. She didn't—*couldn't*—kill Deke."

Sam drew in a deep breath. "Well, Amber's problems aside, do you have any ideas about how all this relates to your flashbacks?"

She spread her hands in bafflement. "Not a clue."

Sam nodded and straightened from her desk. "Don't worry. It'll come."

She tried to smile but failed. "When? Before or after my nervous breakdown?"

"You're not going to break down, Kate. You're too strong."

Both of them started when the telephone rang. "Should we get that?" Kate asked on the third ring. After-hours there was an answering service to pick up calls, but apparently someone at the service switchboard was daydreaming.

Sam reached over and picked up. "Sam Delacourt. Yeah, sure, she's right here." He looked at Kate but didn't pass her the phone. He listened for a moment, then snapped, "Tell them to call Vince Morrison. Right. Good. Hang on. We'll be there in three minutes."

With her bag and car keys in her hand, Kate was rooted to the spot, her heart thudding. Vince Morrison was a cardiologist. "Is it my mother?"

"No." Sam was digging into his pocket for his keys as he flipped the lights out. "It's Leo. He's already at the hospital."

She stared at him, stricken. "What's wrong? What is it?"

"It's a heart attack, Kate." He closed the door behind them and shooed her out. "Come on, I'll drive."

THIRTY

"I don't want to participate in any way, Sam. Don't ask me." Kate got out of the car and slammed the door.

"I'm not asking," Sam said. "I'm telling you." His hand closed firmly on Kate's elbow, and he guided her past the physicians' entrance into the service elevator.

"You may not have to do anything," he said, punching the button. "But Vince Morrison isn't answering his page at the moment, and the intern who's on standby doesn't have a fraction of your experience. For that matter, I don't have a fraction of your experience in handling a heart attack, so if that's what's happening with Leo, you're his best bet right now. And you're going to do what's necessary."

Kate stood trembling as the elevator lifted in a stomach-turning lurch. It was all well and good for Sam to dismiss her misgivings; he didn't have all the facts. All she'd been able to think about on the way to the hospital was the disaster that had followed her handling of Joseph Carmello's case. She closed her eyes. *Dear God, please let Vince Morrison get here soon.*

"I'm scared, Sam," she whispered.

"Me, too," he said, adding in a gentler tone, "You can handle this, Kate. This is the man who's responsible for your decision to become a doctor. Leo himself would have no hesitation in placing his life in your hands."

"This is exactly why I didn't want to do any more

trauma," she replied, wrapping her arms around herself. "If something should happen... If Leo..." She drew an unsteady breath. "I'd never be able to live with myself."

"Come on. You're wasting valuable energy obsessing over something that's not going to happen. Hell, it seems I have more faith in you than you do yourself." He caught her arm again as the elevator opened and urged her down to the double doors of the cardiac-care unit.

She spotted Leo immediately. Two nurses and a young intern stood at his bedside. She saw at once that he was conscious and struggling with pain that Kate knew must be crushing. The intern moved quickly toward them. "Hi, Dr. Delacourt." He shook hands with Sam, who introduced Kate. "Jeez, am I glad to see y'all."

He shoved Leo's chart at Sam and lowered his voice. "I'm in a dilemma here, Sam. The patient displays symptoms of a myocardial infarction, but I'm just not certain. I've given him morphine for the pain, but it's steadily increasing. I've held off on other procedures, trying to get a good fix on what's happening." He glanced at an overhead clock. "I was hoping Vince would show before now. He's in Baton Rouge. No telling when he'll get back. We've done an EKG. It's here." He released a clip and pulled the folded tape from the file.

Kate's anxiety increased as she listened to Jones's rundown of Leo's symptoms and read the EKG. It was a rerun of Joseph Carmello's case. Chest pains, cold sweats, numbness in the left arm. She moved away from the men and headed to Leo's bedside with her heart pounding frantically. He was pale, breathing shallowly. She leaned over and kissed his cheek, and his eyes fluttered open.

"Kate. Good girl. I knew you'd come."

"I know you're in pain, Leo. We're going to take care of it."

"Thanks. To tell the truth, I'd rather be on the golf

course." His lips barely moved in a smile. "But you're here now and we can get down to business. I was afraid that young intern would wait until I was too far gone to do anything except shoot me up with morphine and watch me die."

"Not while I'm here," she said, realizing she meant it.

"Okay, do your thing, girl. I want to live to see your children."

Her heart twisted. "You know I don't have privileges in this hospital, Leo."

"Sam does. Tell him what you recommend and he'll go with it."

"You need the clot buster," Kate said with mounting confidence. Incredibly, her panic was easing. "It's not necessary to wait for the blood tests showing the enzymes. I know what's happening and I know what to do."

Joseph Carmello was another case in another time. She could do nothing about that decision and she would never really know whether she'd made a mistake or not. But here and now with Leo, she did know. Maybe, she thought, looking at his beloved face, this was why she'd had to learn that painful lesson. Maybe it had to have happened so that she would be here to save this man's life.

Sam stood at the foot of the bed with Dr. Jones. "Did you get that, Sam?" she asked. "It can be dripped straight into his IV, so let's get to it."

Sam turned without hesitation and passed the order for the medication to a nurse. Then he stood beside Kate and smiled at Leo. "Hang on, partner. We'll get you fixed up in time to tee off with Bert Landry Sunday morning."

"I'm holding you to that," Leo told him. But he was in obvious pain. Kate directed a quick look at the machine monitoring his vitals. His pulse was too high.

"Heartbeat's a little haywire," Sam observed, touching the older doctor's shoulder. "Relax, Leo. That clot buster's on its way."

Kate held Leo's hand, feeling helpless and wild with urgency. She almost leaped on the nurse when she appeared with the medication. "Get it in the IV, Sam," she ordered. "He's unstable, and we don't want his heart to become too traumatized."

"Gotcha." Sam broke the seal on the medication and attached it to the cord hanging from the IV pole. A tap and the clear liquid began flowing. There were now half-a-dozen people crowded around Leo's bed. All watched anxiously, their gazes shifting from Leo's face to the readings on the monitor. Leo was gray with pain now and only semiconscious.

Kate held fast to his hand, realizing how much she loved this man. Leo had been everything to her in her childhood. He'd sat through her piano recitals, applauded her terrible efforts in school plays, encouraged her academically, supported her decision to study medicine. Kate realized she'd always thought of him as her father, too. In every sense of the word.

"Wow, would you look at that." Ellis Jones stared in amazement at the change in the monitor's signals. "That stuff is really miraculous."

Sam slipped his arm around Kate's waist as she concentrated on Leo's pulse. It was considerably stronger and evening out. "His color's a hundred-percent better," Sam said. "He's breathing easy now, too."

"He is, isn't he?" Still stroking Leo's hand, Kate managed a smile.

"Good work, Dr. Madison," Sam said.

"Thank you, Dr. Delacourt."

And thank you, God.

Ellis Jones rubbed his palms together happily. "I'll call his family in now."

Victoria, not Amber, was the first person to see Leo. Pale and obviously shaken, she made her way toward Leo's bed in the CCU. Kate moved quickly to meet her. "Mother! I didn't know you were here!"

"How is he?" Victoria asked, not taking her eyes from Leo. She reached his bed and took his hand in hers, cradling it against her cheek. "Leo, I'm here, darling. It's Victoria."

Leo managed to nod wearily. "You shouldn't be here, Vicky."

"Don't be ridiculous, Leo. Where else would I be?"

"At home, resting. You know Kate will keep you posted."

"It's not the same as seeing you. And I'm not leaving you, so don't even suggest it." As she spoke, Victoria caressed his cheek, smoothed his hair, twitched at the sheet. "Was it a heart attack, Kate?"

"Yes, but we warded off the worst of it."

"With that new drug, I'll bet," Victoria said. "The one you hesitated over giving the man in Boston."

"Yes, that one." Kate felt Sam's gaze on her but wouldn't look at him. Time enough to explain when Leo made it past the first critical twenty-four hours.

"She saved me this time, Vicky," Leo said, drifting hazily in a morphine cloud.

"Good." Victoria reached over and patted Kate's hand. "Thank you, Kate." She brushed at tears in her eyes. "Are you in pain, my love?"

Leo was having difficulty concentrating, but he managed a smile. "How could I be in pain? I'm full of morphine."

"Good. You just rest. I'll be right here."

Leo roused enough to look disapproving. "No. Go home, Vicky. I'm in good hands."

Victoria suddenly seemed to wilt in despair. "You know you wouldn't be here but for me, Leo. I shouldn't have—"

"Vicky." Leo's eyes opened. "Don't talk rubbish."

"I never meant to cause you pain, Leo."

Leo struggled to concentrate. "Never…pain. No regrets…" He sighed, but the effort to speak was too much. "Have to rest…now, Vicky. Sorry…love…"

Both Kate and Sam frowned at the monitor. Leo's pulse was elevating and his heartbeat showed some irregularity. Kate touched Victoria's arm and drew her back slightly. "Mother, I know you're upset," she murmured, "but let's let Leo rest for a while. He's still critical. The least little thing can trigger arrhythmia, and that could be a real problem."

Victoria seemed dazed as Kate urged her out of the CCU. "It's my fault he's here," she said with a look back at Leo.

"No, Mother, this has been coming on. There were signs. Both Sam and I have been concerned about him."

"He does too much, but he won't listen to anyone," Victoria said. On the way to the family waiting room, she peered anxiously through a window in the corridor that opened onto the front entrance to the hospital. "Where is Amber?"

"She went to New Orleans. I left messages, so she should be calling soon. Stephen said she had to secure the house, and take care of some details regarding her business. Nick drove her."

Victoria sank weakly onto one of the couches in the waiting room. "It's no wonder Leo's heart gave out, with all this…unpleasantness. Certainly I have done nothing to help."

"You didn't choose to become ill, Mother."

"Illness is the least of it. I've been a burden to Leo for years, Kate."

"You've been his best friend, Mother. He loves you."

"No. I was never worthy of Leo's love."

Kate stood for a moment, then simply abandoned any effort to reason with her mother. If she'd ever had any questions about Victoria and Leo's relationship, they were answered now. No married couple displayed more care and concern than what she'd just witnessed between her mother and Leo. The only mystery that remained was why they'd never married.

"Are you sure you won't consider going home and getting some rest, Mother? Sam and I will be here to take care of Leo."

"I'm staying, Kate."

"Okay, if you insist." After a pause, Kate sat on the couch and took her mother's hand. "Sam told me a few hours ago about your tests, Mother."

Leaning back, Victoria closed her eyes. "So tiresome, especially now."

"Not to me, Mama. Never to me." Kate squeezed the thin fingers, finding them even more fragile than they'd been a few days ago. She felt a pang, knowing what was in store.

"You just concentrate on Leo and don't worry about me, will you do that, Kate?" Victoria said.

"You know I will. It's what I intended all along. But I want you to tell me if there's anything you need, anything I can do."

Victoria turned and grasped Kate's hand tighter. "You will let me know the minute I can see Leo again, promise me that?"

"Of course, but you know the rules. You can only see him for ten minutes each hour. They won't bend the rules for anybody in the CCU—not even Leo Castille." Kate leaned over and kissed Victoria's cheek, then stood. "Meanwhile, Sam and I will keep you posted on how he's doing."

Looking drained and exhausted, Victoria nervously adjusted the silk scarf on her head. Her eyes, as she gazed tearfully at Kate, seemed empty and sad. "Tell him I love him, Kate."

"I will."

Kate was still at the hospital at ten the next morning, bone weary, but quietly elated. Courtesy of Sam's hospital status, she had been able to stay in the CCU and personally monitor Leo. At daylight, he'd finally passed the crisis point. A heart catheterization would be scheduled by Vince Morrison within a day or so to assess the damage, but Kate felt confident that Leo was going to be okay. She had done what was necessary and she hadn't panicked. She wanted to sing with the joy of it.

After checking on Leo again, she headed for the physicians' lounge and found it blessedly empty. Waiting for tea to steep, she dropped her head back and pressed her hands to the small of her back to work out some of the kinks. It had been almost thirty hours since she'd slept, and she still had a full day ahead at the clinic. But for the first time since coming home, she was going to work without misgivings.

"Here, let me do that."

Sam's voice came from a spot close to her ear. Not waiting for permission, he put his hands on her shoulders, moving them in a way that sent a delicious lassitude through her nervous system. Pressing both thumbs to her nape, he rotated them, making Kate moan. "Oh, Sam, that feels so good."

"I thought you left an hour ago."

"Only to drive Mother home. I just wanted to check Leo once more before heading for the clinic."

"I've already told Ruby to reschedule all patients for after lunch, so you can take it easy until then."

Had he kissed her nape? It was difficult to concentrate, when all she wanted was to give in to the pleasure radiating through every nerve ending. "I think Leo's going to be fine."

"I think so, too." His hands settled at her waist now, warm and intimate. "Vince approved everything you did."

Kate felt a great, enveloping calm. She'd faced another devil and she hadn't been destroyed.

"See, you worried for nothing," Sam said. His mouth was touching her ear as his arms went fully around her. He was big and close and fully aroused. "I told you so."

She couldn't hold back a little shiver. "It did go well, didn't it?"

"It sure did, Dr. Madison." She sensed his smile, and her own lips curved with joy. Unable to resist temptation, she moved against him suggestively. This time, it was Sam who groaned.

His hands moved beneath her top, seeking her breasts. He unsnapped her bra and, using his thumbs, raked both nipples.

"This is not a massage," she told him breathlessly.

"No," he murmured, swirling his tongue in the shell of her ear.

He turned her to face him and pushed his fingers through her hair. With a glad sound, she gave herself up to the hot urgency overtaking them both. And when he slipped his hands beneath the waistband of her scrubs, she was fumbling at the tail of his shirt, seeking naked male flesh.

"This is nuts," he moaned. "Anybody could walk in."

"Uh-huh." But her arms were tight around his waist and she didn't want to let go. For the second time in less than twenty-four hours, she was tempted to take whatever pleasure was offered and damn the consequences. She—

Her thoughts dissolved as the door opened abruptly. Kate and Sam broke apart, but not before the shocked teenage girl saw enough to guess what was happening. "Daddy!"

THIRTY-ONE

With a curse, Sam stepped in front of Kate to shield her from his daughter's eyes. "What are you doing here, Mallory?"

"The nurses told me where you were." Her stunned gaze went from Sam to Kate, who was scrambling to straighten her clothes. "I wanted to tell you I'm going to the Quarter with LeAnne and I need some money. What is going on, Daddy?"

"Is LeAnne waiting outside?"

"Yes. Answer me, Daddy!"

"Let me walk you out there." Sam put out a hand, but Mallory shied out of reach. Her surprised shock was fading quickly into outrage. She turned an accusing glare on Kate. "You said you and my dad hardly knew each other. You said there wasn't anything between you way back then. You lied to me! You lied!"

Sam reached again for Mallory's arm. "Come on, honey, let me walk you out. I can explain."

"Explain! Well, that would be a trick, Dad," Mallory scoffed, trying vainly to free herself. She threw a disgusted look at Kate. "Are you gonna tell me I didn't see you kissing her? Are you gonna say it didn't mean anything? Well, I know what I saw and it looked pretty hot to me."

Sam sighed. "You can't judge what you saw without

hearing me out, Mallory. Kate and I are friends, we don't deny that. We—"

"Friends!" Mallory cried. "Cody and I are friends, Dad. Stephen and I are friends. And we don't do the kind of stuff you were just doing. It's just like Diane said, she's chasing you. Diane was probably right about everything else, too, but I believed your lies."

"Diane?" Sam and Kate exchanged a look. "What about Diane? What has she been telling you, Mallory?"

"Mom's only been gone a few months, Dad," Mallory said scornfully. "Couldn't you have waited? This is disgusting!"

"Come over here and sit down, Mallory." Ignoring the girl's frenzied resistance, Sam marched her across the lounge to one of the couches and forced her to sit. "Now, let's talk about this rationally."

"You can talk all you want," Mallory said, her expression stubborn. "It's not going to change what I saw. And what I know."

"You don't know anything, and what you saw isn't what you think."

"Oh, yeah? I guess you weren't plastered together like in an X-rated movie. I guess you didn't have your hands in her pants. I guess she wasn't feeling you up, either, Dad. Give me a break!"

Sam's face turned ruddy with embarrassment. Behind him, Kate put a hand over her eyes, wishing to be anywhere else. "I'm sorry you saw that, Mallory," Sam said in a subdued tone. "We—Kate and I—should have chosen a private place for…what you saw." Sighing, he sat down beside his daughter. "Listen, honey, there are things you don't understand. When you're older—"

"Oh, pu-leez." Mallory rolled her eyes. "I know the facts of life, Dad. You've got the hots for Dr. Madison. And it didn't just happen yesterday. Don't try to deny it anymore." She threw a bitter look at Kate. "What I can't accept is how you could like a person who would do what she did. She knew Mom was sick and she still went after you. She tried to break up your marriage, Dad."

Sam put a hand on Mallory's knee. "You're wrong about that, Mallory. I can't allow you to accuse Kate when you don't know the facts." Mallory opened her mouth, but he stopped her. "No, hear me out. My relationship with Kate is private. It didn't begin yesterday, you're right about that. What you're wrong about is believing that Kate deliberately set out to hurt anyone. She never even knew about your mother."

"Sam—" Kate moved forward involuntarily. Distressed, she put a hand on his shoulder. "I don't think—"

"It's okay, Kate." Without rising, he reached up and covered her hand. "This will never be cleared up as long as Mallory blames you for everything." He looked sadly at his daughter. "My relationship with Kate five years ago would have remained strictly professional if she had known that I was married, Mallory. But she didn't know. Because I didn't tell her."

"Daddy..." Stricken, Mallory gazed at Sam through wide, tear-filled eyes.

"I could try and excuse what I did, but the bottom line would still be the same. It was wrong, baby."

Behind him, Kate turned away to stand at the window, looking out. Mallory was torn, wanting to disbelieve her father, reluctant to let go of her resentment of Kate. Sam got to his feet, pushing his hands into his pockets, and looked directly into his daughter's eyes. "You wanted the facts. Now you have them, Mally."

With a wild look, Mallory pressed both hands to her mouth. "You don't realize what you're saying, Daddy."

"Believe me, I do, baby. I'm not proud of the way I behaved then."

"So what Diane told me wasn't true?"

Sam frowned. "What is this about Diane? What did she tell you?"

Mallory glanced guiltily at Kate. "She said Dr. Madison was trying to steal you from us because she wanted to marry you herself, that she didn't care about breaking up a marriage or hurting a person who was dying of cancer."

"When?" Sam demanded in bafflement. "When did you have a conversation with Diane about Kate?"

Mouth trembling, Mallory shook her head mutely. A tear rolled down one cheek.

Sam went to her, hesitant for fear that she'd rebuff him after what he'd admitted, but she threw her arms around him and turned her face into his shirt. "It was when M-Mom was s-sick. Be-before she took the pills. She... Diane...used to come to the house to visit Mom, and that's when she told me."

Sam met Kate's eyes over his daughter's head, then asked grimly, "Told you what, Mally?"

"That...that you were having an affair with...with..."

"With me," Kate whispered bleakly.

Mallory's tawny head bobbed up and down. "And...and then—" she looked at Sam in despair "—then I told Mommy! I didn't mean it to hurt her, but I was just so upset. And I thought she'd d-do something, make you change your mind and stay with us. I—I'm sorry, Daddy. I'm so s-sorry." Her voice rose to a wail. "And that night was when she did it! She took all those pills and she was never the same."

She drew a broken breath, wiping her tears with both hands. "And it was all my fault. So I told you somebody had been to our house and told her all that. I knew you thought it was K-Kate, so I never told you the truth, because I thought she was a bad person. But it was me who told Mom. And I couldn't tell you that. I knew you'd hate me."

"Sweetheart, baby…" He held her close, his hand spread wide on her head, pressing her to his heart. "I could never hate you. I just wish you'd said something. You're not responsible for what your mother did, Mally. You were still a little girl." Something in his voice changed, hardened. "None of this was your fault. You couldn't be expected to know how to handle anything like that."

Mallory quieted down, comforted by Sam's reassurance. She sniffed, swiping childlike at her nose with the heel of her hand. "I wanted to tell you. I made up the words in my head a million times, but every time I looked at Mom, so sick and helpless, and…and…so pitiful, and all because of me, I always chickened out."

Sam took the tissues Kate silently offered and mopped his daughter's tears. "Well, you don't have to worry about this anymore, Mally." He tossed the tissues in a bin at the coffee bar and wondered whether his own guilt could ever be assuaged. He tipped her face up and managed a small smile. "It looks as if I'm going to be shopping for a new nurse."

The girl blinked her long lashes rapidly. "That's better than shopping for a n-new daughter."

"No chance. We're stuck with each other." He tucked a stray wisp of hair behind her ear, then reached into his hip pocket for his wallet. "Now, do you still want some money to go to the Quarter with LeAnne?"

Mallory nodded, darting a shy glance at Kate. "If it's okay."

"It's okay." Sam pulled a twenty-dollar bill from his wallet. "Home by eleven, right?"

Her spirits reviving, Mallory headed for the door. "LeAnne's mom invited me to sleep over. But we'll still be in by eleven. Her mom said." Mallory wrinkled her nose. "She's as strict as you, Dad."

"Want us to walk you down to the car?"

Mallory shot another uncertain look at Kate. "If you want to."

Sam looked at Kate, who nodded. Mallory fell into step beside them. When they reached the front entrance, Le-Anne's mother sat waiting in a sport-utility vehicle with three teenage girls. Sam opened the door and introduced Kate, who answered a few solicitous questions about Leo from the other woman. Before climbing into the vehicle, Mallory stopped and turned, throwing her arms around Sam and hugging him fiercely. "I feel so much better, Daddy. I love you."

He kissed the top of her head. "I love you, too, Mally."

Mallory met Kate's eyes hesitantly. "I'm sorry about all this, Dr. Madison...Kate."

"There's absolutely nothing for you to be sorry for, Mallory." She smiled at the girl.

Mallory nodded, obviously relieved. "Bye, y'all."

Sam and Kate stood watching the vehicle until it disappeared. Then, giving vent to a gusty sigh, Sam planted his hands on his hips. "Are you as pissed as I am, Kate?"

"At Diane? Probably not, because I was only hurt indirectly. But this does explain a lot, doesn't it?"

"I can't go to the clinic and confront her right now," Sam said grimly. "We don't want another murder in Bayou Blanc."

Kate smiled sympathetically. "Maybe you should just settle for terminating her."

"Damn right. Within the hour." Sam sank down on the side of a concrete planter and stretched out his legs. "It's hard to believe anybody would sink so low and then sit back and watch a child assume the blame." He watched a little girl passing by, holding her mother's hand. "After

Elaine was no longer functional, Diane would take Mallory to lunch or shopping, do girl stuff with her. Now I'm wondering what she said to her when they were alone, to make sure Mally didn't suddenly decide to confess everything and put Diane's vindictive ass in a crack."

Kate settled beside him on the planter. "Mallory must have been very confused when I sidestepped her questions about a past relationship with you. I honestly didn't think she needed to know."

"Same here. And I'm not proud of lying about it."

Kate watched an aging couple slowly climbing the hospital steps. "I've always sensed Diane's hostility, but I never thought she'd actually do anything like this. I just thought her attitude was meant to discourage me from picking up where we left off."

He caught her hand and looked directly into her eyes. "I'm sorry, Kate. I never said it before. And I should have. Because I wasn't honest with you, it diminished what we had together. I regret that, along with a lot of other things I did then. Elaine was already sick and desperate. Finding out about us pushed her over the edge. Afterward, I shifted my guilt onto you. You were right about that."

She gazed at their clasped hands. "It's over. Let's put it behind us."

"You mean that?"

"Why not? I have too many really important things on my plate to obsess over the past." She freed her hand and stood. "Besides, we've managed pretty well so far in spite of our checkered past, haven't we?" She gave him a bright smile. "You don't cringe anymore when we pass in the hall at the clinic."

He didn't look pleased. "I assume you don't consider our new relationship one of the 'really important' things on your plate."

She shrugged. "What new relationship?"

He stood. "Kate, what do you call what happened between us in the lounge a few minutes ago?"

She crossed her arms. "Bad judgment. Very bad judgment."

"Don't you mean bad timing?" Suddenly he was almost smiling. "Because just as soon as I can manage it, I'm finishing what we started."

Incredibly, Kate felt herself blush. Her flustered gaze went beyond him. "Isn't that Nick's car?"

Sam glanced behind him at the dark green Explorer pulling into a parking spot, then turned back to Kate with a stubborn look. "So? Let's go somewhere and talk about this, Kate."

"I thought you were hell-bent to go fire your nurse."

"I can do it later," he growled.

"Kate! Sam! Hey, y'all, wait up." Amber rushed up the steps toward them with Nick at her side.

"Hi, guys," Kate said, ignoring Sam's muttered curse.

"I'm glad we caught you," Amber said breathlessly. "You can fill us in about Daddy. He's okay, isn't he?" Her green eyes were anxious.

"He's doing great," Kate said. "We left him in Vince Morrison's care."

"You're sure?" Amber asked, then listened intently as both Sam and Kate gave her details.

Nick's smile suddenly vanished. "Son of a bitch!"

Everyone turned to see a patrol unit pulling into the curved drive, stopping in a No Parking zone. The door on the driver's side opened and Howard Sloan got out. The detective stood for a moment, looking over the roof of the car at the four of them, sun glinting on the mirror lenses of his Ray-Bans.

Nick made a derisive sound. "Looks like Escavez's main man is on the job, boys and girls."

"Maybe he's here about something else," Kate murmured.

"No, he's here to harass Amber." His look became more grim as Pamela LaRue got out of the car. "And he's crafty enough to bring somebody with him who can think."

"I don't want to talk to them, Nick." Amber clutched at Nick's arm as Sloan rounded the car on his way toward them.

"Why are they harassing you, Amber?" Kate asked. She looked at Nick. "Do they have the right to bother her here? Don't they have any decency?"

"It's not about decency, Kate," Nick said. "It's about power, and without Escavez to keep a leash on him, Sloan is going to enjoy wielding it."

"Can't you do something, Nick?" Amber asked.

"You don't have to say anything," Nick told her. "We still have some rights—a proper venue for questioning, to name just one."

Sloan nodded to everyone politely, although his gaze rested for a moment too long on Nick. "Could I have a word with you, Ms. Russo?"

"I don't think so, Detective Sloan," Amber told him, managing a smile. "My father's in the CCU. He's just had a heart attack."

"We're aware of that, ma'am. This will only take a minute."

Amber glanced nervously at Nick, who said, "If you want to talk with Ms. Russo, we'll be glad to set a time and place."

"I guess Santana's your attorney now?" Sloan's mouth slanted with contempt.

"That's right."

The detective shrugged. "It's just one question, Ms.

Russo." Without a pause, he added, "We've got information that your stepson threatened to kill his daddy."

"That's ridiculous!" Amber said, even as Nick's hand closed on her arm.

Sloan began shaking his head, pretending to be perplexed. "Well, me and Officer LaRue, here, have been thinking." Pamela studied the cracks in the sidewalk, ignoring the look zapped her way from Nick as Sloan continued. "Just about everybody claims to be sleeping when Deke was shot...and it was the middle of the night, according to the coroner's report, when it happened."

"What's the one question, Sloan?" Nick demanded.

"The question is this, Ms. Russo." Sloan's leather holster squeaked as he hitched his pants up. "Is there a way you can verify that Stephen was in fact in the house between midnight and 4:00 a.m.? 'Cause if you can't, ma'am, it looks like we're going to have to consider the possibility that it was the kid who might have shot your husband."

"My God, what are they doing, Sam?"

Sam held the door of the clinic open while Kate went inside. "Racheting up the pressure on the family," Sam said, shoving his keys back into his pocket. "Which is where they seem to have concentrated their efforts to find Deke's killer."

"But they've discovered all kinds of nasty things about his personal life. He used cocaine, he liked pornography, he was unfaithful to Amber—he had *tons* of secrets that would have destroyed him if his radio audience ever got wind of them. Why don't they concentrate on that stuff? It was probably somebody in those sleazy circles who killed him!"

Sam stopped at the door of his office. "Apparently the cops believe everything you've just recapped is more than enough motive for someone close to Deke to kill him, Kate."

She followed him inside, slinging her purse at the chair in front of his desk.

He sighed. "If you want to know the truth, I'm more concerned about Stephen being a suspect than Amber. The night I treated Cody after he was shot, Cody told me Stephen said something about shooting his father when they were discussing guns. Stephen was upset over something that had happened that night between Deke and Amber."

"Oh, my God." Kate bent her head, rubbing a spot between her eyes. "This is such a nightmare, Sam. Deke's brutality made both Stephen's and Amber's lives a misery. Now he's dead and their pain just keeps going on and on. But I don't believe either of them would commit murder!"

"Hey, hey…" Sam moved toward her, but just at that instant, Diane Crawford stuck her head around the door.

"Oh, Sam…" She flashed a smile at him before nodding curtly at Kate. "I didn't realize you were here. Your rescheduled appointments start at two. How is Leo?"

"Diane, I was just about to page you." Unsmiling, Sam went to the door and waited for the nurse to step inside. "There's something we need to discuss." With his hand on the doorknob, he looked at Kate. "Kate, would you like to stay and hear this?"

"No." Kate brushed past the nurse, meeting Sam's eyes for a heartbeat. If she hadn't just witnessed the undeserved pain this woman had caused an innocent young girl, Kate might have felt some sympathy for Diane Crawford.

Instead, she walked out, closing the door softly behind her.

* * *

"Stephen, are you asleep?"

"Amber?" Stephen rubbed a hand across his face, then blinked hard to focus on the green numerals telling the time on top of his TV. As Amber slipped inside the boy's room, he scooted over to make room for her. "What's up?"

She sat on the edge of the bed. "Just checking to see how you are." Reaching over, she brushed his hair back from his forehead. "I just left the hospital."

He pulled his knees up, propping his elbows on them. He loved it when Amber came into his room late like this. It used to happen a lot. He sucked in a quick breath. "How's Grandpa Leo?"

"He's okay. He's recovering pretty fast, considering. They're going to do a test tomorrow to see about the damage, but they think it's minimal."

"That's good." He leaned over to turn on the lamp, but Amber stopped him.

"Leave it off. I'm not staying."

"Okay." There was enough moonlight coming in the window to see her pretty well anyway. Chewing the side of his cheek, he watched her wild curly hair all backlit with moonlight. She smelled good—not like the flowery stuff Mallory used, but dark and sexy. He wondered if Deke was watching right now from hell and feeling jealous. He damn sure hoped so. "Are you doing okay, Amber?"

"You mean about Daddy...or about Deke?"

"About Deke."

"Yeah, I'm fine. How about you?"

"I'm great. Never better." So it was a friggin' lie. Who cared? Sometimes he felt sad because there wasn't another living soul left in the world who was related to him. Which meant he was a bona fide orphan. But even when his old man was alive, he'd been an orphan in all the ways that counted. Now Deke was dead and it felt almost the same.

Amber smoothed the sheet stretched over his knees. "What've you been doing with yourself while I've been worrying about Daddy?"

He shrugged. "Just hangin' out."

"You see much of Cody?"

He turned from her, fixing his gaze out the window, knowing what he was going to say was rude. "If you mean do I spend as much time with him as you spend with his old man—hell, no."

"Nick's my lawyer, Stephen. He's helping me cope with the harassment I'm getting from the police here."

"You should get a real lawyer."

"Nick *is* a real lawyer."

He shrugged. "Whatever." He couldn't hold back what came out next. "Are you screwing him?"

"Stephen!"

"Well, are you?"

"No, I told you. He's my lawyer."

"Yeah. Right."

She put a cigarette in her mouth, clicked the lighter, and when it was lit, drew the smoke deep into her lungs. She looked at him again through a smoky haze. "I saw Detective Sloan today."

Stephen snorted. "'Barney Fife.'"

"He came to the hospital, if you can believe that." She studied the smoke rising from her cigarette. "With all Deke's secrets, they seem to be concentrating their efforts on finding his murderer here in Bayou Blanc."

"Figures." Stephen folded his arms over his knees.

Amber leaned over and flicked ashes into an empty pop can beside the bed. "The problem is," she said, drawing again on the cigarette, "that it happened in the middle of the night and it's hard for any of us to vouch for the others."

Stephen pushed the sheet off and scooted around until he was sitting beside her. He didn't worry about being in his skivvies. It wasn't as if she'd never seen him before. "Listen, Amber...you aren't worried about all this, are you?" He put a hand on her hair. He loved to touch her hair. "There's no way the cops can prove we *weren't* all in bed sleeping."

She looked straight at him. "I really was in bed sleeping, Stephen."

"Yeah, me, too."

After a long moment, she sighed and crushed out her cigarette, dropping the butt into the pop can. "They think one of us did it, Stephen."

He rubbed some of her dark curls between his fingers. "Like who? Which one of us?"

"Me, you... Even Nick's a suspect."

"Nick." He removed his hand and flopped straight back on the bed, fixing his gaze on the slowly revolving ceiling fan. "Hell, it works for me."

She shifted so she could look at him. "What do you mean, it 'works' for you? Nick didn't shoot Deke."

"How do you know he didn't? He had motive, he had opportunity, he had cause."

"What are you talking about?"

Stephen raised his hands, ticking points off on his fingers. "Motive, he knew Deke was out to get him for giving Cody access to his service weapon. Opportunity, same as the rest of us. How do we know where he was from midnight to 4:00 a.m.? Plus, he's got the hots for you, Amber."

She was staring at him, horrified. "Don't repeat any of that, do you hear me, Stephen? Those cops are just looking for that kind of ridiculous trumped-up reasoning to pin Deke's murder on somebody in his family. It's awful. I just hate what's happening."

"Nick Santana isn't family, Amber," Stephen said through his teeth. "You and I are family. And Grandpa Leo. Nobody else."

She released a sigh. "This is crazy." She put a hand on his naked belly. Stephen sucked in a quick breath and felt his whole body heat up. "Nick was at home with Cody when Deke was shot, damn it. I was asleep in Victoria's house, Daddy was in his bedroom and you were here. Isn't that right, Stephen?"

"Sure." His heart was going like a jackhammer in his chest. He covered her hand with his, but when he started to push it lower, she pulled away and stood.

"It's late. Get some sleep."

THIRTY-TWO

"For the last time, Sam, where are we going?"

Sam glanced into the side mirror as an eighteen-wheeler pulled out from behind them and thundered past on the interstate. "And for the last time, here's my answer, Kate—wait and see."

Kate looked down at her shorts and T-shirt. "You said casual. I hate it when I'm dressed wrong."

"Here's a hint—I won't need a tie."

Fighting a smile, Kate watched the landscape for a moment, then asked quietly, "What if Leo has a setback?"

"Ah…that's what's really bugging you, isn't it?"

"We're getting farther and farther from the hospital."

"Thirty minutes, Kate." Sam tapped his cruise control and signaled to exit. "Besides, Vince swore to me he would be available, no matter where and when." Slowing at the stop sign, he took a left. "It's been five days. You've practically camped at Leo's bedside. He's stable, and the heart cath showed minimal damage. He'd be the first to tell you to relax."

Kate raked her dark hair back from one cheek. "He is in great shape, you're right about that. To tell you the truth, I worry more about Mother collapsing. She's the one who's camped out by Leo's bedside, not me."

"Nothing you can do or say is going to pry your mother away from him right now."

"I know. Have you ever seen anything like it?"

"Yes, it's perfectly natural for two people who've had such a long relationship. Illness draws them closer."

Kate watched a white crane lift off from the dark surface of a bayou alongside the road. "Amber and I always wondered why they never married. It's plain as day that they love each other. Since both have been ill, they don't even bother to try and hide it. But Mother said the oddest thing the night Leo had his heart attack. She said she'd been a burden to him, that she wasn't worthy of his love. I'm still trying to figure that out."

He slowed again at a secondary road, then reached over and slipped his hand beneath her hair. "Kate, could we not talk shop for just one evening?"

She leaned into his touch, closing her eyes. "I don't consider this shop talk, but okay, if you insist." She glanced around, perking up as she noticed a landmark. "Hey, do you know where we are?"

He gave a low chuckle. "If I don't, we must be lost."

"I'm serious. This is the road that goes to our summer place on the bayou. Just around the curve is where you turn off."

"No kidding."

She looked at him. "Sam, is that— Oh, no, no way. Why would you— Okay, I've been patient long enough. For the positively last time, where are we going?"

"To your summer place."

Her smile held real delight. "Really?"

"Would I lie?" He turned into a white shell-paved lane, and instantly the glare of hot August sunshine was muted by the thick tangle of lush, subtropical growth unique to southern Louisiana.

"Here we are." He pulled the car beneath the rustic Acadian-style cabin set atop tall pilings, then climbed out and went around to open the door for Kate. "Air-conditioning's been on since yesterday, so it should be cool. Food's in the fridge, all ready to heat up in the microwave. Wine's chilling."

She put a hand on her heart. "Oh, Sam."

He grinned and nudged her toward the steep stairs leading up to the cabin's wide veranda. "I was hoping you'd be impressed." At the door, he sorted through a jangle of keys and finally inserted one in the lock, working it a bit. "Victoria said you have to jiggle it sometimes before it turns."

"My mother knows about this?"

He opened the door. "Would you believe it was Victoria's suggestion? When I said I'd like to take you somewhere for the weekend, she thought of the cabin."

"A weekend? Oh, I don't know, Sam."

He pocketed the keys, then put a finger on her lips. "Hush. Don't make any hasty decisions." Leaning over, he gave her a quick kiss, then urged her inside.

Kate looked around with pleasure. "Gosh, I forgot how much I love it here, Sam."

"Hold that thought." He rubbed his hands together. "Okay, wine first," he said, going straight to the bar.

While she waited for him to uncork the wine, Kate wandered around. In the kitchen, fresh French bread was tucked into a basket, a bowl of fruit was placed in the center of the work island, and on the table in the breakfast nook overlooking the bayou was a bouquet of wildflowers. "Who did all this?" she asked, touching a wild iris.

"Victoria sent Rose out first thing this morning."

"Did she?" Kate stood in the center of the great room, turning slowly. "I'll have to remember to thank her," she murmured. She knew how worried her mother was about Leo and Amber. She was touched that Victoria had anything left to spare for her.

"Your mother's your biggest fan," Sam said, pouring the wine. "Why can't you see that?"

"I'm working on it, Sam." She took her wineglass and sat at the bar watching him as he found matches and lit candles set strategically around in the kitchen and great room. Then he went to the fridge and took out a plate of hors d'oeuvres and set them in front of her.

Sam took a seat beside her, studying her profile. "What do you want to do first? Go out on the deck and watch the bayou? Take a nice long bath, play chess? Or," he added, "we could make love."

Kate set the wineglass down carefully. "Is that what this is about—making love?"

He was still studying her. "Would you turn around and go home if I said it was?"

"I don't know."

He stroked the side of her cheek. "I haven't exactly kept it a secret that I want to take you to bed again, Kate, but only if the time is right and you're as ready for it as I am." He pushed away from the bar and went to stand in front of the glass doors overlooking the dark bayou. In the candlelight, he looked brooding and sexy. Kate rubbed her upper arms briskly, suddenly nervous.

"So, is the time right?" she asked, reaching for her wine again.

"If not, I'm going to have to go out to that bayou and swim about forty laps." With a short laugh, he turned and faced her. "It looks dark and dangerous, and I don't know much about wrestling alligators."

She found a smile. "I don't blame you."

Sam finished his wine and set the glass down. "Can we talk about us now, Kate?"

"You want to pick up where we left off five years ago, is that it? Now that you know it wasn't me who precipitated your wife's suicide?"

"It must look that way," he admitted, "but the funny

thing is, I passed that point about fifteen minutes after you came back from Boston, Kate."

"Sam, you don't have to lie."

"It's true. I didn't want to feel anything for you, but I did. I spent that first day telling myself what a vindictive witch you were, how lucky I'd been because I'd found you out five years ago—with a little help from my trusty nurse, as it turned out. But inside me, feelings were stirring, coming alive. I'd been idling along for five years and suddenly I was hitting on all cylinders."

"What are you talking about, Sam? You were hostile from the moment I walked into the clinic!"

"It was self-defense, Kate."

"What?"

"I was looking out for number one," Sam said. "After you left and went to Boston, I honestly tried to put you out of my mind. Sometimes I almost managed it. At the time we met, my life was pretty depressing. Elaine had been sick several years, and looking back, I realize our marriage wasn't built on a foundation solid enough to withstand that kind of pressure. We'd had problems even before she got sick.... Anyway, it was ten times worse after...you. Not only did I have to cope with guilt as I watched Elaine waste away, but I was suddenly a single parent. With Elaine in that state, Mallory had no one but me. Poor kid," he added bitterly.

"Then suddenly you were back in my life, working beside me every day and hating my guts."

"I wasn't hating your guts," Kate replied softly. "I was trying to, but it didn't work."

He looked at her. "Is that the truth?"

She touched his face, cradling his jaw in her palm. "Yes."

"Kate..." He straddled her legs as she sat on the bar-stool. His hands were on her, moving up and down on the bare skin of her thighs. "Tell me it's not too late for us to try again. I want to start over, pretend that time didn't happen. Pretend that my lies didn't ruin the good thing that was happening between us."

She reached out and touched his mouth with her fingers, smiling faintly as he kissed the tips. "I can't pretend that time never happened, Sam."

Alarm darkened his eyes. "Kate, I—"

"Wait. For me, what happened was honest and natural and right. If I do as you say and pretend it never happened, that means I have to throw away the memory every woman cherishes. I fell in love with you then, Sam."

"Kate…" He pulled her forward and kissed her deeply. Thoroughly. With his hands bracketing her waist, he lifted her off the stool and wrapped his arms around her, running his lips over her cheeks and eyes, her temples, her ear; then lower. She lifted her arms with a sigh and put them around his neck, throwing her head back as he buried his mouth against her throat.

Seconds later they were in the bedroom. She hadn't seen the inside of that room for years, and she didn't notice it now. All she saw was Sam, the way he looked at her—as if he were stamping her image on his heart for all time. The way he stripped with ever-increasing urgency, as if now that they'd reached this point he had not a second to waste. And the way he fell on her with an explosiveness that rivaled the moment at the track in the storm.

She didn't have to tell him when her orgasm was upon her. He took her right to the edge and held her when she cried out as she came. Then, with his breath hot and rasping, he was moving again, his body quickening with the urgency of his need. Suddenly he reared up, thrilling her with the deep cry torn from his throat as he erupted into his own powerful climax.

* * *

"So was this a good idea or what?" Sam was smiling his crooked smile, just looking at her.

"The best. Why didn't you think of it before now?"

He touched her lips with one finger. "I did, but for some reason I had the feeling you weren't quite ready."

They lay facing each other, Kate's foot stroking his calf. She felt happy and sated and amazingly calm. She felt safe and right. When she was with Sam, the complications in her life seemed remote, as if they'd happened in another time. She curled a little closer, not wanting to think. But once she'd allowed her problems to intrude, even that tiny bit, they wouldn't go away.

"What's wrong, sweetheart?" Sam was stroking her hair.

"I don't know how I feel about stealing a weekend just for pleasure when there's so much chaos in my life."

"I guess we're talking about your mother and Leo and Amber again," Sam said with a sigh. Rising on one elbow, he held her away so he could look into her eyes. "What could you do for any one of them if you were in Bayou Blanc right now?"

She shrugged. "Nothing constructive, of course. But I wasn't thinking only of them. I was thinking of my own...difficulty."

Sam lay back again, tucking her head beneath his chin. "The flashbacks." His arm was around her, his hand curled so that the weight of one breast rested in his palm. "I guess I should tell you the rest of my conversation with Diane."

"What else is there?"

"Once Diane saw I was serious about firing her, she decided she had nothing to lose by showing me the extent of her jealousy of you. I'd known all along she wasn't keen to have you in the practice, but I was stunned by how far she'd gone to destroy you."

"What did she do?"

"For starters, she called St. Luke's Hospital using my name. Apparently they believed her request for information was a legitimate inquiry from our clinic for the purpose of taking you into the practice. They willingly opened your personnel file."

Kate lay very still, knowing what was coming.

"Somehow, she reached a nurse who'd worked closely with you, I forget her name, but—"

"Jean Sharpe."

"Yeah, that's it. Jean Sharpe." Rising up, he caught her face in one hand to look at her and said dryly, "With friends like Jean Sharpe, Kate, you don't need any enemies."

"I never could win her over."

"That seems an understatement. Anyway, Sharpe told Diane all about your last day in the E.R. at St. Luke's and she didn't pull any punches."

Shifting away, Kate fumbled for the sheet, scooted back against the headboard on a pillow and stared straight up at the ceiling. So much for a sense of safety and rightness when she was with Sam. Saving him the need to say it, she muttered, "So now you know I killed a patient."

"No. According to Jean Sharpe, you were responsible for *three* deaths that day."

Kate closed her eyes. "I can't believe this."

"Funny you should say that," Sam said, reaching up to stroke her hair. "I couldn't believe it, either, so I did a little checking at a higher level. I spoke to several people—the administrator—"

"Charles Winslow."

"Uh-huh. He tap-danced around but finally admitted that you'd had a sterling reputation until the Joseph Carmello incident and that he'd been the one to recommend your leave of absence in case Carmello's family wanted to sue. Incidentally, according to Winslow, they didn't."

"I guess I should be grateful for that."

"Remember Ward Lincoln?"

"Cardiologist extraordinaire..."

"As fallible as the rest of us, it seems. Your decision to withhold the medication turns out to have been proper. Dr. Lincoln withheld crucial evidence from the board that was later revealed in the autopsy."

Kate frowned. "Did you get details?"

"No, I thought you might want to follow up on that personally."

"And the other two patients?"

"'Nurse Ratched' exaggerated," he said dryly. "No one could have saved either of them."

She tapped her forehead. "I knew that up here, but you'd have to have been there that night to understand how devastating it was. It seemed everything that could go wrong did. And then Joseph Carmello was admitted. His case was similar to what happened to Leo, except that Leo was clearly in need of medication to break up blockage. Carmello was a judgment call. His stats showed him hovering in the maybe/maybe-not range."

"Carmello's case won't be the only one when you'll have to make a judgment call that might be fatal, Kate. It happens to doctors."

"I know. I was hoping that if I worked in a small-town practice, those calls would be rare." She laughed wryly. "Oddly enough, folks get seriously ill here in Bayou Blanc, too."

Sam was propped on his elbow, studying her. "I've been trying to decide whether to tell you this part."

"What?"

"Your career in trauma at St. Luke's isn't over if that's

what you want, Kate. I spoke to several people, all of them outranking Winslow. The door's open at St. Luke's if you want to return."

"Really?" She lay back, thinking. A few weeks ago those words would have worked like a magic wand to restore her crumbling life. But that had been when her life as a trauma specialist was her total identity. The complications that had caused her such turmoil had also enriched her life beyond anything she'd expected. What a difference a few short weeks could make, Kate thought, smiling faintly.

"Does that smile mean you're thinking about calling your travel agent to book a flight to Boston?" Sam asked. His tone was light, but there was a watchfulness about him.

She turned to him, pushing the sheet aside so there was nothing between them. "That's not what I'm thinking." She put a hand on his chest, sifting through the dark, curly hair. "That job, those people, my situation at St. Luke's—it all seems like another world. A moment ago I was thinking that a few weeks in Bayou Blanc had changed everything, but it's not the place, it's the people. Mother, Leo, Amber, you..."

He reached for her. "Good, I'll settle for that right now." With his hand cupping her cheek, he kissed her. Stroking her breasts, he pulled back just to admire her, before lowering his head and taking her nipple between his lips. Shuddering with the pleasure of it, she caught his head in her hands.

And then he was readying her again, slipping his fingers into her until she was slick and warm and inviting. When he entered her, she moaned with the joy of it, wrapping her legs around him, feeling the power and thickness of him as he pushed deeper, his eyes locking with hers.

"I love you, Kate," he said as she writhed in orgasm. Then he began to thrust harder, faster heading for that final, savage peak, and with his face buried in her hair, he emptied himself into her.

THIRTY-THREE

Pamela LaRue adjusted the weights on the Soloflex, dropped her towel on the floor, found a comfortable grip on the overhead bar, then began a series of wicked workouts. Her body was at its physical peak, thanks to these grueling sessions; but more than that, working out cleansed her mind and sharpened her ability to focus. As she fell into a good rhythm, she turned her mind to the case.

There was only one case—Deke Russo's murder investigation.

For days she'd been like a mouse in a maze, sorting through a tangle of facts and suspicions. As soon as she thought she had a clear pattern, another piece of the puzzle surfaced and she was forced to think in another direction. The real problem was that she hadn't been able to settle on one prime suspect.

Out of breath, she stopped and sat huffing and puffing. Adding to her stress was Waylon Escavez. The chief wanted to arrest someone for the murder, and he was looking to Pamela to give him the evidence to do it.

Be careful what you wish for.

Well, she'd realized her fondest wish. Escavez had assigned her to work homicides—Deke Russo's, in particular. No money came with the promotion; just pressure, sex discrimination and unrealistic expectations, although she did sense a reluctant respect for her investigative ability—which was something, she supposed. But the downside of her new status—besides Howard Sloan's constant attempts to feel her up—was having to work for the little weasel. Sloan had no credentials for the job, no natural flair for investigation, and he was a chauvinist pig, to boot. However, he was Escavez's man.

She began another punishing routine designed to build upper-body strength. Sloan's position as a desk sergeant had challenged his abilities. As a homicide detective, he was abysmally inadequate. It rankled that any credit for solving the murder would go to him.

Standing, she scooped her towel from the floor and wiped her face. If only she could handle the investigation without Sloan's interference. Escavez—to give him his due—was withholding judgment, but Sloan was convinced that Amber Russo had killed her husband, and like many people with limited intelligence, he allowed no other possibilities to muddy his thinking. For her part, Pamela wasn't convinced that Amber had done it, but, on the other hand, she wasn't convinced she hadn't.

When the doorbell rang, Pamela's first impulse was to ignore it. She looked down at herself with a grimace. Flushed and sweating, she wasn't prepared to entertain visitors, but at this hour, it was probably something work-related. Holding the ends of the towel around her neck, she went to the front door, rising on her toes to check the peephole.

Nick.

For a moment she stood looking at her feet, wishing she had enough willpower to ignore him. Maybe in the next lifetime. The chain clanged as she released it and opened the door.

"Hi," he said. His gravelly voice always made her think of sandpaper and velvet—a too-sexy combination.

On the one occasion they'd made love— She pushed that thought away.

"Nick. What's up?"

"You got a minute?"

Pamela had dated a lot of men, but none of them had made any serious impact on her senses until she'd met Nick Santana. Standing there beneath her porch light looking rumpled and tired and slightly tentative, he was simply the most appealing, most unattainable, most beautifully masculine man she'd ever known. Did she have a minute? My God, Nick could have her whole life if only he wanted it. Stepping back, she held the door wide in wordless invitation.

Thumbs hooked in the waistband of his jeans, he watched her close the door. "You look like you've been working out."

"Yeah, I'm a mess." She pushed her bangs away from her face, wishing for a headband.

"You're fine," he said.

Conversation flagged, and she nodded at his arm. "I notice you've had the cast removed. Any problems?"

"Not really." He stretched out his arm, wiggled his hand. "I was lucky."

"True. Can I get you a beer?" she asked after another too-long pause.

"No. I took advantage of your hospitality last time I was here. I'm not doing it again. But thanks," he added.

She leaned against a table in her foyer and crossed her legs, still hanging on to the towel. There'd been a time when she'd felt comfortable and even confident letting Nick see her in a skimpy top and spandex. Now she was uncomfortable. She couldn't imagine the gorgeous Amber hot and sweaty. Jealousy made her grumpy. "Come on, Nick. Spit it out."

"I heard you got a promotion. Congratulations."

"Yeah, will wonders never cease. Escavez letting a woman into the elite homicide unit."

"For once he made a smart move. I hope you got a nice raise out of it."

She crossed her arms over her waist. "That's a joke, right?"

He frowned. "Don't let him take advantage of you, Pamela."

"Okay, I think I'll go in tomorrow morning and tell him I don't want to work in homicide, that I'll settle for what I used to do—make a lot of coffee, do a ton of paperwork and go out on the occasional dicey domestic-disturbance call. Yeah, that sounds like a plan."

He drove his fingers through his hair, looking away. "I didn't come over to fight with you, Pam."

So she was Pam again. "Why did you come over tonight, Nick? It couldn't be to advise me on my career."

"I wanted to get a feel for how the investigation is going."

"Oh, of course. You don't want to advise me on my career, you want to destroy it."

He was scowling. "Look, maybe I will take that beer."

Without a word, Pamela pushed away from the table and stalked down the hall to the kitchen. Yanking open the refrigerator, she pulled out a bottle, turned and shoved it at him. Nick took it with a slightly chagrined expression, then pulled a chair out and sat down. Removing the cap, he asked, "Will you have one, too?"

"I don't think so."

"Will you at least have a seat?"

"I don't think so."

"Pam—"

With a huff of impatience, she sat down. "I can't reveal evidence we've collected in the investigation, Nick. You know that."

"I'm not asking for that kind of—" He stopped. "Hell, I guess I am. Without compromising yourself professionally, could you answer a few questions?"

"Ask and I'll let you know."

"Is Amber your prime suspect?"

"Not mine," Pamela said. "There're a lot of people who might have wanted to see Deke Russo dead."

"Well, that's something." Nick looked relieved.

"But she *did* have motive and opportunity. You know, of course, that he was violent?"

"Has she admitted that in questioning?"

Pamela's eyebrows lifted. "Oh, I get it. You're going to speak in lawyerese, but I'm supposed to be open and forthcoming."

He waved a hand, acknowledging her point. "I know Deke abused her," he said curtly. Upending the beer, he took a long swallow. "But I don't think she killed him because of it."

"Then why do you think she killed him?"

He gave her a grudging smile. "You're getting good, Pam. Keep it up and Escavez might give you a raise, after all."

His smile faded. "Amber didn't kill him, but I can't prove it yet. Something just doesn't smell right to me. There're too many other possibilities."

"Stephen, to name one," Pamela said.

"No!"

"Leo."

"Never. No way. Impossible." He traced a trail of moisture on the bottle. "How about Deke's acquaintances in New Orleans? Have you checked them all out? How about his coke supplier? Maybe he wasn't paying the right people. Maybe he was being blackmailed."

"Why kill him if that's the situation? No more drug

sales if he's dead. No more blackmail if he's not around to pay."

When Nick threw up his hands, Pamela leaned back and studied him. "I know I don't have the experience you have, but I get the same feeling you do about this. Something just doesn't wash. This murder has an up-close-and-personal feel, doesn't it? But who?"

"It's not Amber," Nick repeated stubbornly.

"You don't want it to be Amber."

"She had everything going for her, Pam. Why would she risk it all by killing him?"

"Why would a woman with everything going for her live with a guy who beat her up regularly?"

"He didn't beat her up regularly."

"I have the hospital reports, Nick. Pull off the blinders, for God's sake!" Pamela watched him stand abruptly and wondered if the only time she would ever see him would be when he wanted something on behalf of Amber Russo.

"I've gotta go," he said, dropping the empty bottle in the trash beneath the sink. "Thanks for the beer."

She stood. "Sure." He would probably go straight to Amber's house. She imagined them together and it hurt. Her voice was low and cool when she said, "You know the way out, Nick. You don't need me."

"What did she say?" Tightening the sash on her kimono, Amber followed Nick from the front door to the den. "I was about to give up and call over there. It took long enough. What happened?"

"Nothing." Nick went to the French doors and stood looking out. It was a stunning night—clear sky with a million stars. He wished his own thoughts were as clear. He'd gone to see Pam because Amber had wanted him to. But he felt rotten about doing it. He shouldn't have put Pam on the spot like that. If Escavez found out he'd been there, that she'd talked to him, she might lose that shitty no-raise promotion. She'd worked hard to get this chance. She deserved it.

"'Nothing'? What do you mean, 'nothing'?" Amber pushed a hand through her wild hair, lifting it up, then dropping it back onto her neck. "You did see her, didn't you, Nick?"

"I saw her. She said Escavez isn't centering the investigation on any single person."

"Oh, so we're all equally suspect, right?" she asked bitterly.

"They don't seem to think Deke was killed by a deranged fan or anyone connected to the darker side of his life."

"How can they know that!" Amber cried. Rushing to him, she threw her arms around Nick from behind, pressing her cheek against his back. "You've got to do something, Nick!"

He covered her hands with his. "Don't you think I'm doing everything I can, Amber?"

"I'm sorry," she whispered, kissing his shoulder, his neck, moving her hands from beneath his to slip inside his jeans. Nick groaned as she found him, cupping the weight of his testicles in her hands. His penis was instantly hard, throbbing painfully as she curled her fingers around him.

"Jesus, Amber." Braced with his hands flat on the door, he dropped his head and gave himself up to raw pleasure.

"Does that feel good?" she asked in a husky voice.

"Too good." Another minute and he'd come right in her hands.

Then she was licking his ear, rubbing herself against his butt. Even through his jeans, he could feel the heat of her. He saw in the glass that she'd let the kimono fall open.

Her breasts were hard-tipped and swollen, pressed tight against his T-shirt. His lust rose like a wild, dark tide.

He turned, going for her mouth in an explosive kiss while his hands streaked over her, stripping her panties down her legs, brushing the kimono aside, tangling in the sash. "Where's Stephen?" he managed, fondling a nipple while his mouth skated over her neck and down, heading for more lush flesh.

"Don't worry, he's out." Cupping her breasts, she offered herself. "Kiss them, Nick. Like you used to."

He kissed one, then the other, inflamed by her words, her whimpers and, as always, by the wildness in her.

On his knees now, as she stood braced by the door, he dragged his mouth over her belly, tongued her navel as she pushed him lower with frantic hands, murmuring words that urged him on, until he was kissing the heart of her.

Her orgasm was as unbridled and tempestuous as it had been when they were seventeen. She would have collapsed from the force of it, but he rose suddenly while she was still trembling, and laid her on the couch. Fumbling with the buttons on his jeans, he freed himself and, with no thought for preparing her, drove into her with one hard thrust. Something inside his head screamed caution, but he was deaf and blind to everything except having her again.

She reared up, grabbing him and pulling him down to devour his mouth in a hot, hungry kiss as he set a frenzied rhythm. She was vibrating like a bowstring in his hands now. Her body bucked and writhed to meet his mindless thrusts. "Now, Nick...*now!*" she gasped, tearing her mouth from his.

Drawing his lips back in a feral grimace, Nick drove into her one last time and, with a guttural shout, surrendered to the mind-numbing ecstasy of his climax.

* * *

Afterward, they lay in a sweating, panting tangle on the couch. Nick's first coherent thought was to get up. Leave. He didn't usually hop right out of bed after he'd made love to a woman, so why this sudden urge to grab his pants and get the hell away from here?

It had finally happened. After weeks of wanting it—hell, after years of fantasizing about it—he'd just had sex with Amber again. Even now, still inside her body, with her hair still tangled in his fist and the taste of her still on his tongue, he could simply move his head a fraction and inhale the scent of her. Why didn't he want to?

Why did it feel like sex and nothing more? What more did he want? What else did he expect?

Feeling depressed and somehow dishonest, he was easing out of her when he heard the sound of a key in the front door. Amber reacted first and instantly.

"Omigod, it's Stephen!" she cried, shoving at Nick in panic.

Muttering an oath, he pushed himself off her, then reached to pull up his jeans. Calling himself every epithet for being criminally careless and stupidly impulsive, he began quickly buttoning up.

"Hurry," she whispered, prodding him toward the hall as she snatched her kimono from the floor. "Go hide in the bathroom, Nick. Don't come out until I say it's okay."

"Come on, Amber. I'm not hiding. I—"

The door slammed and Amber emitted a panicked moan at the squeak of Stephen's sneakers heading their way. "Hey, Amber! I'm home!"

"Just a minute, Stephen!" she called out, giving Nick another shove. "Go!"

"I'm staying, Amber." He was already disgusted with himself for behaving with no more restraint than a teenager. Damned if he'd slink into the closet like an illicit lover. Amber was no longer married. They were both consenting adults.

Stephen appeared, smiling at Amber. "I thought you'd be in bed already. Oh, shit, I woke you up, didn't I?" He glanced at the scattered couch cushions, then a movement from Nick drew his gaze. Quick anger spread over his features, and he turned back to Amber. "What's *he* doing here?"

"He was just leaving, Stephen."

"That's the line you used last time," the boy said, still scowling.

"We were talking about the case, Stephen. Look, go check my car in the garage, will you? I think I left my handbag in it." Holding her kimono tightly around her, she moved toward the archway that led back to the foyer. "Come on, Nick, I'll see you out."

"Wait a minute." Ignoring her order, Stephen eyed them with suspicion. "I don't believe y'all were talking about the case."

Amber sighed, losing patience. "If you won't help me find my handbag, then go to your room and wait for me there."

"You weren't sleeping on that couch, either, were you?" He seemed to take in the total disarray of the room now. The sash of Amber's kimono lay at the French doors where it had fallen in the heat of the moment. And her panties. Stephen's gaze settled on Amber. She was barefoot, her hair was a mess, her lips were swollen. The room itself reeked of sex.

Reading the boy's face, Nick groaned at his own culpability in this sorry scene. "Give us a minute, will you, Stephen?"

"You shut up!" Stephen yelled. Then he turned to Amber. "You were doing it with him, weren't you?" he accused hotly.

Amber fumbled for the missing sash, cursing. "I don't want to discuss this tonight, Stephen."

"You promised me you wouldn't screw him, Amber."

"Stephen, that's no way to speak to your stepmother," Nick chided gently. The boy was emotionally charged and evidently feeling territorial. Nick didn't want to be the one to push him over, but he couldn't let him bully Amber.

"Yes, watch your mouth, Stephen," she warned.

"'Stepmother'?" Stephen gave a harsh laugh and looked at Amber. "Does he really think you're my stepmother, Amber?"

"I *am* your stepmother."

"Bullshit. You know that's bullshit." He glared at Nick. "She doesn't need you, Santana, not as a lawyer and not as a stud!"

Amber put a hand on Nick's arm. "You don't have to listen to this, Nick. Stephen tends to overreact. Jesus, he reminds me of Deke sometimes. Come on, I'll walk you to the door."

"I'm nothing like that bastard!" Stephen cried, moving to block them. On the verge of tears, he fought to keep his mouth steady. "That's not what you say at night when it's just the two of us."

"That's enough, Stephen!" Amber snapped.

There was fire in the boy's eyes as he turned his fury on Nick. "Goddamn you! I'm not gonna just sit still and let you move in, Santana. Things are not the way they look in this family, you better remember that. You can't just walk in and take up where the asshole left off!"

"Stephen!" Amber took a step toward him, but Nick caught her arm.

"I can see you're upset, Stephen," Nick said, "but let me just say this. Maybe not tonight, but later when you feel it's right, we can talk about this and clear up some things."

Stephen's mouth turned down in disgust. "Yeah, well, here's a flash for you, Santana. I don't *want* to talk to you. Ever. Any talking needs to be done, it'll be between Amber and me. Alone." Brushing past them, he stormed off, heading for his room.

Amber made a little grimace of distaste and then wrapped both hands around Nick's forearm. "He is such a trial lately! Come on, he'll settle down in a little while. Halfway through one of his CDs, he'll forget all about this."

"I don't think so, Amber." Still troubled, Nick gazed in the direction of the boy's bedroom.

She gave a light laugh. "Nick, really. Don't worry about Stephen. I can handle him."

Reluctantly he turned and went with her to the foyer. At the door he said, "Walk me to my car, will you?"

Her voice dropped to a husky tone. "I intended to anyway, *chèr*."

He glanced at her feet. "What about shoes?"

"Who needs 'em?" Openly provocative, Amber lifted her hair and let it fall, smiling up into his face. "Remember how we used to do it in your ole pickup and afterward we'd play around buck naked just because we liked to look at each other?"

"I remember." They fell into step, not quite touching. At the car, she stopped and pulled her kimono open, flashing him a glimpse of her exquisite body, her eyes teasing.

Nick removed her hands from the silk and closed the edges. "Amber, have you ever considered the fact that Stephen's feelings for you might be more than the normal affection a boy feels for his stepmother?"

She heaved an impatient sigh and pulled away. "Do we have to talk about this now?"

"Yeah, I think we do. It's not the first time I've noticed his jealousy. Maybe it's normal for a kid to feel he needs to protect his mother when his dad is suddenly gone. But Stephen's behavior seems to go beyond that."

"He's adjusting, Nick. He'll get used to you."

"I don't think so. I don't think he'll get used to any man whom he perceives as a sexual rival where you're concerned."

She smiled, moving close enough to graze his arm with her breast. "And does that describe you, Nick?"

"Did you hear what I said, Amber? You don't seem to realize how serious this could be. It's unhealthy for Stephen to fantasize that way. His whole life could be affected."

"Oh, come on."

"If it is just fantasy," Nick added quietly.

Amber looked away as she pulled the kimono around her. "What does that mean?"

"You tell me, Amber."

She released a short laugh. "Tell you what?" Her gaze was anywhere but on him.

Noting her body language, Nick was reminded of the many guilty suspects he'd observed. The sordid possibility that had formed in his mind made him queasy. He wondered how long the suspicion had been growing and how long he'd been denying it. Denial, it seemed, was becoming a habit in his dealings with Amber.

"What did Stephen mean when he said things weren't the way they seemed in this family?"

She shrugged. "Who knows?"

"And that's it? With just a smirk and a shrug, you're dismissing a very serious situation?"

"Well, what do you expect from me? I can't do anything if Stephen has a crush on me. It could even be considered normal, seeing what a bastard Deke was and how little affection he ever showed to his own kid!"

"Are you saying it's simply that and no more? Stephen has a crush but he's never tried to act on it?"

"You mean has he ever tried coming on to me?" She turned her face away. "What if he has? I've had to handle men's passes most of my life." Bitterness crept into her tone. "I can definitely keep a teenage boy in line."

"He's suffering, Amber. Don't you see that?"

"God, I wish I'd thought to bring a cigarette," she muttered, rubbing her arms briskly. Then, shaking her head, she added, "Everyone suffers when they're fifteen, Nick."

Suddenly weary, Nick turned from her. It was a dark night, with only a sliver of a moon. The stars were as bright as they'd been before he and Amber had slaked the lust that was still uncannily unchanged from the time they'd first had sex. Nick turned to study her beautiful face. She was an erotic dream, a barefoot seductress in green silk. Gifted. Intelligent. Surely a woman like that was not completely without honor when entrusted with a young boy's welfare.

His gaze shifted to Stephen's bedroom window, where no light shone. He felt a deep sympathy for the boy, lonely and isolated in his dark room. What twisted thoughts was he thinking? What inappropriate dreams was he dreaming?

Nick opened the door of his vehicle. Sick at heart, he realized he was afraid to ask Amber to go inside and comfort him.

"Dad, did you ever think of getting married again?"

Nick winced as Cody banged the cabinet drawer after getting out a knife to butter his toast. The sound inside his throbbing skull was like the explosion of a land mine.

He'd almost finished off half a bottle of Scotch the night before without coming close to working out the problem that had driven him to drink in the first place. This morning he was paying dearly. In fact, there was a real possibility that his head would actually shatter and fall off his shoulders if Cody made another sound.

His son slammed the door of the refrigerator and clunked the jelly jar down on the countertop. "You gonna answer me, Dad?"

Nick held himself carefully still. "About getting married again?"

"Right."

"I suppose I've thought of it, yeah."

"Anybody in particular in mind?" Cody snapped a piece of toast from the toaster.

"No." *Not any longer.*

"How come?"

"How come what, Cody?"

"How come you don't have someone specific in mind? Lots of women like you, I bet."

Nick almost smiled. Not quite. "What makes you say that?"

Cody shrugged. "Mallory says you're cool."

"Yeah, well, first I have to find the right lady."

After slathering butter on the toast, Cody juggled the jelly jar from one hand to the other, then around his backside, Michael Jordan-style. "I guess one divorce in a lifetime is enough, huh?"

Clang...clannnggg...clank! Nick cringed as the lid of the jar hit the floor, rolled across the tile and came to a noisy stop at his chair leg.

"Do you have to make all that racket, Cody?"

"What racket?" Biting into his toast, Cody tossed the knife into the stainless-steel sink.

Blam! Another nuclear blast.

Nick got up and moved carefully to the coffeepot. It was funny that Cody should bring this up today. He *had* been thinking of marriage, he realized. Past tense. Pouring himself a refill, he tossed three aspirin back, and, with a grimace, washed them down with scalding coffee. It was painful giving up dreams.

"What's wrong, Dad? Are you sick or something?"

"Headache."

"Yeah, I saw the empty Dewar's bottle in the trash."

Nick resisted the urge to groan and cover his eyes. God, he was a rotten example for Cody. "I overdid it last night, Cody. It's always stupid to drink too much."

"Something on your mind, Dad?"

"Yeah. But it's nothing you need to worry about."

Cody crunched his toast. "Deke Russo's murder, I bet," he said.

"That investigation isn't my responsibility."

"No, but Amber's defense is."

"Yeah."

"And even if you weren't, we're sorta close to the people involved. It seems like we're being sucked into it whether we like it or not."

"Me," Nick said. "Not you, Cody."

"Stephen's my friend, Dad. Like Amber's yours." Cody crammed the rest of his toast into his mouth and dusted crumbs from his hands. "Which reminds me. Stephen's pretty worried, I think."

Nick set his cup down. "What makes you say that?"

"He's always talking about it, like cussing the chief and that Howard Sloan." At the refrigerator, Cody removed orange juice and drank it straight from the carton. "Pamela LaRue, too. He's really pissed at her because he thinks she's zeroed in on Amber and just won't consider anybody else. I told him Pamela's cool. Remember that time she came over here and we cooked out? She was

pretty smart. She knew a lot about your job in New Orleans. I tried to tell Stephen she's too straight to plant evidence or do anything like that just to close a case."

"She'll be happy to know you're defending her." *At
least one of us is fair-minded.*

Cody walked to the trash compactor, stuffed his used
napkin and the empty juice carton inside, then closed it
with a bang. "Wanna hear something funny?"

Head bent, Nick rubbed his temples. "Sure."

"Well, not funny. More like odd."

"What, Cody?" Eyes closed, Nick waited for the aspirin
to kick in.

"I don't know this for a fact, but I get a really bad feeling that Stephen thinks she did it."

Nick's head came up. "Who, Amber?"

"Uh-huh. But he's nuts over her. Really wigged out. I
mean, he loses his sense of... What's that word, Dad?"

"Perspective? Objectivity?"

"'Perspective,' yeah. He loses perspective when it
comes to Amber." Cody laughed and shook his head.
"You know what he told me a coupla days ago? Said he's
gonna marry her. Can you believe that? He says they love
each other! Isn't that the most uncool thing you ever
heard, Dad? She's way too old. She used to be your age,
you know? I mean, she's still your age, but like, that'd
make her old enough to be Stephen's mother, for cri-
miny's sake."

Nick's stomach roiled. Forcing back bitter coffee and
bile, he stood. "I've got to make a call, Cody."

"You feeling okay, Dad? You look... Well, you look
sorta green. You're not gonna hurl, are you?"

Nick put a hand on his midriff. "I'm okay. I've gotta
make a call, Cody."

"Me and Mallory might swim at Ms. Victoria's pool
this morning if it's all right with you."

"It's all right."

"Okay. Hey, Dad..." Cody picked up Nick's coffee cup and put it in the dishwasher. "You know what I like about living with you and all? Like when I drank straight out of the carton, you didn't nag me to use a glass. Same with the iced tea. Mom's always nagging, trying to make me have manners. I tell her I have manners when it counts, but it's a pain having to think about manners constantly. You know what I mean?"

"Your mother's right. I should be more conscientious. We're lucky she even let you stay here after that accident."

"Aw, Dad."

"Which reminds me," Nick said. "Remember your manners at the pool. You're a guest, so behave yourself. Don't leave a mess."

"Take some more aspirin, Dad."

Nick bypassed the telephone on the kitchen wall and headed straight for the garage to use his cellular. At the Jeep, he opened the garage door with a remote to dispel some of the heat, then grabbed the phone from the console, using only his thumb to punch in the number.

It was picked up on the first ring.

"Amber, it's me."

"Nick."

His jaw clenched at the sound of her voice, low and husky, promising the moon and stars. "I need to see you, Amber. Right away."

There was an instant of hesitation. "What's wrong? Is it the case? Has Escavez—"

"It's not the case."

"Ooo, that sounds mysterious, *chèr*. But I'm barely awake, sugar...although I had some lovely dreams."

"Are you alone?"

"No, but it can be arranged."

"How long before you can be dressed?"

"Nick—"

"Just get dressed, Amber. We'll find a private place."
He hung up.

THIRTY-FOUR

Sam and Kate were back in Bayou Blanc by midafternoon on Sunday. Mallory was due home after her weekend with her grandparents around five and both felt they should be discreet about their new relationship in front of the teenager until she had a chance to get to know Kate a little better. Now that Mallory had confessed her secret guilt, Kate felt the girl needed some time to heal first.

"She'll come around," Sam assured Kate, pulling up in front of Victoria's house. "Considering all she's gone through since her mother got sick, she's managed to stay fairly balanced." He looked at her. "That's right, isn't it? Not just wishful thinking on my part?"

Kate was touched by his anxious concern. She leaned over, cupping his face, and gave him a kiss before opening the car door. "I think so. She saw me at the clinic the day after she surprised us in the doctors' lounge. She was shy but friendly."

"Don't get out," she told him as she swung her legs out of the car. "You probably have some things to attend to after being away for the weekend. And I need to check on Mother."

On the way home, they'd stopped by the hospital to see Leo, expecting to find Victoria there, or Amber—possibly both. But Victoria had already come and gone, and apparently Amber hadn't visited at all.

Holding the door open, Kate bent down for a last word

to Sam. "Leo looked a little bit lost shuffling down the hall tethered to his IV pole all by himself, didn't he?"

"Well, he's had a heart attack. It depresses a man."

"I know, I know...."

"Maybe Amber will show up soon. That'll cheer him up."

Kate nodded, then gave him a smile. "See you in the morning, okay?"

He caught her hand. "You aren't going to change your mind, are you?"

"What? And go back to that rat race in Boston? No way."

"Not that. I'm talking about us, Kate."

She smiled. "No, I'm not changing my mind."

"Good." He raised her hand and kissed the backs of her fingers. "See you in the morning."

Kate watched him back the Range Rover out of the driveway before climbing the steps to her mother's front door. Still smiling as she walked inside, she closed the door softly, and only then did she realize that someone was with her mother.

She relaxed slightly. She'd been concerned about Victoria's obsessive need to stay with Leo night and day. The strain of caring for a family member was telling on a healthy person, and Victoria was far from well. But if her mother was well enough to entertain a visitor on a Sunday afternoon, she must be holding up better than Kate had dared hope. Now, if only Kate could get a handle on her own problem, she thought, maybe there would be a chance for real happiness with Sam. But deep in her heart, she knew that wouldn't happen until she'd dragged out into the open whatever was buried inside her.

Still, it was impossible not to feel cautiously hopeful today. Sam loved her. She loved him. In spite of a rocky past, they were together again. Her spirits were uplifted as she headed for the sound of voices in the sunroom.

"He despises me, Victoria! What am I going to do?"

Kate stopped short. Amber sat on the rattan couch sobbing, nearly hysterical. "What's wrong? What's happened?" She hurried toward Amber. "Is it Leo? My God, I just left the hospital. Is he—"

"It's not Leo," Victoria said sadly.

"Who, then?" Kate touched Amber's shoulder. "Is it Stephen? Is he hurt?"

"It's N-Nick," Amber said, her voice rising.

Kate looked at her mother. "Nick? Nick's been hurt?"

"Nobody's hurt, Kate," Victoria said. "Something...ah, distressing has happened. Nick is upset with Amber. He—"

"'Upset'? Why?" Kate looked at Amber in bewilderment.

"He hates me now."

"Nick hates you? Come on, Amber, he loves you."

"Not anymore." After mopping her eyes with a tissue, she said, "I've changed all that now, haven't I, Victoria? I finally had a chance to have a real life, the life I should have had years ago and threw away. Now I don't have anything. Anything! And it's all because of Deke."

Kate looked at Victoria. "Will someone please tell me what's going on?"

Victoria braced her hands on the arms of her chair and tried to stand but couldn't manage it. Forgetting Amber's troubles, Kate rushed over. "Mother, you're trying to do too much. Come on. Let me help you into bed."

"No. Amber needs me." She sank back into the chair, closing her eyes and gasping for breath. Her face was shiny with a fine film of perspiration, and she was deathly pale. Kate took her wrist, automatically noting her pulse.

"Please lie down on the couch, Mother. You're almost at the point of collapse."

"I'm all right. Just give me a minute."

"It's all my fault!" Amber sprang up and began pacing, twisting her hands. "First Daddy and now Victoria. I screw up everything I touch. I never do anything right!"

Kate felt as if she'd arrived in the middle of a play and the plot was completely beyond her. But something was terribly wrong. Her own heart was beating fast with dread. She spoke quietly to Victoria. "What's going on, Mother?"

"You won't understand!" Amber cried. "You can never understand. It would never happen to you, Kate." Her mouth thinned with resentment. "You never screw up— you're too together, too good to ever find yourself trapped in a situation that just…just…overwhelms you!"

"Are we talking about your marriage to Deke?"

"What else!" Openly bitter, Amber turned away.

"And the consequences," Victoria said softly.

"Oh my God…" Kate gripped the back of a chair. "Did you kill him, Amber? Is that what this is all about?"

"No!" Amber stopped pacing. "I wanted to kill him. I *should have* killed him." She wrapped her arms around herself. "We'd all have been a thousand times better off if I *had* killed him, but I didn't. It's not that." She dropped her face into her hands. "It's worse, it's so much worse."

"What could be worse than that?"

"Stephen…" Her voice rose to a shrill pitch. "Oh, St-Stee-phennnn… What have I done?"

"Stephen killed Deke?" Kate was still struggling to piece it together.

"No!" Victoria cried with impatience. "Of course he didn't!"

Amber sank into a chair. "I'm afraid he did. Oh, God, I think he did, and I think I drove him to it!"

"How did it happen?" Kate asked, still confused. "You were sleeping here. Did Stephen confess to you?"

"No, but it's the only answer." Amber wiped her cheeks with both hands, calmer now.

"It's too ridiculous!" Victoria snapped. "The boy would never shoot his own father and then clean up the crime scene. That's not the way crimes of passion are committed. You read it in the papers all the time. A teenager shoots his parents and then calls 911 in tears and says he's done it. No, Stephen was exactly where he said he was, asleep in his bed, with Leo across the hall." Although clearly exhausted by the speech, sheer willpower seemed to keep Victoria upright in her chair.

Kate's thoughts were racing. She walked slowly, thinking as she spoke. "If he did shoot Deke," she said, "are you saying it's because of the abuse, Amber? It would be difficult for any teenage boy to watch his father constantly assaulting a stepmother he adored. And what's this about Nick? He's seen many cases as bad and worse than this. Why would he despise you for defending Stephen?"

"You've got it all wrong, Kate." Amber sat with her eyes closed, shaking her head hopelessly. "God, you're so naive." She laughed harshly. "Nick figured it out last night, but being a sweet guy, he couldn't let himself believe I'd sink so low."

"What are you talking about, Amber?" As bewildered as ever, Kate stood looking at her.

"Think, Kate."

"I'm the naive one, remember?"

"I've been…using Stephen. Okay?"

"You what?"

"I think you heard me."

Kate stared in disbelief at Amber. "You've been having a sexual relationship with Stephen?"

"Oh, God, I feel like such a worthless slut!" Amber cried suddenly, both hands fisted in her hair. "Deke was right when he called me trash!"

"No!" Victoria cried, her lips trembling. Then in a quieter tone, she said, "No, Amber. Never say that. You were victimized by a monster and you reacted inappropriately. It happens."

"How did it happen?" Kate asked, but dread was settling heavily inside her. A moment ago, it was a preposterous notion, defying all reason. Now the whole situation was simply monstrous.

Amber saw instantly that Kate didn't share Victoria's sympathetic acceptance. Her chin tilted defensively. "I didn't mean it to happen, but I was so sick of being humiliated by Deke, sick of his abuse, his hateful digs at me, his eternal efforts to put me down. He criticized my business. He dismissed everything I accomplished as worthless. If we argued, he could always overpower me with his fists." Her voice hardened. "He shouldn't have hit me. Nobody ever did that until Deke. Daddy never spanked me. Not once, did he, Victoria?"

"No," Victoria whispered.

Amber dashed away a tear. "I don't remember a single time Daddy ever raised his hand to me, and my own husband, who was supposed to love and cherish me, was knocking me around before the honeymoon was hardly over. It's disgusting. I hate him! I despise him! I'm glad he's dead! I wish he'd walk in the door right now and I'd kill him again. With my bare hands! I wouldn't need a gun."

"*I'd kill him again.*" With both hands pressed to her lips, Kate was shaking her head as Amber herself compounded her sins.

"And now Nick hates me," Amber said, her mouth beginning to tremble. "He must have figured it all out last night, because he was at my door early this morning. He dragged me to his car and drove like a crazy man to the lake, and that's when he told me Stephen had talked about us."

She looked at them both, her eyes swimming with tears, and gave a harsh laugh. "St-Stephen thinks now that Deke's dead, he and I will get married! Is that a hoot or what? God, Nick was so furious. He was disgusted. He was ranting and raving and threatening all kinds of stuff. He…he…l-looked at me as if I was garbage, Victoria."

Her face crumpled in a kind of bewilderment, appealing to the older woman. "I wanted to hurt Deke. That's why I did it, Victoria. You understand, don't you? I wanted to make him feel as miserable as I was. But I never wanted to—to hurt Stephen." She slipped from the chair to her knees and buried her face in her hands. "Oh, God, I want to die. I…just…want…to die!"

Kate knew she should feel compassion. Instead, she was curiously empty of any emotion. In her mind she struggled to fit Amber's shocking revelations into the already complex puzzle of Deke's murder. She looked at her mother, who sat rigidly erect, white-faced, her lips clamped together. Victoria's thoughts, as usual, were a mystery to Kate.

Kate's gaze returned to Amber. "Did Deke suspect what was going on?"

Amber nodded, pushing her hair from her face. "I never knew that until the night of the festival. I realize now that he was just biding his time to use it against me." She wiped her eyes again, struggling to keep her lips steady. "He threw it up to me after the show. He'd slammed me against the wall in that stupid truck and it was just too much! I screamed that I was getting a divorce. But he said I'd never be able to divorce him because he'd tell the world my dirty secret." Her face crumpled again. "And it is d-dirty. It's the lowest. He was r-right about that."

Kate held her hand over her heart, feeling it race as the implications of Amber's confession roared through her mind. With Amber's career, her reputation and her future all in Deke's hands, she must have been desperate to find a way out. Had she somehow heard Deke come home, slipped out of the house and found him passed out in his car, then seized the opportunity to murder him with his own gun?

Or was it Stephen?

Or the two of them together?

Could it have been Leo?

Amber was now sobbing quietly. "It was never supposed to go as far as it did with Stephen. I didn't mean to...to...actually..." She drew a defeated breath. "It hurt so much how Deke treated me. I just wanted to find a way to make him pay, to hurt him back. Stephen... Stephen was just...there. Deke's son, the perfect weapon."

Kate felt sick. "Stephen wasn't a weapon, Amber. He was a vulnerable boy. He was your stepson."

"I wasn't thinking, Kate! Okay? I was just so furious with Deke!"

"He was a devil."

Kate turned in surprise as her mother spoke. With trembling hands, Victoria levered herself out of the chair and went to the window wall of the sunroom, which framed a view of Leo's house. "I know what a devil looks like and I know how a devil talks. I know what a devil can do to a woman's soul, and Deke Russo was a devil."

Kate's chest hurt with the force of her heartbeat and a fear of impending doom. "Are you talking about my father?" she asked, almost holding her breath.

"I'm talking about John Madison." There was bitterness in her tone and hatred in the rigid set of her shoulders. "I can't bear to think of him as your father, Kate. He was as vile a man as the devil ever created. He was guilty of all those transgressions you name, Amber. And more. Believe me, I understand how a woman can be tempted to kill."

Putting her hand on her throat, Kate wondered if she could bear to hear what else her mother might say. Dread coiled in her stomach, forcing her to sit down.

Victoria spoke quietly. "He was a vicious, evil man, John Madison. I didn't know it until we were married, however." Her lip curled in scorn. "His father had been a monster, and John dedicated himself to keeping up a time-honored family tradition."

With one hand she fondled the cord hanging from the blinds. "He named that evil yacht *Mayday*. I begged him not to. I feared that a name like that was tantamount to tweaking the tails of the gods. The very word meant disaster. Wasn't he afraid? John laughed. Ridiculed me for harboring a silly superstition. But, of course, he ridiculed anything and everything I did." Looking down at the cord in her hand, she laughed without humor, almost without sound. "Looking back, *Mayday* seems a prophetic name."

Almost in a trance, Kate concentrated every atom of her being on the images suddenly flashing in her mind. She could see the water, gulls circling the yacht in a blue, blue sky. She could see the polished fittings of the cabin and the tiny kitchen—all things a wide-eyed child of six would notice.

"There was a horrible fight." Kate didn't realize she'd spoken. The words just came out as her memory suddenly returned like a rush of seawater.

"Yes. We were too far from shore to get help when it happened," Victoria said, her voice a monotone. "John had been drinking. Like Deke, he couldn't hold his liquor.

Only a little and he'd get testy. A lot and he got down-right mean. It was late afternoon, time to begin dinner preparations in the galley. Caroline and Leo were up on deck. The two of you were sleeping. We were going to have french fries with our steaks, because John insisted. He liked french fries, therefore we would have them. The pot with hot oil was on the galley stove.

"You were going to be starting school, Kate, and I wanted to find a job. I was slowly starving to death emotionally, but I thought I could save my sanity if I could just maintain some contact with other people—sane people. And I made the mistake of choosing that afternoon on the yacht to mention it to John. I thought with Caroline and Leo on board, he would be forced to hear me out…possibly even see reason."

Her laugh held bitter irony. "What a disastrous miscalculation on my part. He was furious. A job meant independence, in his view. The idea was intolerable to John Madison."

Victoria turned around, facing them, but she seemed to be seeing that day and other people. "Even after flatly declaring the subject closed, he couldn't let it be. He kept at me, poking and prodding. I flared up, finally. Like you, Amber, I'd just had enough. He struck me then—a hard, backhanded blow that sent me flying." She lifted a shaking hand and covered her eyes. "Leo, of course, came to my defense, being the only other person on board who could.

"They fought like animals. They fell to the floor, rolling and tumbling, grunting and gouging. Cursing. It was terrifying. John was bigger and insane with rage. I thought he was going to kill Leo, and if he did, I knew none of us would be safe on that yacht. Caroline was on deck, screaming in terror. I couldn't think what to do—until I remembered the gun."

The gun.

"You took it from the cabinet above the sink," Kate murmured, seeing her mother that day with total clarity, unlike in her flashbacks.

"Yes. I took it down." Victoria drew a deep breath. "But I was afraid to use it. They were locked in a death struggle on the floor, and I didn't want to kill Leo by mistake."

"And then my father grabbed something...." Kate's mind was racing, the scene as vivid as if it had happened yesterday. "Something with a wire handle..."

"A lantern, the yacht's emergency lantern."

"Yes. And he swung it around. It hit Leo on the side of his head."

"It stunned him," Victoria said. "Then John fell on top of him and began choking him. I screamed and screamed. Begged. Cried. I waved the gun at him and told him to stop or I would have to shoot. But he just laughed. He looked up at me as he was choking the life out of Leo, and he laughed! So I shot him."

I saw it.

Kate stood, blinking as if awakening from a deep sleep. "The bullet went in here...." She touched the exact spot where Cody had been shot. "He wasn't dead. He got up and came at you. I screamed and screamed."

"I had to shoot again. The force of the bullet slammed him against the galley stove, and the hot grease flamed up. A towel and some other flammable articles caught fire. It seemed just seconds before the place was engulfed in flames."

Kate rubbed a spot on her forehead, frowning, trying to recall everything. "I was standing on those steps leading up to the galley." She glanced over at Amber, who was listening in horrified fascination. "Amber never knew anything. Leo had to wake her to get her life jacket on.

We'd taken them off before falling asleep, although we knew we weren't supposed to."

"Was everyone wearing a life jacket?" Amber asked.

"Of course. Everyone, that is, except John. We—Leo and I—decided it was not necessary to take the time to put him in a life jacket. He was dead. And by then the fire was out of control."

"What happened to my mother?" Amber asked.

Victoria clasped her hands together, almost prayerlike, but they were shaking badly. "Caroline was with us when we jumped into the water, but somehow she was trapped underneath the boat. Leo dived again and again trying to free her, but when he finally brought her to the surface, it was too late."

"I can understand now why you never wanted to talk about that day," Kate said.

Victoria's eyes were dark with regret. "You were both so young. I couldn't see what possible good could come from your knowing the ugly details." She frowned, looking beyond them both. "But you know that old saying. 'The road to hell is paved with good intentions.' These things have a way of lingering, intruding when we least want or expect them. Perhaps if I'd told the truth, if you had both been armed with the knowledge of what happened that day, it might have strengthened you. If Amber had known the consequences of abuse, maybe she would have walked away from Deke sooner. If we had discussed what you saw that day, Kate, and made peace with it, there might have been no basis for your nightmares and no mystery regarding your flashbacks. Perhaps there would have been no flashbacks."

Neither Kate nor Amber could find an answer to that.

"Leo agreed to keep your secret," Kate said.

"It was just good luck that no body was ever found," Victoria said. "On the other hand, if his body *had* been found, Leo and I would have been free of that evil secret all these years."

"True," Kate agreed. "It would have made no difference legally. It was self-defense."

"I call it poetic justice," Amber said.

"Except that Caroline Castille died, too," Victoria replied, examining her hands. Kate watched her staring at her fingers and guessed that her mother saw them as somehow stained with the blood of her neighbor. She now understood Victoria's words about being a burden to Leo and unworthy of his love. She was beginning to understand the depth of her mother's guilt.

Victoria smiled sadly. "So you see, Amber, I know how it feels to hate your husband. To resent his brutality. I understand fantasizing about ways to escape. To get even. To hurt him as he hurt you. I know how a woman can be driven to behave inappropriately." She sat down abruptly, touching her forehead with an unsteady hand. "I'm sorry," she said. "I'm afraid I'm going…to…"

Kate sprang forward, too late to prevent Victoria from slipping out of the chair and falling to the floor. "Mother!" Kate felt for a pulse and found it weak and uneven. "Go and get my bag, Amber! It's on the desk in the study. And then call 911!"

Amber dashed away to obey. Kate gently tucked a knitted throw around her mother and slipped a small cushion beneath her head. "It's okay, Mama," she whispered. "Hold on. We'll get you to the hospital in just a few minutes."

Victoria's eyes fluttered open. She appeared dazed, then managed to grope for Kate's hand. "Kate, I want… I need to tell—"

"No more talk now, Mama, please." Managing a smile, Kate squeezed the delicate bones. "All those hours at Leo's bedside have just about done you in, plus you've dredged up memories that have to be painful. Let it all go, Mama. We'll get you to the hospital and soon have you on your feet again."

"Too late…" Victoria's lashes fluttered and she stirred restlessly. "Leo must—"

"Here!" Amber thrust the black bag at Kate and scrambled to the telephone on a small glass table. As Kate pressed the stethoscope to her mother's chest, Amber frantically dialed 911.

"Tell them to hurry!" Kate called, her own fear rising sharply. Her mother was slipping away.

"They said ten minutes," Amber said a few seconds later, dropping to her knees beside Victoria. Snatching her hand, she kissed the older woman's fingers, holding them tight against her heart, looking at Kate. "Is she going to be all right?"

"I don't know. She's very weak. I don't know how she's held up so well until now. We'll just have to pray."

"It's my fault," Amber said, pressing the back of Victoria's hand to her cheek. "It was too much for her, knowing what I've done. If I hadn't run over here whining…"

"You can't know that, Amber. Her cancer's spread. This was bound to happen sooner or later."

"Then let it be later!" Amber cried. "Please don't die, Victoria," she begged, kissing the older woman. "I need you. I can't face this without you. Don't leave me, Victoria! Please…please hold on, Victoria."

Kate gazed at her mother's still, waxen features and fought an angry urge to remind Amber that her pleas were selfish and self-centered. Then, as quickly as the impulse rose, it died. Weren't her own wishes just as selfish? Really frightened now, Kate touched her mother's cheek and whispered her name. But Victoria was beyond hearing.

THIRTY-FIVE

Stephen lay on his bed with his hands clasped beneath his head and stared at the ceiling fan. He blinked in sync with it a couple of times, trying to freeze-frame it, making it look as if it had stopped. He did that sometimes for kicks—played stupid games. To keep from thinking real thoughts.

But real thoughts bugged him anyway.

The CD player blasted a number he'd played about fifty times today. A song about sex and suicide. It was kind of off-the-wall shit, not serious. Like who'd want to kill themselves over love? When you're dead, there's no more nothing. Especially sex. And he couldn't think of anything that felt better than sex. That was about the only thing he and his old man had in common. Deke liked to do it, too, only he was too stupid to know that what he had at home was a thousand times better than any of those bimbos he was always fooling with. He grunted in disgust. Like any of those sluts could touch Amber.

He rolled off the bed and got to his feet. A lot of really mean shit had come down lately. He used to think that if Deke somehow croaked, life would be a lot better. It showed how screwed up a person's thinking could get. Deke was dead and the whole frigging world was turned upside down. Look at Leo, so upset he'd had a heart attack. And Victoria might be dying. But worst of all, any day now, Amber was sure to be charged with murdering

Deke. He didn't know how many hours he'd spent trying to figure out how he could somehow keep the cops from zeroing in on her. He would have done it for her, damn it. All she'd had to do was ask.

He got up to change the CD, and in the abrupt silence heard the sound of a car outside. His heart jumped, hoping it would be Amber coming home. He parted the blinds and saw a police car pulling into the driveway. He held his breath, the new CD forgotten. Maybe they were just turning around. Maybe they'd change their minds and go away. Maybe pigs would fly.

The door chimes rang. Tossing the CD aside, he headed down the hall to the foyer. There were two of them, he noted through the bevelled glass. "Barney Fife" and Pamela LaRue. Fife, he could handle. Pamela scared him. He'd heard Santana say she was a first-class detective. Throwing the lock, he opened the door only a crack. Nothing said you had to let them inside your house.

Pamela smiled. "Hi, Stephen."

"No one's home. My grandpa's in the hospital."

She nodded. "I know. We wanted to speak to your stepmother."

"She's not here."

Pamela glanced beyond him as if to check, but before she spoke again, Howard Sloan demanded, "Where is she?"

"What do you want with her?"

"Just answer the question, kid."

Stephen shrugged. "I don't know where she went."

Pamela poked a card through the crack. "Give her this, will you, please? And have her get in touch. We just have a few questions."

"What kind of questions? She's told you everything she knows. She's got a lawyer. You should be calling him, not coming here like this out of the blue."

Howard Sloan smirked and cocked both hands on his skinny hips. "Listen to this, Pam. The kid sounds more like a lawyer than a lawyer."

"Just tell her we'll expect her to get in touch, Stephen," Pamela said quietly. "Okay?"

Stephen watched them walk back to the police car, climb inside and drive off. When he looked down at the tiny white card with Pamela's name on it, his hand was shaking.

Amber slipped from Victoria's room and hurried down the hall. Public telephones were tucked in an alcove near the elevators, and all were blessedly unoccupied. She dialed quickly, glancing at her watch. Lunchtime. He made it a point to have lunch with Cody every day. Maybe she'd be lucky and catch him.

He picked up on the first ring. "Nick!"

"Amber."

She winced at the coolness in his voice. "I'm at the hospital, but I've been thinking about you, Nick."

"How's Leo?"

"He's coming along fine. He spends almost every minute with Victoria."

"I heard. Kate must be upset."

"We're all upset. As if I didn't have enough on my conscience, I now feel responsible for Victoria's collapse, too."

"'Responsible'? How?"

"Well, I was upset over you, so I went over to talk to Victoria. You made it plain what you think of me, Nick, and I just needed...somebody. We talked about...things. Victoria became agitated telling Kate and me about the day my mother and John Madison drowned on the yacht, only John didn't drown. She killed him, Nick."

"Who?"

"Victoria. She shot her husband. It was very weird, the way it happened. It wasn't murder or anything. It was self-defense. After she told us, she just sort of collapsed."

"Victoria killed her husband?"

"Yes. He was fighting with Daddy, who was trying to protect Victoria after John attacked her."

"That's some story."

"Yeah. All these years Kate has never been able to remember much about that day. Suddenly it all came back to her. Everything at once."

"Sounds like an interesting hour."

Eyes closed, Amber rested her forehead against the cold metal of the telephone. Her tone very low, she whispered, "Nick, I know you think what I did was despicable."

Silence.

"I want to see you, Nick."

"I'm pretty tied up with things right now, Amber."

"Nick, don't hate me. I really need you right now. Don't desert me! Victoria's sick, and Daddy... He can't be here for me now. So what'll happen if you walk away, too?"

"I'm your lawyer. I won't walk away."

"But you want to."

He sighed. "I'm doing what I can to sort out the leads we've got. Not that I'm making much progress."

She heard the frustration in his tone and was hopeful. If he still cared enough to work on her defense, he couldn't hate her, could he?

"It's a bitch of a case, Amber. If you feel I'm not doing a good job for you, you're free to get someone else."

"I don't want anyone else!" she cried. "You know that. I want you to help me prove I didn't kill Deke, and I want us to still be friends." Twisting the telephone cord in one hand, she allowed her voice to drop huskily. "I want us to be more than friends, Nick. You're not just my lawyer. We proved that Saturday night, didn't we?"

"Saturday night was a mistake, Amber. I don't think it's wise to get personally involved. I shouldn't be distracted if I'm going to give you an adequate defense against a murder charge."

"We're already involved!"

"One sexual mistake doesn't make a relationship, Amber."

"It wasn't a mistake. It... It was...special, Nick. Don't deny it."

"I don't want to debate this with you, Amber."

"You can defend me and we can still—you know—we can still be close."

"No, we can't," Nick said firmly, then added, "I'll keep in touch. If something comes up and I need you, I'll call."

Head bent, she pressed the receiver to her lips and whispered, "I'll always need you, Nick."

There was no reply.

"She's weak but she's stable, Kate." Taking her arm, Sam guided her away from the crowded nurses' station toward Victoria's room. "She's coherent. She knows what's happening. I've prescribed morphine on demand, which she controls. It will keep her comfortable."

Kate pressed her fingers against her lips. "It's the end, isn't it, Sam?"

"You of all people know that's impossible to answer, Kate. She's been incredibly strong to this point. Some cancer patients show a remarkable will to survive. We'll just have to wait and see."

"Wait and see," Kate repeated. Leaning against the wall with her arms folded, she stared at her shoes. "I've said those words so many times."

Sam glanced at Victoria's chart and frowned. "I

wouldn't have predicted something like this so soon. Did something else happen when she collapsed?"

Something else? Kate wondered how much to reveal. She was still stunned by her mother's confession and the sudden recovery of her own memory. And then there was Amber's dark secret. "When you dropped me off, I went inside and found Mother and Amber together. Amber often runs to Mother when she's upset. We talked about her abuse by Deke, among other…things. I now know the reason I've been plagued by those flashbacks." She gave a hollow laugh. "I'm not sure figuring it out was a good thing."

Sam bent a little at the knees to look into her face. "You want to explain that?"

"My mother shot and killed my father in self-defense on the yacht that day, Sam. And I saw it all."

"Kate…" There was shock and sympathy in Sam's eyes.

"Yeah. I was floored, to say the least." She rubbed her arms briskly and told Sam the whole sordid story. "Mother must have thought it would be reassuring to Amber to know that she, too, had been an abused wife, so she put herself through the anguish of telling the story and it was simply too much for her."

"I'm so sorry, sweetheart." Sam slipped an arm around her waist, and Kate clutched his wrist as a rush of tears blinded her for a minute.

"The good news is that I know I'll never have another weird flashback. They're gone. Don't ask me why, but I just know it. Still, I didn't want to be free of them this way." Her lips trembled as she tried to smile.

"Maybe Victoria believed her confession would free you as well as reassure Amber."

"She said as much." Kate blinked and wiped the outer corners of her eyes. "I think it's true."

"She's a remarkable woman, your mother."

Kate nodded, swallowing a lump. "I know. I just wish I'd come home sooner. I wish we'd had more time together."

"For everything there's a season," Sam said. "Maybe the time just wasn't right until now, Kate."

For a time they stood in silence. Her mother had the very best care in Sam; she had no problem acknowledging that now. For a few seconds she closed her eyes, standing close to him as if to absorb his strength. She inhaled the essence of the man she loved and drew courage from it.

"I'm going in now," she told him. "I'll be staying, of course. You're heading back to the clinic?"

"Patients are waiting. But if you need me, just call. I mean that, Kate."

Kate nodded and managed a smile. "I know."

Pushing the door open silently, she entered Victoria's room and was unsurprised to find Leo sitting beside her bed. Tethered to his own IV pole, he'd wedged a chair into a space near the machine that bleeped Victoria's vital signs in a soft, reassuringly even cadence. He held her mother's fingers in his. Ignoring her duty to scold him for wandering from the cardiac-care unit, Kate walked over to him and squeezed his shoulder wordlessly.

"Kate." He reached up and covered her hand. "She was asking for you a few minutes ago."

"I was talking to Sam." Both looked at Victoria. "Is she resting well?" Kate asked.

"So-so." He leaned forward and touched Victoria's cheek. "Look who's here, Vicky."

Victoria stirred and her eyes fluttered open. "Kate…"

"Hi, Mama. They'd better be treating you right or I'll be all over them like a bad habit."

"That's my Kate. A fighter."

"Where's Amber?"

"She slipped away a while ago."

Kate sat down in a chair on the opposite side of the bed and gazed at her mother. She'd seen death up close many times, but nothing ever prepared anyone to watch a loved one die. With her mother's confession in the sunroom, many of Kate's childhood questions had been answered. It was a strange gift—the knowledge that her father had not been a good human being—but she acknowledged at the same time that her mother had been careful over the years not to give Kate a false impression of John Madison. He'd remained a shadowy figure, neither good nor bad. In every sense of the word except biologically, her father had been Leo Castille.

Watching him now, gently stroking Victoria's hand, Kate knew that fate had been kind.

THIRTY-SIX

"Hi."

"Oh...hi, Stephen." Amber was barely inside the front door when Stephen was beside her. She sighed inwardly, tossing her handbag on a chair beside a small table in the foyer.

"I've been waiting for you," he said with a hopeful expression on his face.

"I've been at the hospital."

"How's Grandpa Leo?"

"He's good, but Victoria's not so good."

"Oh."

Moving past him, she went into the den and pulled a bottle of wine from the built-in wine rack beneath the bar. "Open this for me, will you, Stephen?"

"Sure." He got the corkscrew from a drawer. "Did you come straight from the hospital?"

"Why do you ask, Stephen? Am I going to have to start accounting for my every move to you like I did with Deke?"

"I wasn't checking up on you," he said with a hurt look. "You know I wouldn't do that."

"Uh-huh." She selected a wineglass and set it on the bar. Reaching for her cigarettes, she tapped one out and lit it, savoring the smoke. "I'm really bushed, too. I don't know what it is about sitting in a hospital room that's so tiring. No smoking, either. Has Nick called?"

"No."

"Are you sure?" She went to the answering machine and checked for herself. "You didn't erase anything, did you?"

"I didn't erase anything, okay? What's so important about Nick Santana, anyway? You don't need him, Amber. Don't you remember how we talked about the way it could be if only Deke wasn't around? Well, he's gone, but Santana's ruining everything!"

She blew smoke out impatiently. "Come on, Stephen, that wasn't serious. All that talk was just...talk. You know, fantasy stuff. This is the real world now."

Near tears, he handed her the open bottle. "It wasn't just talk to me, Amber. I meant every word. I want to take care of you now. I'll probably inherit a lot of money from Deke. Did you think of that? It'll be ours. You'll never have to worry about anything again."

"Half of it's mine anyway, darlin'. It's the law in this state." Amber poured the wine, sniffed it, then took a small taste. "And don't worry about taking care of me. Things have worked out fine, provided I don't get arrested for murdering the creep. It's like we discussed a few days ago—we're both free now. What's done is done, and I think we should just put it all behind us, Stephen. You'll find a really nice girl and forget all about me."

"Stop talking to me like I'm a kid, Amber!" When she heaved a heavy sigh, he made a sound of anguish, thrusting bony fingers through his hair. "I won't forget about you, Amber...ever! I already know a lot of nice girls, but they're not you." He stopped, dropped his hands to his hips, walked a few steps in frustration, making a tight circle before stopping in front of her again. "What was this all about if it didn't mean we could be together?"

She looked askance at him through a screen of smoke. "What do you mean, 'all this,' Stephen?"

Clearly agitated, he scrubbed a hand over his mouth and shifted his feet. He looked at her, then away, then back again. The thought in his mind was too awesome to be spoken. "You know, Amber."

She tapped ashes from her cigarette with a frown. "Did you kill him, Stephen? You can tell me if you did it. I—"

"No!" He stared at her, aghast. "You know I didn't!" There was a beat or two of silence while their gazes locked. Then Stephen's eyes narrowed. "He told you to say that, didn't he? Santana wants you to try and confuse me, doesn't he? He thinks because I'm a kid I'm too stupid to see through a scheme to try and break us up. Isn't that right?"

Eyes closed, Amber shook her head wearily. "No. That's so wrong, Stephen. Nick doesn't know anything about this. He's still trying to figure out ways to keep that Pamela LaRue person from building some kind of trumped-up case against me and somehow getting me indicted for a murder I didn't commit!"

Suddenly, Stephen put out a hand. "Quiet. Someone just drove up." He looked toward the front door. "It's the cops again."

"Again? What? Have they been here before?"

"Yeah, a couple of hours ago."

She gave him an exasperated look as the door chimes rang, and with a frown, set her wineglass down and made her way around him to the foyer. She swore when she saw Pamela LaRue waiting on the other side of the door. After a slight hesitation, she opened the door.

"Officer LaRue, isn't it?" Amber checked the police car parked in the driveway, but nobody else was in sight.

"Hello, Ms. Russo. I noticed your car was here, so I hoped to have a word with you. May I come in?"

Beyond her, Amber spotted Nick jogging toward the house. Inside, she went weak with relief. Everything would be all right now. "I assume this is official business?"

"It is." Pamela's eyebrows rose in polite inquiry. "If I could just come inside, Ms. Russo..."

"I also assume this is about Deke's murder?"

"It is."

"Then I'll have to ask you to wait a moment until my lawyer arrives." She directed a bright smile past Pamela's shoulder. "Here he is now. Hi, Nick, you're just in time. Officer LaRue wants to interrogate me some more."

Only slightly winded after jogging half a block, Nick propped his hands on his hips to ask, "What's up, Pamela? My client doesn't answer any questions without counsel present. And that's me. So what's the situation here?"

If Pamela was annoyed, she gave no sign. "The chief sent me to ask Ms. Russo to come to the station. I don't have a warrant for her arrest," Pamela said hastily when he bristled. "I was hoping she'd come along voluntarily."

"On what grounds, Pam?" Nick demanded, clearly irritated.

Pamela looked at him. "Are you advising her to refuse?"

"Unless you can show reasonable cause otherwise, yeah."

"Why is that, Nick? Does she have something to hide?"

"Nick..." Amber touched his arm. "Maybe I should just go. But I want you to be with me."

After looking at her, Nick blew out a breath. "Come on, Pamela, let's have the charges."

"No charges, Nick. It's just to get some information."

"Is that legal?" Amber asked.

"Yeah, it's legal," Nick said shortly. "Not always the best move in an investigation, but it's legal." He was still looking at Pamela. "Three guesses whose idea this was."

Pamela spread her hands. "Sloan's. The chief went along with it."

Nick rolled his eyes.

Pamela looked at Amber. "It'll be best if you cooperate, Ms. Russo. Naturally, Nick—your lawyer—can be present."

"I want it noted that I object," Nick said. "This is a fishing expedition. That jerk doesn't have one goddamn shred of evidence."

"Ms. Russo?" Pamela waited for a sign from Amber, who nodded when Nick grunted.

"Okay, but I'll drive her," he said. "Tell 'Barney Fife' we'll be there within the hour."

"I was told to bring her in personally, Nick. And right away," Pamela said quietly.

"What, in cuffs?" Nick demanded. "Maybe you oughtta get out the ankle chains, too." He threw up his hands. "I know, I know. It's not you, Pam." He touched Amber's arm. "I'll be right behind you, okay?"

Suddenly Stephen angled his way past Amber and stopped in front of the officer. "You can't do this! You've got it all wrong. Amber wouldn't kill Deke! She's innocent." He looked desperately at Nick. "You're supposed to be innocent until proven guilty, isn't that right? Why are they doing this?"

"It'll be okay, Stephen," Nick said, but he had a grim look on his face.

"Your stepmother will be fine," Pamela said, reaching for Amber's elbow. "Try not to worry."

"But she didn't do it!" Stephen cried. Standing at the top of the steps, he watched Amber stumble on the way down, steadied by Nick, who walked close beside her until they reached the police car. Stephen watched as Pamela backed the vehicle out, then pulled away from the house. Through the rear window, he could see Amber and Nick sitting close together. Amber was crying.

When they were out of sight, he rested his forehead against a porch column and gave way to his own anguish.

The interrogation room at Bayou Blanc police headquarters was a six-by-six closet. Nick tolerated Sloan's clumsy questioning for an hour before he succeeded in convincing Chief Escavez that there was not one iota of evidence sufficient to justify detaining his client.

"The man's an idiot!" Nick fumed to Pamela, pacing in the hall while waiting for Amber.

Pamela poured coffee into a mug and offered it to him. "He's convinced of your client's guilt," she said. "And he doesn't intend to be distracted by anything that doesn't support his take on the case."

Nick gave her a sharp look. "Are you considering another suspect?"

"I've never been convinced of Amber Russo's guilt. You know that." Pamela stared thoughtfully into her coffee. "Nick, have you ever had a case where you know there's a vital clue, a key that somehow unlocks the mystery? And it's dangling out there, just beyond you?"

"Every detective has had cases like that, Pam. It comes with the territory."

She laughed shortly. "Oh, great. It's a hazard of the job and doesn't necessarily mean anything."

"I didn't say that. I've had hunches that have broken a case for me. I've also had hunches that meant exactly nothing."

She leaned back against a counter. "I know the missing link is staring me in the face, but I just can't put my finger on it." She gazed at the floor. "I've turned Deke Russo's life upside down. He had a ton of secrets—but nothing he might be murdered for."

"Maybe he knew somebody else's secrets," Nick said, then frowned as the thought took hold. Amber's revelations about the truth of the boating accident years ago were still on his mind. Some secrets could be deadly. He was telling Pamela about it when a deputy motioned to him from the front desk.

"There's a call for you, Santana. It's your boy, Cody."

Nick frowned. Cody wouldn't call him here unless there was a real problem.

"You can get it at my desk, Nick," Pamela said, pointing out a work station conspicuous for its neatness among the other cubicles in the squad room. Nick lifted the receiver.

"Dad, it's me."

Nick instantly picked up the tension in Cody's voice. He turned away from curious eyes. "What's up, son?"

"Stephen told me to call you, Dad." The boy's voice was definitely shaky.

"Stephen did?" Nick found himself glancing at Pamela. "I'm here with his stepmother, Cody. Does he want to give her a message?"

"I'm not sure." Cody drew a breath and rushed on. "Dad, you're probably not gonna believe this, but—"

Nick heard sounds of a scuffle and then an angry curse from Stephen. Worried now, he spoke sharply. "What's going on, Cody?"

"It's me, Santana." Stephen's voice was unsteady but laced with bravado. "I've got my dad's gun. I let Cody make the call, but he won't be talking anymore. I want to speak to somebody there, but not that stupid Sloan. Maybe Pamela LaRue."

Nick's heart kicked against his ribs. His first thought was to drop the phone. He'd known for a couple of days that Stephen was a desperately unhappy boy. Now, because Nick hadn't acted fast enough, Cody's life was in danger. He drew a calming breath.

"You don't need a gun to talk to these people, Stephen. Put it aside before someone gets hurt and Pamela will be happy to talk to you."

"I want them to let Amber go. She didn't kill Deke, I did!"

Nick had a fresh new idea about who'd murdered Deke Russo, and it wasn't this kid. "Listen to me, Stephen. Amber isn't under arrest. Chief Escavez is letting her go right now." Nick forced the panic from his voice. "What you're doing isn't necessary."

"You're lying. They don't take people to jail for nothing. She said they were trying to pin this on her and she was right. But she didn't do it, I tell you. I did it!"

"Okay, okay, Stephen. I'm going to tell Pamela that. She's standing right here and she'll go straight in and tell the chief." Nick signaled to Pamela, who nodded and hurried to the chief's office. As Escavez's bellow echoed through the station, Nick prayed for the right words to reason with Stephen.

"Where is Cody right now, Stephen?"

"He's sitting here. He's okay. For now."

"Will you let me talk to him?"

"No. Not until I see Amber. I want her to come over here. Then we can talk about letting Cody go."

Nick pinched the bridge of his nose and tried to remain calm. "Can we talk about the gun, Stephen?"

"It's a Glock. Belonged to my dad. He's got guns and shit everywhere."

Familiar with the weapon, Nick groaned. The Glock was big and powerful, accurate in the hands of someone skilled in its use—as Stephen was, no doubt, thanks to his father. "Be careful with it, will you, Stephen?"

"Nothing's gonna happen like last time."

"I'm holding you to that, Stephen."

"Are they letting Amber go?"

"Yes." Nick turned as Escavez and Howard Sloan burst out of the office. "Like I said, she's not under arrest. We would probably have been on our way home within the hour anyway."

"But they'll just keep hounding her because they think she did it! And they're wrong. I did it, not Amber! I snuck out of my room that night and he was in his car, dead drunk, and I knew the gun was in the glove box and I took it out and I shot him."

"If that's the way it happened, the police will want that in a formal statement. You can come in to the station and give it to them. You don't need to hold Cody hostage, Stephen."

"Before I let him go, I want Amber to come here," he said stubbornly.

Just then Amber came out of the interrogation cubicle with Pamela. Scanning the room, she saw Nick and hurried over. "Pamela said Stephen's got a gun and he's threatening to hurt Cody. Is it true?"

Still holding the phone, Nick raised a hand to silence her. "Amber's here, Stephen. Do you want to talk to her?"

"No! I want to see her! Bring her over, and I don't want you to try and come inside with her, you hear me?"

"Stephen? Stephen!" Nick hit the disconnect on the telephone several times, then slammed down the receiver. "Shit! He hung up!"

Catching Amber's elbow, he hustled her in front of him toward the exit. "Come on. He's holding Cody at gunpoint and I don't think it'll take much to panic him."

"What's wrong with him?" Amber cried, looking at Nick in disbelief. "Is he crazy?"

"Not crazy," Nick said. "Just confused and hurting and desperate."

"If he's got a gun, do you think I ought to go in there?"
Amber asked with an anxious look at Nick. "What does
he want with me?"

A partner in suicide. The thought lodged itself in the
back of Nick's mind. It would explain Stephen's insistence on seeing Amber, even knowing she wasn't under
arrest. The boy's whole life had been one tragedy piled
upon another lately, and there'd been precious few folks
to offer emotional support. It didn't take a psychiatrist to
see this as a desperate cry for help by Stephen. But with a
little luck, maybe they could avert another tragedy.

Sam left the clinic that day as soon as he heard about
the hostage situation. Before heading to the hospital to tell
Kate, he drove by the house on Vermilion Lane and spoke
briefly to Nick and Chief Escavez. Television crews from
all three stations in New Orleans were lined up in front of
the house. Sam checked on Mallory, who was pale and
fearful for both Cody and Stephen. In a few short weeks,
both boys had become her good friends.

Stephen was still insisting that he wanted to see Amber
and no one else, and no amount of talk by the chief or any
of his staff—including the trained hostage negotiator
flown in to Bayou Blanc, could budge him. Sam left to go
to the hospital to try and reassure Kate and Leo, who
would be frantic over this latest tragedy.

No one said anything in front of Victoria, but she
seemed to sense something was going on and was especially sensitive to Leo's agitation. It was clearer than ever
to Kate, after learning how the *Mayday* had sunk, that Victoria considered Leo and his daughter her family, and her
mother wasn't the kind of person who would appreciate
being kept in the dark when her family's well-being was
at stake. Kate consulted with Sam and Leo, and after

briefly telling her mother about the ongoing drama, she turned on the television set above the bed.

It was clear that tension was mounting among the chief and his men. Kate saw Pamela LaRue's face as she conferred with Nick, both of them trying to evade the intrusive eye of the TV cameras. From Pamela's expression, Kate guessed Nick wouldn't be alone in his anguish if something happened to Cody.

Amber sat alone in the back seat of a police cruiser, smoking. Her television image was grainy and indistinct. From time to time, the camera caught her profile, but she seemed determined to avoid a direct shot. This was one public appearance Amber hadn't sought and wouldn't appreciate, Kate thought. She must feel overwhelmed—first Deke's murder, then her own role as a suspect, and now Stephen's desperate act. Was her concern for Stephen and Cody, or was she fearful of new damage to her career ambitions?

Feeling disloyal and depressed, Kate turned away from the images on the screen and went to stand beside Sam. Sensing the turmoil of her thoughts, he slipped both arms around her waist and she let herself lean against him for just a few moments.

Leo stirred in his chair. Although gray with fatigue, he had refused to go to his own room. "Sam, you were there," he said suddenly. "You talked to Nick. Why do you think Stephen keeps insisting on Amber going inside? He knows she wasn't charged with Deke's murder. Why is he doing this?"

"I don't know, Leo. I wish I could answer that."

Suddenly the voice of the reporter on camera changed. Accepting a note, he scanned it quickly, then looked up into the camera to speak. "We've just been given some new information from Det. Howard Sloan, spokesman for the BBPD. According to Sloan, the hostage situation has become far more deadly. Russo has now issued an ultimatum. If his stepmother, Amber Russo, refuses to join him within the next thirty minutes, Russo says he will kill young Cody Santana and then turn the gun on himself." Dropping the note to his side, the reporter looked gravely into the camera. "Ladies and gentlemen, this is one very desperate and confused boy."

An *abused* boy, Kate thought. She guessed that Amber hadn't told the hostage negotiators what she'd done, but Nick knew, and with his son's life at stake, would be careful with such explosive information. Kate herself hadn't yet decided what to do about Amber. She'd planned to talk it over with Sam, but there hadn't been time. Telling Leo would only have added to his heartbreak. Was he strong enough to bear it? Glancing at her mother, Kate saw that Victoria had guessed her thoughts.

"Full circle," Victoria whispered woodenly. "The evil has finally come...full circle."

"Our whole world is falling apart, eh, Vicky, darlin'?" Leo said in a broken voice. Lifting Victoria's hand, he held it to his unsteady lips.

Victoria drew in a trembling breath and closed her eyes. A small smile whispered across her lips. "Always my knight...in shining armor, Leo. But it can't...end this way." Beside her, the machine bleeped a little faster.

"We...can't let the boy do this. Too much death...too many secrets." One hand brushed restlessly at the sheet. "If I'd spoken before...Kate would have slept innocently as a child. Instead...nightmares. Fear. Insecurity. When I exposed her to the violence in my marriage to John Madison, I sentenced her to a lifetime of anxiety. I...set the stage...for her flashbacks. I...programmed her...to break down under the...stress in her job."

"Mama..."

"Let me finish, child." When Leo touched her cheek,

Victoria drew a fortifying breath. "I killed my husband, John Madison...that day on the boat." Her gaze moved to Sam. "When you...leave here...tell them that." After taking a moment to catch her breath, she said, "I killed Deke Russo, too."

Kate gasped, clutching Sam's arms at her waist. When she would have started toward her mother, Sam restrained her. Bending near her ear, he whispered, "Let her talk, Kate. She needs to do this." And Kate realized that Sam didn't seem shocked. How long had he known?

"I believe you guessed that...didn't you...Sam?"

"Not exactly, Victoria," he said gently. "But it did cross my mind."

"Confessions," she whispered, her eyes closed. "Doctor-client privilege."

"That's right."

"As bad as Leo."

Leo pulled her blanket up. "Isn't that enough for now, Vicky?"

"Must...tell it all." She fumbled for Leo's hand again. "I told Leo about...shooting Deke...the night of his... heart attack. That caused it."

"No," Leo said, tears glistening in his eyes.

"Yes. I...knew how Deke abused Amber. Saw the signs. Bruises...insults...jealous rages. Worst of all... Stephen. I begged her...to leave him. To divorce..." Victoria's breathing was shallow, her strength waning. "Amber...couldn't. Like me...trapped." Tears now leaked from the corners of her eyes. "That day at the pool...Stephen told me he...sometimes wanted to...kill his father...to free Amber. I didn't know what... road...his thoughts were taking. I just knew his life...and Amber's...would be ruined if they...couldn't get away."

Kate gave a moan of distress. "You should have told someone, Mother. It was too much for you to bear alone."

Victoria shook her head weakly. "I'm...dying... anyway.... Atonement... Tried to...clean it up.... Couldn't... Didn't want Amber...Stephen...to see."

"Oh, Mother."

"Now, go...tell that...obnoxious...Escavez...who killed Deke Russo. Stephen truly believes...Amber's guilty. I'm...afraid if she goes into that...house, he'll shoot her and himself." Exhausted, she leaned her cheek against Leo's hand. "Time...to stop...the violence."

Kate went with Sam to the hostage scene, which teemed with activity. Parish police had joined the city force, most of whom were busy with crowd control. Adding to the circus atmosphere was a frenzied media. Overhead, three helicopters circled the site.

Nick stood with a knot of negotiators that included Chief Escavez, Howard Sloan and Pamela LaRue. Kate and Sam were blocked by a barrier of yellow police tape, but Nick saw them and hurried toward them. Pamela LaRue came with him.

Sam addressed Nick directly after a polite nod at Pamela. "We just left Victoria Madison's room at the hospital," he said. "We've got information that Escavez needs to hear, Nick. We might be able to clear this up and get Stephen to turn your boy loose."

Nick gave Kate a quick glance, but it was Sam he addressed. "It was Victoria, wasn't it? Did she confess?"

Kate covered her mouth. She was still badly shaken by her mother's confession. "How did you know?"

"It was after Amber told me Madison was an abuser and that Victoria had shot him that day on the boat. But we don't have any time to waste. Pam, get them past the tape, will you?"

"I don't know if this will fix the situation here, Nick," Pamela said, lifting the tape herself after a quick aside to the cop guarding the scene. "We can tell Stephen, but will he believe us? He wants Amber in there."

"She could be walking to her own death if she agrees to go to him," Kate said. "I think he knows the relationship he wants with her can never be. He could be suicidal."

"That's my fear exactly," Nick said. Removing his baseball cap, he plowed a hand through his hair. "And I don't want Cody to be sacrificed to his sick fantasies!" His features were a grim mask of fear and frustration. Turning, he regarded the house, his eyes full of turmoil. His next words tore at Kate's heart. "If something happens to Cody, it'll kill me."

Pamela spoke quietly. "I think we should give Amber a chance to say whether or not she'll do as Stephen asks."

"It'll be a waste of time," Nick said bitterly.

There would be no happy ending for Amber in this man's life, Kate thought sadly. "Why don't you go over and ask her, Nick?" Kate suggested. "If she'll do it for anyone, she'll do it for you."

All eyes turned to the police car where Amber sat unmoving except for the arc of her cigarette. Nick was silent, thinking that he'd been exactly Stephen's age when he'd first fallen in love with Amber. What kind of fate had brought him to this moment? Again he lifted his cap, re-settled it, then blew out a resigned sigh. "Kate and Sam, go tell the chief about Victoria's confession. Pam, try again to get Stephen on the phone. Stall him while I try to appeal to Amber." His jaw set, Nick left them to make his way through a sea of blue uniforms to the car where Amber waited.

When he opened the door, Amber turned to look at

him. "Nick." She stamped out her cigarette in the ashtray before asking, "What's happening? They won't tell me anything."

Nick got into the car, turning so that he faced her. "Nothing's changed, Amber. Stephen wants you to come inside. He won't release Cody until you do."

"So he still has the gun?"

"Yeah." Nick picked up her hand, looking down at his thumb moving over her fingers. "Amber, you're the only person who can save my son."

"I can't believe Stephen's thinking anything can be solved this way!" Amber cried. "He's hurting a lot of people."

"Stephen isn't thinking about anybody's pain except his own," Nick said, striving to keep an even tone. "You came into his life when he was lonely and needy, Amber. Now you can do the thing that will save him again. All he got from Deke was harshness and criticism. You gave him love. After that, well, it went in a wrong direction, Amber. You know that, and the world will know it soon. There's no keeping a lid on these things."

"My career's over." There was a sulky tone in her voice. "Here in New Orleans, at least."

He felt like shaking her. "But it's Cody's life that hangs in the balance now! He's an innocent in this, Amber. I'm asking you to go into that house and try to persuade Stephen to put down that gun and let my son go."

"You hate me now, don't you, Nick?"

He stared at their hands while he considered his answer. Amber viewed everything in terms of her own wants and desires. "I don't know what I feel now, Amber—except an overwhelming fear for Cody. I don't think I can survive if I lose him."

She turned away to stare out the opposite window.

"He's going to kill me and then he'll kill himself. You know that, don't you?"

"Maybe you can convince him he has a reason to live."

Amber pulled her hand from his, turned and regarded the front door of Leo's house. Nick could read no emotion on her face. "I knew it was going to come to this," she murmured. "I knew there would be a price to pay for what I did."

She turned and met Nick's eyes. "Victoria wanted me to leave Deke, but I'm like her. I couldn't find the courage."

"Victoria killed Deke," Nick said. "She told Kate and Sam just minutes ago."

"Did she?" There was only a moment of mild surprise.

Nick looked at his watch. "It's six minutes to Stephen's deadline, Amber."

Amber reached for her purse, opened it and studied her reflection in a small compact. She retouched her lipstick, fluffed her hair and smiled brightly at Nick. "Wish me luck, *chèr.*"

The hostage scene at Leo Castille's house formed the backdrop for WDSU-TV's action reporter, who stood facing the camera, ready to read from flash cards held by a member of the news crew. Much of the crowd was gone, although some lingered to watch the media wrapup. Several police cruisers were still on the scene as the chief of police pulled away with Howard Sloan at the wheel.

Smoothing his styled hair, the reporter stood waiting for his cue, then assumed a solemn look.

"The scene here is much calmer now that Stephen Russo has given up both his hostage and his weapon. There was no bloodshed, thanks to the courageous action of Amber Russo. Stephen Russo never wavered in his demand to see his stepmother, who is the widow of the late popular radio talk-show host, Deke Russo. Just half an hour ago, Amber Russo entered the house, and within minutes, hostage Cody Santana came out, shaken but unharmed. Cody is the son of New Orleans homicide detective Nick Santana, who was seriously injured while on duty in March of this year. Santana was recuperating here in Bayou Blanc."

The reporter paused, drowned out as one of the helicopters overhead made a final pass. As soon as he could be heard again, he continued. "There had been some speculation that Amber Russo was involved in her husband's murder. Only this morning she'd been subjected to intense questioning by Bayou Blanc police officers investigating Russo's murder. But in a stunning twist, Police Chief Waylon Escavez announced that Victoria Madison, a woman who was acquainted with the Russos, confessed to the murder.

"To add more drama to the amazing events unfolding here today, we've just learned that Victoria Madison passed away in the hospital twenty minutes ago. According to a hospital spokesperson, Madison was suffering from advanced carcinoma. Madison, Amber Russo's godmother, died peacefully just as the Russos emerged from the home of her neighbor. Ms. Russo's father was at her side."

EPILOGUE

"Sam, wake up!"

Sam muttered something unintelligible and snuggled closer to Kate. Laying her book aside, Kate fumbled for the TV remote on the bedside table and punched the button to bring up the volume. She stared in disbelief at the television screen as Amber Russo was greeted by a grinning Jay Leno. She settled into the seat Leno offered, then smiled directly into the eyes of millions of America's late-night viewers.

Kate shook Sam's arm, which was draped across her midriff. "Sam, wake up. You're not going to believe this!"

Sam stirred just enough to crack one eye open. "Is it morning already?"

Laughing softly, Kate dropped a kiss on his ear. "No, but you've got to see this, Sam. Talk about leading a charmed life!" Eyes glued to the TV, Kate shook her head in amazement.

Sam groaned and buried his face in the pillow. "Do you realize I've been at the hospital for the past eighteen hours, Kate?"

She shook his shoulder again. "It's Amber, Sam. She's on 'The Tonight Show'!"

"'The Tonight Show'?" Groggily, Sam eyed the TV.

"Shh! They're talking about her new program."

"What new program?" Rubbing a hand over his face, he propped himself against the headboard.

Leno was plying Amber with questions about her new media venture, "Ambrosia!" The show would air daily from Los Angeles and was scheduled to follow Oprah. Flashing a bright smile, Amber told him the focus would be on women's issues. Today's women needed advice on how to manage a gracious lifestyle while juggling home and career, but "Ambrosia!" would stand out because in every show, Amber planned special features highlighting the problems facing women of the nineties—child care, divorce, blended families and abuse, to name only a few.

"Oh, Amber..." Kate murmured, a hand to her lips.

"Hell, why not?" Sam said with a short laugh. "She's an authority on all of the above. She gives the term 'blended families' a whole new meaning."

Kate was shaking her head. "When she gets around to doing that segment, she probably won't mention that her stepparenting drove Stephen to a psychiatric hospital."

With a grunt, Sam pulled Kate next to him, and together they settled back to watch. Two years had passed since Stephen's desperate act, and the memory of that day was still painful to everyone. Kate recalled it in almost surreal detail, packed as it was with shock, denial and emotional loss. It had also been the day that Sam had persuaded her to set the date for their wedding.

Somehow, in the midst of everything, he'd sensed she needed something solid, something hopeful and good to hang on to as her world was shaken to its very foundations. They'd been married just one month later and had moved into Victoria's house—Kate's house now. Kate's and Sam's and Mallory's. She knew her mother would have been pleased.

"You've got to hand it to her," Sam said in amazement

a few moments later. "She's a woman who lands on her feet—no matter what."

"I guess people have forgotten she used to be married to Deke Russo," Kate said.

"Out of sight, out of mind," Sam observed. "And now that she's in L.A., she'll never look back."

"That's hardly true for Stephen," Kate reminded softly. "I haven't had a chance to tell you that Leo and I went to see him yesterday. Mallory and Cody went with us."

Sam paused. "How is he?"

"Coming along, but still far from complete recovery. I keep thinking Amber will surely have to pay someday for what she did, but she seems to have everything she ever wanted."

"Not everything. She wanted Nick Santana."

"And Nick walked away."

Kate turned off the TV and shifted until she was face-to-face with Sam. "You know something, Sam...?" She looked beyond him for a moment. "When Amber was talking to Leno tonight, I was searching for a hint of the person I grew up with. We were almost sisters, but I never knew her, did I? And that's sad."

Sam slipped his fingers into Kate's hair and brought her lips to his. "Let it go, sweetheart," he murmured. "Amber made her choices and you made yours. She looked happy on that TV screen tonight, but she looked the same when she was married to Deke, and you know what she was hiding then."

"In spite of everything, I hope she can find peace."

"Yeah." Sam tucked a strand of hair behind her ear. "But you know what they say, 'What goes around comes around in this life.' As Victoria said, 'Full circle.'"

A tiny chill ran up Kate's spine. She hoped not, for Amber's sake. Victoria would have wanted her to be happy, to escape the past as Kate herself had finally done. Comforted by that thought, she moved into Sam's arms and lifted her face for his kiss.

New York Times bestselling author

ELIZABETH GAGE

brings readers an unforgettable novel about the destructive forces of love and obsesssion.

Rebecca Lowell is the perfect wife and mother—on the surface. But underneath she's living a life of polite, well-bred, never-to-be-mentioned desperation.

Then her daughter, Dusty, brings home her young fiancé. He's everything Rebecca could wish for her daughter. For herself...

An unstoppable chain of events starts with one bold act, one sin committed in an otherwise blameless life.

Confession

Gage's writing is "...utterly captivating." —*Kirkus Reviews*

On sale mid-January 1999 wherever paperbacks are sold!

MIRA

If you enjoyed this story by
international bestselling author

Karen Young

**Don't miss the opportunity to pick up her
previous title from MIRA® Books:**

#66306 GOOD GIRLS $5.99 U.S.☐ $6.99 CAN.☐

(limited quantities available)

TOTAL AMOUNT	
POSTAGE & HANDLING	
($1.00 for one book, 50¢ for each additional)	
APPLICABLE TAXES*	$ _____
TOTAL PAYABLE	$ _____
(check or money order—please do not send cash)	

To order, complete this form and send it, along with a check or money order for
the total above, payable to MIRA® Books, to: **In the U.S.:** 3010 Walden Avenue,
P.O. Box 9077, Buffalo, NY 14269-9077; **In Canada:** P.O. Box 636, Fort Erie,
Ontario L2A 5X3.

Name: _____

Address: _____ City: _____

State/Prov.: _____ Zip/Postal Code: _____

   ***New York residents remit applicable sales taxes.
   Canadian residents remit applicable GST and provincial taxes.

MIRA

Look us up on-line at: http://www.mirabooks.com   MKYBL1